DAW

No. 1728

$7.99 U.S.
$10.99 CAN

W9-CZK-802

ISBN 978-0-7564-1327-9

9 780756 413279

50799

S ▷ EAN

HEROINE COMPLEX

SARAH KUHN

DAW
No. 1728

Praise for Sarah Kuhn's *Heroine Complex*:

"The superheroine we've been waiting for; the urban fantasy we deserve. Sarah Kuhn is the total package: comedy, tragedy, and sincerity. Grab your cape. We're saving the city."
— Seanan McGuire, *New York Times*-bestselling author of the October Daye series

"This book is so much fun. It's a really neat take on the superhero/sidekick relationship . . . a crazy entertaining ride."
— Charlie Jane Anders, author of *All the Birds in the Sky*

"Smart, sexy, and filled with beautifully fleshed-out/kick-ass women, *Heroine Complex* is the kind of read that sticks in your brain like a fanged cupcake. . . . I adored it."
— Amber Benson, author of *The Witches of Echo Park*

"Every page of Sarah Kuhn's novel delighted me immensely. . . . Kuhn's writing is bouncy and engaging, and Evie is very clearly spun into a captivating character."
— Book Riot

"Onomatopoeias? Check. Snarkiness? Check. Kick-ass Asian-American superwomen saving San Francisco from demon-possessed cupcakes? Check and check, Kuhn's *Heroine Complex* is a ridiculously fun read."
— *RT Reviews* (top pick)

"Sarah Kuhn's *Heroine Complex* is a delight."
— Leigh Bardugo, *New York Times*-bestselling author of the Grisha trilogy

"I can happily admit that *Heroine Complex* is the kind of unabashedly fun and emotional novel I've been looking for . . . one of the most genuinely satisfying novels I've read in years." — Women Write About Comics

"*Heroine Complex* must have superpowers of its own to be this good. . . . The action scenes sparkle and the sex scenes simmer. There's something for everyone in this rollicking tale of kissing, cupcakes, and karaoke."
— Lightspeed Magazine

Also by Sarah Kuhn

HEROINE COMPLEX
HEROINE WORSHIP

HEROINE COMPLEX

SARAH KUHN

DAW BOOKS, INC.
DONALD A. WOLLHEIM, FOUNDER
375 Hudson Street, New York, NY 10014

ELIZABETH R. WOLLHEIM
SHEILA E. GILBERT
PUBLISHERS
www.dawbooks.com

First Mass Market Printing, July 2017
1 2 3 4 5 6 7 8 9

For Mom: still my favorite superheroine after all these years.

CHAPTER ONE

I AM NOT *a superhero.*

This was the only thought I could muster when a cupcake with fangs launched itself at my head.

"Evie, duck!" The voice rang out through the sugar-laced air. "And whatever you do, don't stop filming!"

"I'm on it, boss!" I yelped. I bobbed out of the cupcake's path and flung myself behind a counter, my tailbone colliding with the floor of previously pristine bakery Cake My Day. That floor had been a spotless expanse of ivory up 'til about fifteen minutes ago, when a posse of demons leapt through their portal of choice, assumed pastry form, and started acting like a bunch of assholes.

I peeked over the countertop, tightening my grip on my phone. Its plastic case was slippery with palm sweat. It was a cold sweat, though. No warmth. *Never* any warmth if I could help it.

I finally located my boss, held the phone aloft, hit record/livestream on the video app, and managed to get her in frame as she spun around to deliver a solid roundhouse kick to another fanged cupcake. When confronted with the power and sheer stylishness of her thigh-high leather boots, the cupcake split in half, sending frosting pinwheeling outward.

I couldn't help but imagine her name popping up over this bit of footage in cartoony bubble letters:

AVEDA JUPITER

She is a superhero.

Aveda landed from the kick, her ponytail making a heroic *whoosh* sound as it flipped through the air. Her lithe frame was encased in a skintight confection of black leather and silver spandex, just glittery enough to fall on the right side of the "tacky" divide. With her raven hair pulled into a tight ponytail and her eyelashes heavy with silver mascara, she looked like an intergalactic cheerleader.

Personally I thought the whole ensemble screamed of overkill, but what did I know? I was wearing jeans, a hoodie, battered Chuck Taylors, and a T-shirt with a cartoon duck on it. I was not exactly an authority on looking fabulous.

I was, however, an authority on using my phone to document *Aveda* looking fabulous. As her personal assistant, it was my duty to fulfill her every need, cater to her every whim, and get splattered by demonic cupcakes. Usually while cowering behind countertops.

I was pretty good at all these things, but right now I was mostly good at getting splattered. A cupcake landed with a *sploosh* next to me and sank its tiny fangs into my wrist.

"Hey!" I protested, wincing at the sharp stab of pain. I batted the cupcake toward my foot and kicked it hard. It skittered across the floor, then snapped its fangs at me right before smashing against the bakery's back wall and exploding into a blizzard of crumbs.

"Yeah, fuck you, you 'roided out Cakey Monster," I muttered, narrowing my eyes at the remnants of the stupid thing. "Why'd you have to imprint on something so messy?"

I surveyed the damage to the bakery. Letta Wilcox, Cake My Day's hopelessly emo owner, wasn't going to like this. She'd worked hard to make the place a wonderland of calorie-laden carbohydrates, a haven where San

Franciscans could stuff their faces with everything from delicate petits fours to massive layer cakes, all topped with sparkly frosting. Adding to the fairyland vibe was Letta's collection of porcelain unicorns, a rainbow menagerie of beasts that dotted the countertops and lurked behind the tower of cookies in the display case.

Now the whole place was trashed: the cookie tower had toppled, the display case was a pile of glass shards, and the frosting was fucking *everywhere*.

And the evil cupcakes kept coming, spitting themselves out of that just-opened portal with the force of tennis balls being relentlessly whacked over the net by a Wimbledon-caliber superstar.

I pressed my hoodie sleeve against my wrist, sopping up the blood oozing from the demon bite. A solitary bite was nothing to worry about, but if I wasn't careful, those cute little cupcakes would scent my blood, swarm me like piranhas, and chomp me to death. No matter what form the portal demons took, they were always insatiable in their need to eat everything in sight. And they loved human flesh the most.

Recently Aveda had tried to capitalize on this by slashing a cut next to her collarbone before going into battle so the demons would scent her blood, go after her, and *boom*—she'd take 'em down. I found this a bit extreme, but she'd waved me off, noting that "a little blood is a small price to pay when it comes to saving human lives."

Well, when you put it *that* way . . .

"Evie!" Aveda's voice pierced my thoughts. "I told you not to stop filming!"

"Like I said: I'm on it." There was no trace of annoyance in my tone—only soothing placation. It was a tone I'd spent the last three years perfecting. (And luckily I'd made the decision to livestream without sound. Aveda's fans didn't need to know that she usually *required* soothing placation during battle.)

I turned back to the screen, attempting to hold my phone steady as Aveda blasted through a series of cupcake missiles with a single punch. I had just managed to zoom in for a particularly flattering close-up when a figure clad in a frothy lace dress smashed into me, her head clonking against my shoulder. I nearly dropped the phone.

"Oops! Sorry, love!" the figure exclaimed.

"Watch it, Lucy." I readjusted my sweaty grip. "This primo footage of our fearless leader is being broadcast live to thousands of San Franciscans. You know, for all her fans who want to feel like they're right here with us. Watching the amazing Aveda Jupiter kick demon ass in person."

The battle livestream had been Aveda's idea. I knew she was hoping her fans would be particularly wowed by a spinning backhand move she'd recently added to her repertoire. It looked pretty awesome to me. Then again, all her moves looked awesome to me, mostly because I couldn't conceive of doing them without falling on my ass.

"And I'm here to help with that," Lucy purred, gesturing at my phone. "If only to get Miss Fearless Leader to stop yelling at you for two seconds. I was merely attempting to slide in next to you in cool superspy fashion." She fluttered her eyelashes and flashed me the patented Lucy Valdez Smile of Supreme Innocence.

Others might be taken in by that smile, given Lucy's tiny stature and typically adorable ensemble: vintage frock, knee-high stockings, patent leather Mary Janes. For me the effect was somewhat ruined by the knowledge that she had six daggers of various sizes concealed on her person. And possibly some nunchucks. As Aveda's weapons expert/personal trainer/occasional bodyguard, she was in charge of such things—but I was pretty sure she carried all that stuff around on her days off, too.

"Has Boss Lady tried her spinning backhand yet?"

Lucy asked. "She insisted on prolonging last night's training session way past both our bedtimes just to make sure she had it exactly right."

"I think it's coming . . . now." I gestured to Aveda as one last mob of cupcakes swarmed her, their fangs tearing at her costume. She took a step to the right and whirled into that forceful spinning backhand, taking them out one by one: *Splat! Splat! Splat!*

Frosting exploded everywhere. I ducked, but managed to hold my phone steady.

The effect of the move was stunning. It was like watching old-school Wonder Woman Lynda Carter go into her trademark spin. Only instead of emerging with a costume change, Aveda racked up demon kill points.

Aveda glowered at the mess of the bakery. "Take that, you befrostinged fiends," she growled.

Hmm, not her best catchphrase. I mentally patted myself on the back for the whole "filming without sound" thing.

An eerie silence descended over us as the portal closed, its glittery gold haze narrowing into a thin line, then disappearing entirely.

"Looks like all is quiet on the baked goods front," Lucy said, gesturing to our suddenly silent surroundings. "So . . . yay?"

"Yay," I agreed, tapping end on my phone screen, cutting the livestream. "Our little friends got bored with their latest toy pretty quickly this time 'round. Though the cleanup crew still has to come in, make sure we didn't miss anything."

"*I* didn't miss anything," Aveda said, brushing frosting remnants from her sleeves. "Now let's see the footage. You recorded in addition to livestreaming, yes?"

"Yes," I said, passing her the phone. "And you know, you also saved the world again and stuff. Maybe take a moment to enjoy that."

"It was nothing." She flashed me her dazzling Aveda

Jupiter Smile of Triumph—the one the public loved so much—then focused on the screen. She liked to study every kick and punch the moment battle ended, as she was "in the right headspace to properly focus on bettering my fighting skills." For a moment she beamed, her pride in her moves evident. Her expression warmed further as she watched herself land in position, watched her ponytail fly like a glorious flag behind her.

"Yes! Nailed it," she said, tapping the screen as her spinning backhand replayed. "Oh, what's this?" She frowned as my phone emitted a series of *dings*.

"That's to alert me about your name being mentioned on Twitter and other social media platforms," I said, taking the phone back from her. "Since this is the first time we've attempted a battle livestream, I thought you'd like to see the immediate fan reactions."

"Clever, Evie," Aveda said, peering over my shoulder. "So what are they saying?"

I pulled up the app that tracked social media mentions and scrolled through.

"Thank u for saving the city again, Aveda! We love u 4ever!"

"Whoa, the demons took CUPCAKE form this time? That is crazypants from crazytown!"

"Good thing we have Aveda Jupiter around to keep this crazytown from being eaten alive!"

"Maybe cut the close-ups next time, though. Am I the only one who noticed . . . her face?"

I tried to hit close on the app, but it was too late.

"My what?" Aveda gasped in my ear. "What's wrong with my . . ."

She whipped around and peered at her reflection in the ruined display case. Finally I saw it, this thing that was about to upset her more than a whole army of ferocious cake monsters ever could. It was a bright pink half-sphere dotting her left cheekbone, the one sour note in her otherwise flawless visage.

Oh, no.

Oh, shit.

It was—

"A. *Zit*," she hissed, her voice low and cold. I could tell she was milliseconds from blowing up, but trying to rein herself in.

Ugh, how had I not noticed the zit? I kept a full complement of makeup stuffed into my various hoodie pockets in order to prevent moments like these. The little fucker must have bloomed in the heat of battle.

Okay, okay, maybe I could still keep her from falling into the impending rage spiral . . .

"You're covered in demon bites," I said, soothing voice in full effect. I gestured to the blood dribbling all over Aveda's costume. "How is one little zit worse than that?"

"Wounds are heroic. Zits are weakness!" she snarled, flinging her arms out. Her hand smacked into a porcelain unicorn perched on the counter, sending it on a death-defying leap to the floor.

"Whoa." Lucy came to the rescue, catching the poor unicorn just in time.

"That is not a saying. That is not a *thing*," I said. But as I scrolled through the social media mentions, I could see that the public—at least the nastier ones who seemed to delight in posting their word vomit on the internet—agreed. Mixed in with the glowing remarks about Aveda's city-saving skills were various snarky comments about the "monstrosity" on her face. Had she even bothered looking in the mirror before going into battle? Maybe that's what scared the demons off? Perhaps she'd been indulging in a few too many actual cupcakes lately? Come to think of it, her costume *was* looking a little tight on the backside . . .

There was even an #AvedasGinormousZit hashtag. And it was already trending.

"Did anyone mention my spinning backhand?" Aveda asked. Underneath the steel of her tone lurked something else: a thread of genuine hurt that no one had bothered to notice the thing she'd nearly killed herself perfecting. The thing that would help in her quest to, you know, save the city.

I kind of wanted to hug her, but showing her I'd glimpsed any weakness would only hurt her more.

"Let me see what I can find," I said, scrolling through the app again.

"No. Forget it!" she growled. "Dammit. I've been working on that move for months. It takes down three times the demons three times as fast. I *timed* it."

"I know," I said, trying to make my tone even more gentle, more calming. "I'm sure everyone will see that once they've had a chance to watch the footage a few times. Speaking of which, we can digitally remove the zit from all rebroadcasts. And it's really not that bad—"

"Not that bad?" Aveda's arms reached full-on flail as her voice twisted into a hysterical squeak. "You know Little Miss Reporter Maisy will focus on this shit rather than the fact that I just took down a whole portal's worth of demons. And what about the fan meet-and-greet tonight? Or the benefit tomorrow? My face has to be perfect! *All of me* has to be perfect!"

She shook her head emphatically, as if this would banish all zits ever from planet Earth.

"Get your priorities in order, Evie!" she shrieked. "This is a complete disaster!"

Seething with frustration, she yanked her hair out of its ponytail and scrutinized her expression once again in the display case. "Where did you even come from?" she snarled at the blemish. "I haven't eaten french fries in *seven years*."

One of her flailing hands swept out, knocking a whole parade of unicorns to the floor. This time there were just too many of them; Lucy managed to save only a couple from plummeting to their doom.

Aveda whipped around, pointing an accusatory finger at us.

"And sometimes," she said, "I just *really want french fries*."

With that, she turned and stomped toward the door.

"Are you coming?" she barked over her shoulder. "I have to greet my public. And *then* I have to get back to work."

I could already hear her muttering under her breath about the different techniques she was going to apply to the spinning backhand to make it absolutely flawless. So powerful no one would be able to say jack-shit about any imperfections that dared show up on her face next time.

"My word." Lucy gently placed one of the unicorns she'd saved on the counter and patted its head. "Given the choice, which would you rather face, darling: an Aveda Jupiter tantrum or our sugary little demons?"

"The demons," I muttered without hesitation. We both watched as Aveda flung the bakery door open with such force, the foundation of the building seemed to shake. "Always the demons."

CHAPTER TWO

"YOU KIND OF have the world's worst job."

A reporter said this to me once while waiting for Aveda to make her grand interview entrance. I was scrubbing at an especially nasty patch of demon goop on Aveda's leather pants, my face twisted in concentration as I battled the crusty ooze.

"Maybe," I retorted. "But I'm kind of the best at it."

It was a quippy response to a quippy observation, but it was also true. Much as I might joke about preferring the demons, I was the only person who knew how to handle Aveda's canyon-size diva mood swings. And what can I say? I was proud of that.

She took care of our fair city and I took care of her. I was her babysitter, confidante, and therapist, all rolled into one. The way I saw it, I was doing my civic duty and getting paid for it.

Yes, I realize that's not how "civic duty" works.

"Is that why you don't quit when you've gotta clean disgusting shit like that?" the reporter pressed.

Well, sure. Also 1) I needed a steady job to amass enough cash so my little sister, Bea, could go to college, and the well-paid pickings for PhD Program Dropouts Who Only Have Experience Working in Academia were basically nonexistent and 2) said job gave me the routine and safe space I required to maintain my sanity and 3) Aveda had saved me pretty much every time I'd needed saving. And there had been one time in particular when I'd *really* needed it.

I may have been a total cowering-behind-countertops type, but I was also very loyal.

I didn't say all that to the reporter. Instead I gave him a conspiratorial smile, like, "Look, my superhero-adjacent life is just as fabulous and cray-cray as your wildest imaginings, sir! It's way too exciting to quit! And you can print that shit!"

He did not print that shit. I was a little disappointed.

There was a crowd to greet us when we emerged from Cake My Day. Lucy had herded the bakery's customers outside when we'd arrived on the scene, and they were still milling around, buzzing about the terrifying nature of demon pastries. They'd been joined by a slew of fans and press types. Luckily Cake My Day's heavy white curtains had prevented anyone from witnessing Aveda's snit (zit) fit.

When the door flew open, everyone cheered.

Aveda adjusted immediately, plastering a smile on her face. I noticed her brush her hair over her cheek, covering the zit. She beamed out at the crowd, glowing with heroic charm and grace. You'd never know that just minutes earlier, she'd been smacking porcelain unicorns around.

"Saved us from the demon swarms again, didn't you, Aveda?" a girlish voice piped up from the crowd. Maisy Kane, founder of San Francisco's popular gossip blog Bay Bridge Kiss, elbowed her way to the front. "What would we do without you?"

"That's a question you'll never have to answer," Aveda said. "Protecting San Francisco is my duty, my love, and my life."

A pleased murmur rippled through the crowd and I

couldn't help but smile, even though I knew Lucy was rolling her eyes behind me. That was one of Aveda's patented sound bites. She spit it out at every press conference and the public ate it up like, well, cupcakes.

"Were there any demon escapees this time? Any increased danger to the city my readers need to know about?" Maisy tilted her head, her hair—light pink, quite a change from last month's forest green—swaying back and forth. "Because I'm sure none of us want a repeat of the incident from last month. You know, wherein two demons somehow escaped from their portal site, bred like bunny rabbits, and proceeded to utterly destroy the sourdough bread factory by the waterfront."

"As you must remember, I evacuated the factory and eradicated the demons before anyone was seriously harmed," Aveda said, standing up a little straighter. Her hair fell away from the zitty spot. I reached over and discreetly brushed it back into place. "And that incident occurred because a misguided citizen happened upon a pair of demons who imprinted on stuffed toy kittens and thought he could keep them as pets. He's lucky his lapse in judgment only cost him a hand."

The crowd nodded in agreement. That idiot citizen *had* been lucky. His actions served as a useful reminder: no matter how cute the portal demons might appear, they were vicious little motherfuckers.

"'Only cost him a hand'—oh, Aveda! You are a gosh-dang hoot!" Maisy giggled, easily transitioning from hardnosed reporter to eager fangirl. She peered at Aveda from behind the (probably fake) lenses of her cat-eye glasses. "We so have the same sense of humor. It's like we're best friends!"

She nudged her actual best friend—Shasta, owner of hip local lingerie boutique Pussy Queen, who was glued to her side. Shasta was nearly always glued to Maisy's side, but like me, she tended to blend into the background. Unlike me, I got the sense this wasn't intentional. "Shast! Aren't I always saying how we'd be best friends?"

"Yes," Shasta said, her eyebrows rising into the impenetrable fortress of her Bettie Page bangs. "Always."

I tried to catch Shasta's eye to give her a nod of sidekick solidarity, but she avoided my gaze.

"In any case, it's important to remember my key tips on demon-related safety," Aveda said. "Number one: if you witness a portal opening, evacuate immediately and contact Aveda Jupiter, Inc. The easy-to-remember number—"

"Cleanup crew's here," Lucy whispered. I turned to see Rose Rorick leading her team into Cake My Day's side entrance. As head of the San Francisco police department's Demon Unit—a special squad in the Emergency Service division—Rose was responsible for cleaning up any leftover mess after Aveda had saved us all yet again. That meant capturing and/or squashing lingering demons, collecting any supernatural detritus they might have left behind, and scanning the area to make sure the portal was totally closed. I gave Rose a little wave and she responded with a stoic head nod. I grinned. A stoic head nod from Rose was the equivalent of a bear hug from someone else.

"Hey." Lucy nudged me. "How much longer is Boss Lady going to pontificate for?" She nodded at Aveda, who was still droning on about demon safety measures.

"She has two more points to cover," I whispered back. "And be forewarned: once we're away from her adoring public, The Aveda Jupiter Tantrum will be back in effect."

"The zit has not been forgotten," Lucy murmured.

"The zit will never be forgotten. All other zits shall cower in fear and immortalize it as their one true god."

"Goodness." Lucy giggled. "Such drama."

It was total drama. But when it came to The Aveda Jupiter Tantrum, there was nothing but drama.

Here's the thing about The Aveda Jupiter Tantrum: just like the leaves on the trees and the frost on the mountains, it has a natural life cycle. It's no good trying to truncate or disrupt said life cycle. The frost will come back harder and you'll be buried underneath the snow and probably forced to cut off a limb in order to survive.

The only thing to do was wait.

After we'd wrapped up the Q&A, Lucy and I wordlessly trailed behind Aveda as she stomped her way back to Jupiter HQ—a crumbling Victorian in the Lower Haight—and tornadoed into the second-floor gym. Staring at the sticky trail of demonic cupcake frosting she left in her wake, I heaved one very long, very gusty sigh. I'd have to clean that up later. And demon-based fluids had a persnickety way of dribbling into the scratches gracing our weathered hardwood floors. They stubbornly wedged themselves there until I flopped onto my stomach and picked them out with my fingernails.

Aveda's boots would also require meticulous hand-washing, I realized, remembering how they'd gotten covered in frosting during battle. That job was always a pain. The buttery leather was delicate and I needed to make sure it survived the cleaning without getting scratched. Otherwise she'd just go buy another pair.

Thanks to personal appearances and endorsement deals, Aveda Jupiter made a more-than-decent living. Unfortunately she was phenomenally bad at managing her money and thought nothing of dropping a few thousand bucks on shoes that were identical to the dozens of pairs she already owned. I wasn't about to complain, since she overpaid me quite handsomely for my menial assistant duties, but I tried to keep her in line by coupon-clipping, balancing the books, and doing everything in my power to ensure she didn't actually *need* another pair of boots.

That reminded me: bills were due in a couple days. Yet another thing to add to my ever-growing to-do list. Said list existed only in my head, a giant mental bulletin board containing a mishmash of multicolored sticky notes with my tasks, Aveda's schedule, and various notations I'd made tracking her mood swings and Tantrum info. To anyone else it would probably look like a mess, but I knew where everything was. I kept fastidious track of each sticky note and its place on the board and I made sure the pieces that represented my tasks were checked off in a timely manner. My mental board wasn't as flashy as Lucy's extensive knife collection, but it kept HQ running in a reasonably efficient manner.

I reined in my sighs, trudged up the stairs, and plopped myself outside the gym door, prepared to weather the storm. I needed to be ready to provide support whenever The Aveda Jupiter Tantrum wound up to a big finish, and self-pity was definitely not part of the equation.

"Here, love, sustenance." Lucy returned from her foraging trip to the kitchen and plunked a bowl of Lucky Charms into my hands. "But let the record show: I highly disapprove of you eating that garbage for every meal. You must have scurvy by now."

I inhaled the intoxicating scent of processed sugar and chemicals. "Then why are you enabling me?" I dipped a finger into the bowl, searching out the nefarious purple marshmallow bits and casting them aside.

She sat down next to me, primly tugging her lacy hem over her knees. "There's nothing else in the kitchen. Which means I have to starve."

"I'll put extra kale and kale-like things on the shopping list for you," I said, giving my cereal one last purple-check. It was all clear, so I dug in, savoring the way the sawdust-like texture crunched against my teeth. "Wasn't Nate supposed to do a grocery run last night?"

Thwack!

The sound of Aveda's fist smacking into her boxing bag jolted us out of our conversation.

I suppose I should be grateful The Aveda Jupiter

Tantrum usually involved heavy working out rather than whining, but Aveda's intensity when it came to attaining the physical perfection required of a superhero was a little scary sometimes. Not to mention the fact that she had a tendency to destroy boxing bags at the rate of roughly two per Tantrum.

Much like the boots, they added up.

Thwack! Thwack! Thwackthwackthwack!

Better add "budget for new boxing bags" to the to-do list, then.

"I've told her she can't go so hard after a demon takedown," Lucy said. "Her muscles are cooked. Should we go in?" She nodded at the door.

"Not yet." I shoveled more cereal into my mouth and got a bite that mixed pink and green marshmallows with the perfect ratio of sawdust bits. "We don't have to get her out for the party until seven and we have . . ." I checked my watch. "Approximately twenty minutes 'til she cycles through her rage levels, embraces a feeling of helplessness, and asks for my assistance."

"Or you could storm the gym, tell her to stop acting like a perfection-obsessed loon, and take a stand against her piling all her diva crap onto you." Lucy idly twisted one of her long, honey-colored locks around her finger. "Just for example."

"The ability to accept any and all diva crap is a highly valued skill in personal assistants." I scraped my spoon across the bottom of my bowl, scavenging for stray sugar granules.

Lucy snorted. "Then you must be *very* valuable. But really, darling, the way she lit into you during her little screaming jag today—"

"Luce. We've been over this. Saving the city from packs of bloodthirsty demons is stressful; sometimes she needs to vent. And my special gift in life is knowing how to absorb, defuse, and contain said venting. I am an expert at handling her and this is *how* I handle her." I set my empty bowl to the side and checked my watch. "And we've got eighteen minutes left, so let's get back to more important things. Like the groceries. Did Nate forget to go to the store?"

Lucy sighed, apparently willing to let the matter drop for now. "He's been buried in his basement lair for the past twenty-four hours. Obsessively mapping out our latest round of demon portals, trying to find a pattern."

I rolled my eyes. "The pattern is that there is no pattern. The pattern is also that he needs to remove the gigantic stick from his ass and go on the damn grocery run."

Lucy smiled. "Not to mention the fact that he should be thanking you on a daily basis for even having a basement lair to call his own?"

"Have I ranted that rant before?"

"A few times, love."

"Mmm." I closed my eyes and allowed my head to fall back against the wall—then winced when a new series of angry *thwacks* rang out from behind the gym door. "Then I'll spare you."

It was true, though: full responsibility for Jupiter HQ went to me. I found the Victorian, I scouted it, and I got the small business loan that allowed us to buy it off its former dot-com millionaire owner five seconds after the second (or was it third?) tech bubble burst. The instant I saw its faded pink wallpaper and scratched floors, I knew it was perfect—weird and rickety enough to project proper superhero mystique, but cozy enough that Aveda could call it home. It also had something very few San Francisco living situations do: space.

Enough space for Lucy to knock out a few walls and make the second floor into a makeshift gym. Enough space for Nate Jones—Aveda's physician/demonology expert/annoying non-getter of groceries—to forge a creepy mad scientist lab in the basement. And most importantly, enough space for the small arsenal of

workout equipment, beauty products, and high-end designer shoes that made Aveda . . . well, Aveda.

I heard a series of determined grunts from the gym.
That meant Aveda had moved on from the bag to her
push-up/pull-up/sit-up routine. I checked my watch
again. She must be reaching her final rage level, which
meant about seven more minutes.

"Why are you two loitering out here?" A gruff voice
boomed down the hall. "We need to debrief regarding
today's attack."

"Or maybe," I said, frowning at the black-clad figure
striding toward us, "*we* need to remember when it's our
turn to get groceries, Nate."

Nate came to a stop, his six-foot-four frame looming
over us like an angry tree. He crossed his muscular arms
over his broad chest and glowered at me through decep-
tively mild-mannered-looking wire-rimmed glasses.
Given that his face was made up of sharp angles—from
the high cheekbones to the too-long nose—his glower
tended to be pretty intimidating. Lucy claimed his in-
congruous combination of brawny physique and up-
tight, nerdy demeanor made him "weirdly hot in that
cute scientist meets broody thug way, if you're into that
kind of thing." Given her own preferences, I knew she
wasn't, so I was pretty sure she was just saying that in the
hope that I'd suddenly take notice and smash myself on
top of him.

Lucy was very invested in my non-sex life. You know,
in that she encouraged me to drop the "non" part. Maybe
because she thought I needed extracurricular activities
that didn't involve Aveda. Or maybe she wanted me to
chime in with my own juicy details when she shared her
exploits. Honestly? I was happy just to listen.

In any case, I wasn't into the Nate kind of thing either,
especially since our working relationship contained so
much glowering. I met his dark eyes without flinching.

"And before you make your next not-so-incisive observation: we *are* working," I said.

"Did you get the stone?" he asked.

"There wasn't one."

His glower deepened. "There wasn't one, or you didn't bother to look for it?"

"We were a little busy with the demonic cupcake fighting to look for anything. And as you haven't even bothered to notice, our boss is in the middle of a crisis." I pointed to the gym door. The grunts had intensified. Push-ups/pull-ups/sit-ups were almost done; kettlebells would be next.

He raked a hand through his unruly shock of hair, making it stand on end. "I've told you: those stones are crucial to my research."

"And I've told *you*: the number one priority for this organization is Aveda. It'd be nice if you expressed some facsimile of concern for her well-being after a big demon battle instead of fixating on your 'experiments.'" I actually made air quotes around "experiments." Something about his condescending, know-it-all tone always brought out the contrary three-year-old in me. "And anyway, if we missed a stone, Rose will send it to us."

"Which will take at least twenty-four hours, which is time that could've been spent studying the specimen—"

"If finding the stones is so important, why don't you join us on the missions? Get your hands dirty." I gestured to my frosting-spattered jeans. "Actual fieldwork might be better research than, say, locking yourself in the lab and ignoring the rest of us for days on end."

He stiffened. "And what, exactly, do you know about scientific research? Unless you mean researching Aveda's favorite shade of lipstick."

"There's definitely a science to that." I resisted the urge to roll my eyes. I knew he didn't get my jumbled mental bulletin board way of doing things. If something wasn't written down in an official-looking spreadsheet, he thought it didn't count.

Hmm. Maybe if I scrawled "get the damn groceries" on one of his spreadsheets, he'd consider it a task worthy of his notice.

Anyway, I was only half joking about the lipstick science side of things. My job might not seem important to him, but considering his severe lack of interpersonal skills, I doubted he'd be very good at it.

His glare shifted to the side. "What's this?" He grabbed my hand and pushed my hoodie sleeve up, revealing the welt on the inside of my wrist.

"One of the cupcakes bit me," I said, pulling away. "No big deal."

"I have a salve for that," he said, grabbing my wrist again.

"I don't need a salve." I yanked my hand away and tugged my sleeve down. "It'll heal on its own."

"It'll heal faster if you use the salve—"

"Let's get back to worrying about Aveda," I interrupted. "She's the one who was in the thick of battle and all?"

He frowned, looking like he wanted to say something else. Instead he abruptly switched topics. "Letta Wilcox is in the foyer. She's waiting for you to tell her what the portal means for the future of her bakery."

"Shit." I glanced at my watch for the umpteenth time. "I need to be here when Aveda's done. Otherwise her rage cycle will loop back up to the top again. And that'll keep her working out 'til at least three a.m."

"I can talk to Letta." Lucy scrambled to her feet, her pixie-ish features taking on an enthusiastic cast.

"Hey." I hopped up and jutted an arm out, blocking her. "Stick to the script. No trolling for dates."

Her eyes widened with unconvincing innocence. "I would never . . ."

"Right. You think I haven't noticed the big, flirty eyes whenever we stop by Cake My Day for a communal cookie? Which you then don't eat?"

"She's a redhead," Lucy said, as if that was a perfectly acceptable defense.

"Can we save this round of slumber party gossip for non-work hours?" Nate said.

"Can you save your man-bitchery for no time ever?" I shot back.

"I will be perfectly professional," Lucy said. "Remind me: what is 'the script'?"

I pasted a soothing smile on my face and clasped my hands in front of me, going into my well-rehearsed act.

"So your place of business has been selected by the Otherworld as a demon portal site," I droned. "Really it's nothing to worry about. I realize your first reaction might be complete and total panic, but I ask you to remember the facts . . ."

I held my hands out in the manner of a children's show host about to impart a Very Important (and Super Calming) Lesson.

"Yes, the very first Otherworld portal—the one from eight years ago—made a total mess of San Francisco and, yes, the demons who came through were of a distinctly humanoid variety and may have been part of an invasion attempt, at least according to our most respected demonology scholars. But those demons died pretty much immediately upon entering our world, and we haven't seen anything like them since. The demons who have come through every subsequent, way-less-crazy portal are very different—not at all humanoid and usually take the form of the first thing they see, albeit with the added bonus of fangs and/or claws. And while they're still totally dangerous, they aren't smart enough to organize any invasion-level plans. Plus Aveda Jupiter always takes 'em down."

I paused here for another reassuring smile. I some-times threw in a hand pat at this juncture, but decided Lucy would improvise her own touchy-feelies.

"And?" Nate prompted.

"And . . . sometimes, the demons will bring a distinctive-looking token with them when they slip through: a piece of stone with gibberish scribbled on it."

"Not gibberish!" Nate protested. "Possible messages from the Otherworld."

"Gibberish," I said. "Gibberish that's never given us any actual useful information. If you happen to spot one of these, please collect it and send it to Aveda Jupiter, Inc. so our resident annoying scientist can log it in one of his many spreadsheets."

"I'm assuming I can switch up the wording a bit," Lucy murmured.

I studiously avoided Nate's thunderous gaze, winding up to my big finish.

"It is unlikely that your portal will reopen: once the thing closes, it seems to be a done deal. That said, the fact that you played host to a real, live Otherworld por-tal often means your establishment will become a sought-after tourist attraction, much like that drag bar on Turk that weathered a vicious attack from demonic high heels, so . . . congratulations! Should you have any further problems, feel free to call, email, or tweet us here at Aveda Jupiter, Inc. and we will be happy to perform any necessary acts of superheroism."

"'Congratulations'?" muttered Nate. "Really?"

"It's an ironic 'congratulations,'" I said. "Breaks the ice."

"That is the most illogical thing I've ever—"

"Because your grasp of human relations is so amaz-ingly—"

"Guys." Lucy waved her arms, her lacy sleeves flap-ping like excitable snowflakes. "I got it. I—"

"*Eviiiie.*" The wail came from deep within the gym,

the cry of an animal stranded in the desert with no food or water or high-end moisturizer.

That wail was the final stage of The Aveda Jupiter Tantrum.

And that was my cue.

ZITASTROPHE!

Aveda Jupiter Conquers Cupcakes . . . but Falls to Face Volcano!

by Maisy Kane, Bay Bridge Kiss Editrix

Bonjour, 'Friscans! Your pal Maisy was first on the scene today when Aveda Jupiter dispatched the dastardly demons gracing the latest Otherworld portal. The little bastards took on cupcake form this time and I nearly fell into a diabetic coma from the sugar shock of it all! (Kidding! Diabetes is no laughing matter—get yourself tested!) Even though A. Jupes had things well in hand, I must express a smidge of concern for her health. Girl seems to have developed a monster blemish on her face—and at exactly the wrong moment, what with the big ol' party happening tonight!

As my readers may recall, Mayor Mendoza is set to present everyone's fave superheroine with the key to the city—an honor her fans have been clamoring for forever! They're already lined up around the block, eagerly awaiting the ceremony and fan meet-and-greet, wherein A. Jupes will sign autographs and be her usual fabulous self . . . or as fabulous as she can be, considering that crazy-ass zit! (A, honey, call me! I can recommend an ace skin care regimen.) My sources say we'll also be getting appearances from a pair of San Francisco's finest local celebs: Tommy Lemon (Mr. Big Time Movie Star) and Stu Singh (The Gutter's beloved old codger of a piano player). And of course, your pal Maisy will be on the scene to document the most thrilling goings-on and face volcano eruptions! (Kidding! But seriously, A, invest in some decent blush.)

Shasta's Corner! Shasta (Maisy's bestie) here. Don't forget: all organic lace bras are 50 percent off at Pussy Queen this week. Come on down and prepare to get down. (Editrix's Note: Shast, that "joke" is as fresh as a pair of granny panties. Not kidding.)

CHAPTER THREE

THIS IS GONNA *be a bitch to clean up.*

Yes, fine, I'll admit it: My first thought upon entering the gym was not very assistant-y.

It was a total mess, though. As I'd predicted, two loyal boxing bag soldiers had fallen to Aveda's merciless blows. One was still hanging from the ceiling by its ropes, determined to stay at least sort of upright. Unfortunately a hole had been punched clean through the middle. The other had been knocked free from its moorings and was deflating on the floor in a sad pile of black vinyl.

Weights, jump ropes, and Aveda's fabulous boots were scattered all over the sweaty mats that covered the floor. I allowed myself a mournful look at the boots, which were now smeared with a sticky mix of frosting, blood, and the sand that had once served as the boxing bags' filling. Definitely not salvageable. Not even if I gave them the most meticulous of hand-washings.

Sand had also gotten all over the floor. It crunched under my feet as I made my way over to Aveda. She was sprawled against the far wall, glaring steadily at the bag with the hole in it. As if the sheer power of her glare would somehow make the zit vanish and render her whole and awesome again.

I tried to summon the words to tell her she was still awesome, zit be damned. To remind her of her bravery and city-saving mojo and the fact that she was strong enough to punch a hole through an entire boxing bag.

But none of that would register until we'd fixed the zit problem. For Aveda Jupiter, anything less than perfection at all times and in all areas was bullshit. And it was my job to fix the bullshit.

"It's . . . still . . . there," she growled, pointing to the zit. "I have to go to that party tonight. What am I going to do?"

I knelt down next to her and studied the zit, doing my best to hide my dismay. It had grown brighter and more toxic-looking over the past hour, meaning she'd picked at it.

"Okay," I said, reaching into the depths of my hoodie pocket. "We're gonna full-coverage foundation this bitch." I pulled out a makeup compact and dangled it in front of her, as if trying to hypnotize a cranky cat with yarn. "This stuff is like magic."

"Right." Nate hulked his way into the gym. "And clogs the pores to such a degree that you will continue to develop skin imperfections in the same area for years to come."

"Stop! Helping!" I sang out, popping the compact open and dabbing makeup on Aveda's cheek. I might be able to get a glamour for her later, a bit of actual magic that would further conceal the blotch and enhance her overall look, but this would have to do for now. Slowly but surely the zit faded underneath a hefty layer of Skin Tone #67 until it was nothing more than a barely visible spot. Aveda's shoulders relaxed, her expression turning peaceful under my ministrations.

Now we were safely into the aftermath of The Aveda Jupiter Tantrum: that moment of serenity before she whiplashed back to imperious mode, conveniently forgetting that an obstacle had dared cross her path in the first place. I felt my own shoulders relax as she leaned into me like a toddler getting food swabbed from her face.

Naturally, Nate had to interrupt our nice moment.

"What," he growled, "is that?"

"What?" My eyes swept over Aveda's face. "Do you see another zit?"

"No." He brushed stray sand out of the way and lowered himself to the floor next to Aveda's feet. "That."

I turned to where he was gesturing, prepared to roll my eyes at whatever minor source of irritation he'd managed to pinpoint.

Instead my eyes nearly bugged out of their sockets.

Aveda's left ankle was . . . well. It barely looked like an ankle at this point. It had swollen into an angry, mottled sphere that looked ready to rise up, detach itself, and club the rest of her leg to death.

"Did she fall at the bakery?" Nate demanded. "Why didn't you tell me?"

"Of course not!" I snapped. "She never falls—wait, did you fall?"

I swiveled back to Aveda. She was holding one of her hands up, trying to use her telekinesis to levitate the compact away from me. Telekinesis was her actual superpower, but it was so weak she could barely do anything with it. We downplayed it in all our press materials and she rarely showed off in public. Her ass-kicking abilities, as she'd be quick to remind you, came from hard work, intense physical training, and an obsessive willingness to avoid carbs.

The compact twitched between my fingers, but didn't move further. I handed it to her.

"I didn't fall." She examined her concealed zit in the compact's mirror. "Well. Not at the bakery."

Her voice was disinterested, as if Nate and I were discussing something unrelated to her. "I might have slipped while I was practicing a jump-kick combination."

She gestured vaguely at the sand-covered floor.

"But it's no big deal. I just need to rest for a minute." She shut the compact and met my eyes. Her gaze was regal, fully restored to pre-Tantrum imperiousness.

I remembered what Lucy had said about her muscles being "cooked." Apparently she had finally pushed them too far.

"But . . . but . . ." I sputtered, gesturing to her ankle. Nate probed the blob with his fingertips. "Aren't you in pain?"

In an instant, the imperiousness turned to steel.

"Aveda Jupiter does not feel pain."

I couldn't think of a good comeback. Over the years Aveda had trained and honed and sculpted her body into a perfect weapon, impervious to heat and cold and all manner of demon attack. I was convinced she had also figured out how to block her sweat glands, since perspiration never seemed to grace her brow.

That was why something like a zit was so monumental. Her body had found a way to disobey her.

It seemed like she had always been this way, commanding and unbreakable. It was easy to forget that before she was Aveda Jupiter, she was little Annie Chang—that when we first met, we were nothing more than a pair of perfectly average five-year-olds growing up in the East Bay suburbs. We'd initially come together over the fact that we were the only Asian Americans in Mrs. Miller's kindergarten class and our parents sent in food for afternoon snack that the other kids deemed "weird." In Annie/Aveda's case, it was her mom's handmade soup dumplings, pockets of boiling hot meaty yumminess our classmates rudely shunned for scalding their tiny little mouths. They made fun of Aveda for days, claiming she had tried to "burn their faces off." A week later my dad took it upon himself to craft spam musubi. Personally I found it to be the perfect comfort food, the spam-nori-rice combination salty and savory and hearty in a way that spoke directly to my soul.

My classmates did not agree.

No one would touch the musubi on the basis that the spam looked pink and fleshy enough to be "human meat" and also "seaweed, ew." I could still remember my face getting hot, the start of tears burning behind my eyes, as the rest of the kids started up a chant of *"Hu-man meat! Hu-man meat!"* The spam glistened in the light, all sweaty from sitting out for so long.

And then little Annie/Aveda pushed her way to the front. Her pigtails, usually perfectly symmetrical, were askew and her eyes were lit with something I now recognized as a potent brew of rage and bravado.

"Human meat looks absolutely delicious to me!" she'd screamed.

And then she'd proceeded to gobble down every single freaking spam musubi while the rest of the class watched. She was like a tiny child version of the Tasmanian Devil crossed with Pac-Man. In the midst of her cramming snacks into her mouth, she'd looked over and given me a nod: *This is for you, okay? I'm doing this for you. Because I remember what it was like when they made fun of* me.

All the attention and the whispering from the other kids had transferred over to her, the assembled five-year-olds switching easily from mocking me to regarding her with a mix of shock, fear, and "dang, that girl is *crazy*" awe.

I'd hovered around and rubbed her back when she'd thrown it all up in the bathroom right after. It was the first time she'd saved me. The first time I'd comforted her afterward. It bonded us for life.

We were inseparable after that, which meant we were also together that fateful night so many years later. We'd both just turned eighteen—our birthdays were within a week of each other, but we always had our joint celebration on hers—and were in the process of getting drunk on cheap wine from Mrs. Chang's secret stash. I'd anticipated passing out on the shag carpet of Aveda/Annie's bedroom mid-tipsy-giggle.

I did *not* anticipate an earthquake that sloshed our crappy wine all over the carpet and opened up that first big portal to the evil alternate dimension known as the Otherworld. Or that said portal would result in a bunch of San Franciscans getting superpowers.

Demonologists later hypothesized that the powers had been somehow transferred to humans from the demon corpses found around the portal wreckage, and while superpowers from badass demons sounded way cool in theory, the vast majority of the powers turned out to be pretty unimpressive. Like barista Dave down at the Sunny Side Café could subtly alter the temperature of a room if he thought about it hard enough, but all that really meant was he never had to pay for air conditioning. Or, you know, local vintage boutique owner Shruti Dhaliwal found she had the ability to grow her hair as long as she wanted on cue—which enhanced her unique signature style, but wasn't exactly world-saving.

The actual number of superpowered San Franciscans was fairly low—less than a thousand—but that didn't stop certain wild-eyed individuals from trying to claim they had suddenly gained powers whenever a new portal opened up. These claims were always disproved, chalked up to wishful thinking or flat-out fabrication. The smaller portals, it seemed, just didn't have the same juice.

Aveda's power was just as weak as the rest, yet where others saw party tricks, she saw an opportunity to finally pursue her true calling: protecting the people of our fair city. She'd been quick to loudly and firmly establish herself as the city's sole hero.

That's right: she'd basically called dibs.

A couple other wannabe heroes tried to challenge her, most notably our old junior-high acquaintance Mercedes McClain, who'd been gifted with a sort of human GPS ability. But Aveda trained harder and longer and was always first on the scene whenever a new portal opened up. Plus she had better outfits. The public loved her immediately.

With protecting San Francisco off the table, others blessed with superpowers took a variety of paths, but none of them involved fighting the supernatural. Mercedes, for instance, relocated to Los Angeles, refashioned herself as Magnificent Mercedes, and used her human GPS ability to foil carjackers and put an end to dangerous high-speed chases. My friend Scott Cameron's power enabled him to access and manipulate bits of Otherworld magic, so he made a decent living selling spell-casting services online—usually to people looking to ensnare their crush of choice with a love token. (I liked to refer to him as "the Sorcerer Supreme" after Marvel Comics' magic-wielding Doctor Strange, which he thought was funny even though he didn't get the reference.)

And as for me . . . well. The less said about me, the better.

"Nathaniel, get me a bandage," Aveda said, snapping her fingers. "I should start prepping for the party."

"You're going to need some kind of crutch," I began.

Nate snatched a towel from the gym's rack, folded it into a neat square, and slid it under Aveda's ankle. "She's not going anywhere," he said. "This looks like a severe sprain."

"So it's not broken," I said.

"It might as well be," he said, getting to his feet. "I'm going to get my supplies and patch her up and then we'll move her to the ground floor bedroom."

"No," Aveda said, her mouth flattening into a thin line. "The party tonight is a must."

"No parties," he said. "You have to stay off your feet, and for much longer than tonight. No fighting, no work-outs, no nothing."

"*I* can't do nothing!" she snapped. "I'm a beacon of hope to this city. They depend upon me, and I must maintain a certain image of heroism for them. And they've been anticipating this moment—Aveda Jupiter triumphantly holding that symbolic key aloft—for *months*. Imagine how it will look if I don't show up!"

"Maybe there's a compromise," I said.

"No." Nate's tone took on an air of finality. "Aveda needs to take this seriously or risk permanent damage to that ankle. She will sit here and breathe and that's it. Likely for four to six weeks."

He frowned at me, as if all of this was my fault. "Don't let her move until I get back."

And with that, he stalked out the door.

"I keep telling him he needs to work on that bedside manner," I said, attempting to lighten the mood.

Aveda didn't hear me. Her eyes were glued to Nate's retreating back.

"No," she hissed. "This is not happening."

I laid a soothing hand on her arm.

"There must be a solution here. Maybe we can Skype you in for the party."

"No!" She sliced a defiant arm through the air, nearly smacking me in the chest. "I have to be *present*. A face on some shitty little computer screen isn't going to make my fans feel special. They want *me*, Evie. In person, in-teracting with them."

She planted her hands on the floor and attempted to push up, her face turning purple from the strain.

"Don't just sit there," she growled. "Help me!"

"Nate said not to move," I protested. But I was already allowing her to drape her arm around my neck, was al-ready hauling both of us to our feet as my undeveloped muscles screamed at the weight of her body sagging against me. She wouldn't stop trying to stand until she saw it was impossible, so I might as well speed up the process.

"I can walk," she insisted. "I'll show him!"

I managed to drag us into a standing position. We were a two-headed monster, me quaking uncertainly as I battled to keep us upright.

"To the door!" she rasped, her arm tightening around my shoulders.

I attempted to sway forward, but it was no use. Our two-headed monster configuration could barely stand, much less move. I made it half a step then felt my legs give way as my foot slid through the sweat-and-sand mess coating the floor.

"Gaaaaaaaah!"

I wasn't sure who cried out, her or me, but suddenly we were both on our asses and her face was twisting in pain. She disentangled herself from me and tried to push herself up again.

It didn't work.

"Dammit!" she shrieked, pounding her fist against the floor. She leaned back against the wall, biting her lip. Her eyes locked on mine, frustration swirling in their coal-black depths.

"Okay," she said. "So I can't stand up. Apparently."

"Right," I said, as if she had come to this very smart conclusion on her own. "We should wait for Nate to come back. Then we can figure out a game plan." I hesitated, not sure how to bring up the next bit. "And we'll need to call Mercedes."

"What? That is the last thing—"

"Aveda! You just admitted you can't even stand. And if you're incapacitated in any way, we're supposed to call her so she can temporarily take over demon-fighting duties. Otherwise the city—"

"The city needs Aveda Jupiter," she sniffed. "Not some half-assed imitation."

"Are you afraid your fans will suddenly convert to Team Mercedes? Because that's crazy—"

"Yes." She interrupted me a little too quickly. "It *is* crazy. It is also of utmost importance that my fans feel safe, and me being my usual invincible self is what makes them feel that way. I've never taken so much as a sick day. And I'm not about to start."

She frowned. And slowly the frustration in her eyes morphed into something else: a shrewd glint, a spark of something that was very likely an idea.

Oh, God. Not an idea.

"Evie," she said, "remember the summer between third and fourth grade? When we got obsessed with that one movie?"

Now she was in a reminiscing mood? "*The Parent Trap*? Mills, not Lohan?"

"Yes. We borrowed each other's clothes, got the same haircut . . ."

"Serenaded everyone in our general vicinity with an off-key version of 'Let's Get Together'? I remember."

Seriously, why was she on this tangent? I wondered if she'd also hit her head.

"What does that . . ."

Her lips curved further. She cocked her head to the side, waiting for me to figure it out.

Wait. Panic flared in my chest. I swallowed hard, shooing it away. Panic was not in my wheelhouse.

But surely she wasn't suggesting . . .

"Evelyn Tanaka," she breathed. "You can be *me*."

Okay, so yes. She was *totally* suggesting that.

"Um." My voice was calm and controlled, even as my hands fisted at my sides. "Let's discuss the many reasons why this is a bad idea. Number one: we look nothing alike."

Though we're both twenty-six years old, my dark brown tangle of curls was the antithesis of Aveda's smooth sheet of raven hair, my freckled nose the blotchy version of her clear skin. Her eyes were a startling black, mine a half-assed hazel. Her features were angular and elegant, mine rounded off and occasionally cute. We did have similar builds—short and slender—but hers was one straight, athletic line and mine curved here and there, punctuated by decent-size breasts and hips.

"We're both Asian," she said dismissively. "That's enough for some people."

I rolled my eyes. She was Chinese, I was half-Japanese. Even our Asian-ness didn't match.

"And doesn't Scott have something that will help? Some kind of glamour token thing?" she added.

"What about after the party? I can't fight. I can barely run without keeling over. And I don't exactly have your charisma."

"I know, but—"

"The point is, I definitely can't be you for four to six weeks."

She waved a hand. "I'm sure Nathaniel's exaggerating the seriousness of my injury; I should be back on my feet by tomorrow. This'll just be for tonight. So I keep my promise to the fans." She smiled brightly, a bit of that trademark imperiousness creeping back into her eyes. "Aveda Jupiter *always* keeps her promises."

I took a deep breath, forcing my hands to unclench. My palms had gotten sweaty again. I had to pull out the last weapon in my arsenal: the biggest reason this absolutely, positively was not going to work.

"Can we please remember I can't be the center of attention? That kind of thing puts way too much pressure on me," I said, making my voice extra calm, extra soothing. "Everything else, whatever you need—someone to clean costumes, someone to clean toilets, someone to hold the wind machine so your hair blows out behind you in the most becoming fashion—I'm here. I'm always here. But we've talked about why I need to stay out of the spotlight. Especially at something like a party. With all those people. We've *talked* about that."

"Don't be such a drama queen," she said. "It's just the fans. They're perfectly normal. Regular schmoes!"

"Aveda—"

"And you'll have Lucy with you. She'll keep back the worst of the lot."

"Aveda—"

"Please." Her hands clamped on my shoulders. "Please, Evie. I've always been there for you, haven't I? Now I need you to be there for me."

Her gaze bored into me, single-minded and intense.

I felt my resolve start to crumble. The truth was, she *had* always been there for me. After the spam musubi incident, she'd declared herself my playground protector. Any would-be bully who so much as looked at my crayons was greeted with a blood-chilling glare and an "Oh, I *wouldn't*." She'd held fast to that role through the years, fiercely guarding my lunch money once we graduated to first grade, making sure my hair didn't look totally stupid at our first high school dance, and insisting on having "a nice little chat" with the funeral home when they'd tried to charge me up the ass for Mom's burial. (I was pretty sure the "chat" had been neither nice nor little—after that, the funeral home director cowered whenever Aveda so much as looked at him.)

And of course, she'd been there for that night three years ago, when *I* was the one tantruming and she was the one doing the comforting.

She'd saved me yet again.

"Are you listening?" She shook me a little. "You're the only person I can trust with this. Evie, please . . ." She hesitated. I looked up, meeting her gaze. The intensity had faded and her eyes were pleading, almost teary. "Remember," she said, "we're like *The Heroic Trio* . . . except there's only two of us. You remember that, right?" Her voice quavered a little.

I sighed, covered one of her hands with mine, and squeezed. "Of course."

Seeing that shred of naked vulnerability flaring in her eyes . . . well, it was disconcerting. And it reminded me, suddenly and viscerally, of our days as totally mundane preteens, stealing booze from her parents and watching *The Heroic Trio* on a loop. It reminded me of that flash of hurt I'd seen earlier, when she'd asked if anyone had mentioned her spinning backhand.

It reminded me that I was probably the only person who knew that piece of her—the piece that was *capable* of being hurt—existed.

"All right." I gently extricated my shoulders from her claw-like hands. "I'll do it. But this has to be the only time. Okay?"

Her head bobbed up and down, her eyes flooding with relief. "Yes, yes, of course. Like I said, Aveda Jupiter always keeps her promises."

"And as far as *The Heroic Trio* goes: this means I'm the Michelle Yeoh," I added. "This settles it once and for all."

She let out a surprised, croaky laugh. "Fine," she said, a trace of amusement creeping into her voice. "You're Michelle. And I love you for it."

I gave her a half-smile and slumped against the wall. My jeans felt gritty with the sand from the destroyed boxing bags.

It's just another task, I thought. *Just another thing for Aveda. Add it to my to-do list.*

I had a sudden flashback to that reporter telling me I had the world's worst job.

But dammit, I thought, squaring my shoulders, *I'm still the best at it.*

From the official website of Demon City Tours:

Demon City Tours
For the Bold Traveler in Search of Something Different!

Are you looking for a vacation that puts the "super" in supernatural? Do you like your wildlife extra "wild"? Would you enjoy witnessing the true "power" of superpowers?

Come visit beautiful San Francisco, the only spot in the world where adventurous tourists can encounter real, live demons!*

Take one of our tours of former Otherworld portal locations and thrill in the carnage wrought by demon attacks!** Learn about the city's first big portal from our knowledgeable guides! Visit the HQ of famed San Francisco superheroine Aveda Jupiter and catch her in ass-kicking action!***

Our tours will give you a sense of one of the most unique cities on the planet: its supernatural history, its demon infestations, and the heroine who keeps its residents safe!

No need to make reservations in advance: we accommodate walk-ins and same-day requests!

*Demon sightings not guaranteed. Attacks are unpredictable in terms of both time and place . . . which just makes them more exciting, in our opinion! In case of attack, it is recommended guests take out travel insurance.

**Extra surcharges may apply for certain locations. Guaranteed stops at Blue Bird Vintage, Holistic Tea House, and Greg's Crazy Toys, all of which have roped-off areas with meticulously preserved, 100 percent authentic wreckage from their respective demon attacks.

***Aveda Jupiter sighting not guaranteed. Select photo ops may be available, pending Ms. Jupiter's busy schedule. Tour vehicle stops in front of HQ, but guests are not permitted inside. In the event that Ms. Jupiter is not available, Demon City Tours will offer guests the opportunity to meet other superpowered residents of San Francisco.

Most Recent Reviews of Demon City Tours:

"As a longtime comic book fan, I thought it'd be awesome to tour the one city where you can see actual demons, instead of just boring animals or scenery or whatever. But this was actually kind of boring, too. There were no demon attacks the week I visited and the 'former Otherworld portal locations' are museum-like: musty, dusty, not that exciting. And we didn't even get to meet Aveda! They subbed in some 'superpowered' guy named Dave who can make a room hot or cold on demand. I got the idea after, like, two minutes. Sounds like things were pretty exciting eight years ago, when that first big portal opened up. But now? I gave it five out of five 'mehs.'"
—Drea L., McMinnville, OR

"Our group got to see the very end of an Aveda Jupiter takedown! I've been following her exploits on the Holding Out for a Heroine website and she was just as tough and kickass as promised. Although . . . I still don't quite get what her power is? Other than being tough and kickass? I guess I can see why her main fame is with SF residents and superhero fanatics. But hey, that just meant more room on the tour bus for me!"
—Steven R., Bangor, ME

CHAPTER FOUR

I HATE CRYING. To me, it is a useless action, a sign of weakness, and a total waste of time. Think about it: in those moments you spend allowing salty rivers of angst to stream down your cheeks, you could be fixing whatever caused your tears in the first place.

I first came to this conclusion the summer Aveda and I turned eleven. Neither of us was interested in boys yet, and we were content to spend entire afternoons on dorky activities like making up our own theme songs using the battered Casio keyboard we scored at Goodwill.

It was also the summer we discovered *The Heroic Trio*.

Let me back up a little.

While Aveda appointing herself my playground protector was great for me, it wasn't always so good for her. Mouthing off to bullies got her in trouble with teachers. That, in turn, got her in trouble with her parents, who had very specific ideas about what a good firstborn Chinese-American daughter should be: demure, studious, and on the doctor track by age five. Aveda had a temper. Aveda had a theatrical streak. Aveda insisted on shouting down bitchy little Kelly Graham when she made fun of our "weird eyes" after we kicked her ass in dodgeball during second grade recess. (I was prepared to slink off once the teasing started up. Aveda told Kelly her "whole face" was weird, so she should probably shut up about other people's eyes.)

I loved her for all of this. And while she basked in my admiration and reveled in protecting me, she desperately wanted adoration from her parents as well.

She couldn't control her outspokenness, and even though she gave it her all, she could only manage Bs in math and science. That kept her off the doctor train, so she was always searching for something else she could be The Absolute Best at. Something that would impress her parents and force them to finally accept her as their perfect daughter.

She put together impeccable outfits, color coordinating her socks with her ponytail holders.

She trained until she was the only kid in our class who could do three whole pull-ups.

She ran for class president every year—and usually won.

I cheered her on through all of it, my outfits and attitude never nearly as fabulous. I couldn't even do one pull-up. But I was always *there*. That was how I defined myself: by being reliable and loyal and present. I patted her on the back, iced her injuries, and picked the occasional bit of lint off her stylish sweaters.

None of Aveda's feats were quite enough to win the approval of the elder Changs, who regarded these non-demure, non-doctorly accomplishments with a stern "Mmm" and a suggestion that she request extra credit homework in math.

It wasn't until that summer—the summer of *The Heroic Trio*—that she finally found a purpose. And in a way, so did I.

We'd been allowed to trek into San Francisco that day and were dragging our preteen limbs through muggy July, our hands sticky with melted ice cream. Aveda spotted a poster displayed outside the Yamato Theater—a grotty establishment that mostly showed old Hong Kong action movies. The poster featured three Asian women striking badass poses.

"Evie, look," Aveda breathed, smashing her nose against the display case. "Asian lady superheroes." She ran her sticky fingers over the title. *"The Heroic Trio."*

"Cool," I said, my voice thin and weary. We'd had a long day of running around in the sun and I could feel myself sugar crashing from the chocolate double-scoops we'd just crammed into our gaping maws. "Annie, it's getting dark. We should head home."

She whirled around and planted her hands on her hips. "We need to see this *now*."

Even then she was bossy.

I didn't get home until after dark and was grounded for a week, but the movie was worth it. As we watched those three Asian lady superheroes kick and punch and badass their way across the screen, Aveda's sweaty hand crept over the armrest and clutched mine, her grip tightening until I thought she might break my fingers off. But I didn't mind. My own heart felt too big for my body, beating against my breastbone so hard that I was sure it was mere seconds away from bursting clean out of my chest. We knew we were witnessing something big enough to knock our world off its axis: superheroes who *looked like us*.

Most eleven-year-olds would've taken that as "awesome, there's finally a character I can play while everyone else is Spider-Man and Wonder Woman." Aveda took it as, "I can *be* that. And I'm going to." Finally she found a goal to channel all of her considerable energy into, something that combined everything she was good at: charisma and fashion and athletics and protecting the downtrodden.

Even though she didn't get her power until years later, her life mapped itself out from that point, sitting in a dust-mite-infested theater and crushing my hand. From then on we were *"The Heroic Trio* . . . except there's only two of us."

While Aveda connected with the kicking ass/taking names/wearing awesome leather bodysuits with matching accessories parts of the movie, I was all about a more intimate bit involving Invisible Girl, the member of the Trio played by Michelle Yeoh, who we later witnessed being amazing in *Supercop* and *Crouching Tiger, Hidden Dragon* and tons of other Yamato favorites. In the scene I replayed in my head, Invisible Girl held her cute, bespectacled love interest as he died. A single, beatific tear slid down her cheek . . . and then just like that, she was back to the business of saving the world. One tear was all she needed.

To me, that was more badass than a perfectly executed roundhouse kick—or the stylish boot doing the kicking. Because as happy as I was to have someone like Aveda as a protector, I was still a bona fide wuss. I cowered behind her like nobody's business. I started sniffling whenever bullies so much as looked at us. I cried at the drop of a hat, and it was never that winsome-eyed situation that makes kids look so adorable. No, when I cried, it was an ugly, scrunched-up, snotty red face type of deal. I wanted to be brave like Aveda, but when the chips were down, I could never keep it together. Not even a little bit. I still retained the memory of that deep humiliation welling up inside of me when those kids started in with the "human meat" chant.

So while Aveda decided in that moment to be a superhero, I decided I would never cry again. That was how I could be brave. That was how I could fight back. Of course, Aveda and I had an ongoing argument about which of us was actually Michelle Yeoh, since she was clearly the coolest.

I usually let Aveda win.

But in my heart of hearts, I knew it was me.

From that day on, whenever I felt my face start to scrunch up and go red, I simply thought of Michelle and her badass single tear. And that was that. I even remained stoic—my eyes barely misting over—during the entirety of my mom's funeral.

That's why, when confronted with something as gut-churning as being forced to impersonate my superheroine boss at a party, I didn't allow myself the possibility of tears. Instead I breathed deeply as I climbed the rickety stairs to my apartment and focused on using my Soothing Inner Voice—the one I superimposed over my thoughts on those rare occasions I allowed myself to get stressed. Soothing Inner Voice was cool and modulated and never wavered from the same disaffected monotone. She sounded like she'd be adept at everything from guiding you through jury duty to delivering GPS instructions.

It's just a party. It's. Just. A. Party. Justaparty. Yoga. Flowers. Oprah.

Ah, yes. Soothing Inner Voice also liked tossing in references to things that were generically calming.

I unlocked the door and charged toward my bedroom, only to collide with one very angry sixteen-year-old girl.

"Bea!" I exclaimed at my younger sister/roommate. "What are you doing home?"

"Apparently I'm waiting for my babysitter," she seethed, her eyes narrowing as she towered over me. Bea had gotten all the leggy genes from our Irish mother. "Seems I need to be watched over like a toddler—or a *prisoner*—while you go out and party."

Her gaze hardened into a glare. The Tanaka Glare. Our mom had had it perfected: narrowed eyes that seemed like they were shooting tiny judgment lasers into your very soul. I never mastered it, never quite internalized my mother's will of steel. But when Bea made that face, she looked so much like Mom that I always stopped breathing for a second.

"It's a work thing," I said, taking a step back from her. I willed myself not to back away any further. She would pounce on any smidgen of vulnerability like a mountain lion tearing into a gazelle. But it was tough to stand my ground. When she was really mad, Bea's anger swirled around her in an almost tangible cloud of teenage resentment.

And she was mad a lot lately.

I decided to go on the offensive. "Aren't you supposed to be in school right now?"

She huffed over to our thirdhand couch and collapsed onto it, her cap of purple-streaked black hair swaying back and forth as she shook her head. She'd added the streaks recently, an attempt to piss me off. I actually thought they were kind of cute.

"Toddlers don't have to go to school," she said. "And neither do prisoners."

"Actually many prisons do have educational enrichment programs . . . okay, not the point," I said hastily as she opened her mouth to retort. "But, seriously, tonight is a boring, just-for-work type thing. And I only invited Scott over so you wouldn't have to be by yourself."

That was at least half a lie. I wanted someone around to keep Bea from breaking the lock on our liquor cabinet, inhaling half the contents, and stumbling down to The Gutter, the hole-in-the-wall piano bar where Lucy and I often indulged in an after-work beer. Last week she'd done that very thing—and then proceeded to serenade the disinterested crowd with a few drunken verses of Adele's "Rolling in the Deep."

"You guys can play Xbox or something," I continued, trying to sound cheerful.

"We don't have an Xbox!" She sprang to her feet and stomped toward her room, then stopped in her tracks and turned, Tanaka Glare zeroing in on me.

"God, I love it when you try to parent," she growled. "I suppose I should be grateful for those few seconds when you unglue your lips from Aveda's ass and pretend to pay attention to me."

"Yes, I have a job. That's so we can eat. And you don't

have to live in a cardboard box on Telegraph." *And so you can go to college and have a fighting chance at turning out normal. Unlike me.*

"A-ha!" she shrieked. "Now we're on to the Martyr Technique. Totes effective."

"What's effective?"

I turned to see a familiar figure leaning against the doorframe, lopsided grin bisecting his boyish features.

"Hi, Scott," I said. "Bea and I are just . . . chatting."

"Hey, Bug," he said, inclining his head in Bea's direction. He was the only person who could get away with calling her by her childhood nickname. "Are you ready to kick my ass on Xbox?"

Bea's face turned deep red and for a second, I wondered if she was going to pull the classic "I'm gonna hold my breath 'til I get my way!" trick. All things considered, she really was kind of a toddler.

"We. Don't. Have. *An Xbox!*" she spat out, lobbing each word like a grenade. Then she turned on her heel and stomped off.

"So." Scott loped into the room. "I shouldn't have texted her about me coming over, maybe? I was trying to position it as not a babysitting situation. Even though that's what it is."

"It's not you. Ever since she turned sixteen, it's like she's realized she's supposed to resent me for every single thing that's gone wrong in her life."

Like Mom dying of cancer when she was only twelve. Like Dad leaving two months later.

Really I was the only one left to resent.

He smiled back, but his eyes were laced with concern. "Do you want to—"

"Talk about it? No. I'm just saying: if you like, you can lock her in her room and call it a day. I have other things to worry about right now."

Peace, said Soothing Inner Voice. *Pictures of baby animals.*

Ugh. I needed to dissolve the gigantic ball of anxiety that had taken up residence in my stomach, pressing against my insides and forcing my breath out at a pace that was starting to recall hyperventilation. I briefly cursed myself for turning down Aveda's long ago invitation to move into Jupiter HQ. Lucy and Nate lived there, but I wanted to have a "normal" living situation for Bea. But running home and tangling with her and then having to run back to HQ . . .

Well. It was only adding to my Anxiety Ball and increasing the odds of hyperventilation. I could practically hear my boss snitting in my head: *Aveda Jupiter does not hyperventilate!*

But how did normal people get rid of stress?

Soothing Inner Voice piped up with an uncharacteristically enthusiastic comment: *Alcohol!*

That wasn't a bad thought. Maybe if I took the edge of my mood off, I'd be able to float through the party without incident.

"Come on, Scott," I said. "Let's have a beer."

I headed into the kitchen and fiddled with the all-new, supposedly durable lock on our liquor cabinet, liberating a pair of Coronas.

"Why, Evelyn Tanaka." Scott hoisted himself onto the kitchen counter in one fluid motion. "Are you boozin' it up at . . ." He glanced at his bare wrist, as if a watch might magically appear. "Something like four in the afternoon?"

"I'm relaxing." I passed him one of the beers.

"Relaxing with warm beer? Not terribly delicious."

I shrugged, popped the cap off, and took a swig. I wasn't a fan of warm beer either, but locking it in the liquor cabinet kept it from Bea's grabby hands.

As I felt the crisp tang on my tongue and the burn in my belly, I realized the me of three years ago would've so disapproved of this casual bit of afternoon alcohol consumption. Then again, the me of three years ago was always stressed out beyond belief: wrapped up in the halls of academia, never subverting the dominant paradigm, exactly, but talking about it a whole lot. Studying her ass off, working toward a PhD, hoping to become a universally lauded professor of popular culture studies. Never really thinking about where all that stress might lead.

If she had been thinking, like, *at all*—

Well. It was best not to dwell on that. After all, the me of today had managed to organize her life into a series of compartments, all with manageable stress levels.

She knew how to handle every step of an Aveda Jupiter Tantrum.

She knew how to kick a demon cupcake across the room without losing her cool.

She knew how to adhere to a humdrum routine: keeping her to-do list bulletin board up to date, eating the same bowl of Lucky Charms for every meal, and wearing the same outfit every day.

And, I thought firmly, *she could certainly handle one little party.*

"So what's Annie making you do tonight?" Scott asked. "Extra patrols? Extra boot-polishing? Extra telling her she's extra beautiful while she gazes at herself extra long in the mirror?"

I realized the fingers of my right hand were drumming a manic beat on the countertop and curled them into a fist.

"You know plain old 'Annie' hasn't existed for years," I said.

He shrugged, blue eyes sparkling impishly. "She'll always be little Annie Chang to me. The only sixth-grader in history who managed to get elected seventh-grade class president."

He took a long pull on his beer and leaned back farther, propping himself up with one elbow. He was sprawled all over the countertop, yet managed to look perfectly comfortable.

Then again, in our fourteen years of friendship, I'd never seen Scott look anything *but* perfectly comfortable. Back in sixth grade he'd been absorbed into the inseparable duo that was me and Annie-Aveda after cracking us up with inappropriate comments during the sex ed section of biology class. He was our mascot, our surfer dude sidekick, our goofy big brother who reveled in running a destructive hand through our gelled-into-submission hair-don'ts.

"I actually need another favor," I said, remembering the other reason I'd asked him over.

"Oh . . . ?" He waggled his eyebrows at me and leaned back farther, his frayed T-shirt riding up to reveal a swath of tan ab muscles.

"Not that," I said, rolling my eyes extra hard at him. "The one time was enough."

"I maintain that prom night shouldn't count. We were both virgins, drunk on the heady cocktail of spiked punch and formalwear. And the backseat of my mom's dog-scented Volvo isn't exactly the most romantic locale."

"And I maintain that panting your way to not-quite-orgasm amid a pile of golden retriever hair is enough to render the person you're panting with hopelessly unsexy forever."

He grinned, but I knew he agreed with me. One night of teenage pseudo-passion had done nothing to change the warm, sibling-like vibe between us. I could acknowledge he had matured into an objectively gorgeous man—all lean, golden muscle and sandy hair that was just long enough to fall over his forehead—but I appreciated his abs in the distant way one might admire fine art in a museum. They inspired no visceral reaction that might prompt me to take a closer look.

Though if I was being honest, I sometimes wondered if I had trained those responses out of myself entirely. Wild sex didn't go with my well-ordered approach to life, so I had simply cut it out. Lucy often suggested I was wired with a Dead-Inside-O-Tron, which controlled my lack of lustfulness.

Anxiety stabbed at my insides again, sending a wave of nausea spiraling through me. I gripped the edge of the countertop. I *had* to make this stop.

"I need a glamour," I blurted out.

Scott's expression shifted, concern passing through his eyes. He sat up straight, regarding me keenly.

"You never answered my question. What is Annie making you do?"

I took a swig of my beer and manufactured a quick smile. "It's this party thing she wants me to go to. Not a big deal, but she's freaking out extra hard today."

"A party," he said, sounding out each syllable. "Is that really the best idea? For you?"

I toyed with the discarded cap of my beer bottle.

"I can handle it. Whatever she wants, I always handle it."

But even as the words spilled out of my mouth, a sliver of doubt niggled at me. Could I handle *this*?

"You know," I said. "I might be able to handle it better if you'd just try that spell already."

I tried to make my tone light. But he saw right through me.

He slid off the countertop and rested his hands on my shoulders, the concern overtaking his expression entirely.

"I've told you over and over again: it's too dangerous," he said. "Everything I do magic-wise is basic, simple— enough for people to pay me a few bucks for a fun party trick, but hardly earth-shattering. That spell is outside of the realm of anything I've ever tried before. You could end up hurt. Maimed. Or worse."

I shrugged out of his grasp. "I was kidding."

I wasn't. Someday I'd convince him to try that spell. Someday I'd be normal.

"You can say no to Annie," he said. "You know that, right? You don't have to go along with every single thing she says and put up with every single demand she piles on top of you just because she's . . . her. If she wants you to do something that's going to put you in danger . . ."

"No." I shook my head a little too vehemently. "It's nothing like that."

"I don't understand why you stick with her," he continued. "Why can't you find another job, one that's not so—"

"I like this one just fine," I said firmly. "I'm good at it. And you know I need stability."

"'Stability' equals a crazy boss who orders you around in an increasingly crazy manner?"

"Stability equals dealing with a brand of crazy I *know*."

He blew out a long, frustrated breath. I knew he didn't understand. Though Scott could still reminisce about pre-fame Annie Chang with affection, the two of them had experienced some sort of falling out when Aveda started making a name for herself. These days they could barely stand to be in each other's company. I'd never pressed either of them for details, but I knew it had to be bad: mentioning Aveda's more outlandish behavior was the only thing that shocked Scott out of his relaxed state.

There was no way I could explain to him that, in a weird way, I found it comforting that I could always depend on Aveda to be so . . . Aveda-like. We'd known each other so long, we were practically part of each other's DNA. And with Mom and Dad gone and Bea well into her unpredictable teens, she was the closest thing to stable family I had.

So yeah, maybe her latest request was sending me into an Anxiety Ball–inducing tizzy. But no one else would've gone to bat for me with that greedy-ass funeral director. No one else would have eaten all those spam musubi. I knew that in my bones.

"Scott," I said, trying to get us back on track, "this is

really no big deal. It's a small party. In a large space. And very well-ventilated, I'm sure."

"And you need the glamour for . . . ?"

I shrugged, schooling my features into as passive an expression as possible. "She wants me to look nicer than usual. That's all."

He studied me for a long moment, then finally nodded and reached into his pocket. "This one will work." He held out a wooden token about the size of a nickel. His features had relaxed, which meant he'd bought my lie. Anxiety Ball pressed against my internal organs again, as if to scold me for deceiving one of my oldest friends.

"When you're ready to use it, hold it in your palm and visualize what you want to look like," he said. "But remember, it only lasts for three hours. And keep it safe: it's for you and only you to use."

"Of course." I nodded, trying not to make my sigh of relief too obvious. Scott tended to keep a tight rein on the glamour tokens so people wouldn't use them for nefarious purposes. Like, say, disguising themselves as someone else and robbing a bank or something. The fact that he trusted me with one made me feel even guiltier. "Thank you." I accepted the token and slipped it into my pocket. "And you know, Aveda's always saying she'd love to have someone with your talents on staff. Maybe the two of you could talk about—"

"No." His normally carefree smile was tight. "Not in a million years. And for the record, I think you look fine the way you are."

I ran a self-conscious hand through my curls and smiled back, an awkward silence descending between us.

"You are a fool for not hitting that, darling," Lucy always said whenever Scott joined us for a beer at The Gutter. Once again she was way invested in my non-sex life. "You know I feel the same way about cocks as I do about cauliflower: weird shape, kind of gross. But this one is right in front of you and it can be quite relaxing to—"

Wait! Relaxing . . .

I met his clear blue eyes.

Sex! chirped Soothing Inner Voice. *Sex relieves stress!*

Okay, so there was that comfortable sibling vibe to consider, but maybe if I focused hard enough, I could produce a sexy response to Scott's theoretically sexy abs. We were two sexy twenty-something adults now, and if I could get myself to feel that special, sexy way, maybe we could have a dog-hair-free quickie on this sexy counter-top, thereby dissipating my unsexy Anxiety Ball and sending me on my way to this stupid party and—

Oh my God. What was wrong with me? One unexpected task from Aveda and I was ready to re-create awkward prom night sex, potentially trash a longstanding friendship, and scar my baby sister for life should she hear any of our tepid cries of pleasure.

Besides, I was getting nothing. No sexy feelings at all, no matter how hard I stared at his abs. Dead-Inside-O-Tron was cranked up to eleven.

"You could use the glamour to mess with her." Scott smiled, dissipating the momentary awkwardness between us. "Make yourself look like someone even more famous. Maybe Angelina Jolie could be at this party, steal Aveda Jupiter's thunder."

I let out a laugh that was supposed to sound tossed off but came out strangled.

"No," I said, as Anxiety Ball delivered one last kick to my gut. "My game plan is to be as un-thunder-worthy as possible."

CHAPTER FIVE

"I'M AFRAID MR. SPARKY was unsalvageable."

"Darling, that is tragic. Isn't it tragic, Evie—er, Aveda?"

"What?" I snapped to attention. "I thought the porcelain unicorn's name was Mr. *Sparkly*? With an L?"

Letta Wilcox turned to me, auburn topknot shifting mournfully back and forth as she shook her head. The combination of her sylph-like limbs, porcelain skin, and sad demeanor always reminded me of Galadriel posing as a goth kid. Mopey Elf.

"Both Mr. Sparky and Mr. Sparkly lost their lives in today's battle." Letta heaved a sigh. "They were brothers. I picked up all the pieces, but gluing them back together is gonna be impossible."

Lucy scooted closer to Letta. "Such a shame," she said. "I want to let you know, that I—er, *we* are here for you."

Lucy, Letta, and I were in the roped-off celebrity VIP section of Whistles, Union Square's latest terrible tourist trap of a restaurant, waiting for the fan meet-and-greet to start. The big key to the city ceremony would take place after I'd successfully interacted with each and every fan.

I was hoping for something resembling "successfully," anyway.

The fans themselves had already formed a meandering line in the non-VIP section, a seething mass of humanity that threatened to overwhelm the not terribly spacious space. And I'd been wrong about the well-ventilated part. The thick scent of fried mozzarella sticks and sweat hung in the air like a greasy cloud. I'd seen Maisy flitting around earlier and vowed to avoid her at all costs. The last thing I needed was a bungled "exclusive Aveda Jupiter quote" showing up on her blog.

Letta was there to deliver desserts, but as soon as she tried to leave, Lucy attached herself like a piece of double-stick tape. "I didn't find one of those stones for you guys," Letta said. "I thought the demon cupcakes might've left it in my best vat of chocolate, but there was just . . . nothing." She heaved another sigh.

"Look at you, being so helpful during your time of crisis," Lucy purred.

I suppressed a very un-Aveda-like eye-roll and allowed myself to zone out from their conversation so I could focus on the matter at hand.

Which was breathing.

Aveda had a specific ensemble in mind for her big night. And said ensemble involved a corset that could charitably be described as "ribcage-pulverizing."

I'd argued against the corset's necessity. Predictably, I'd lost.

"It's steampunk," Aveda trilled as I was being prepped, pinched, and squeezed into my party outfit. Shoehorning Aveda into her ensembles was usually a task that fell to me. But since I was the one being shoehorned, Lucy did the honors, lacing me into the blue satin corset. This outfit centerpiece was offset by a white blouse, knee-high boots with whimsical buttons shaped like clockwork, and a pair of very tight leather pants. Aveda wanted me to strap goggles on top of my head to enhance the overall steampunkiness, but even I had my limits.

"I let the fans vote on my new costume and Sexy Steampunk trounced Goth Lolita two to one," Aveda continued. "They will be expecting it."

Her gaze swept over me and I could practically see the gears whirring in her brain, cataloging every bit of my body that was rejecting the corset. We could usually wear the same size clothes, but they hung a little differently on me. And the corset didn't so much hang as crush.

"So suck it in," she ordered.

"I am," I gasped. "But, you know, the me version of you likes to eat the occasional carb. And the glamour will smooth out any wrinkles."

Though Scott's glamour token couldn't conjure, say, an entire outfit, it would make the corset ensemble appear to fit me the way it fit Aveda. But it didn't change the way the clothes *felt* against my struggling-for-breath body.

Aveda's gaze cut through me in a way that made me feel even more out of breath. Despite her opposition to being an invalid, she took to the role reasonably well once she was set up in the downstairs bedroom. She was icing her ankle, which was now bandaged in a compression wrap and elevated on a pillow. With her perfect posture and impeccable black satin pajamas, she projected a heightened version of her trademark air of queenliness. She might be injured, but she was prepared to make up for it by reigning over us with twice the usual amount of gusto.

"I don't like this," Nate interjected, pacing the room like an oversize tiger trapped in a cage. "The half-baked plan you two have hatched is reckless."

"Your faith in me is way too encouraging," I retorted.

"That is not what I meant," he snapped. "I was merely suggesting—"

"And no one asked for your suggestions. This isn't a science-y thing. This is an *operations* thing," I said, resisting the urge to punctuate my sentence with "so, nyah."

Aveda and Nate still couldn't seem to agree on how long she'd be incapacitated. She insisted she'd be ready to go after a good night's rest. Nate was sticking with his four to six weeks mantra.

I was tuning both of them out and trying to come up with a plan wherein I sneaked a call to Mercedes and Aveda was somehow okay with it.

I tried to keep myself focused and breathing as Lucy finished lacing me up, as I used Scott's glamour token to morph me into Aveda, as I was finally hustled out the door and over to Whistles.

Despite the restaurant's name, there didn't seem to be an actual whistle theme to speak of. No collection dotting the walls, no wacky whistle-themed food items, no "Mr. Whistle" managing the place.

Instead every available surface of Whistles was covered with pictures of cats. Cats batting at yarn, cats in costumes, cats reenacting key scenes from *A Midsummer Night's Dream*. No space was allowed between these artistic masterpieces. They were pasted edge to edge, wallpapering the place in adorableness. The one non-feline decoration was a life-size statue of Aveda situated in the middle of the restaurant, a garish hunk of plastic—bright red costume, jet-black hair, painted-on grin. I knew she had campaigned extra hard for that statue—the newest in a line of high-end collectibles—to make an appearance at this event.

I shuddered. I had managed to all but stamp out my claustrophobia over the past three years, but this cave of yowling kitty mouths was testing me, particularly when combined with the buzz of the crowd and the cheese-sweat smell. I tried to think about yoga and other calming things, but all I could see were the walls of cats, ready to close in on me while the corset rearranged my internal organs.

"At least I got her number," Lucy said, snapping me out of my thoughts. She nodded at Letta's retreating back. "But the girl blows hot and cold. Which would be fine if the blowing weren't so metaphorical." She winked at me, gunning for a laugh. I was focused on calming my nerves and didn't have the strength to give it to her.

"Does that . . . can you use that saying?" I sputtered. "How would it work?"

"I'm not here to give you Gay Lady 101," Lucy sniffed. "Anyway. You have to help me choose a crowd-pleaser for my next big karaoke jam at The Gutter. Once Letta witnesses me doing my thing, she'll be putty in my hands."

That was probably true. Lucy was a superstar down at The Gutter. She had an impressive voice and an even more impressive sense of showmanship, sprinkling her performances with seductive nods to the crowd, soulful hands to the heart, and a thing I called "the stare-fuck." When deploying the stare-fuck, she singled out an attractive lady in the crowd, locked eyes with her, and sang like there was no tomorrow. She usually ended up going home with that person.

"What should I sing?" she pressed.

"I don't know," I said, tugging at the fluttery cuffs of my blouse. "Why don't you ask Stu?"

I jerked my head toward the far left corner of the room, where Stu Singh, the grizzled old piano player from The Gutter, was serenading the crowd with tinkly instrumental versions of show tunes.

"Try 'Walkin' After Midnight,'" a smooth voice piped up. "Patsy Cline always equals classic crowd-pleaser."

"Rose!" I smiled, pleased to see a familiar face. Instead of her uniform, she wore a suit that complimented her broad frame and a crisp white dress shirt that contrasted nicely with her dark brown skin. "So great to see you!"

"Aveda," she said, regarding me coolly.

Oh, right. I was Aveda. Who probably wouldn't be so effusive to the head of a team she often referred to as "redundant."

"So," I said, racking my brain for what Aveda would say. "Are you here for the fan meet-and-greet?"

"No," Rose said. "The mayor requested my attendance. To show that we're all in the supernatural crime-fighting business together."

I thought I detected a hint of sarcasm, but with Rose, I couldn't be sure. Her deadpan was deader than most.

If it *was* sarcasm, I couldn't really blame her. Rose and her cleanup crew worked hard, but never got a fraction of Aveda's glory and fame. I'd tried to get Aveda to throw them a mention at one of her press conferences, but she liked preserving the illusion that she didn't need any help when it came to keeping the city safe.

I suppose it was true that Aveda didn't need *much* help, though the U.S. government had initially seen things differently. Back when that first portal opened up, the government had gone a little crazy: a special demon task force was formed and installed in San Francisco, a hefty military presence was brought in, and large sums of money were dumped into developing technology to predict, detect, and contain the portals. There was even talk of evacuating and nuking the entire damn city if another big portal opened up.

But then? Nothing happened.

Okay, not *nothing*. The smaller portals kept on keepin' on, the non-humanoid demons threatened to eat the city on a regular basis, and demonology scholars continued to study, dissect, and theorize 'til they turned blue in the face. And as for all that expensive tech? Most of it ended up being next to useless. Rose and her team used a few scanner-type gadgets to make sure the portals were closed and staying that way, but no amount of tech could predict where and when the portals were going to occur in the first place. Some weeks were multiple-portal-type deals and some weeks boasted a grand total of zero.

Still, the threat of invasion seemed to have passed and the smaller portals remained confined to San Francisco, and that was enough for the government to shrug and go, "Welp, guess this is just another thing to add to San

Francisco's already astronomical quirk factor." The task force still maintained an office in the city and Nate submitted any new findings to them on a monthly basis. And Rose's cleanup crew was always on hand to back Aveda up.

Not that she ever acknowledged that.

"Hey, Rose," I said impulsively. "Great job at the bakery today."

Surprise flickered through her eyes. "Thank you." She straightened her spine and gave me a stiff chin bob. "I need to go check in with the mayor." She turned to Lucy. "Try the Patsy Cline."

"What? Oh, sure thing," Lucy murmured. She cocked an eyebrow at me as Rose left us. "Going a bit off script, aren't you? Aveda Jupiter isn't in the habit of delivering accolades to others."

"One time won't hurt," I said. "And maybe don't tell Aveda I did that."

"Dudettes!" Tommy Lemon stomped up behind us. "They're about to let the fans past our illustrious velvet rope!"

Being an actual movie star (albeit one who usually starred in lowbrow comedies wherein he donned a foam suit and played an alien, animal, or elderly version of himself), Tommy was the only San Franciscan who could match Aveda in celebrity-ness, and Whistles management had thought he'd make a fine addition to tonight's event. I knew Aveda thought differently.

"Time to look alive!" Tommy said, bugging out his already buggy eyes.

I squelched the unease in my gut. My brief interlude with Rose had been calming, but now the oppressive walls of cats were back on my radar and really getting to me.

They're just nice, regular folks, Soothing Inner Voice reminded me as Lucy and Whistles' lone security guy started letting people past the rope, a few at a time. *Just like Aveda said. Nothing to worry about.*

"Ms. Jupiter?"

An awed-looking twelve-year-old girl popped up in front of me. She opened her mouth to speak again, but couldn't form any words beyond "uhhhhhgghhh." She thrust an Aveda Jupiter trading card at me, her eyes the size of dinner plates.

I smiled and took it from her, trying to look as beatific and serene as Aveda always did at public appearances.

"Why, thank you . . . ?"

"Amy!" she squeaked.

"Amy!" I scrawled my best approximation of Aveda's signature on the card. "Do you have a question for me?"

"Only one question per fan!" Lucy barked, hovering behind Amy. "And no touching!"

"I really want to be a superhero when I grow up." Amy peered at me gravely. "How do I do that?"

"Uh . . ."

The real answer was, of course, "be involved in a freak supernatural accident and let your psycho obsessive nature do the rest." Instead I took as deep a breath as my corset would allow and said, "Stay in school."

She tilted her head to the side, the awe fading.

"That's it?"

"Yup!" I plastered a grin that was more like a grimace across my face. "You can do it!" I handed her the trading card and ended with a double thumbs-up.

"Okay." She looked at me skeptically. "Well, thanks."

"'Stay in school'?" Lucy clapped a hand over her mouth as the now severely disillusioned Amy toddled off. "Why not lead with 'crack is wack'?"

"Shut up," I snarked, tugging at my corset. "This thing is cutting off the oxygen flow to my brain."

Of course, Maisy chose that moment to flit her way over to us. "Ooh!" she exclaimed, a delighted gleam dawning in her eyes. Shasta stood behind her, scowly as ever. "Is your new costume not working out, Aveda? 'Cause that's a scoop if I ever heard one."

"Clothing *is* oppressive to our natural forms." Tommy leered. I took a minuscule step away from him.

In an instant, Maisy's phone was in her hands, her thumbs tapping away at the keyboard. "Punked by Steampunk," she murmured. "Something like that."

"That's a good one," Shasta said.

"Er, no," I said, with more force than I intended. Aveda wanted press, but not the kind that made her look silly or indecisive. "The new costume is great. I was just making a hilarious Aveda-style quip."

"Got it." Maisy nodded. "I hope we can hang out more so I learn to read you like a true friend. Know when you're kidding and when you're not."

"You can't kid a kidder," Tommy said, guffawing at his own non-joke.

"Whatever that means," muttered Shasta.

"Wait . . ." Lucy swiveled away from me, every muscle in her body tensing. Her gaze zeroed in on a giant dude forcefully pushing his way through the line, eager grin plastered on his face, Over the Moon for Jupiter! tee pulled tight over his mountainous torso. He shoved a few fans at the front of the crowd aside and stomped up to the velvet rope.

"Aveda!" he bellowed, his voice a donkey-like honk. He leaned in a little too close, sending bits of spittle flying at my face. "You have to settle a bet for me. My friend didn't think I'd have the balls to ask this question, but I am so gonna!"

"Hey!" yelled a peevish-looking woman near the front of the line. I noticed her hair was arranged in a passable imitation of Aveda's flowing locks. "No cuts, dude!"

Disapproving murmurs erupted from the rest of the line, the tension percolating as they craned their necks to get a better look at the loudmouth rule-breaker.

"Sir!" Lucy stepped in front of me. "You'll need to go to the end of the line if you want to talk to Aveda. You can't just—"

"UberAde or PowerThrust?" Giant Dude raised his voice to drown out Lucy.

"Um . . . what?" I tried to decipher the strange collection of words he'd just spit out as the outraged din from the line got louder.

"Your favorite sports drink!" he bellowed. "It's UberAde, right?"

"No!" Hair Doppelganger yelped. "C'mon, everyone knows it's PowerThrust! It says so on her trading card!"

"But she endorses *UberAde*," countered Giant Dude. "Aveda, you look really hot on the new billboards, by the way."

"Endorsing something just means she was paid to drink it!" growled Hair Doppelganger. "It says nothing about personal preference!"

"I believe Aveda has way too much integrity to endorse something she doesn't love. Isn't that right, Aveda?"

He fixed me with a knowing look and crossed his arms over his chest, waiting for confirmation of his genius.

"*Sir.*" Lucy took action, vaulting herself over the velvet rope and landing in front of Giant Dude. In one swift motion, she wrapped a hand around his left wrist and twisted it behind his back, sending him to his knees.

"Yooooooooow!" he yelped, his voice thinning into a pathetic whine. "Police brutality!"

Lucy started to drag him through the crowd. She might not have superpowers, but she was wicked strong.

"I'm not police, darling," she said, baring her teeth.

"Golly!" Maisy's thumbs were flying over her phone keyboard. "Your bodyguard is gosh-dang adorable, Aveda! You have got to tell me where I can find one of those!"

"So he still gets to meet Aveda after breaking the rules?" Hair Doppelganger snarled, as Lucy deposited Giant Dude at the end of the line. "How is that fair?"

"Technically, he already met her," Lucy said.

"Jupiter Bodyguard Entangles Fan in Devastating Dustup!" Maisy exclaimed, typing on her phone again.

"Surely that's the least interesting story from this event," I protested weakly. I realized my hands had balled into tight, sweaty fists.

It was still a cold sweat, though. Nothing to worry about.

Definitely nothing, Soothing Inner Voice said. *Think about yoga.*

"I think we need to cut this fan interaction bit short," Lucy murmured, resuming her place at my side. "Why don't you tell them we're about to start the key ceremony?"

I nodded. I could do that. Then hold the key triumphantly aloft and I'd be done. Home free. Able to resume my life of complete wallflowerism.

I took a deep breath, unclenched my sweaty hands, and began.

"Hey, you guys—"

"Wheeerrre is sheee?"

The bleat of a voice emerged from nowhere, stabbing its way through the crowd.

"Whersh—where's *my sister*?"

Wait . . . what? Make that the bleat of an all-too-familiar voice.

I turned around slowly, as if to protect myself for as long as possible from what I knew I was about to see.

But there she was. Light of my life, pain in my ass: Beatrice Constance Tanaka. My baby sister. Perched on Stu Singh's goddamn piano.

As Bea leaned forward, her miniskirt hiked into wardrobe malfunction territory, and poor Stu aimed his eyes directly at the floor so as not to catch a fleeting-yet-unfortunate glimpse of her underwear.

How did she fucking get here?

"I didn't know Stu was gonna let people sing with him," Tommy breathed. "I woulda volunteered my mad skillz."

A thread of panic slithered its way through my stomach, wild and wormy. Lucy's hand closed around my upper arm.

"It's all right," she said through gritted teeth. "Let's just get her out of here."

As if prompted by a sisterly sixth sense, Bea's head whipped in my direction, her glittering green eyes landing on me.

"Aveda!" she shrieked. "Oh em gee! Do you know where my sister is?! I am gonna siiiiiing for her!"

"Oh my good gosh-dang!" Maisy squealed. "Do you guys *know* this rug rat?"

"Of course not," I stuttered. "She's a fan. Shows up at all my appearances."

"She looks a bit young for that bottle of bourbon she's swigging from," Shasta sneered.

Shit. I was pretty sure I recognized said bottle as the same one that had previously resided in my locked—or so I thought—liquor cabinet.

I was going to murder Scott. Well, maybe Bea first. Then Scott.

"We'll go over there together," Lucy whispered. "You talk her down. I'll provide the muscle."

I nodded and raised my voice to address the crowd. "Not to worry, folks! Aveda Jupiter is always here to help, no matter how small the peril."

That sounded so much better in my head.

My hope was this declaration would cause the crowd to immediately revert to chitchatting among themselves. But the silence only thickened, the weight of several hundred human eyes boring into me and Lucy as we climbed over the velvet rope and threaded our way through the crowd. Kitty eyes, too, since I couldn't seem to escape the stare of all those damn cats. Everyone was way too interested in the drama swirling around the girl on top of the piano.

Bea always had that effect on people: a certain charisma

that seemed to hypnotize whatever room she inhabited. It was what made her one of the most popular girls at her school. Unlike me, she was simply incapable of hiding. Usually I admired that quality.

At the moment, I found it supremely unfortunate.

Breathe, Soothing Inner Voice reminded me. *Your heartbeat is even, even, even.*

I breathed with each step across the room. In and out, in and out. Dammit, that cheese-sweat stench was still all too present.

"Bea," I hissed, as we finally reached the piano. "You need to get down *now*."

She turned toward me, gaze focusing and unfocusing.

"Aveda," she slurred. "Where's Evie? I want her to hear my song!"

"And I'm pretty sure she would want you to get down from there," I said firmly. "Let's go." I reached over, my hand closing around her wrist.

"No." She wrenched away. "SOOOOONG." She rose to her knees and gave Stu Singh a half-assed "let's get started" motion.

"Don't you dare," I snapped at Stu.

He touched the brim of his signature fedora, letting me know he was cool with that.

"Peoples!" Bea bellowed, throwing her arms wide. "If my sh—sister were here . . . she'd want me to stop. But I say . . . never. No matter how much it emb—embarrasses her."

"Beatrice." I was acutely aware of the titillated murmur sweeping through the crowd. I swore I could also hear the enthusiastic sound of Maisy's thumbs hitting her phone screen. "Stop."

"C'mon, Bea." Lucy hoisted herself onto the piano and maneuvered within grabbing distance of Bea's ankle. Bea dodged, but Lucy was nothing if not nimble: her arm jutted out and latched on to Bea's leg.

"Nooooooooooo!" Bea wailed, her fingertips scrabbling against the piano top.

I darted around to the other end of the piano, dancing from side to side, trying to get myself into position so I could help Lucy corral Bea's squirmy body. Weirdly the murmur of the crowd seemed to be increasing in volume, taking on the menacing hum of a swarm of angry bees.

What could they possibly be buzzing about? I thought frantically as Lucy finally dragged Bea off the piano and shoved her into my arms. *This situation is getting less scandalous by the minute.*

"It's glowing!" someone cried.

Glowing? Bea wasn't—wait a second.

I whirled around and I saw it. The telltale golden swirl of a new demon portal. Opening up directly over the VIP section.

Holy shit. Holy fucking shit.

"Stay here," Lucy hissed. "I'll get closer to the portal."

I nodded mechanically as she darted off through the crowd. Dealing with a new portal hadn't been part of the plan. Then again Bea also hadn't been part of the plan. This whole "plan" was spiraling into disaster and there was nothing I could do except watch helplessly as my palms got sweatier and sweatier and—

No, Soothing Inner Voice ordered. *Stop. Think. It'll be okay.*

My palms were so sweaty, Bea nearly slipped out of my grasp. I tightened my hold on her.

"AVEDA!"

I turned in the other direction to see Giant Dude barreling toward us, arms waving as he shoved his way through the crowd.

"I'LL HELP YOU!" he bellowed. "LET US VANQUISH THE YOUNG INTERLOPER TOGETHER!"

Whoomph!

A blob of bright colors swooped out of the portal and

landed a few feet from us with a *thud*. I squinted at it as it took shape.

Oh . . . oh, fuck. It was . . .

It was another Aveda statue.

The demons had fucking imprinted on Aveda's swag statue.

The statue advanced on us, lurching forward with menacingly creaky steps, its painted-on Aveda grin a parody of her million-watt smile. I saw the telltale glint of demon fangs.

"Oh my God!" someone shrieked. "The evil Aveda statue is gonna kill us all!"

Whoomph! Whoomph! Whoomph!

Three more statues dropped from the portal. "Make that *statues*!" someone else yelled.

The crowd parted for the Aveda statues and the screams started, a wall of noise overtaking the claustrophobic space. People pushed and shoved at each other, but there was nowhere to go: the sheer mass of the crowd made exiting impossible. Bea sagged against me, eyelashes fluttering, apparently ready to pass out now that the drama was in full swing. I glanced down and noticed she'd scraped her knee, probably while flailing around on the piano. And there was a little bit of blood.

Even a little bit would be enough to attract the demons' attention.

Shit.

"Get away from Aveda, youngling!" bellowed Giant Dude, still gunning for Bea. "She has demon-busting to do!"

I froze, panic thrumming through my entire being. My senses were overloaded and it was just all too much and there was nothing Soothing Inner Voice or yoga breathing or any of that bullshit could do about it. I couldn't move, couldn't think.

Giant Dude barreled at us from one direction, a mountain of fanatical human launching itself forward.

And the Aveda statues bore down on us from the other side, their lurchy steps ominous and zombie-like. I stared at them for a moment. Bea was bleeding. Why weren't they swarming us in their usual piranha-like fashion, fangs already sinking into our flesh, ripping us apart—

God, why was I visualizing that?

The crowd had managed to mostly get out of the way, allowing both the demon statues and Giant Dude a clear path to me and my sister. I had no idea where the fuck Lucy had vanished to.

The thick air pressed against me and those kitty-covered walls felt like they were closing in, their tiny mouths threatening to swallow me whole. I tried to breathe, but the corset pinched me, stealing every bit of air. Sweat bloomed anew on my palms.

Only this time, it wasn't cold sweat.

No. That wasn't possible. It could only be cold. It had to be cold. I had to *make sure* it was fucking cold—

Nonononononononono.

Giant Dude reached us and clamped a meaty hand on Bea's shoulder and my formerly Soothing Inner Voice quickly and viciously morphed into an entirely different kind of thought.

No . . . NO ONE FUCKS WITH MY SISTER.

My palm sweat spiked in temperature, a jolt of heat, bright and burning and hot . . . hot, hot, hot, way too fucking hot . . . *hot* . . .

Flame shot out of my hand in a blur of orange and red and yellow, whizzing across the room with a mighty *whoosh*, and obliterating the Aveda statue demons one by one: *Bam! Bam! Bam!*

The demons exploded, but the fire kept going, crashing into the *actual* Aveda statue.

Baaaaaaaaam!

It went up in flames, the chemical-heavy scent of plastic drenching the air.

I braced myself for the screams. The stampede toward

the door. The feeling of helplessness I was all too familiar with.

But then the flames disappeared in a puff of white
mist and Lucy emerged from behind the remnants of the
statue, clutching a fire extinguisher.

"What . . ." Her lacy dress was tangled around her legs.
And her eyes were full of terror.

"Lucy . . ." I whispered.

But it was lost in the din that started as a slow clap and
built into genuine applause. Bea sagged more heavily
against me, snoring in earnest.

I glanced up at the ceiling. The portal flattened into a
line and winked out of sight.

"Holy cats!" shrieked Maisy. "Is that a new power?"

"I'm tweeting it!" yelled Hair Doppelganger.

"You shouldn't do that before Aveda's ready to answer the fourteen kazillion inevitable questions!" countered Giant Dude.

"Which she'll be doing in my gosh-dang exclusive interview!" interjected Maisy. "Isn't that right, Aveda?"

As they all continued to shout and murmur and buzz,
I said nothing, my gaze still locked with Lucy's. Bea
chose that moment to start awake.

"Mmm," she snuffled, rubbing her cheek against my
shoulder. She raised her head and squinted.

"Wha' happened?" she slurred. Her eyes sharpened as
she took in the smoke lingering in the air and the charred
remains of the Aveda statue. A bit of sobriety crept into
her gaze. "What did Evie burn down *this* time?"

AVEDAPOCALYPSE!

Who's the New Girl on Fire?
by Maisy Kane, Bay Bridge Kiss Editrix

Aveda Jupiter never received the key to the city at tonight's shindig . . . but as it turns out, sweet 'Friscans, she had a big surprise for us! Apparently, the beloved Daughter of San Francisco can make FIRE. Like, with her HANDS.

No word on whether this is a new development or merely a trick A chose not to bust out 'til this very moment (and really, Aveda-girl, you couldn't give your pal Maisy a heads up?), but rest assured I'll be the first to know. And you, dear readers, will be the second!

Sadly for us, this means we may now have to share our glorious superheroine with the rest of the world. I mean, yes, non-Bay-Area-ers are familiar enough with A as a kickass local demon slayer, but I can't help but think having a show-offy new superpower—a superpower so obviously better and stronger than any we've seen before—puts her in the running for International Celeb status.

In other words? This changes everything.

Shasta's Corner! Shasta (Maisy's bestie) here. Want to look as cool as Aveda? Then check out Pussy Queen's brand-new selection of corsets. Fire power not included. Haha. (Editrix's Note: Shast, when you actually write out "haha," it kills the gosh-dang joke.)

Chapter six

"OFF, OFF . . . get it *off*!"

The fingers of my right hand clawed at my back as I burst into Jupiter HQ, trying to free myself from the corset. An errant curl fell over my eyes. Three hours were up and my glamour had worn off.

"Evie, love. Hold still and we'll get it off!"

Lucy trailed behind me, dragging half-conscious Bea with her. I motored into the foyer, the force of my stomping feet sending one of the gear-like buttons from my boots to the hardwood floor with a *clang*. But even the sheer realness of that sound wasn't enough to bring me back to Earth.

Scott was waiting for us in the foyer, his usually relaxed shoulders rigid with tension. I stopped abruptly, sending another button to the floor. *Clang*.

"What are you doing here?" I gasped. "And how could you—"

"I'm sorry." He held up his hands in placation. "We left the liquor cabinet unlocked. And Bea took advantage. And then climbed out her bedroom window."

Shit. In my overeagerness to squelch Anxiety Ball, I had forgotten to relock the liquor cabinet. So this fiasco was my fault.

"I came over to see if I could help," he said.

You could've helped earlier, I thought. *Why wouldn't*

*you try that damn spell? I've begged you to for years and
it might've stopped me from . . . from . . .*

I tamped down on my rising anger, hauled Bea from
Lucy's grasp, and shoved her at Scott. "Take her. Patch
up her knee and put her in one of the upstairs bedrooms
and go home. We'll talk later."

I brushed past him and marched toward Aveda's bedroom. My breathing sped up as my brain cycled through
an array of horrifying thoughts.

*What if Lucy hadn't been there? What if the statue had
been bigger? What if there had been more demons?
Whatifwhatifwhatif.*

By the time I flung open the door of Aveda's bedroom,
my breath was coming and going in shallow gasps—the
gasps of someone who was being slowly but surely buried alive.

"Aveda," I wheezed.

She was perched on the bed, ensconced in her mountain of pillows, her face lit by the glow of the iPad in her
hands. Nate was leaning against the dresser, his expression flummoxed, as if he couldn't begin to comprehend
what had just happened.

I couldn't, either.

When Aveda saw me, her eyes went wide and shiny.

"Evie," she breathed. "My brilliant, beautiful Evie.
The tweets and Facebook posts about your little adventure are uh . . . may . . . zing." She beamed at me. "You
finally embraced your true self. And at just the right moment. I know you've always been a little shy about the
whole 'I have an insane fire power that could potentially
kill millions' thing, but—"

"Whoa," Lucy said. I'd forgotten she was right behind
me. "Hold the flippin' phone. You have what, now?"

"What did you think that was, Luce?" I croaked.
"Cheap-ass memorabilia doesn't spontaneously com-
bust like that."

"My special collector's edition life-size replica statue

was cheap?" Aveda said. "We're going to have to speak to the manufacturer about that."

"Let's get back to the matter at hand." Nate pushed off from the dresser and started pacing the room. "Evie, Aveda said you would explain all of this?"

He turned to face me, his harsh features morphing into something that resembled concern. On him, it looked really fucking weird.

The absurdity of the night hit me full force and a hysterical laugh rose in my throat. I squelched it, but the effort forced my breath out in gasps again. I could only choke out a squeak expressing my most primal desire.

"Off."

Nate crossed the room in two strides, wrapped one of his giant hands around my corset ribbons, and yanked. I heard the satin rip and then suddenly, miraculously, the corset was on the floor and I was gulping precious oxygen into my lungs. The flouncy white blouse billowed around my torso. I breathed so deeply I started to get light-headed and felt myself tipping forward.

"Hey." Nate grabbed my elbow. My air-deprived brain focused on his hand, warm and solid. I unclenched my fists. I needed to calm down. Where the hell was my Soothing Inner Voice?

"An explanation would be good, love," Lucy said gently.

"Okay," I said, my breathing slowly returning to normal. "Okay."

I removed my elbow from Nate's grasp and hobbled over to Aveda, perching myself on the foot of her bed. I glanced at her out of the corner of my eye, wondering if she'd help me with this explanation. But she was too busy scrolling through her Twitter feed.

"Incredible," she murmured. "The pictures of you—er, me—all lit up have already gone viral."

So I was on my own then.

I folded my hands in my lap, focusing on taking deep breaths.

"It's like Aveda said," I began. "I have an insane fire power. That could potentially kill millions."

I lowered my eyes to my lap, not wanting to witness the inevitable horror that was surely dawning on their faces.

"I got it when Aveda and Scott got their powers," I continued. "Back when the first portal opened. It didn't seem serious at first. There were a few . . . minor incidents." I twisted my fingers together, calling up the memories. "I figured out it was tied to moments when I would have these big, crazy bursts of emotion. And so I decided I would just not have those feelings anymore."

"You stopped feeling?" Lucy said, her voice skeptical.

"Sort of." I still couldn't look at them. "I mean, I am Asian. We know from emotional repression. It worked out pretty well. Until grad school. And Richard."

"Guh, Richard." Aveda chose that moment to interject. "He was such a . . . dick."

"Yes." Our eyes met and I couldn't help but exchange a wry smile with her. "I remember that being your pet joke. In any case, he was also my professor slash secret boyfriend in my Gender Archetypes in Modern Cinema class."

My eyes drifted to my lap again. I could practically feel Nate and Lucy's judgmental eyes boring into my bowed head. I powered forward, trying to get through the story.

"We had a moment over my paper on the female power dynamics in *Crouching Tiger, Hidden Dragon*. One thing led to another and . . . well. Anyway. As it turned out, Aveda was right about his dickishness. He was also boning a whole cross-section of faculty and fellow students on the side. Until the day I caught him and Ms. Clarion, the too-cool-for-school Human Sexuality professor, doing it behind a stack of encyclopedias in the campus library."

"Human Sexuality?" Lucy murmured. "Really?"

I gave her a look.

"Sorry," she said. "It's kind of on the nose."

"When I saw them, I felt this stab of rage. More than a stab. Like a full-body feeling. Like I couldn't see anything else, couldn't feel anything except this soul-deep throb of pure mad."

I clenched my fists in my lap. I didn't like what came next.

"Before I knew what was happening, fire was shooting out of my hands and destroying the shelf behind their heads."

I uncurled my hands, forcing them to slacken.

"No one was killed, but . . . but people got hurt. A few of them had to go to the hospital. There was running and screaming and everyone was so terrified . . ." I shook my head, trying to erase the images. "The library burned to the ground. I knew I had to leave school. I had no idea what to do next. I was lost and scared and I showed up on Aveda's doorstep later that night in hysterics. She calmed me down and she offered to let me work for her." Recalling that moment, I felt a small rush of warmth. "She saved me."

Aveda perked up, smiling benevolently from behind the iPad. "That was before I had actual staff," she mused. "Evie was my first."

"I've kept my fire under control since then," I continued. "There have been little flare-ups, but nothing like that. Nothing for the past three years. I made my life ordered. I never allowed myself to get stressed or upset. Not until tonight."

I looked up, searching their faces. Nate's expression was hooded, revealing nothing. Lucy, on the other hand . . . her eyes were wide and she was trying to hide how unsure she was. I knew that look, but it had never been aimed in my direction before. It was for demons. For girls who blatantly copied her signature fashion. For outsiders.

"This power," Nate said, his voice thoughtful, "do you know the exact moment it triggers, once you have this so-called 'big, crazy burst of emotion' or—"

"Oh, no." I held up a warning finger. "You are not turning me into a science project. We're going to focus on fixing this situation. Oh, and we'll need to see if the cleanup crew made it to Whistles post-portal." I'd been freaking out too hard to even think about checking in with Rose. I had no idea if she'd hung out long enough to witness the craziness. I frowned, a stray thought worming its way through my panic.

"There was something weird about the demons tonight," I said.

"Weird how?" Nate said.

"It was the way they moved. Or didn't move." I shook my head in frustration, trying to put it into words. "They were slow. Lurchy. Bea's knee was bleeding and they didn't immediately swarm us."

Nate's brow crinkled. "But they kept moving toward you, yes?"

"Yes. I mean, they were still obviously attracted to the blood, but they weren't as fast as they usually are."

"Perhaps it had something to do with the composition and weight of the statues they imprinted on," he said. "If they were moving as a statue might move—"

"But the demons always move the same way," I interrupted. "You might not be a aware of that since you're never on the scene with us, but—"

"People!" Aveda snapped her fingers. "Let's not get distracted. We need to discuss our course of action."

"Right." I stood up and folded my hands in front of me, trying to make my tone as brisk and businesslike and personal-assistant-y as possible. "This isn't so bad. I'll draft a press release saying that this was a fluke—some kind of power surge—and then we'll call Mercedes—"

"No," Aveda said. "Really, Evie, you're missing the most obvious plan of attack."

"Which is . . . ?"

"Look!" Aveda shoved the iPad in my face. The screen displayed her Facebook fanpage. She pointed to a new thread of comments.

"Aveda: You lit a fire under my heart!"

"Kewl new POWER . . . what else can it do?"

"That was fierce, Firestarter!"

"You may have gotten the supervillain power of the lot," Aveda said. "But look what happens when you let loose. We get headlines. And not just on Maisy's blog." She smiled at the iPad screen. "I'm getting new Facebook fans from all over the world."

She lowered the iPad and scrutinized me for a long, uncomfortable moment. Her eyes took on a ferocious gleam.

"You have to keep pretending to be me," she said. "At least until . . ."

I flapped my hands incredulously. "Until what?"

"Until I can get my own fire power, of course!" She smiled in a "that settles it" kind of way. "Mayor Mendoza just announced that he's rescheduled the key to the city ceremony for two months from now, and I figure I'll definitely be ready to go by then."

"You can't just get one," I sputtered. "They don't hand them out like free samples at Costco."

"I'm aware that it might not be easy, but I'm sure I can accomplish anything I set my mind to," Aveda said, steel creeping into her gaze. "It's just a matter of doing the work."

I jerked my head at Nate. "Tell her! Tell her it's medically impossible to get your own fire power!"

But he just stared at me. His expression had gone all inscrutable again. I turned back to Aveda.

"And like I said, I can't call it up at will! I don't even know how it works!"

"You'll figure it out."

"Aveda! This whole me-being-you thing was only supposed to happen one time. You promised—"

"And things have changed. It's like Maisy said: this changes *everything*. Imagine what I could do with a fire power. This could take the Aveda Jupiter brand to a whole new level, which, in the end, means heightened protection for the city and continued employment for all of us." Aveda reached over and took my hand, her expression turning intense. "I know you can do this. Remember: you're my Michelle Yeoh. You don't need tears. You don't need anything except that incredibly powerful ability you've been suppressing for so long."

She squeezed my hand, her gaze boring into me. When she'd called me Michelle earlier, it had been earnest, a genuine plea born of desperation. Now it seemed calculating, like she was thinking of what exactly she could say to get me to agree to this insanity.

"And remember, Evie: I've—"

"—always been there for me. I know."

Oh, man, did I know. She was my oldest friend. She was my *Heroic Trio* compatriot. She had been there when I needed her.

And she sure as hell knew how to manipulate me.

After many attempts to dissuade Aveda from going through with her plan, I gave up, changed into one of her spare pairs of sweats, and dragged myself upstairs to check on Bea. My sister was sprawled facedown on the bed, her violet-streaked hair fanning around her head like a rage aura.

I eased myself onto the bed and smoothed her hair off her face. Her eyes fluttered open. She was drowsy, but in the process of making the turn to sobriety. In sleepiness, she was more like the Bea I remembered from before our parental situation explosion: a girl who hadn't yet experienced tragedy and was still open to the possibilities life had to offer.

"Evie," she murmured, guilt creeping into her eyes. "Did Aveda tell you about . . . ?"

"Yes. But I'm too tired to punish you right now. And it was half my fault for leaving the liquor cabinet unlocked, so let's call it even?"

"Okay." She pressed her lips together. "But I think I'm coming down with something . . ."

"You're going to school. Do this one thing for me so I can feel like I'm not completely ruining your teenage development."

"But I'm not feeling . . ." Her eyes slid to the side. After a long pause, a mumbled series of words slipped out of the corner of her mouth. "I got an email. From Dad."

Oh.

"Oh," I said, unable to think of anything more eloquent.

Our dad couldn't cope with his grief, so he took off on a spiritually dubious "vision quest" two months after Mom died. He'd gone back to Oahu, where he was from, for a bit. But after that, he was all over the globe. Once in a while we'd get a sparsely worded postcard or email from an exotic location ("Peace, love, and llamas" from Peru; "Find your inner gladiator" from Rome). As maddening as this was, I always felt a stab of romanticism whenever one of his notes came our way. He loved our mother so much, her death broke him into a million pieces. Now he was a larger-than-life figure who only communicated in single sentences from lands so far away, they seemed imaginary. Nothing would ever bring him back to the real world. Not even us.

On those rare occasions when he chose to get in touch, it always threw Bea's world off its axis.

"What did it say?" I asked.

"The usual. Something about his new 'spiritual wellness' training with someone called 'Yogini Lara.' I can't handle being around people right now, Evie. School is too much." She let out a dramatic sigh.

"I know." I stroked her hair again. "You still have to go to school, but why don't we hang out tomorrow night? Masses of junk food. All the bad movies you can handle. Just you and me and a cross-section of the city's best take-out menus."

She peered at me through clumpy mascara. "I guess," she said, doing her best to reinstate her disaffected veneer. "That could be fun. Or whatever."

"Okay!" I said, infusing my tone with false cheer. "Get some sleep, then. Looks like we're staying here tonight."

But her eyes were already drifting closed.

I lay down next to her. My breathing slowed to match hers, uniting us in a rare moment of peace. I had just begun to drift off when I heard the door creak open and footfalls leading someone over to the bed.

"Evie . . ."

"Scott," I murmured. "I told you to go home."

"I know," he said. "But I wanted to see how you were doing. The glamour I gave you—it was for more than what you said it was for. Obviously."

"Yes," I admitted, hoping that would be the end of it.

Naturally, it wasn't.

"Evie."

This time his tone had a trace of disapproval to it. Scott's protective big brother side always came out at the most inconvenient of moments.

"I'm fine," I murmured, keeping my eyes shut. "Everything is . . . totally . . . fine . . ."

I pretended to fall asleep, hoping that would make him leave.

There was a long pause, then, "We're not done talking about this."

Maybe it would be totally fine, I thought, as I heard

the door close behind him. Aveda was currently lit up by a heady rush of social media feedback, but surely she'd see things more clearly in the morning. Surely I could talk her out of this crazy plan. Surely.

I let my head fall against Bea's shoulder, our breathing matching up in a perfect rhythm until I finally slept.

CHAPTER SEVEN

IN THE PANTHEON of Comforting Smells, I ranked Mc-Donald's french fry grease in the top five. Maybe top two, even.

In seventh grade Aveda and I went on fry runs every Wednesday after school, cramming piles of those golden grease sticks down our throats while gossiping about the latest developments in our social circle (which was mainly just us and Scott). I hadn't eaten fries since converting to my Lucky Charms-only diet. But I still liked the smell.

I awoke to that french fry scent, a sleepy smile spreading over my face as the greasy aura invaded my nostrils. Then my eyes snapped open and panic replaced comfort.

Aveda had banned carbs from HQ, my Lucky Charms arsenal being the one notable exception. Therefore the presence of that smell indicated something was very wrong. And speaking of wrong . . .

The events of last night came flooding back. My freak-out. The fire. Aveda's plan.

Shit.

I rolled out of bed. Bea's side of the mattress was rumpled but empty, which I hoped meant she'd already gone to school. I opened the door to the hallway and looked back and forth, attempting to discern where the mysterious fry smell was coming from.

"Morning, love!" Lucy bustled down the hall and snagged my arm, pulling me along with her. "Aveda wants to see you."

"And I want to see her," I said, my brain diverting from the fry smell to the speech I was preparing. All I had to do to talk Aveda out of her plan, I reasoned, was play on her vanity. There was only one Aveda Jupiter. Accept no substitutes! Remember *Highlander*! Etcetera! There was no way I could step into her formidable shoes, and not just because the five-inch heels would send me sprawling. And if we had to call on a lesser hero like Mercedes for a bit . . . well, that would make the public appreciate Aveda Jupiter even more.

"Luce," I said, as she dragged me toward the stairs, "you're very peppy this morning."

"Aren't I always?"

"Yes, but . . ." I hesitated. "Last night, you seemed kind of scared? Of me?"

"I was momentarily shocked, but I'm over it. I think your suppressed power is rather cool." She flashed me a devilish grin. "I'm devising a Total Superheroine Workout Plan for you: running, kickboxing, Pilates. Piloxing. It will be intense."

"Intense?" I was pretty sure I'd never exercised. Like, in my life.

"If we're going to pull off Aveda's scheme, we have to get you into tiptop shape," Lucy said. "Scott's glamours might help you look the part, but you also need to be able to run up a flight of stairs without losing your breath." She cast a sidelong glance at me. "And," she added, worry creeping into her voice, "if we're going through with this, I need to keep you safe."

I couldn't help but feel touched. Underneath all the bravado and ill-timed flirtations, Lucy was a softie.

"Now let's talk about something more important," she said, veering back to perky. "Like: have you had any sex since this horrible-sounding Richard person? I know we've joked about your Dead-Inside-O-Tron and surely you would have confided in me about any recent exploits. But three years of vaginal hiatus seems extreme."

"Lucy! No. Nothing since then." I hoped she'd let me leave it at that. I did *not* want to discuss Richard. The truth was, sex with him had never been that exciting. He'd often insisted on discussing "the way mainstream fictions reinforce dated gender roles" right in the middle of the act, claiming nothing was quite as stimulating as "robust academic conversation." I disagreed and faked more than a few noises of passion just to get him to shut up. In retrospect I wasn't sure why a person who'd failed to inspire my libido went on to inspire so much rage. Maybe in addition to being pissed about his secret second girlfriend, I'd been furious he'd never managed to give me an orgasm.

"Three barren years. So tragic," Lucy said. "Speaking of tragic, Letta isn't responding to my texts. I still need you to help me pick out that deal-closing karaoke number."

We reached the bottom of the stairs and she gave me a shove toward Aveda's room. "In the meantime, I'm going to put the finishing touches on your workout regimen. And it's going to involve honing your own deal-closing skills. You must use this whole fake superhero thing to *get some*."

She made a not-at-all-subtle hip-thrusting motion.

Was this part of being Aveda? Your friend ordered you to have sex via X-rated mime?

Another reason I wanted no part of it. That and the exercise. And the whole "I could possibly kill people with fire" thing.

Seriously, of all the people in all the world, I was probably least equipped to be a superhero. Or even impersonate one.

I squared my shoulders and marched into Aveda's bedroom.

"Oh, there you are!"

Aveda beamed at me from her perch on the bed and waved me over with a french fry. Which was inexplicably clutched in her hand. As I entered the room, my eyes darted to another unexpected element: Scott. Sitting in a rocking chair next to the bed.

I looked from the fry to Scott and back again. It was hard to say which element of this little scene weirded me out the most. Nate, at least, was ever reliable, leaning against the dresser with his usual scowl in place.

"Scott," I said. My brain grasped a possible explanation. "Are you here to do a healing spell on Aveda's ankle?"

"No," he said. "You know that sort of thing is way outside the range of my abilities—"

"Scott and I have come up with a most excellent plan for you," Aveda interrupted. She popped the fry in her mouth and rooted around in the McDonald's bag sitting next to her.

"Plan?" I stared dumbly at her and Scott and couldn't help but flash back to them sitting side by side in our junior high cafeteria. He had always reveled in needling her, in trying like mad to get her haughty exterior to crack. Usually this translated into something like stuffing his mouth full of grapes and offering advice for her sixth-grade presidential campaign in a garbled cartoon voice ("Free nuts for all, Annie! Capture the rabid squirrel vote!"). I'd egged him on by giggling until my sides hurt. She'd responded by giving us A Look and going back to her work. In retrospect, it had probably seemed like we were ganging up on her by refusing to take her seriously.

And now they were ganging up on me.

"You two don't even get along," I blurted out. I picked irritably at the cupcake demon bite on my wrist. It had already almost healed.

"We're getting along for your sake, Evie," Aveda said sternly. "Isn't that generous of us?"

"I've been trying to get ahold of you all morning," Scott cut in. "Annie called me—"

"Aveda," Aveda corrected through a mouthful of fries.

"Annie. She has an idea."

"An idea I strongly oppose," Nate grumbled.

"It's the spell!" Aveda shrieked. "The one you've been begging him to try for years. I've convinced him to give it a go!"

That pretty much stopped my entire thought process.

"The depowering spell?" I said, my voice small and quavery. I turned to Scott. "But you always said—"

"Everything I've always said holds true," he said. "I still think it's too dangerous."

"At least we agree on something," muttered Nate.

I ignored him. "Then why now?" I asked Scott. "Why are you willing to—"

"Because you and Annie clearly need some kind of intervention," he interrupted. His voice was low, tight, controlled. He frowned at me and suddenly it felt like we were the only two people in the room. "How could you let her convince you to go through with that charade at the party? How could you . . ." He shook his head, as if he still couldn't quite believe it. "Maybe if I finally give you what you want, you'll feel less tethered to this version of 'stability.'" He gestured to our surroundings. "And maybe that will make the two of you reevaluate this toxic, codependent bond you've got going on."

"Since when are you so melodramatic?" Aveda said. She rolled her eyes and poked him with a french fry. "What Scott's not getting to is the fact that I made him see the spell in a whole new light." She thwacked him in the arm with the fry. "Go on, tell her!"

Scott batted her fry away. "Annie and I have an idea that might make the magic that goes into this less dangerous. Normally this kind of spell—like a healing spell—is beyond the scope of what I can do. I can manipulate small bits of magic to create equally small things—the glamours, the love tokens—but I can't just up and eliminate something. Especially something as huge as an injury or a superpower."

"But?" Aveda prompted.

"But if I can take something that already exists and, rather than eliminating it, move it somewhere else—"

"Scott's going to put your power *in me*!" squealed Aveda, no longer able to contain herself. She dragged a pair of fries through a ketchup splotch on a napkin. "I told you: freakin' brilliant! I'm saving your life again!"

"But it will take some time," Scott said. "I have to make sure all elements of this spell are going to work and that means—"

"He estimates it'll take four to six weeks!" chirped Aveda. "Perfect timing. I'll be all healed up by then. So you only have to be Aveda Jupiter for a little bit longer."

She looked at me expectantly. I gnawed on my lower lip, my brain awhirl.

Scott was going to try the spell. *The* spell. The one I'd been begging him to try forever. If he succeeded, I'd be free of my long-held curse.

In short, he'd finally make me normal.

But was "normal" enough of a reason to risk calling forth the fire I couldn't really control? To willfully put myself in danger?

I opened my mouth to tell Scott that I was, in fact, not intent on going through with this and was about to successfully talk Aveda out of the whole thing and—

"I know you're worried about going out there as me, what with the demons and all," Aveda said, as if reading my thoughts. "I know *you*, Evie. And while I may have gotten carried away in my thrill over seeing you finally fulfill that Michelle Yeoh-an heroic promise after all these years, don't worry: I realize you don't actually want to *be* Michelle forever, and I will do everything in my power to protect you." She gave me a smile that actually verged on reassuring. "Rest assured, Lucy will take a more active role whenever there's actual danger or demon-fighting to be done. She'll keep you safe. She has all those weapons and she knows all my best moves, even if she's not as skilled at them. You won't even have to *use* your fire power. The public's already seen it in action; now it's just a matter of keeping up the heroic Aveda Jupiter appearance while my ankle heals and Scott figures out the transfer."

Normal. Normal. *Normal.* That single word pulsed through my brain, overwhelming any further protests I might have had. "Normal" was something that hadn't been even remotely within my grasp for years. Now here it was: a beautiful possibility. I could already anticipate the sweet, crashing sensation of relief I would surely experience once I didn't have to worry about the fire ever again.

God, what would that even be like?

"When you think about it, Evie, this whole fire thing is more suited to my superheroing lifestyle, anyway," Aveda said. "Imagine how much more awesome my spinning backhand will be with a fist of flames."

That was probably true. The fire was nothing but wild, unpredictable danger to me. To her, it would be a new weapon in her artillery, a powerful force she could use to enhance her already kickass moves and level up her demon slayage. Although . . . she would need to rein in those diva mood swings. Maybe once Scott figured out the transfer, I could delicately recommend some good therapy.

Okay. I could do this. True, the party the night before hadn't gone as planned, but it had at least given me a little practice being a fake superhero. Lucy would be there for me the whole way through, and at the end of this little adventure, I'd finally get what I wanted more than anything.

Normal.

"I don't know why we're even considering this." Nate's rumble of a voice cut into my thoughts. "Evie hasn't had a chance to think about the ramifications of—"

"*Evie* thinks this is a fine plan," I interrupted. "And it's my decision, isn't it?"

He gave me an exasperated look. "Which is one of the many reasons you should take some time to think it through."

"I have thought about it. I've thought about pretty much nothing else for the past three years. And I know this is right."

"But Scott himself correctly points out that it could be dangerous," Nate pressed. "And he's never tried anything like this before." He turned his scowl on Scott. "What makes you think you can go from treacly love spells to pulling an incredibly complicated power out of a human being?"

"As I already explained—" Scott began.

"We need to look at this from every possible angle," Nate interrupted. "To collect more data, to—"

"No." My voice was clear and firm. "*We* don't need to do anything. *I* trust him." I inclined my head toward Scott. "And this is the perfect answer for both me and Aveda. End of story."

Scott nodded, his eyes unreadable. "Then I'll get started," he said, standing and striding out of the room.

"Wonderful!" Aveda clapped her greasy hands together. "I'm glad you decided not to be a stick-in-the-mud about this, Evie. See, Little Sis: she's not always a stick-in-the-mud."

I realized Aveda was grinning at a spot beyond my shoulder. I turned to see Bea standing in the doorway. Well, Bea trying to back away from the doorway.

"Beatrice, what are you doing here? 'Here' not being anywhere near school?" I said.

She gave me an insolent look. "It's an in-service day."

"Right." I narrowed my eyes. "In-service."

Ignoring me, she crossed over to Aveda's bed and plopped herself down, snagging a fry.

"So, Evie," she said, feigning nonchalance, "I hear you've become an overnight master of superheroic disguise. But I guess that wasn't worth mentioning to me, huh? Can't trust your frakballs crazy Little Sis with important info like that."

Goddammit. There hadn't been a good moment to relate my adventures to her last night. And I'd planned on getting out of further adventuring until the whole spell thing came up. But if I tried to explain this convoluted bit of waffling, she'd never believe me. For her, it was always easier to believe I was trying to make her life difficult.

"Anyway," Aveda said, glossing over the sudden tension in the room, "tonight's gonna be a blast for you, Evelyn."

"Tonight?" I mentally scanned my to-do list bulletin board. What was on Aveda's schedule for tonight?

"Aveda," said Nate, "under the circumstances, considering that you aren't . . . you, I think we should—"

"No cancelling." Aveda gave him a cool look. "League of Social Betterment Through Bettering Oneself events are crucial to the Aveda Jupiter image. And it'll be fun for Evie. She gets to wear an amazing dress."

League . . . dress . . . Oh, right.

"The benefit," I said, the event finally coming into focus in my mental calendar. "Aveda, I can't. Bea and I have plans tonight."

I tried to meet Bea's eyes, hoping this would get her to cut me some slack. Instead she shot me a full Tanaka Glare.

"Not a problem," Aveda said. "I can take care of Beatrice. She and I will have this place all to ourselves. She already did a great job fetching me breakfast." She waved a fry around. "Since I don't have to wear that dress tonight, I can indulge a little, right?"

"Hanging out with Aveda sounds good to me," said Bea.

"But—" I started to protest.

"Stop right there." Aveda held up a hand. "Aveda Jupiter must attend the benefit. And people." She frowned at her now-empty fast food bag, then picked it up and waved it around like a grease-soaked flag of surrender. "Someone get me more of these."

I had forgotten about the dress.

It was an odd thing to forget. While Aveda claimed League of Social Betterment Through Bettering Oneself events were crucial to her image, they also tended to be packed with self-congratulatory types. This brought out her competitive edge even more than usual. And that meant her dress had to be the best.

Aveda usually loved nothing more than shopping for beautiful clothes, but her demonbusting/promotional appearance schedule had been more packed than usual lately, so the task had fallen to me. I'd dedicated myself to the quest for the perfect dress, scouring vintage shops and the internet and even the ninety-nine cent bin at Goodwill. I'd finally found just the thing at an out-of-the-way estate sale in San Leandro: a daring gown that had once graced the body of some eccentric old lady whose overflowing mansion of possessions clearly belonged on *Hoarders*.

As I admired my pre-glamoured self in the mirror, I had to admit: the dress was pretty great, a confection of glittery beads sprinkled over pearly tulle, like a swirl of Cake My Day's sparkly icing. The tulle wrapped itself around my body like a second skin and plunged low in the front. I wouldn't wear anything like this of my own volition, ever—but I was literally not myself.

I was incredibly, irrefutably, uncharacteristically *hot*.

Or I would be, once I put the glamour token to use. Because I'd be at the benefit for longer than three hours,

Scott had given me an extra one. At some point I'd have to slip off to the bathroom to refresh my Aveda-ness.

In the meantime, I needed to figure out the buttons. The gown fastened up the back in a series of tiny pearl beads that started at the tailbone and snaked up my spine. No matter how much I bent my body into various twisty positions, there was no way I could reach them all.

I contorted my torso, my fingers scrabbling at the minuscule buttons and the even more minuscule loops they were supposed to fit into. I tried turning my head, but that just made my neck cramp. After a few moments of attempting to twist myself into a button-reaching position, I gave up. I was getting sweaty, and sweat, as Aveda would be quick to remind me, definitely didn't go with this dress. I stretched my right arm around to my back so I could hold the dress semi-closed. Then I slithered over to the doorway, each small step reminding me that the hip-hugging skirt restricted movement in a way that bordered on painful.

Between this and the corset, I was starting to wonder if all Aveda's outfits were so cumbersome.

I needed . . . well, I needed me. A version of Assistant Me to help Aveda Me into these binding clothes.

I made it to the doorway and peered into the hall. I'd opted to change in one of the vacant upstairs bedrooms. Because Aveda currently couldn't do stairs, this ensured me a moment of peace to collect myself. But I hadn't counted on the buttons issue.

I looked left, looked right, hoping Lucy or even Bea would magically spring out of the woodwork.

Nothing. Silence. Well, silence interrupted by the swish of tulle rubbing together as I adjusted my grip, trying to keep the back of the dress closed. Then I heard something else: a heavy footfall connecting with the stairs.

Clomp. Clomp, clomp!

Unless she was flinging her entire tiny body quite forcefully against the stairs, definitely not Lucy.

Clomp, clomp.

And despite her noisy state of teenage rebellion, probably not Bea, either.

Clomp!

Scott?

No, of course not, I thought as the large, scowly figure emerged at the top of the stairs. *It would have to be him.*

Given my current state of near immobility, I couldn't afford to be picky.

"Nate!" I waved to him from the doorway. "Can you help me with . . . wow. What are you wearing?"

Like me, Nate had a uniform of sorts: black, black, and more black. The idea that he owned clothing in other shades was completely foreign, yet here he was in a beautifully cut charcoal gray suit. The jacket hung nicely off his broad shoulders, softening his thuggish appearance and giving the shock of dark hair falling onto his forehead a rakish cast (as opposed to its usual cast, which translated to "I do not own a hairbrush"). For a second, I could almost see the off-kilter attractiveness that Lucy was always going on about.

I mean, almost. Let's not get crazy. This was still *Nate* we were talking about.

"A suit," he said.

I cocked an eyebrow, indicating he needed to elaborate.

"I'm . . . escorting you," he relented, shoving a hand through his hair and taking it back to hairbrush-needed land. "Aveda decided you could use some extra security. In addition to Lucy."

"So she's forcing you to leave your lab for the night?"

He met my gaze. "I volunteered."

He *volunteered*? I tried to keep the shock from registering on my face. Nate never went anywhere. He was a total hermit. The only instance I could recall of him actually standing outside was the day he'd shown up on Aveda's doorstep two years ago. I'd mistaken him for a bodyguard hopeful (Lucy had snagged that position several days earlier), but as he'd been quick to inform me, he was the illustrious Nathaniel Jones, the renowned physician and demonology scholar whose paper on the science of superheroism had caught Aveda's attention earlier that year. Given his unique combination of talents, she'd simply had to have him on staff. I'd known about all this, of course, but I hadn't known what Nathaniel Jones looked like; unlike other famed demonology scholars, he shunned public appearances and lectures and his photograph never appeared alongside his published papers. I suppose all of this contributed to some kind of self-aggrandizing air of mystery. I mostly just found it aggravating, especially since his need to stay indoors meant he always conveniently "forgot" when it was his turn to do simple household errands. You know, all that "get groceries" type of minutiae that might seem beneath his notice, but was key to keeping HQ up and running.

"Okay, then," I said. "Your first escort duty is to help me with these buttons."

I shuffled back into the bedroom without waiting for his response. After a moment of silence, he clomped in after me.

I stood in front of the mirror and gestured awkwardly toward my back with my free hand. "I can't reach."

He took the back of the dress from me hesitantly, contemplating the buttons.

"I'm not sure . . ." he said, his gruff tone wavering. "Perhaps Lucy would be better at . . ."

"It's not that hard," I interrupted, irritation pricking my sweaty skin. "Aren't you always dissecting demons and stuff? Compared to that, this should be a piece of cake."

He adjusted his grip on the tulle. "First you might want to . . ." He gestured at something.

"I might want to what?" I tapped my foot, my

impatience rising. That *nyah* quality crept into my voice. He always seemed to bring the *nyah* out.

"Your, um . . . bra. Is showing."

He ducked his head, focusing on the buttons.

"Oh."

My cheeks flushed as I glanced down at my chest, which was encased in hot pink lace. While my T-shirt/jeans uniform was pretty basic, I liked to make my own fun via neon underwear. After setting the library on fire, brightly colored unmentionables were about the biggest thrill I could handle. They were cute, they did not induce anxiety, and no one ever saw them except me.

Well. *Usually* no one except me.

Anyway Nate was right. A faint pink outline was visible through the thin material of the dress. I might as well have pasted a flashing SEE BOOBS HERE sign over my chest.

"Thanks," I said, pulling the front of the dress against me. I unhooked the bra with my other hand and tossed it on the floor. "I guess I can go braless with this dress, right? It doesn't leave much to the imagination anyway."

I twisted back and forth, trying to determine if there was visible nipple. It was borderline. The effect of my bigger-than-Aveda's breasts would be softened by the glamour, though.

Nate suddenly seemed even more preoccupied with staring at the buttons.

"Hold still," he said, some of that signature gruffness creeping back into his voice.

I forced myself to stop moving and he started doing up the buttons. My foot tapped again and I hastily stilled it, trying to remain immobile while he worked.

"I pulled some of my recent analyses for you," he said abruptly. "Regarding common factors in the last two months of demon attacks."

"Uh . . . what?"

While I understood the medical doctor keep-Aveda-healthy side of Nate's job, the demonology scholar part seemed as gibberish-riddled as his precious portal stones. In addition to dissecting whatever demon specimens came our way, he was always running various technobabble-y tests with names like "multiple regression analysis" and "structural equation modeling," claiming this would help him discover links between the portals. As far as I could tell, the only link he'd come up with so far was that the portals appeared in totally random fashion and produced scary, hungry demon swarms. Which I could've told you without the fancy tests, since I was always there on the scene.

"You mentioned observing oddities in regard to the Aveda statue demons last night," he said. "I thought looking at my recent data might give you further insight. Perhaps you'll see a connection."

I shivered, remembering the statues advancing on me and Bea. "Last night you didn't seem to think I was clear on what I saw."

"It's not that I don't believe you," he said. "But you were describing your impressions of the event, and impressions are not exact data. Additionally, because you were in a heightened state, your thoughts were a bit . . . muddled. I am merely trying to eliminate various possibilities to get a better idea of what you deemed out of the ordinary."

I bit back a retort about my "muddled" thoughts and tried to call up a more detailed memory of the statue demons. Maybe my stressed-out brain had imagined the weirdness. Anyway, last night's mess seemed like it had happened forever ago and I had plenty to think about at the moment without fixating on whatever I thought I'd seen.

"It was probably just a fluke," I said.

"Sometimes a fluke can be the first sign of an important pattern—"

"This is really not important right now," I said. Not when I had to worry about going out in public as Aveda without setting anything on fire again. "And if you want to collect more data, then seriously: come with us when the demons attack. Check out the scene, observe them in person, analyze what you see with your own eyes. I mean, if you're going to break the seal on the whole going out in public thing, that seems like it would be way more useful than attending some silly benefit."

That shut him up, at least for the moment.

"Why did you volunteer anyway? To escort me?" I pressed. "You never escort Aveda." I sounded vaguely accusatory.

"I'm concerned," he said.

"That I'll fuck everything up like I did at Whistles?" I said.

"Your power is unpredictable. If I go with you, I can monitor your moods, your reactions. See if we can figure out a trigger."

"So you want to make me an extra-toasty lab rat. I should've guessed."

I tamped down on my irritation. Why couldn't he leave well enough alone? We'd already come up with a perfect solution: remove the power from me, put it into an actual superheroine, cut to me fulfilling my long-held dream of being *normal*. I didn't need to spend time delving into the hows and whys and wherefores of the fire power. I needed to get the fire out of me—and into someone who could actually handle it—as soon as possible.

Not that he'd ever understand that. He never seemed to understand anything that didn't involve a nice, neat little column of numbers.

"Why aren't you more interested in finding the exact trigger?" he countered. "'Crazy bursts of emotion' is maddeningly unspecific."

I shrugged, causing the tulle to shift in his hands. He pulled it back into place.

"That's the best way I can describe it. Haven't you ever had a feeling you couldn't define? Or articulate?"

He didn't respond, so I barreled on. "It's a certain kind of heightened feeling, like an emotional burst that overwhelms all logic and thought. It takes over to the point where I'm unaware of anything else. I don't really know how else to say it. I just know when it's happening."

"But we could try to quantify it—"

"Quantify it? You want me to do tests with my feelings?" I snorted. "Now there's a recipe for disaster. Anyway, if Scott's spell works, I won't have to deal with this much longer. So what's the point in trying to 'quantify' anything?"

"The point is, you could really do something with it if you wanted to. Learn to control it. Act like a naturally curious person who wants to figure out why you are the way you are."

Wow, really? My irritation flared. He'd been aware of my fire for less than twenty-four hours, and already he thought he knew better than me. As if I hadn't spent the last three years locking myself down, controlling my impulses, and establishing my safeguards. As if I didn't hear all those terrified screams ringing through the library whenever I allowed my mind to wander during cold, sleepless nights. As if I didn't know myself all too well.

But that was his way, wasn't it? To immediately assume he knew everything about everything without actually experiencing it in real life.

"I know why I'm the way I am," I snapped. "Demon portal, freak occurrence, maybe you're familiar? I *know.* And I also know I don't want to be this way."

"But you haven't even tried it," he said, his voice twisting in frustration. He frowned at me in the mirror. "You've wasted all your energy suppressing it. All of these years, and you've never even—"

"Wasted?!"

I yanked myself free from his grasp and whirled around. He wasn't done with the buttons and the dress hung half open. How dare he judge me from behind those cold, clinical scientist glasses? He was supposed to be *helping* me. And helping meant contributing to the whole Get the Fire Power Out of Evie ASAP plan, not asking five million irrelevant questions and acting all superior when it came to dealing with my own actions and feelings. When it came to the very real danger I posed to people. My stomach knotted just thinking about it.

"All that 'wasted' energy means I haven't burned anything down since the library," I growled. "How has this not penetrated that supposedly gigantic brain of yours? I destroyed an entire building. I could have destroyed people. I don't want something that allows me to do that. I don't."

I willed my hands to relax at my sides. I would not allow myself to flare up over *him*.

He stared back at me, his eyes unreadable behind those damn glasses. I slid forward, the dress still restricting my every move, and jabbed my index finger into his chest.

"You want a tip on how the fire power works?"

I leaned in closer, giving him a glower that was as good as the ones he usually gave me.

"Don't make me *angry*."

I turned on my heel and shuffled indignantly out of the room, my half-buttoned dress flapping behind me. I'd like to think I accomplished this with at least a little bit of dignity and a touch of haughty attitude.

Maybe Aveda was rubbing off on me after all.

HOLDING OUT FOR A HEROINE Q&A:
Magnificent Mercedes

Here at the Holding Out for a Heroine blog, we track the latest and greatest in superhero news—and that includes spotlighting those in and around the supes community! Today we welcome Mercedes McClain, aka Magnificent Mercedes.

HOfaH: Please tell our readers about your power and how you utilize it.

MM: I have what I like to call a "human GPS" ability, which enables me to track vehicles, determine the best routes between locations, and "see" traffic.

HOfaH: You can see traffic *in your brain*?!

MM: That is correct, yes.

HOfaH: And does that mean you can track anything with a GPS locater on it? Like house arrest monitors and stuff? Because that seems like it would be totally useful in a superheroing career—

MM: No, just vehicles.

HOfaH: Oh. Huh. That's—

MM: Still very exciting, I know. My power is particularly useful in my adopted home city of Los Angeles, where I am able to assist the police in apprehending car thieves and/or individuals who otherwise misuse their right to the automobile. Additionally I've been making inroads as far as clearing up the city's serious gridlock problem.

HOfaH: And you could totally help the pizza delivery dude find the best way from Santa Monica to the Valley during rush hour, right?

MM: I *could*, but as a superheroine, you must make difficult decisions regarding what is and is not a worthy use of your power. And pizza delivery falls into the "not" category.

HOfaH: I disagree, but let's move on! So obviously you're part of the only group in the world that has superpowers: that select number of San Francisco residents who got their abilities eight years ago when the big portal opened up. But not everyone chose to fight crime. In fact, most folks just kept doing whatever they were doing pre-portal. What inspired you to take this on?

MM: I've always had a finely tuned sense of right and wrong and the desire to put good out into the world. Also most people's powers were . . . how can I put this nicely? Just not all that powerful. Relatively mundane. Only a handful of us saw the potential in what we were given and were therefore able to choose this path. I feel very blessed.

HOfaH: Blessed! I love that. Hey, have you ever thought of changing your codename to "The Lost Angel" or something? Because you live in Los Angeles and you're "lost" from San Francisco and then "angel" kind of goes with "blessed" . . .

MM: I wouldn't say I'm "lost" from San Francisco. I wouldn't say that at all.

HOfaH: Then why didn't you stay? You could've fought demons alongside Aveda Jupiter instead of chasing cars around and stuff!

MM: I don't do anything "alongside" anyone. Besides, my work is very important—

HOfaH: So that's why you left? Because Aveda outshone you and you had to go somewhere else to get that kind of attention?

MM: No, of course not—

HOfaH: What do you think of her new fire power? Word is, it's finally gonna break her through to huge international fame!

MM: I very much doubt that.

HOfaH: Why?

MM: Well, we don't even know much about this new power yet. It could be temporary. A flash in the pan.

HOfaH: She's sure making the most of it, though, eh?

MM: Mmm.

HOfaH: At the very least, this could definitely increase the world's awareness of supes in general! I mean, most of you are local celebs at best, right?

MM: . . .

HOfaH: Hey, maybe more demon portals will finally open up in locations beyond San Francisco? And then maybe people everywhere could get superpowers, too? That'd be way cool, right?!

MM: I don't think that would be cool at all.

CHAPTER EIGHT

THE MOMENT I set foot in the ballroom, I was blinded by glittering light. Thankfully it wasn't portal light. There was nothing supernatural about it, unless you counted what was surely an out-of-this-world price tag.

The League of Social Betterment Through Bettering Oneself was known for their splashy events: bacchanalias of such jaw-dropping excess, even Hugh Hefner would be like, "Hey, maybe take it down a notch." I found this amusing, since the League was supposedly based around the principle of finding ways to be less wasteful in our everyday lives, their website littered with such statements as: "Go green!", "Take a bus/bike/unicycle!", and "Save the red panda!" (Fuck the regular panda, I guess.)

I couldn't recall what this particular benefit was supposed to be benefitting, but every League benefit had a theme, and tonight's shindig—situated in the vast ballroom of one of the Financial District's generically sumptuous hotels—was simply entitled "Space." (Maybe it was benefitting red pandas . . . in space?)

Strings of twinkly lights sweeping across the ceiling made for a passing imitation of a starry sky, and gargantuan rocket ship sculptures were positioned all over the room. In the far right corner someone had erected a wax model of what appeared to be an alien-esque villain who . . .

Wait.

I squinted at it. With its swooping horns and voluminous robes, it bore a striking resemblance to *The Heroic Trio*'s chief bad guy, aka The Evil Master. In the movie he plotted to take over China (not necessarily the world—just China) via an ill-conceived scheme that involved stealing babies. As hokey as he might have been for adult viewers, he scared the shit out of the wide-eyed tween versions of me and Aveda.

I must have been hallucinating. That was simply too obscure a reference for this crew. League members always let it be known that they were way too socially conscious to own anything as vulgar as a television.

I blinked several times, trying to avoid disorientation from the lights, and gripped Nate's arm so I wouldn't topple over in my ridiculous shoes: five-inch, sparkle-encrusted high heels that threatened to snap my ankles off every time I moved. Nate and I hadn't spoken since I'd stalked out on him. I'd found Lucy, who had helped me finish buttoning my dress, and then he'd clomped back to my side at the appointed time. Even though he was a pain in the ass, I was grateful for his oversize solidness as the seizure-inducing lights flashed on and off. I knew he wouldn't let me fall.

"So we're trying to go stealth, here," I said, attempting to convey confidence I didn't feel.

"You can't do stealth in that getup," retorted Lucy, casting an approving look at my dress. "Yowza."

She grinned at me and adjusted her own dress, a 1920s flapper number with a matching headpiece. Probably not your typical bodyguard gear, but she looked wonderful.

"Maybe not so much stealth as sort of under the radar," I amended. "I can be an under-the-radar guest of honor, right?"

The League ladies dominating the scene were undeniably fancy, but these weren't stock trophy wife types.

These were San Francisco fancy ladies: younger, trendier, more in tune with the latest in fig stuffings and the best oldey timey-looking filters for your camera phone photos.

"Oh my goodness! That dress!" Maisy Kane sang out. She trotted toward me, champagne flute in one hand, phone in the other. Shasta trailed behind her, looking decidedly less peppy.

"You always have the best fashions, Aveda," exclaimed Maisy. "The steampunk getup last night was to die for. But this little number takes the gosh-dang cake."

"Where did you get it?" Shasta asked, curving her bright-red-lipsticked mouth into something that was probably supposed to resemble a smile. A suppressed challenge flickered through her eyes: this was a test.

I scoured my brain. Had Aveda come up with a backstory for this dress? She definitely wouldn't want me telling people it had once graced the body of a pack-ratty old lady.

Aveda Jupiter does not shop secondhand.

I stood there blankly, trying to put together a piquant tale of the dress's origin, something befitting a fashionable superheroine.

Shit, shit, shit. My brain was a big, blank thing, a vast field of nothingness. I couldn't conjure a simple sentence. I was too afraid it would be the *wrong* sentence, which would then be plastered in accusatory all-caps on Maisy's blog. A hummingbird-like buzz of panic thrummed through me and I anticipated the sweat that was about to bloom on my palms.

Less than twenty-four hours had passed, and here I was, on the verge of fucking up our stupid plan. And not because of the whole destructive fire power thing. Because when confronted with the prospect of socializing while wearing an uncomfortable dress and impossible shoes, I apparently couldn't deal.

My eyes darted to Lucy, who was mouthing something at me, but the too-bright lights made my vision blur. My fingers flexed instinctively against Nate's arm, trying to maintain my grip as my palms started to sweat.

No. No sweat. Stop that. *Stop it.*

Maybe I should pretend to pass out. Swoon. Faint. Ugh, no. Aveda would hate that.

Aveda Jupiter does not show weakness. Aveda Jupiter lives a healthy lifestyle, which does not include something so pedestrian as fainting. Aveda Jupiter thinks you are being an idiot right now.

Suddenly a hand covered mine, big and warm and solid. My head jerked up to meet Nate's gaze, his dark eyes boring into me. He cocked his head and raised an eyebrow as if to say, "Well? You're not gonna sink us on a fashion question, right?"

"Local designer," I heard myself blurt out, the words haphazardly stringing themselves together. "Don't recall the name. She's new to the scene and specializes in organic fibers."

Maisy beamed and even Shasta looked moderately impressed. I guess I passed?

Almost imperceptibly Nate's fingers squeezed mine. Yup. I passed. Sweet relief flooded through me, knocking my anxiety-inducing chest hummingbird on its ass.

"Aveda," Maisy sang out. "We are so dang thrilled to nab you for our little do. How does one take a night off from superheroing? Do you have a wee sidekick type who fills in for you?"

If only she knew.

"I'm ready to bust out of here and fight demons at any moment," I improvised. "This dress . . . breaks away. If you know what I'm saying."

Lucy clapped her hand over her mouth, eyes dancing with merriment. Nate suddenly had to clear his throat.

"Scandalous!" Maisy roared with laughter. "Aveda, babe, you have got to save some of these witty nuggets for our exclusive interview. About your new power. Which you are definitely giving to me, right?"

"Oh, well . . . I . . ."

"I'll have my assistant call your assistant and set a time for us," Maisy said, bulldozing right over me. "What's the name of yours again? Ava? Eva? Ellie?"

"Evie," muttered Nate.

"Right." Maisy snapped her fingers. "The mousy little thing with all the hair. You should do something about that whole . . . situation." She waved a hand around her head to indicate my unruly curls. "Our assistants are visual representations of our brands, are they not? I can recommend a good blow-out person."

I bit my lip to keep from giggling. Really, this was all just too weird. I glanced up at Nate, trying to catch his eye to share my amusement. But his eyes were fixed on Maisy, a scowl brewing on his face. I elbowed him in the ribs. Scowly was not a good look for Aveda Jupiter's escort.

"In the meantime you simply must try the gouda-stuffed date," Maisy said. "It's to die for."

She plucked a brown blob from a waiter's passing tray and thrust it into my hands. I hesitated, studying it. I was unused to non-Lucky-Charm foodstuffs.

But that sweet relief was still coursing through my veins, making me borderline giddy. And Maisy and Shasta were staring at me again, their eyes wide with expectation. And at this point, I'd leapt so far out of my comfort zone, what was one more thing?

I popped the date in my mouth.

"Wow . . . *wow*. That really is to die for," I exclaimed, as the bright, earthy flavors exploded on my tongue.

As Maisy might say, hot dang. That was good. That was actually *delicious*.

My relief morphed into something purer, something downright enthusiastic. Huh. Not a feeling I was accustomed to. But as I had to keep reminding myself, I wasn't me. I was Aveda Jupiter. And Aveda Jupiter could totally get enthusiastic about fucking delicious dates, right? I dropped my hand from Nate's arm and reached for the tray again.

"Yes, have another, have another!" squealed Maisy, clapping her hands. "Have the whole dang tray. Your escort will be happy to hold it for you."

Maisy snatched the date-laden tray from the waiter and shoved it at Nate. He pinched it between his fingers like it was covered in dead things.

"Listen, *Aveda*," Lucy said, muffling a giggle. "I'm gonna scope the perimeter. You enjoy those to-die-for dates."

"Mrph!" I agreed, my mouth full of delicious blobs.

"Make sure you grab one of the VIP gift bags," Maisy said, linking her arm through mine. "I did up something special for you guests of honor."

She leaned in and gestured to the wax model on the other side of the room. "There's a mini-replica of that statue over there in each bag. I commissioned them from a local props guy. The other League ladies have no idea it's from this old Hong Kong movie called *The Heroic Trio*."

"*The Heroic Trio*?" I blurted through my mouthful of dates. "You know *The Heroic Trio*?"

"Of course I do!" she said. "I watch it all the time over at the Yamato Theater."

"They still play it at the Yamato? I haven't been there in . . . well, it's been ages!"

Actually Aveda went to the Yamato every Friday for the early matinee. She always wore a glamorous "disguise" in the hope that someone would recognize her and tweet some kind of "celebrities: they're just like us!" nonsense. She hadn't told me the Yamato had resurrected *The Heroic Trio*, though.

"Every other Monday night!" said Maisy. "They just don't make movies like that anymore, do they?"

"No!" I agreed, shoveling more dates into my mouth. "They most certainly do not."

Nate looked at me like I'd sprouted another head. I ignored him. The giddy feeling was surging through me now, emboldened by the intoxicating taste of gouda-stuffed dates. And the fact that I was getting my own replica of The Evil Master.

"That's actually the movie that inspired me to be a superhero," I said impulsively. "Maybe we could go see it at the Yamato one of these Mondays. We could do the interview then?"

"I'd love to," she said, squeezing my arm. "And for the photo shoot, we simply must style you as Invisible Girl—a skintight red jumpsuit capped by a gorgeous mane of Michelle Yeoh-esque hair!"

"Want to let the rest of us in on whatever it is you two are whispering about?" Shasta said.

"Nothing important, Shast," Maisy said, giving me a wink. "Just asking Aveda to divulge all her superheroine secrets. Which she'll never give up, I'm sure."

"Never!" I agreed, letting loose with a tinkling laugh. On me, that laugh would sound strange. But as rendered in Aveda's voice, it was just right.

"Aveda," Nate said. "We've been standing in this same spot for a while. Perhaps you'd like to see more of the party?"

I suppressed my eye-roll. Couldn't he see I'd finally just gotten comfortable in my Aveda-esque skin? That this spot was actually working out pretty well? Why did he always have to be so *annoying*?

"I'm fine right here!" I snagged a flute of champagne from a passing tray and used it to wash down my last mouthful of dates.

An all-new feeling blossomed in my stomach, as light and fizzy as the champagne bubbles.

I was Aveda Jupiter. I was not mousy. My hair looked amazing.

Could it be? No. No way.

And yet, as a smile spread slowly over my face, I had to acknowledge that this was actually happening.

For the first time in years, I was enjoying myself.

After a few more champagnes, my bladder screamed bloody murder and it was time to refresh my glamour, so I detached myself from Maisy and Co. and set out for the bathroom. Nate gave me a dark look that indicated he didn't like me flitting off on my own, but honestly: what punk-ass demon was gonna take me down while I peed?

As I teetered down the hall in my high heels, my thoughts wandered back to finding an unexpected *Heroic Trio* kindred spirit in Maisy. I wondered what her opinion was on Thief Catcher's stylish goggles. Or Invisible Girl's inner torment and change of heart. Maybe I could ask during our interview. My champagne-fizzy brain took a surprising amount of delight in the idea and I nearly giggled to myself.

I was so lost in my swirl of thoughts that I teetered around the corner and almost smacked into someone.

"Oh! Sorry!" I exclaimed. Then I actually did giggle.

The person grunted and lurched away from me, continuing their quest down the hall.

"Wait! Sir . . . Ma'am!" I squinted at the person's retreating form. I couldn't make out gender, they just looked like a multicolored blob. Was I *that* tipsy?

"Wait!" I called again. But they continued lurching away. Shit. I didn't want some kind of "Drunk-ass Aveda Jupiter mowed me down at a charity event!" tweet going viral. I shuffled after them as fast as my binding skirt and wobbly shoes would allow. As I shuffled, I squinted at the person's back again. There was something odd about the way they moved. Something familiar.

I squinted harder. Black hair. Tight red outfit that

wasn't exactly a dress, but definitely wasn't a suit. It looked more like a spandex body covering. My sense of déjà vu intensified.

Where have I seen that before?

The realization hit me like a splash of cold water, sobering me up.

The Aveda statue demons. That . . . person looks and moves like an Aveda statue demon. That . . . person is an Aveda statue demon! But I got all of them, I'm sure of it. I saw them all burn. So how is that possible? How is it here?!

My heart sped up and I gathered the bottom of my skirt in one arm and kicked off my shoes.

"Stop!" I yelled at the figure. "Stop or I'll . . ."

Or I'll what? Club them to death with my stupid shoes?

I brushed that thought aside and took off after the figure. The figure's lurching sped up and it heaved itself through a doorway and out of sight.

"Dammit," I muttered, increasing my speed. I propelled myself down the hall and through the same door. I looked right, looked left. I was in a bathroom, surrounded by gleaming whiter-than-white surfaces.

So I had successfully arrived at my original destination, but where was that thing? "I know you're in here!" I yelled. "Show yourself!" My voice echoed off the shiny white walls. Otherwise there was silence.

What the hell?

I stomped over to a stall, lifted my skirt higher, and kicked the door open. Nothing. I frowned, moved to the next stall, and kicked that door open, too. Also nothing. Inspection of the third, fourth, and fifth stalls all produced the same result. I was alone.

I shook my head, trying to clear it. Had I imagined the whole thing? Had my body responded to an unusual-for-me amount of alcohol and rich food by hallucinating a lurchy blob ducking into the bathroom?

Had being Aveda Jupiter already driven me completely fucking crazy?

I looked down at my bedraggled form. *Well, shit.* I couldn't go back out there like this. My skirt was bunched up and there was something that looked suspiciously like a rip near the hem. Plus I had no shoes.

I heard the bathroom door creak open and hastily flung myself into the stall just as two sets of high-heeled footsteps clicked through.

"—so slut-tastic," one of the high-heeled interlopers was in the midst of saying. "'Local designer' my ass. That sparkle-motion bullshit was clearly mass-produced in, like, *Asia*."

As my heartbeat began to slow and I forced myself to breathe evenly, I realized I recognized those nasal tones: Shasta. Giving me a bad review. With vaguely racist undertones. She was probably jealous 'cause me and Maisy were planning on going to the movies together. She seemed like the possessive friend type.

"Sweatshop material, fo' sho'," snarked her companion, whose voice I couldn't quite place. "And did you see how many dates she stuffed into that huge mouth of hers? I thought superheroes had to be fit."

"If she lets out a few seams in that dress, maybe she'll be able to avoid all the nip slips," said Shasta. "Not that you can't see everything already in that little number, it's practically transparent. I don't know if you noticed—"

"I sure gosh-dang did. I even snuck a picture."

Oh. Now I recognized that girlish lilt. Maisy.

"You are so bad," shrieked Shasta. "My God, she looks naked. You have to blog that shit. Your hits are gonna be off-the-chain insane!"

"I am so blogging it," Maisy assured her. "But do you think I actually have to go to that movie with her? The Heroic Whatever? I mean, I suppose it's an opportunity to cozy up to San Francisco's beloved daughter. Writing about her all the time is fine, but it's still not quite enough to further my association with her and therefore my celebrity status." I could practically see her preening in front of the mirror.

"And you want to transcend her status, even—yes?" Shasta cooed adoringly. "You want to be celebrity royalty. Who cares about San Francisco's beloved daughter, when you could be, like, San Francisco's beloved princess? I mean, you already have the style and grace for it."

Ugh, seriously? Shasta had the whole ass-kissing thing down to a science. I imagined Maisy ruling over her own blog monarchy and almost gagged, then remembered I was trying to stay silent and clapped a hand over my mouth.

"All right, all right, I'll suffer through the movie," Maisy groaned. "Getting close to her is the first step in transcending her or whatever. But really, who knew Aveda Jupiter had such juvenile taste?"

"Anyone who saw her in that dress!" crowed Shasta.

Their cackles bounced off the walls of the bathroom, echoing in my ears, forming a wall of banshee-like noise that threatened to smother me. My face flushed and the tulle of my ruined dress was itchy and abrasive next to my skin. My sweaty fingers grappled at those teeny pearl buttons, trying to loosen them, but I still couldn't reach.

And as their laughter spiraled into hysterics, I felt something even more foreign than the sweet fizz of enjoyment that had overtaken me earlier.

The beginnings of tears. Pricking at my eyes, threatening to escape.

"Stop it," I muttered to myself, blinking hard. Seriously? I was going to start crying? Over these two-faced bitches who apparently derived all their pleasure from ripping other women apart? And, okay, it might also have something to do with the fact that I'd just hallucinated a demon and chased after it and ruined my damn dress in the process. But still.

My phone chose that moment to buzz from its sequined clutch prison.

Shasta and Maisy were clacking their way out the door, but I took extra care to keep my voice down as I answered the phone.

"Hello?"

"Eviiiiiiiiiiiiie. Evvvvvvvvie. Evelyn."

"Aveda?" I whispered, my near-tears and demon hallucination momentarily forgotten. "Are you drunk?"

"What? No. *No*. Of course not." She let out a laugh that went on too long. "We have a little sitcher—*situation* back at HQ."

"Which is . . . ?"

"It's Beatrice. She is . . . hmm. How do I put this? Completely effing wasted."

"What?! How is that possible? You're supposed to be watching the Barden Bellas take nationals. And other wholesome activities."

"I know. I know. IknowIknowIknow. I thought it would be fun for us to brew some fruit punch—"

"Punch?! Aveda, Bea's not ten—"

"Hush, youse! I'm a little behind on what the kidsh—*kids* like these days. Anyway, she told me she was adding a special ingredient."

"Which she no doubt obtained from our unlocked liquor cabinet yesterday," I muttered. "Aveda, you're supposed to be the adult, here. You couldn't supervise her?"

"Meeeeeeeeeeeeh," she whined. "Now you're all mad at me. I knew I shouldn't have called."

"I'm not mad," I lied. "Sit tight. I'll send help."

I hung up before she could respond and punched in Scott's number.

"Evie?" He sounded confused. "Is everything okay? I haven't made much progress with the spell yet—"

"Not why I'm calling," I cut in. Now that I had An Important Task, I latched on to it fiercely, determined to put the craziness of two-faced Maisy and the imaginary Aveda statue demon aside. "I need you to go over to HQ and handle an Aveda disaster."

"A disaster," he repeated slowly. "Evie, just because I agreed to do this spell, it doesn't make me one of Aveda's flunkies. I can't be around her."

"You were around her this morning. In fact, you guys teamed up on this whole plan thing."

"That's for you," he interjected, his tone sharp. "I'm trying to save you from your fucked-up relationship with her. Maybe if I take away your fire power, you'll finally have the guts to leave. Find another job. Find another *life*." He took a deep breath, as if trying to calm himself. "But me showing up for that doesn't mean you can pull me into whatever craziness she's managed to stir up."

"It's Bea, too!" I yelped. "Aveda's supposed to be babysitting and Bea somehow managed to get both of them drunk and I'm stuck at this stupid party in this stupid dress and I'm worried they're going to hurt themselves or, like, destroy San Francisco or—"

"All right, all right." His voice turned weary, but the sharpness was still there. "I'll go. But don't call me next time. Not if it's about Aveda. I mean it."

"I—" I spluttered. But he'd already hung up. My hand clutched the phone in frustration and I had a sudden vision of squeezing hard enough to make it shatter. *Evie smash.*

"Goddammit," I growled, stuffing the phone back into my clutch.

My dress constricted further against my skin, tighter and itchier than ever, and every crazy-making thing of the last fifteen minutes—my demon hallucination, Maisy's cackling laugh, Aveda's drunken slurs, Scott's harsh tones—played back through my brain, each individual track fighting for attention, louder and louder until there was nothing but noise. The flush that had overtaken my face burned its way through my body like wildfire and my breathing started to come in panicked gasps and I couldn't stop sweating.

I stumbled out of the stall, trying to slow my breathing. The tears came roaring back, flooding my eyes, determined to escape.

No. No crying. Invisible Girl would not *approve.*

I staggered over to one of the sinks and grabbed the edge, gripping hard, blinking the tears back.

At least Shasta and Maisy cleared out. At least there's that, I thought. *No one here to see my barely controlled freak-out. Which isn't even a freak-out yet. Definitely not a freak-out. It's . . . it's . . .*

I caught a glimpse of myself in one of the tiny circular mirrors above the sink. It was so tiny I could only see a small swatch of my face. One panicked eyeball. Half a gasping mouth. A few tendrils of hair escaping from my sophisticated updo, curling around my . . . wait! *Curling?!*

I'd forgotten to refresh my glamour.

I gripped the sink harder, squeezing my eyes shut, trying to think of nice things, calming things.

Fuck. Fuck. Fuckfuckfuck.

And suddenly I was holding nothing but air.

My eyes flew open to see the sink hanging precariously from the wall by a single bolt. It creaked ominously and the bolt detached, sending the whole contraption crashing to the floor with a resounding *crash.*

Before I could process this, water exploded from the now-bared pipes, splattering aggressively onto the floor.

I tried to leap out of the way, but the last pipe burst just in time to spew in my direction, drenching me. I heaved myself out of the water's path, frantically clawing at the heavy ropes of wet hair plastering themselves over my eyes.

"What on Earth is taking so long in here?"

My head jerked up and I saw Nate bursting through the door, glower firmly in place. He stopped abruptly, his expression morphing into total confusion as he took in the water sluicing out of the wall, the sink on the floor, and my bedraggled self. The tulle of my dress now hugged my body in a way that crossed the decency line and landed me in near-pornographic territory.

"I . . . came to get you. So you can, uh . . . announce the winners of the silent auction," he said. His eyes couldn't help but wander. Forget the "slips" Maisy and Shasta were so scandalized by. Now there were just straight-up nipples all over the place.

"Don't look at that," I gasped, crossing my arms over my chest. "Get out of here. I'll fix this and get cleaned up and meet you back in the ballroom and . . . and . . ."

My words petered out in a pathetic little whine. He kept standing there, staring at me.

I felt exposed, exhausted. The tears I'd managed to keep at bay for the entire disastrous bathroom stint took advantage of my moment of weakness and spilled over.

And I'm cold, I realized. *Really, really cold.* My teeth started to chatter.

"I fucked it all up," I blurted out. My voice caught on something that sounded dangerously like a sob. "I can't even do a simple Aveda night out. I thought I'd girl-bonded with Maisy, but she thinks I'm a carb-crazy loser in a slutty dress. And I actually like this dress, so what does that say about my, what do you call it, taste level? And Bea managed to terrorize what I thought was a non-terrorizable space and Aveda let it happen. And Scott . . . I don't . . . I don't know why he had to get so mad at me. And then . . . then . . ."

I hiccupped and gestured helplessly at the ruined sink.

"You melted the sink off the wall?" His voice was a low rumble, a gentle version of his usual harsh tones.

I looked at the sink. The water had stopped pouring out of the pipes and the sink's shape was different than before: blobby and deformed, like an abstract painting come to life. I brought one of my palms close to my face, examining it. Even though the rest of my body was freezing, my hand felt as if I'd just touched a stove.

"Yeah." I stared at my palm and hiccupped again. "I guess that's what happened."

Nate took two wide steps, closing the gap between us. He shrugged out of his suit jacket and wrapped it around my shivering body.

"Aveda would have killed it tonight." I resumed my babbling as he adjusted the jacket over my waterlogged form. "She would have schmoozed it up like a champ. She would have somehow, through sheer force of will, gotten those bitches to be her best friends. She would've made herself the hero of this sink disaster. And she would have pulled off this dress like nothing else."

And she never would've hallucinated a fucking imaginary demon and thrown her shoes away trying to chase after it. I was too embarrassed to even vocalize that part.

I bit my lip, snuffling and shaking. Nate unhooked one of his cufflinks and used it to pin the jacket closed around me.

"We need to get you warm," he said.

He frowned, intent on getting the jacket to close fully, unpinning and repinning the cufflink. I absorbed the cocoon-like warmth, the silk lining whispering over my skin. It smelled clean, fresh—like soap and spearmint and the air after a rainstorm.

"If we can trap some heat around you and get you out of here, you should be okay," he said, readjusting the cufflink. He bent his head and leaned in closer, trying to get the pesky cufflink to cooperate, his breath warming the patch of exposed skin near my collarbone. A jolt of electricity ran through me, shock at the unexpected heat.

I wanted to start babbling again, but the words died in my throat. And as his fingertips closed over that cufflink, they brushed against that same patch of skin—that exposed, sensitive bit the jacket just wouldn't seem to cover—and the electricity coursing through me intensified into a lightning bolt of pure feeling that shot through my body, arcing from head to toe and making a few very important pit stops in between.

"Sorry," he murmured, still concentrating on the cufflink.

I barely heard him. I was too focused on this new feeling, a feeling so foreign—more than enjoyment, more than tears—that I had to stop and parse it for a full minute before I could identify it.

Lust.

Wait, what? Seriously? *Lust?!?*

But there was no denying it. My eyeballs were fastened to his long, graceful fingers closing over that cufflink, and I was making a special note of how long and graceful they were, how they seemed at odds with his big hands, his big body. I had the dim realization that I'd never been this close to him, never had cause to study him in such detail. Whenever we were standing next to each other, we were usually fighting.

But now I was silent: unable to stop breathing deeply, unable to stop trying like mad to get more of the scent of his jacket into my lungs. My heartbeat sped up and I wondered if he could hear it. To me it seemed like the loudest thing in the room.

Heat flooded my cheeks. I should have been grateful for the extra warmth, but all I could think was, *What the hell is wrong with me?*

If I was going to feel lust for someone after all this time, why did it have to be him? Why not someone who didn't aggravate me? Why not someone I wasn't constantly at odds with? Why not someone I actually *liked*?

I gulped in a few mouthfuls of air, which only served to make me dizzy.

It's because you're vulnerable and cold, I thought wildly.

You're not used to being vulnerable or cold. You've just experienced emotional overload and he's close and warm . . . and . . . and . . . Dead-Inside-O-Tron is malfunctioning. Or something. Oh my God, stop looking at his hands. Stop it.

"Aveda might've faked her way through small talk with those two awful women, but that's all it would've been," Nate said. "And she wouldn't have been able to make herself the hero of the sink disaster because there wouldn't have been a sink disaster. Because she can't do what you do."

Finally satisfied with the jacket/cufflink configuration, he nodded briskly. "Let's sneak out. There appears to be an alternate exit behind that." He gestured toward a partition I hadn't noticed before at the far end of the bathroom. The partition was so whiter-than-white it practically blended in with the wall, but if I craned my neck, I could see the top of a doorway peeking out from behind it. "Based on the layout of the building, it probably leads into a back hallway," Nate added.

"Okay." I scraped a hand over my eyes, trying to shake off the strangeness that had overtaken me. I had to get my control back. It was the only thing that was going to get me through this whole Being Aveda Jupiter deal. Hell, it was the only thing that had gotten me through life so far.

Nate patted the pinned cufflink one last time, then stood up straight, putting some distance between us. Okay. That helped. I took in a few deep breaths. "We'll make up a story about Aveda getting called away on a demon emergency," I said. "I can spin a press release that makes her look extra-heroic."

"Yes." One side of his mouth tipped up in a ghost of a smile. "And Evie. What you were saying about Aveda . . . pulling things off. You look nice."

I shook my head, still trying to get my bearings back. "What?"

He placed a hand at the small of my back, guiding me toward the door. "The dress. You look nice in the dress."

"Oh . . . Well." I smiled ruefully. "You mean Aveda does."

He reached over and gently tugged a sproingy lock of my still-damp hair. I realized my glamour had worn off completely.

"No," he said. "I mean you."

DRESSBACLE!

Aveda Shows Us Some Skin!
by Maisy Kane, Bay Bridge Kiss Editrix

Morning, 'Friscans! As it turns out, Aveda Jupiter's ready to reveal a whole lot more than a new power! Girl was rockin' quite the daring number at last night's League soiree and when I say "daring," I mean, "Holy cow, A-babes! Those perky nips are a superpower all their own! And hey, maybe ease up on the fancy date snacks—those suckers are like 90 percent lard and that dress is already tight enough to pop!" (Kidding! But seriously, A, I'm happy to provide fashion consultation free of charge. Your new power seems to be a megahit with my readers—not to mention a whole slew of brand-new fans from all over the world! Greetings to those of you reading BBK for the first time!—so you want to be extra careful about the image you're putting out there, eh? You don't want your fans getting the idea that you're all boobs, no brains. Kidding! But definitely call me. We have an exclusive interview to do, remember?)

A. Jupes also had to leave us a bit early due to a "demon emergency." I can't help but wonder if said "emergency" involved the hunky mystery man who was escorting her last night. No word on the identity of Mr. Tall, Dark, and Frowny, but can I just say, RAWR. Your pal Maisy may not approve of A's fashion mishaps, but she definitely approves of those biceps!

Now, before I sign off, a final word of warning for my dear readers: I've received tips that stray demons from Whistles—the ones who took the form of Aveda's glorious swag statue—have been sighted around the city! Seems a few of them escaped A's notice. No casualties yet, but keep an eye out and be extra-super-careful! Being chomped to death by the mirror image of San Francisco's Beloved Daughter would be a fate worse than death! Well, actually, it would just be death, but you get what I'm saying.

Shasta's Corner! Shasta (Maisy's bestie) here. I've got nothing to add, but Maisy's line about "nips" was pretty funny, right? (Editrix's Note: Ugh, Shast! It's like you're not even trying.)

CHAPTER NINE

"EVIE! GET IN HERE!" Aveda's voice blasted from the bedroom.

"Goodness." Lucy winced. "Why can't her lungs be broken, too?"

I dragged myself down the hall, leaving Lucy to fend for herself. We'd just returned to HQ after "a little morning run," which was part of Lucy's Total Superheroine Workout Plan. I definitely didn't like it. After stumbling around a park trail for an hour, I was drenched in sweat and all my limbs felt like they were about to fall off. I'd have to figure out a way to tell her I wasn't interested in exercising ever again.

I found Aveda in what was becoming her regular perch: in bed, surrounded by pillows, focused on the iPad in front of her. Nate was staring out the window, scowl in place. The half-smile from last night must've been a fluke.

He turned from the window and goggled at me. "What happened to you?"

"Yeah, yeah." I swiped a hand over my face, wiping away excess sweat. "A far cry from last night's boob-tacular number, I know."

He opened his mouth, but couldn't seem to think of what came after that, so he went back to looking out the window.

"Explain this," Aveda said, thrusting the iPad in my direction. I dutifully accepted and scanned Maisy's latest blog post. And then my heart dropped.

"Other people saw the statue demons!" I blurted out.

Nate turned away from the window again. "What?"

"The Aveda statue demons from Whistles!" I said, pointing to the screen. "I saw one last night at the benefit and now other people are reporting sightings around the city!"

"Back up," he said, frowning. "You saw one? Why didn't you say anything?"

"Because I thought I imagined it—"

"Which you did," Aveda said, waving a dismissive hand. "Honestly, Evie. You know how this works: our citizens are often so traumatized by seeing all those demons spilling out of a portal, they start dreaming up sightings in the days after. And clearly you were *very* traumatized from that night at Whistles, so you're also affected. Didn't you destroy them all?"

I called up my shaky memory of the Whistles incident. My fire had blazed through all of those statue demons, leaving nothing behind.

"Yes, but . . ."

But what?

I frowned, trying to make sense of it all. Last night I'd been convinced I was hallucinating. But now . . . I wasn't so sure. And after seeing one of the statue demons again, I couldn't help but go back to the idea that there was something super-weird about the way they moved—

"I'm sorry these last couple days have been so trying for you," Aveda said, interrupting my thoughts. "But we need to have a discussion." She tapped her index finger against the iPad. Her silver nail polish was starting to chip and a piece flaked onto the screen.

Nate glanced at the iPad screen and did a double take. "Wow," he said. "There's a picture of . . . us."

"Of you and Aveda, you mean," I said. "Don't worry,

you're not identified. No one knows the illustrious, mysterious, never photographed Nathaniel Jones went to something as frivolous as a party."

I noticed Maisy hadn't posted a photo with actual nip slips. Maybe she didn't want to fully piss off her "good pal" Aveda.

"We need to *talk*," Aveda pressed, "about all the publicity I—er, you as me—seem to be getting."

The wheels in my brain creaked, trying to figure out what she was getting at. I was still stuck on the statues. What, exactly, had I seen last night? "Publicity's good, right?" I said. "Isn't that why you made me go to the benefit?"

"There's publicity, and then there's the right kind of publicity." She frowned at me. "Now. My Social Media Guru recommends a press conference to refute some of this chatter popping up online. First of all, you need to say you were wearing that dress as a tribute to your . . . er, *my* dead mother. That it was originally hers and that's the only reason you would dream of wearing something so revealing."

I stifled the urge to roll my eyes. Now clearly wasn't the moment to tell her that Maisy could easily refute that explanation, thanks to the local designer story I'd oh-so-cleverly improvised. Otherwise it might've worked. According to our official press documents, Aveda's parents—hardscrabble Chinese immigrants who had once run a humble dim sum eatery—were killed in a freak cable car accident before baby Aveda had a chance to know them. In reality Philip and Linda Chang were comfortably ensconced in Pleasanton, played golf three times a week, and had both recently retired from their professions of choice (accountant and pharmacist, respectively). Aveda claimed that story simply wasn't dramatic enough for a superhero's origin, but I knew the truth: despite her finding a purpose in *The Heroic Trio* and striving to attain it, her parents still withheld their approval at every turn. She worked her ass off to be the perfect superheroine, but she wasn't perfect in a way *they* deemed worthy. She still wasn't a doctor, she wasn't married or even close to it, and her chosen livelihood was tastelessly flashy and glory-chasing.

In truth, they were embarrassed by her.

Maybe that's why the adoration of the public mattered so much.

"Second, you will clarify that you aren't dating anyone—particularly not 'mystery men'—because Aveda Jupiter is far too busy saving the world to have time for such pedestrian endeavors." Aveda crinkled her nose, as if disgusted by the very notion. "Third, you will casually drop in a mention of your insanely high metabolism, which allows you to cram as many dates down your throat as you want."

She set the iPad down and gave me a frosty look.

"And, please, in the future, Evie, try to embody behavior that is more becoming of Aveda Jupiter. Being me is a big responsibility. And this is simply not up to my standards."

I took a deep breath, tamping down on the unhinged feeling welling up in me. I had the urge to blurt out every single thing in my overstuffed brain. Like the fact that she'd loved the dress when I'd first brought it to her. Or the fact that taking an escort to the benefit had been her idea. Or the fact that I had *so* seen that statue demon, dammit.

At least . . . I thought I had.

My toe started tapping on the floor of its own accord, seemingly detached from the rest of my body, and I felt adrenaline spike in my veins.

It's fine, I told myself. *Let her talk. She's probably going stir-crazy from being trapped in here. From being bedridden. From being unable to* be *Aveda Jupiter. That's the one thing that gives her meaning and purpose and drive and now she can't do it, and that's got to be frustrating as*

*hell. She's micromanaging the shit out of me so she has
control over something. And she's probably overcom-
pensating with the attitude a bit. Or a lot. Whatever.*

It's fine.

"You can actually do your press conference right
now," Aveda continued, examining her flaking nail polish. "My Social Media Guru has noted mentions on
Twitter of strange activity at the Yamato Theater. Everyone's freaking out because the movie stopped in the
middle with no explanation and they can't find anyone
to restart the thing. It's probably nothing. You know our
dear citizens think a new portal's opening up whenever
they feel so much as a light draft in the room. But me
putting in an appearance reassures them that they're
safe. And this will give you the opportunity to bring up
the talking points we just discussed."

She smiled at me in her "that settles it" kind of way.

"Aveda," I said. "What if it's not nothing? What if
there is an actual portal with actual demons and I have
to fight them? What if I have to, like, punch something?
I don't know how to do that."

"Don't be silly." She turned back to her iPad. "There's
no mention of anything even remotely portal-ish in the
tweets, and if you're really concerned, you can take Lucy
with you. I've been through this kind of thing a million
times and it's always a false alarm. People just want to
see Aveda Jupiter. You worry too much."

"No." My toe tapping increased to double-time, beating
against the floor with the ferocity of a heavy metal drum-
mer during a shred-tastic solo. "I think I worry the exact
right amount. We should think this through and discuss—"

"Oh, stop being so emotional," she said, giving me a
look. "Really, Evie. Arguing with me about the best
course of heroic action? Going on about some statue
demon hallucination? These little outbursts aren't just
unbecoming of a girl posing as a superhero. They're unbecoming in general."

"I . . ."

"Take that phone call from last night," she continued. "You didn't need to get so upset. I had it under control."

"You called *me*! You were drunk and you let Bea—"

"We were having a good time. I think she's starting to see me as a big sister figure."

The adrenaline flowing through me turned vicious and icy and my toe dialed up its manic tapping. And before I could stop it, rage built, taking me toward that feeling of unhingedness again. I felt my hands clench. I tried to slow my breathing, to remember how I usually calmed myself when Aveda was being unreasonable.

It's fine, I thought, trying to repeat my mantra from a few minutes ago. *Finefinefine. So she accidentally let your little sister get her wasted and is now covering by saying it was all in good fun and is trying to claim said sister for her own and come to think of it, this is extra-crazy behavior, even for her—*

CRASH.

I swung around to see a parade of burly men in coveralls hauling stacks of boxes past the bedroom door and down the hall. My eyes went to the source of the crash: shards of broken glass splayed out all over the hallway. One of the coveralled men guiltily tried to sweep it into an overflowing box. I squinted at the shards, which looked familiar.

"Aveda," I said, trying to keep my tone steady. "Is that my lamp? The one that's usually in my home?"

"Hey, boss." One of the coveralled men stuck his head in the bedroom doorway, addressing Aveda. "My guys are moving a little slow today, but rest assured: we'll get it done."

"Thank you, Frank," Aveda said. "Your work is much appreciated."

A sickening realization took root in my stomach. I turned back to Aveda. "*Annie.* What . . . is . . . going . . . on?"

Nate frowned at Aveda. "You didn't tell her?"

"It's better this way," Aveda said. "Especially with her heightened emotional state." She didn't even look up as she started to address me. "Evie: I'm moving you and Beatrice in here. I think you'll agree it's for the best. You've been practically living here the past couple days anyway. And now you can receive my instructions properly and I can look after Bea while you're busy being me." She finally deigned to look up from her iPad, gifting me with a dazzling smile. "Not to worry, I didn't move your furniture—just your clothes and favorite knickknacks and decorations, so it really feels like home. You can still sublet your old place if you like. It'll be wonderful for everyone."

"And you just *decided* this." I looked back at the movers merrily jostling my stuff down the hall. Another *CRASH* rang out.

My wheezing took on a snorty, labored sound. *Why am I letting her get to me? My one true superpower is I never* let *her get to me.*

And then, just when I thought things couldn't get any worse, my sister bustled into the room.

"Bea . . ." I stared at her in confusion. She had her phone in one hand and a clipboard in the other.

"Hey, guys." Bea nodded at Aveda. "Boss, the tweets about the movie 'mysteriously cutting out' . . ." She made little air quotes around her clipboard. " . . . have increased eighty percent in the last forty-five seconds. Evie needs to glamour up and get out of here before the 'Where's Aveda' hashtag really takes root."

I glanced over at Nate, but he looked as bewildered as I did.

"Do you even remember that school is a thing at this point?" I blurted out.

"School's for nonstarters, Big Sis," Bea said. "I have a job now."

"Job?"

I heard Nate muttering to himself. "Social media . . ."

He put a hand on my arm and an idle thought plopped into my head: Maisy was right about one thing. His biceps were *very*—

For fuck's sake. What was wrong with me?

"That's what Aveda meant just now," he continued, "when she started talking about the Social Media Guru."

"Yeah, keep up, oldsters." Bea snapped her fingers at us. "The world keeps turning while you age. Aveda and I had a good talk about her social media presence while we were hanging out last night and we agreed my talents were being wasted in the public school system."

"Wasted?" I sputtered. "Was that before or after you got tanked on spiked punch?"

"I mean, your idea for tracking mentions during Aveda's battles wasn't bad, Evie, but there's so much more to be done in that arena," Bea said, as if I hadn't spoken. "Oh, hold up . . ." She frowned at her phone screen. "The hashtag is imminent. People are pissed about the movie cutting out and the Yamato employees seem to have vanished. They *really* want Aveda. You've gotta get over there, Evie."

I opened my mouth, closed it. Stared at her some more. Thousands of stray thoughts were warring in my head. *Hallucinations . . . statue demons . . . social media . . . biceps . . .*

I took yet another deep breath. If I wasn't careful, those thoughts were going to mix themselves into emotional stew and cause me to burn HQ to the ground.

So I forced my hands to unclench and did the only sensible thing I could think of: I backed out of the room and pointed myself toward the Yamato.

CHAPTER TEN

I THOUGHT I was done running for the day.

Given how wrong I'd been about everything this Being Aveda Jupiter gig entailed, I needed to cut it out with the dumbass predictions.

Thud . . . thud . . . *thud*.

My feet, encased in thigh-high platform boots that seemed to weigh ten pounds each, plodded against the Yamato Theater's threadbare carpet. Aveda insisted her Galactic Warrior Princess costume was best for this situation, so I was clad in a tight silver minidress, a flappy cape that kept getting tangled around my arms, and the monstrous boots. Every single element of this getup seemed designed to prevent me from achieving my ultimate goal, which was forward motion.

As I thudded laboriously down the aisle, I was hyperaware of the scrutinizing gazes from the packed house of moviegoers. They'd been shocked into silence by . . . well. Something so evil, no one could properly convey it on Twitter, apparently. Only the occasional rustle of someone nervously twisting a candy wrapper punctuated the air. I didn't see the telltale portal glow drifting above our heads, though, so Aveda was probably right: it was nothing more than hyperactive imaginations at work. All I had to do was give them their desired dose of Jupiter and I'd be done.

I hadn't set foot in the Yamato in years, but it looked exactly the same as it had on that fateful day when Aveda and I first witnessed *The Heroic Trio*. It was untouched by the renovations that had turned other theaters into Death Stars of high-tech movie-going—no IMAX, no 3D. It was locked in a time capsule of lo-fi mustiness, a dated haven for anyone who didn't want to fork over half their paycheck to see the latest blockbuster reboot based on a line of shitty toys. The only modern-type thing I spotted on my thudding journey was a faded cardboard standee of Tommy Lemon at the theater entrance, urging you to see his new movie with a cheesy grin and an exaggerated thumbs-up.

I landed in front of the screen and swiveled around to face the crowd, my legs wobbling atop the platform boots.

"She's in place." Lucy's voice crackled in my ear. "Now what? I see no evidence of . . . well, anything."

My freak-ass ensemble was topped by a rhinestone-encrusted plastic tiara, which Bea had rigged with an earbud and camera. The possibility that she secretly possessed high-tech talents and could use them for her own nefarious purposes scared the living crap out of me. Not to be outdone, Nate had asked her to add a couple of other elements to my outfit: a heart rate monitor, body temperature sensor, and a few other things I didn't even want to know about, all designed to give him metrics on my every move.

The tiara's camera ensured that Aveda and Nate could see and hear everything I was about to do from HQ, while Lucy observed from the back of the theater, her own earbud connecting her to our communication system.

My eyes swept the crowd, a mixed bag of school-skippers, stoners, and slackers. Their eyes were fastened on me, wide and expectant.

"Make an introduction." Aveda's voice crackled

through the tiara. "Aveda Jupiter knows how to put on a show."

I raised my voice. "People of Earth!"

"Ugh, that's terrible," said Aveda. I heard Lucy smother a staticky giggle.

"People of Earth," I said more firmly. "I'm here to save you from . . . from . . ." I glanced at the movie screen, a swath of white nothingness, silent and benign.

"What exactly am I saving you from?" I said, turning back to the crowd.

"That's barely a speech!" squealed Aveda. "Milk the drama! And then get to my talking points!"

"Stop distracting her," growled Nate.

"Miss Jupiter?" A girl in the front row raised her hand, her face obscured behind Coke-bottle glasses and a raggy mop of dirt-brown hair. She looked about fourteen.

"Yes?" As I raised my arm to point at her, I got tangled in my cape again. I twisted free and settled for giving her an officious nod. "Er, citizen?"

"We were watching the latest Tommy Lemon movie," the girl said. "The one where he disguises himself as a giant baby? And all of a sudden the movie stopped."

"I told you: false alarm," Aveda's voice hissed in my ear.

"Citizen," I said to the girl. "That doesn't exactly sound like an, ah . . . Aveda Jupiter–level emergency. Why didn't you all just get a refund?"

"Don't tell them to leave!" Aveda squealed. "Stop wasting time and talk about my insane metabolism!"

"Well, Miss Jupiter," the girl continued, her voice taking on the cadence of a straight-A student gunning for extra credit, "we looked for someone to restart the movie. But we couldn't find anyone. And then we were trapped."

"Trapped?"

"We couldn't get up. From our seats. We still can't."

She demonstrated, wriggling around, trying to detach
herself from her movie theater chair. It held her in place,
as if the rear of her pants was covered in glue. "And
then . . ." Her eyes shifted back and forth behind her
thick glasses. " . . . right after that, all our phone signals
were blocked. So we couldn't even tweet about it, Miss
Jupiter!"

I looked out at the crowd of people anxiously clutching rumpled popcorn bags. Messy-haired girl's eyes
bored into me. I wanted to say something that would
instantly reassure her, make her feel safe. I scoured my
brain for the right words, but it was too busy trying to
puzzle out what all of this meant.

No portal, no demons. Just a bunch of trapped moviegoers with malfunctioning smartphones.

"Aveda," I whispered in the direction of my tiara, "this
is bizarre—"

BOOM.

A thunderclap reverberated through the theater, in-
citing scattered gasps in the audience. I whipped around,
nearly toppling over in my giant boots, looking for the
source of the sound.

Suddenly the lower corner of the movie screen popped
forward like a 3D effect—like someone was trapped behind the screen, trying to break free. I jumped back, my
heart rate ratcheting upward.

What the hell?

Screams rippled through the crowd. Just a few at first,
but they built to a fever pitch as a giant fisted hand burst
through the screen. The hand opened and expanded,
each fingertip sporting a deadly looking claw.

"The movie's starting again! You can finally get to my
talking points!" yelped Aveda. "And wow! What an incredible special effect."

"Not a special effect," I snapped, lunging backward.

A different shape popped through the screen, an oversize head with protruding fangs. As the thing scanned

the crowd, a malevolent glare etched itself across its face. I forced myself to focus on the details of the shape, willing my heart rate to settle down. And that's when I noticed this terrifying visage sported a trace of the familiar: the protuberant ears and buggy eyes marked it as the usually friendly face of Tommy Lemon. The face I'd seen two nights earlier at Whistles.

Well, not the exact face. There were the fangs, for one thing. And his skin was sort of gray and pockmarked and flaky, like he was in really desperate need of moisturizer.

"HOW. DARE. YOU." His voice boomed, but it didn't quite match up with his mouth: the effect was distorted, eerie. I noticed a black smudge on his index finger and tried to home in on it, to get a better look. His taloned fingers swiped forward, his aim wild and uneven. I jumped back, the screams of the crowd echoing in my ears.

"Evie, get them to listen to you!" barked Aveda. "Tell them it's just a movie!"

"Pardon me, love," Lucy chimed in. "But this doesn't look like 'just' anything."

"It's a supernatural presence," Nate said. "It has to be."

"It looks exactly like Tommy," Aveda retorted.

"You can't ignore what's right in front of you," Nate countered. "I'm telling you—"

"You don't tell me anything," Aveda said. "Anyway, we need to get Evie to follow instructions—"

"Shut up!" I snapped. "All of you."

"MY MINIONS," wailed the grotesque version of Tommy. "NOT MINION ENOUGH."

I tilted my head at the screen. "What's that, Mr. Lemon?"

The Tommy thing responded with another wail, then extended his claws even farther. His movements were labored, lurchy. One of his claws swiped dangerously close to me, snagging my cape.

"RAWWWWWWR!" he bellowed triumphantly.

"Oh yeah, that's real," I gasped, trying to twist away. "Definitely fucking real."

He yanked on the cape, dragging me back. I planted the soles of my boots on the carpet, trying to pitch myself forward.

"Dive, Evie! Low to the ground!" yelled Aveda, apparently accepting that I was in actual danger.

"Lucy! Help her!" Nate barked.

"I'm sorry, but I can't seem to move," Lucy said, her voice frustrated. "Evie, try transferring your weight—"

"Stop . . . talking . . ." I gasped. My arms pinwheeled as I attempted to gain traction, tangling further in the folds of the cape.

My feet slipped from under me, skidding along the carpet, *thunkthunkthunk*. I pitched one foot forward, trying like mad to plant again, and wrenched my left arm free from the cape's folds. The Tommy Thing yanked harder and the cape pulled tight at my neck, strangling me. I smacked my hand against my neck, my fingertips grappling at the cape's collar. My breath got shorter and a sudden, idiotic thought popped into my head.

This is about the dumbest way for a (fake) superhero to bite it: death by cape strangulation.

I redoubled my efforts, leaning as far forward as I could while grasping at my neck, trying to find the cape's snap closure. My fingertips slid helplessly over the slippery material of the collar . . . then finally, blessedly, hit a circular piece of metal. I yanked with all my might and heard the satisfying *clack* of the snap coming loose. The cape slid off my shoulders and I pitched forward, falling to my knees.

"DAAAAAAAAAAAAAAAAH!" howled the Tommy Thing.

I rolled over, trying to get my breath back, my hands slamming against the soda-stained carpet. The Tommy Thing glared at me, crumpled the cape in his gargantuan paw, and tossed it to the side.

"Nicely done!" Aveda crowed. "That was a Michelle Yeoh–level action heroine move, Evie. Now while you have everyone's attention, let's get to those talking points!"

"Fuck this," I muttered. I struggled to my feet, my eyes never leaving the Tommy Thing. Then I ripped the tiara-camera off my head, chucked it to the ground, and crushed it under one of my ten-pound boots.

I heard a faint, pissed-sounding "Evvvvvvv . . ." amid the cracking of the plastic.

"Tommy," I said, my voice ringing loud and clear through the theater. "What do you want?"

"GRAAAAAAWWWRRRR!" he screamed.

"NO." I stepped forward, trying to inject a little swagger into my stance. The boots helped. I found myself adjusting to them, using them to give me height and power. "Cut it out with the incoherent bellowing. Use your words."

He cocked his misshapen head at me. I took another step forward.

"You said something about minions?" I coaxed. I realized I was using the same placating tone I usually used on Aveda.

He clasped his taloned mitts together, looking unsure. "MINIONS BAAAAAD." He extended a claw at the audience. "NO LAUGHING."

"Laughing?" I turned to survey the crowd, trying to figure out what he meant. I realized they didn't seem all that scared anymore. Most of them avoided my gaze, their eyes shifting from side to side. They looked almost . . . guilty?

"Um, you. Citizen." I pointed at the messy-haired girl who had helped me out before. "Any idea what he means?"

"Well," she said, "the movie, Miss Jupiter. It wasn't that funny."

My face must have looked extra-bewildered, because

her words started coming out in a rush. "I mean. I loved the last Tommy Lemon movie—the one where he pretends to be a Saint Bernard so he can mother an abandoned litter of puppies? That was hilarious. But this one, it just . . . it . . ."

"BABIES FUUUUNNNNNY!" wailed the Tommy Thing.

"Middle-aged men dressed as babies are *creepy*," the girl insisted. "No one wants to laugh at that."

"NOOOOOOOOO . . ."

I twirled back around to face the Tommy Thing, who was thrashing around the screen, in the throes of what appeared to be a gigantic tantrum.

"Let me get this straight," I said, striding forward. Maybe I was imagining it, but my feet seemed to be getting used to the giant boots. "You popped out of the screen and scared all these people and got all clawy and growly because they didn't like your movie?"

"GRAAAAAAAAAWR!" he growled in the affirmative.

"Oh my God." I gave him my best disdainful look. It wasn't quite The Tanaka Glare, but it was something. "That is the stupidest fucking thing I've ever heard. You've made millions of dollars dressing up in various asinine disguises and slopping it on the screen for people to consume. You got everyone here to give you their money. And you're upset because they don't automatically think you're a comedy genius for slapping a bonnet on your head and drooling all over the place?"

He crossed his bulbous arms over his chest, pouting.

"You can't control audience response," I continued. "I wrote a paper on this in grad school. Once the artist puts the art out into the world—"

"RAAAAAAAAAAAAAAAAAAH!"

The Tommy Thing's arm shot out of the screen again, pawing savagely in my direction.

"Hey." I hopped backward, out of his reach. "If you would just listen . . ."

"MRAAAAWWRRAAAAAA!" His arm extended, claws slashing. His movements were still on the labored side, but he was big and powerful enough that it didn't matter. The audience screamed in terror. I dodged once, twice. Then felt something heavy land on my foot. I wrenched my foot back, hot ribbons of pain shooting up my leg. I gritted my teeth, ignoring the pain, my gaze falling to my left boot, which now sported a gigantic claw mark. And more than a little bit of blood.

Dammit. I had actually begun to grow fond of those boots.

The Tommy Thing roared again, his arms extending into the audience, claws slashing. Shrieks rippled through the crowd, nearly drowning out his roaring.

"Hey, we can move!" the messy-haired girl cried. "The seats aren't holding us anymore!"

"THEN EVERYONE GET OUT OF HERE!" I yelled.

Apparently I'd forgotten the rule about screaming "fire" in a crowded theater.

People stampeded for the exits, everyone climbing over each other. The mob was an ugly thing, a mass of terrified faces, grabbing hands, and crumpled popcorn bags.

"EVERYONE, GO STAND IN THE BACK!" I amended. "IN AN ORDERLY FASHION."

The Tommy Thing reached his claws out farther, trying to get at the mob.

"Hey!" I snapped my fingers at him. "Right here. We were talking."

His eyes went to me, narrowing with malice. I shuddered, feeling the full weight of his gaze, the pure evil that seemed to thrum through the theater and straight into my soul.

"That's right," I murmured. "Focus on me."

I closed my eyes as his arm extended, his claws slashing toward me.

I can do this, I told myself. *I can save all these people. If I can get him to concentrate purely on me, take me out, maybe his rage will be satisfied. And then maybe ...*

Wait a minute. What the hell was I thinking? A realization smacked me upside the head.

He might have unabashed rage, but my rage was better.

My eyes flew open. I dodged his slashy claw just in time.

"Forget the fear, Evie," I muttered. "Focus on the anger. Anger leads to hate. Hate leads to you blowing stuff up."

I darted out of the way of his claw again, hopping back and forth. I was vaguely aware of shooting pain in the foot wearing the ruined boot, but I did my best to ignore it.

"Goddamn, Tommy Lemon," I said, turning my voice into a growl. "Forget this movie. Your last movie sucked even harder. I took my sister to see it and she wouldn't talk to me for a week. Our relationship is damaged enough and you made it worse."

His claw narrowly missed my left hip. "You're a symbol for the worst kind of mediocrity!" I continued, darting behind a row of theater seats, dragging my aching foot behind me. "So lazy you can't come up with a concept that's half original. You keep dressing up as stupid things and making the same stupid movie. I wanted to stab myself during that last one! *Stab myself!*"

"RAAAAAAAR!"

I ran-limped down the row of seats as his claws slashed out for me again, destroying the seats one by one. The stuffing exploded out of them in angry clouds of white polyester: *bam, bam, bam.*

"You're a hack!" I screamed. I landed in the center aisle, dancing out of his way. "And I do *not* need your bullshit today. My crazy boss just moved me into her house against my will, I'm being forced to take orders from my juvenile delinquent of a sister, and I'm either hallucinating or not hallucinating demons, depending on who you talk to." I raised my hand to point at him, my index finger jabbing defiantly at the screen. "Also? *You ruined my shoes*."

Rage surged through me and for the first time, my blaze of anger was shot through with satisfaction. I welcomed the heat in my palm. I encouraged it. I set it free.

A bright burst of flame arced from my hand, catapulted itself toward the screen, and hit the Tommy Thing squarely between the eyes.

"RAWWWWWWR—" His screams were cut short as he exploded, what was left of the movie screen caving in on itself with a *ripppppp* and leaving nothing but a big, black hole.

I took an involuntary step back. In the back of the theater, someone started a slow clap. It gained strength, more and more people joining in, until it crescendoed into full-on applause.

"Aveda Jupiter is *on fire*!" shrieked a little voice. Messy-haired girl again.

I stared at my palm, then looked up at the destroyed movie screen.

"Yeah," I murmured to myself. "That just happened."

CHAPTER ELEVEN

I COULDN'T STOP EATING. Loaded potato skins were my new best friends. Also stuffed mushroom caps.

Lucy and Nate eyed me with awe (and, okay, maybe a little disgust) as I crammed another forkful of over-salted, over-cheesed goodness into my mouth.

"Oh, God," I moaned, licking sour cream off my fingers. "Don't get me wrong, saving all those people was nice, but this might be the best reward for Evil Tommy Lemon slayage."

They just kept staring at me.

"Guys, I'm kidding. And Aveda says *I'm* the stick-in-the-mud."

"We're confused, Evelyn," Lucy said. "Your diet normally consists of processed cereal products. Between the fancy dates last night and this feast . . ." She gestured to the artery-clogging spread in front of me. "Your taste buds seem to be undergoing some kind of shift."

"Or your metabolism is," Nate said, leaning forward and resting his elbows on the table. "This latest incident of excessive hunger was preceded by a meaningful use of your fire power at the Yamato. Maybe using your power depletes your system in ways you weren't previously aware of."

"So my need to eat potato skins is science," I said. "It

can't be that I'm, like, enjoying them. Once again, science explains it all!"

I gave him a mocking look. He held my gaze for longer than necessary and I flashed back to last night's moment in the bathroom: his fingertips brushing against my skin, my heartbeat ratcheting upward. A flush crept up the back of my neck and I quickly averted my eyes, allowing them to roam the dank atmosphere of The Gutter, San Francisco's seediest piano/karaoke bar.

The Gutter was a place where I felt like I could hide. The lighting was bad, the red velvet tablecloths were worn to patchiness, and the clientele was beyond geriatric. Kevin, the owner, presided over the grimy bar with gusto. I watched as he planted his hands on his hips and frowned at someone's (undoubtedly pedestrian) drink order. Somehow he managed to make even that minor a movement look simultaneously disdainful and fabulous, his tight BLATASIAN AND PROUD T-shirt flowing sinuously over his three-hundred-pound frame. Kevin—who was indeed a mix of Black, Latino, and Asian and enjoyed making people guess exactly how much of each—knew how to rock an empowering message tee.

And as usual Stu Singh was perched behind his scratched-up baby grand, signature fedora in place. Karaoke requests hadn't picked up for the night, so he plunked out his own composition, a melancholy little tune Gutter regulars had been hearing for the past few months.

After Nate patched up my foot, which turned out to bear nothing more than a medium-size cut, Lucy declared we had to celebrate my Yamato triumph. I demanded we go to The Gutter. Then I demanded five orders of potato skins. Those gouda-stuffed dates had opened my eyes to the potential wonders of non-cereal foodstuffs. Call them the gateway dates.

Surprisingly Nate agreed to come with us, but Aveda

still couldn't move around easily and said she needed her beauty sleep. I'd thought Bea would try to wheedle me into taking her underage ass back to the scene of one of her most recent alcohol-infused crimes, but she'd said she had "a lot of work to do analyzing today's media metrics." I didn't know what that meant. I was just happy she hadn't started a fight.

"So," I said, slathering guacamole on my last potato skin, "let's talk about something more interesting than me." Once I'd emerged from the heat of battle and wasn't preoccupied with, you know, *not dying*, something had niggled at the back of my brain. Something I couldn't quite put into words. I decided to try anyway.

"What *was* that Tommy Thing today?"

"What do you mean?" Nate asked. "As you pointed out in the moment: obviously a demon, not a special effect. Even Aveda came around to that line of thinking."

"A demon for sure," I agreed. "But didn't it seem like a different kind of demon than usual?"

"They're always different, though, aren't they?" Lucy said. "They take the form of the first thing they see. And in this case, that seemed to be that dreadful cardboard Tommy standee at the entrance of the theater."

"Right," I said. "But its skin was kind of weird and it chose to make itself very large—"

"Which has happened before," Lucy mused. "Sometimes they don't get the texture or proportions exactly right. Remember that hair salon attack where Aveda had to battle strangely massive bottles of shampoo?"

"True," I said. "But what's really weird is there was no 'they.' No swarm. It was just the one demon."

"I am conducting an exhaustive search of all past demon sighting reports to discern whether a single demon sighting has occurred before," Nate said. "Perhaps I can connect today's sighting to—"

"It's not just that, though," I said. "He also didn't immediately jump out of the screen and try to eat me."

"You weren't bleeding, initially," Nate said. "Not until he got your foot. And while demons may attempt to attack when you aren't bleeding, they're most vicious when they scent your blood—"

"I know," I interrupted. "I've seen all of that up close and personal. Many, many times. But the weirdness of this particular demon goes beyond that, even. The way he acted, the way he moved . . ."

Suddenly it hit me. The thing I'd been trying to articulate, the connection I couldn't quite grasp.

"He moved like the Aveda statue demons!" I yelped, slamming my fist on the table. Nate and Lucy jumped a little. "Slow and lurchy, not swarmy and piranha-like. But the way he interacted with me wasn't like the Aveda statues at all. Or any demons we've seen before, really. We had, like . . . a conversation. Sort of. And there were times where he reacted like the real Tommy Lemon might. I mean, he was mad because people didn't like his movie—"

"And then tried to kill everyone," Nate said. "Which *is* in line with the way the demons usually act."

"But the way he was talking about it was . . . nuanced," I said. "I mean, in between the growly sounds. He seemed genuinely upset that people weren't laughing."

"What are you trying to say?" Nate asked.

"I don't know." I shook my head, trying to put my thoughts into some kind of coherent order. "I really don't know. All this stuff contributes to this overall . . . feeling I got from him. An impression. That he was different."

Nate met my eyes. "Impressions—"

"Aren't exact data," I interrupted. "Yes, I know."

"Perhaps the demons are getting more creative," Lucy said. "It seems logical that an evil species would be content with things like bitey little cupcakes for only so long."

"There *were* oddities about the attack today," Nate said. "But we should start with the facts—"

"'Oddities' meaning the force field that kept people stuck to their seats and me frozen in the back of the theater?" Lucy said, wincing. "Evie, if I haven't said it enough already: I'm sorry I couldn't get to you. Whatever that thing was, it was holding me in place. I couldn't move until it released the crowd—and then I was just trying to corral them, get them under control. They were such an unruly mob—"

"We've seen force fields before," Nate interrupted. "Though they are very erratic and I haven't been able to find a pattern yet. Sometimes they're visible, sometimes not. Sometimes people can move in them, sometimes not. And sometimes it's a mix. For instance, there was one at the attack a month ago at the bicycle shop: Aveda was the only one who could move through it, but she said it was like punching molasses. No, I meant like the lack of a portal—"

"That's right, there was no portal!" I exclaimed. "So where did that Tommy Thing come from?"

"Maybe you missed the portal, love," Lucy said. "You were running around quite a bit. Or it could've been behind the movie screen."

"There was no portal," I said firmly. "Rose and her team inspected the site after the attack and she confirmed it."

Nate nodded thoughtfully. "I need to put this information in a spreadsheet."

"Forget the spreadsheet!" I sputtered, my frustration bubbling over. "We have to think beyond spreadsheets. We have to put all these *impressions* together, because they might actually mean something. Are the demons evolving? Changing?" Dread bloomed in my chest as a horrible new thought occurred to me. "Could this be a new invasion attempt by those human-shaped demons that tried to get through the first portal? Because the Aveda statues and the Tommy demon? Human-shaped.

Very, very human." I was babbling now, spurred on by my runaway train of thought.

"That's definitely not it," Nate said. "These most recent demons still followed the pattern we know: they imprinted on a statue and a cardboard standee. And those are still objects."

"But they're objects that represent human forms," I countered. "They're similar objects, even."

"So maybe they're targeting certain types of objects now?" Lucy said, her brows drawing together. "Because that does seem different. Like, smarter?"

"It's still not the same as the humanoid demons that came through the first portal," Nate said. "Those demons were shaped like humans to begin with. Now as to the rest of it: yes, the idea that our usual demons are evolving is worth further exploration."

"So wait—now you're agreeing with me?" I said, not bothering to hide my surprise.

"I wasn't disagreeing with you before," he countered. "I was trying to get you to put your impressions in more concrete terms."

I shook my head, my frustration morphing into annoyance. "So I have to phrase my observations a certain way in order for you to consider them valid?"

"No, I . . . I'm just trying to understand . . ." He frowned and blew out a long, exasperated breath. "I'm surprised you want to discuss this at all. When I tried to talk to you about the strangeness with the Aveda demon statues before, tried to get you to look at my most recent analyses, you didn't seem interested."

"Right, because . . ." I trailed off. It was true; I had brushed aside his attempt to talk to me about the statue demons earlier. But the reasons weren't things I could share with him. It was because . . . because I was being shoved into so many new high-stress situations, I didn't trust my own eyes. Because I was trying to deal with those situations as best I could while also not setting anything on fire and that took up all available space in my brain. Because I was overwhelmed by the possibility of finally achieving normalcy: the one thing I wanted most in the world. Because he tended to discount whatever I was saying in favor of information that could be understood as hard data and he always brought out my most immature side and my first response was to counter whatever he was saying anyway.

Why did I let him irritate me so much?

"In any case, we simply don't have much data beyond a few oddities right now, which is not enough to form a full-fledged hypothesis," Nate continued.

"But we definitely have oddities, like, going on," I said. "Oddities are *happening*. 'New and improved demons' isn't exactly number one on my birthday wish list, so I think we should keep talking about all this and *try* to form that hypothesis. And I will be sharing my impressions, even if they aren't exact data."

I shot him a challenging look, expecting him to counter with some kind of snotty, superior retort. Instead he just nodded and said, "Okay."

"Glad we settled that," Lucy muttered, her eyes shifting from me to Nate and back again.

I frowned at Nate, willing the perfect comeback to form on my tongue. But he had already moved on to other things, his eyes roaming the bar as he lifted his beer bottle to his lips. And as I continued staring at him, I found myself oddly distracted by those lips: the pleasing way they curved around the beer bottle, the surprising fullness I'd never noticed before. Just as I had been momentarily and irrationally obsessed with his hands the night before, his lips were now embedding themselves into my consciousness as something worthy of being stared at and I didn't even have a sub-zero body temperature or near nudity to blame and, seriously, what the hell was wrong with me?

"Team Aveda, right?"

I tore my gaze away from Nate's stupid lips to see a familiar figure standing in front of us.

"Shasta!" I exclaimed. "What are you doing here?"

"And where's your Evil Overlord?" Lucy said.

"Maisy's busy writing up the Yamato incident," Shasta said. She planted a hand on her hip then shifted awkwardly from foot to foot. Without Maisy standing next to her, she looked strangely adrift, as if she was trying for some kind of defiantly bitchy pose, but didn't quite know how to position her body.

"You guys were there today?" I said.

"Naturally." Shasta shot me a withering look. "We're always on the scene when Aveda Jupiter does something noteworthy."

"Right," I said, remembering the bathroom conversation about Maisy "cozying up" to Aveda from the night before.

"Anyway, Maisy knows you guys hang out here, so she sent me to get a quote," Shasta said. "No one's answering the phone at your HQ and our emails haven't been returned." She gave us what was probably supposed to be a disdainful glare. It looked more like she had indigestion. "Do you cretins have something I can bring back to her?"

"'Cretins'?" Lucy muttered under her breath. "That's the best you can come up with, as far as sassy insults go?"

"Apologies for the lack of response; Aveda's getting some much-needed rest," I said, kicking Lucy under the table. "She'll send out a statement ASAP, but in the meantime, you can let Maisy's readers know that she's very proud to have saved the city once again."

"You should write that down, love," Lucy said, flapping a hand at Shasta.

"No need," Shasta said, attempting to morph her glare into a smirk. It retained the same "indigestion" vibe. She glanced over at Nate, who was still occupied with his beer. "How about you, anything to add? You're always so quiet."

He stared back at her. "'Always?'"

"Well, at the benefit last night," Shasta said. "That's the only time we've seen you out with Team Aveda and Maisy was wondering . . . you know what, never mind."

I rolled my eyes. Obviously Maisy was still trying to get the scoop on "Mr. Tall, Dark, and Frowny."

Shasta turned back to me. "Make sure Aveda gets us that statement. In a timely fashion."

"So odd to see the toady away from her queen," Lucy said as Shasta stalked off. "She looks like a detached limb."

"It's tough being attached to someone with an outsize personality," I said, watching as Shasta grabbed a cocktail napkin from the bar. She glanced around, frowning, then marched over to Stu Singh and whispered something in his ear. He handed her one of the golf pencils the bar's patrons used for karaoke slips. She scribbled on the napkin. Apparently she needed to write down my quote after all. Without Maisy around, Shasta's haughtiness seemed oddly defanged. Maybe it was all part of a "Maisy's sidekick" act she wasn't very good at, but didn't know how to drop. Maybe augmented bitchiness was her version of the soothing voice I used with Aveda. "Who knows what Maisy's like behind closed doors?" I added.

"True. Probably almost as bad as she is out in the open," Lucy said.

I laughed. Dealing with Shasta—a very assistant-y sort of task, after all—had relaxed me. I felt comfortable, glad to be back in my uniform: jeans, T-shirt, neon undergarments (electric orange this time). Glad to be wearing my own unnotable face.

I allowed my heart to lift a little. This was supposed to

be a celebration, after all, so enough with the freaky demon talk and sudden lip obsession. I was here to have fun, dammit.

I signaled the server for another round of potato skins.

By the time Scott showed up I had moved on to nachos. Beautiful, beautiful nachos. I'd also scored some spam musubi, which Kevin had recently added to the appetizer selection in an attempt to, as he put it, "get some true mixed-race dishes on the menu." I savored the taste of my OG comfort food, alternating bites of musubi and nachos with reckless abandon. It was like I'd never had food before.

"Bea told me you guys were here," Scott said, plopping himself into the lone empty chair at our table. "I have some updates on the spell."

He hesitated, then leaned in to whisper in my ear. "Sorry about what I said on the phone last night. And the way I've been reacting to this in general. I just . . . I want you to be safe." He squeezed my shoulder.

"I know," I murmured back. I patted his hand reassuringly. "It's okay. I'm glad we're working on the whole safety thing together." I raised my voice so the rest of the table could hear. "So what are the updates?" I said, lifting a fully loaded nacho to my lips.

Scott leaned back, draping an arm over my chair. "I think I've figured out part one. I have an idea of how to take the fire out of you. But I'm still working out the specifics of the transfer."

"Can we test it?" I asked, stuffing the nacho in my mouth. "Part one, I mean."

"That's not a good idea," Nate interjected. "If the spell is as dangerous as Scott keeps claiming—"

"Then we should let *Scott* tell us about that," I said. I resisted the urge to give him a glare. We'd just reached a rare moment of agreement, thanks to our discussion of demon oddities, and I was trying my best to be an adult and not mess that up.

I turned to Scott. "We need to get on this," I said. "There's a possibility that the demons are going through some sort of change, and if that's the case, we need to get the fire into Aveda as soon as possible. So she can handle the situation."

"Noted," Scott said, squeezing my shoulder again. "But no tests 'til I have a better handle on things, okay?"

"It can't merely be a better handle on things," Nate said. "If—"

"Please stop nitpicking every little thing Scott says," I said, attempting to keep my tone from veering into testiness. Did he have to act like such a superior know-it-all when it came to *everything*? And was he still pushing the idea that I shouldn't go through with the power transfer at all? I sopped up leftover potato grease with my last nacho. "I trust Scott, he'll handle it, end of story. He's trying to move our master plan forward, here."

Nate frowned at me, then muttered, "I would have more essential data to contribute to this process if *someone* hadn't destroyed the tiara."

This time I did glare at him.

Being an adult was overrated.

"Gah." Lucy, who had apparently zoned out from our discussion, leaned so far back in her chair that it almost tipped over. "Do you see that?"

She gestured to the entrance. Letta, mopey as ever, had just sauntered in with some equally depressed-looking friends. They scanned the room and headed over to the bar, where Shasta had plunked herself down and was now nursing a martini. I wondered how long she was allowed to be away from Maisy.

"Letta's ignoring me," growled Lucy.

"Maybe she didn't see you, Luce," I said.

Lucy shook her head. "This is not acceptable. She

hasn't responded to my last three texts, either. I have to pull out the big guns."

She snatched a request slip from the abandoned table next to us and filled it out with gusto.

"You've been agonizing over the Letta-bedding song choice," I teased. "Did it just come to you?"

"You inspired me, Evie." She nodded at her slip with satisfaction. "So this particular song is also for you: demonbuster, firestarter, and heroine of the day. You want to join me up there?"

She inclined her head toward the piano.

"You know I never do," I said. "But I'll watch."

"All right, then. And by the way, the showstopping performance you're about to witness will also qualify me for that."

She pointed at a bright yellow flyer pasted to the wall above the bar. It announced an upcoming Ultimate Karaoke Battle, a duel to the musical death featuring two lucky souls deemed to be the best of The Gutter.

"Everyone already knows you're the best of The Gutter," I said.

She shrugged. "Might as well reinforce the notion." She grabbed Scott's arm. "Come on, Scotty. I need help with this one."

"Your surfer boy sure is game for a lot," Nate observed, watching Lucy drag Scott away.

"He's not mine," I said quickly. "I mean. I guess he used to be sort of . . . ours. Mine and Aveda's. But not anymore. Not really."

But as these words spilled out, I found myself contemplating the idea of Scott and me. After all, Dead-Inside-O-Tron appeared to be . . . well, considering last night's Bathroom Incident, it was safe to say "on hiatus." Scott was one of my oldest friends, he was sweet and supportive, and he loved Bea. And except for last night's stressed-out phone conversation, we never fought. Maybe if his spell worked and I finally became normal after all these years, we could have something. It wouldn't be a totally supernatural-free something since he still did magic for a living, but he wasn't like Aveda. He didn't let his power define his entire identity.

Hell, maybe he was right. Maybe I could find another job, another life. And maybe that life could be with him.

I watched his ass as he loped up to the piano. It was a nice ass. Really nice. Well-shaped. An ass that . . . um . . .

So not working. No sexy feelings whatsoever. Apparently, Dead-Inside-O-Tron wanted to malfunction only when it came to certain people.

Nate and I sat there in silence as Lucy handed Stu Singh her request slip. I gazed mournfully at my now-empty plate while he sipped his beer with those perfect lips.

Why was I thinking about his lips again?

Goddammit, Dead-Inside-O-Tron.

Nate set the beer down and studied me, looking like there was something he wanted to say.

"I don't want to talk about it," I said.

He gave me a quizzical look.

"About why I shouldn't let Scott go through with this depowering spell," I said. "I know you think it's a bad idea—though I can't imagine why, especially given this possible demon evolution—and I know you really want to convince me with science. But right now, I would rather just . . ."

I trailed off as the plinky opening chords from The Bangles' "Eternal Flame" wafted from the piano. I smiled. Lucy knew me well.

". . . listen to the song." I gave him my own attempt at The Tanaka Glare. Even without a mirror, I could tell it wasn't as good as Bea's version.

"Okay."

"Um, what?" I blinked in disbelief. "That's the second time you've responded with a simple 'okay' rather than backtalk. Are you feeling all right?"

His mouth quirked up in a half-smile. "Just fine."

I sat back in my seat, perplexed. "If we're not going to argue, what the hell are we going to talk about?"

He set down his beer and spat out a short, harsh bark of a laugh—a bizarre sound I was pretty sure I'd never heard before. He leaned forward, setting his elbows on the table.

"Why don't you tell me why you like this song?"

I hesitated. Was he making fun of me?

"You just smiled," he said. "When the song started—you smiled. You don't do that very often."

I turned toward the stage, where Lucy had draped herself over the piano in classic siren fashion. She tossed her hair back from her face, pointing straight at me, belting out the big notes.

I felt that unhinging inside of me again, that recklessness I had been overtaken by earlier in the day. I tried to block it, tried to get my usual control back, tried to call up Soothing Internal Voice to advise me against allowing my words to spill out. But like Dead-Inside-O-Tron, Soothing Internal Voice seemed to be on extended hiatus.

Two days of being a fake superhero and my internal safeguards were thoroughly fucked. So my mouth opened and I started blabbing.

"It's the song I was always waiting for." I curled my hands around my ice-cold beer bottle. "At school dances? You know how you were always waiting for that certain song, hoping the DJ would magically read your mind? Maybe that was just me," I added as a hint of amusement flashed through his eyes. "Annie—er, Aveda and I found an old Bangles cassette tape at Goodwill. We must've listened to it a thousand times."

I paused, picking at the label on my beer. It flaked off in satisfying bits of gluey paper. Talking to him this way was weird. But as long as I was talking, I wasn't thinking about his lips.

"We both thought it was a perfect slow dance song . . . shut up!" I said, as his mouth started to curve. "You aren't allowed to laugh at me. We were twelve."

My eyes wandered back to the piano. Lucy and Scott were tearing it up, hands over hearts, singing to each other like their lives depended on it. The senior citizen audience ate it up, their gray heads swaying back and forth.

"I'd wait for it, every junior high school dance. And the DJ never came through with the mind-reading. The song was too old to be relevant but not old enough to be vintage cool."

I decimated the remainder of my beer bottle label, arranging the remnants in a pile. "Then we were at our first high school dance. We were freshman, the lowest of the low. And this dance had something we'd never seen before: a live band."

I picked at my pile of label pieces, snagging glue underneath my fingernails.

"I wouldn't shut up about the song that night. I kept obsessing about it. Like, if they somehow managed to play this one song during the first dance of my high school career, freshman year would be automatically awesome."

I pushed my label pile to the side and looked up, meeting his eyes. He was biting his lip kind of hard.

"You *are* allowed to laugh at that," I said, grinning in spite of myself. He didn't laugh, but he smiled back, taking a final swig of his beer and setting the empty bottle on the table.

"So? What happened?" he asked.

"Aveda kept hounding the band guys. Which I didn't want her to do. I didn't think it counted if we *made* it happen. But she was a lot like she is now."

"Relentless."

"Yes. So finally she's had enough. The band guys are ignoring her, pretending like they can see right through her, which was *never* okay with her, even back then. So she climbs up on the stage . . ." I smiled at the memory. "And while the lead singer dude was basking in the screams from hormone-crazed groupies, she slips in front of him, commandeers the mic, yells, 'this one's for you, Evie,' and proceeds to sing 'Eternal Flame' in its entirety. A cappella."

Nate's eyes widened in disbelief. He leaned forward and our knees touched. I surreptitiously moved my legs to the left, putting a microcosm of space between us.

"Was it amazing?" he asked.

My smile widened. "It was terrible. But it was just so . . . her. It was her way of being there for me yet again. And it was all anyone could talk about for the entire week afterward."

Nate laughed. "And your roles were forever set after that?"

I attempted to pick the glue out from underneath my fingernail. It wedged itself farther in. "What do you mean?"

"She loves the spotlight. And you insist on staying in her shadow."

I gave him a look. "Way to reduce us to easily digestible *90210*-ian stereotypes. Which, by the way, is something I wrote a thoroughly eviscerating paper on in grad school. What's next, bargain basement psychoanalysis about how I need to discover my own uniqueness and break away from my personality-squelching friend?"

"No. Your personality is abundantly clear." He gave me an attempt at a half-smile, but I was in no mood to receive it. I leaned back in my chair, crossing my arms over my chest.

"But," he continued slowly, "you have an almost pathological desire to shrink."

"Shrink?"

"You saved an entire theater full of people today." His stare bored into me, making me squirm. "And all you can think about is getting rid of the very thing that allowed you to do that."

I shook my head, struggling to tamp down on the frustration burning through me. He'd lulled me into semi-pleasant conversation only to start badgering me about his pet topic once my defenses were down. That had probably been his plan all along. How could I make him understand that the fire wasn't something I could even imagine wanting? That I would never, ever see it as this really cool science thing he'd somehow built up in his mind? That yes, I was proud of what I'd done at the Yamato . . . but thinking about calling up such a destructive force on the regular filled me with deep, soul-shaking terror?

Once again he was acting like he just automatically knew what was best for everyone. What was best for *me*.

"I told you—I don't want to talk about that," I hissed.

"Why not?" He leaned forward. Our knees brushed again. "Why won't you even think about what you might be capable of?"

"Because I already know," I growled. "I *told* you: I already know."

"I don't think you do," he snapped. "What about today? You got mad at Aveda and you didn't set anything on fire. Whereas with Tommy, you called it forth when you *wanted* to. And last night, the incident with the sink. You were under extreme stress and your hand got hot, but there were no actual flames. Isn't it possible that your heightened emotional state of the past couple days is forcing your body—your entire system—to learn some measure of control?"

"What, so you've tracked all my moods in one of your neat little spreadsheets? Maybe done a whole analysis on me feeling all my feelings?"

"So you're for analysis and discussion when it comes to these new demon oddities, but not when it comes to your own power?" He raked a hand through his hair in frustration. "You confuse and confound me."

"Tracking the new demon oddities is something that will *help* people—and so is giving my power to Aveda," I said. "It's all part of the same 'keep everyone and this whole damn city safe' thing. And anyway, I've made the decision! We have a plan and we're on the path! We don't *need* further analysis!"

"All I'm saying is that when you actually use your power—"

"I don't want to use it! I want to be normal!"

"But you're *not* normal—"

"*Stop.*"

I scrambled to my feet. An uncomfortable flush spread through my body, making me feel like I had invisible bugs crawling underneath my skin. "Why do I keep trying to explain this to you? You don't listen. You just want to make me into one of your science experiments."

"That's not true—"

"For your information, I'm proud of what I did today," I barreled on. "But whether I want to do it again is my choice. Just mine. Full stop. You think you somehow know better than me when it comes to my own power, but I've thought about this plenty—obsessively, even. About how dangerous I could be and what I might do if I let things get out of control. How many people could end up . . ."

Dead. I couldn't even say it out loud. I shook my head, trying to clear it.

"I didn't ask for your opinion and it would be really fucking great if you kept it to yourself. Your *data* doesn't trump my real life experience."

I turned on my heel and stomped off, my full-body flush so intense, I wished I could shed all of my skin.

I made a sharp right into the hallway leading to the bathrooms. I leaned back against the wall, breathing hard, my fingertips brushing the faded business cards that papered the corridor walls. I focused on my breathing until it was all I could hear.

My breath would not slow, no matter how much I willed it to. I instinctively curled my palms at my sides, waiting for that trademark heat to flare.

It didn't come.

I opened my fist and stared at my palm. What the hell? I couldn't help but think about what Nate had said.

Some measure of control.

"Evie."

My head snapped up and I was greeted by the sight of Nate standing in the hall's entrance. He shifted from one foot to the other, as if he couldn't decide whether he should step through or not.

I heard the opening chords of "Eternal Flame" plinking through the air again. Stu Singh must have mixed up his sheet music and looped Lucy and Scott back up to the top.

"I'm sorry," he said.

"You're . . . what, now?"

He met my gaze and a ghost of uncertainty flitted across his face. He finally took a step toward me.

"I'm sorry. I wasn't . . . I didn't mean . . ." He raked a hand through his hair. "Shit. I'm really bad at this."

"Terrible," I said. I meant for it to come out haughty and defiant, but it emerged as a trembly whisper.

"I only want you to realize . . ." He trailed off and hesitantly reached down to take my hand.

"It's not hot," I blurted out.

He looked at me blankly.

"Um, my hand. I just got mad at you. Really, really mad. And it's not heating up at all."

He stared at my palm. Then his fingers curled around mine and his eyes drifted back to my face, his gaze piercing right through me.

And suddenly I didn't care about my palm or my

power or "Eternal Flame" or anything but the intense study of his perfectly formed mouth.

His grip tightened on my hand. I squeezed back, our intertwined fingers crushed together, producing an unmistakable heat of their own. His other arm snaked around my waist, pulling me against his hard, unyielding wall of a body, and I breathed deep, taking in that scent of soap and spearmint and rain. He smelled *so fucking good*.

My free hand splayed against his chest and I found myself gathering the front of his shirt in my fist, yanking him closer, and finally closing the last few millimeters of space between us, crushing my lips against his. His mouth moved over mine, hot and demanding and tart with the taste of beer. I ripped my hand from his and tangled my fingers in his hair, devouring him with an urgency I didn't know I was capable of. Only one thought pounded through my hazy brain: *if I stop kissing him for even a second, I will probably die.*

His hands slid to my hips and he scooped me up, my eager form colliding with the beautifully muscled planes of his body. My legs wrapped around his waist. All I wanted was *more*: more of his scent, more of his tongue stroking against mine, more of his hands running all over me in a way that made me wish my clothes would spontaneously disintegrate.

I wanted him in a desperate, single-minded way I'd never wanted anything else.

He stumbled forward, propelling us down the hallway and into The Gutter's supply closet. As the door swung closed behind us, we slammed against a creaky metal shelving unit, my ass colliding with a stack of binders. I yelped, breaking our kiss. Nate cursed and lifted me higher, settling my backside onto one of the shelves. Keeping one arm wrapped around my waist, he used his other arm to sweep the binders to the floor.

He turned back to me, raw hunger emblazoned on his

face. Both of us were breathing hard, a duet of gasps that threatened to drown out the other duet that was still wafting through the bar. Our eyes met and we paused as a tiny bit of reality pierced the weirdness of the moment: here was this man I saw every day, this man I fought with every day, this man I had oft proclaimed to be the most irritating person alive, and all I wanted to do was rip his clothes off in the supply closet of a filthy piano bar. If we were going to stop and laugh and acknowledge how ridiculous the situation was, this would've been the time to do it.

Instead we started kissing again.

His lips traveled to my neck, finding that sensitive hollow where throat met collarbone and marking the spot with enticing little nibbles. I inhaled sharply, a shiver coursing through my entire nervous system. My arms jutted out on either side of me, my hands gripping the cold metal of the shelf. My legs tightened around his waist and I found myself grinding into him, gasping when I felt how hard he was. He groaned into my neck, a primal sound that shaped itself into my name.

Keeping one arm locked around my waist, he skimmed his free hand over the curve of my breast, then grasped the neckline of my T-shirt and yanked it down. The fabric ripped and I barely had time to register the rush of cold air sweeping over my half-exposed chest before his big hand cupped me, his thumb moving the bright orange lace of my bra aside to stroke my nipple. A moan escaped my throat as he kissed his way down my neck, across my collarbone, blazing a trail to that hardening peak of a nipple and finally claiming it in his perfect mouth.

Chills rocketed through my body and I arched against him, the pleasure intensifying with every swirl of his tongue, every graze of his teeth. I didn't recognize the sounds coming out of me. I'd never sounded like this, never felt like this. I'd never allowed myself to.

I threw my head back, my eyes closed, wanting to feel his lips against every inch of my skin. So hot and good and hot and . . . hot . . . *shit.*

"Nate . . ."

My eyes flew open just as the fire exploded from my flailing hand. It careened past the shelf, over a box of creepy plastic hands and feet Kevin used as Halloween decorations, and smacked into a tattered poster sporting Stu Singh's smiling face. The edge of the poster caught fire, Stu's grin highlighted by ribbons of red and gold.

"What . . ." Nate pulled me closer, his lust-dazed eyes widening in confusion.

"Fuck!" I unwrapped myself from him and hopped to the ground, ripping what was left of my abused shirt from my body and using it to smother the flames. Stu grinned at us, a little singed but mostly unharmed.

I turned back to Nate. His eyes drifted to my mostly naked torso.

I had no idea what to say.

Luckily anything I might've said was drowned out by the blare of the fire alarm.

Nate's face snapped back to a more alert expression, as if someone had doused him with cold water. He snatched an XXL hoodie emblazoned with THE GUTTER! :) (part of Kevin's attempt at swag) off one of the lower shelves and wrapped it around me, then shoved me toward the door.

We rolled through the bar area with the geriatric crowd, pouring out the exit and into the crisp night air. I turned to face Nate, pulling the sweatshirt around me. It was so big, it gaped open, exposing my near nudity to the displaced senior citizens. One of them, a lady with a severe helmet of steel gray pin curls, gave me a disapproving look.

I opened my mouth. I still had no idea what to say.

This time Lucy saved the day.

"You guys!" Her lilting voice cut through the mob, and I whirled around to see her trotting toward us, Scott loping behind her. "Can you believe they cut off my song?" she said. "I was just getting really into . . ."

She trailed off. "Evie, love. What happened to your shirt?"

CHAPTER TWELVE

"RISE AND SHINE, Supergirl!"

I cracked one eye open. And saw a pair of purple ankle boots bouncing up and down in front of my face.

"Bea," I croaked. "Get your shoes off the bed."

"Blah." She bounced one last time, then plopped down next to me. "You are no longer the boss of me, Big Sis Stick-In-The-Mud."

I kicked her foot, which was rubbing dirt and germs all over my clean sheets. It was Saturday, so at least I didn't have to needle her about going to school. Which she probably wouldn't have done anyway.

"I am still *a* boss of you."

"Blaaaaaaah," she repeated, adding a little flourish at the end. She stuck her tongue out at me, but moved slightly, dangling her feet off the edge of the mattress. "Maybe you could cheer up for two seconds? I mean. It's so exciting!" She grinned, her eyes—rimmed today with a truckload of electric blue liner—going all sparkly. It was the most sunshine I'd seen from her in months.

"What's exciting?" I asked. "Your new room?"

I had to admit the rooms we'd been given at Jupiter HQ were much nicer than any rooms we'd ever occupied before. I'd initially been set on moving me and Bea back out immediately, but everything had happened so fast the day before, and after seeing how nice the rooms were, I couldn't help but admit that living here for a little while wasn't a terrible idea.

The walls of my new digs were painted a pristine eggshell and light streamed in from the window facing the street, giving the whole affair a womb-like glow. And the bed was a queen-size oasis of sturdy box springs and downy pillowtop. But even the comfort of this sweet little room couldn't help me last night.

After Nate, Lucy, and I stumbled home from The Gutter, I found my new room and attempted to go to sleep. Funny thing about sleep: it doesn't come easily when a fucking highlights reel of your latest closet tryst won't stop playing on a loop through your head. Even after an ice-cold shower, I could still feel the imprint of Nate's hands all over my body.

What the hell was I thinking?

I didn't have *that much* to drink. And really, I was way too old to be affected *that way* by "Eternal Flame."

I could only chalk up our encounter to yet another unfortunate side effect of superheroing: the adrenaline rush resulted in impulse control that was best described as "poor" and decision-making that was best described as "really, really shitty."

"My room is fine but hardly exciting, Ignoramus Rex." Bea snapped me out of my thoughts. "I'm talking about this."

She brandished her phone, its turquoise sequined shell glittering insolently as she waved it back and forth.

"Hold it still," I said, squinting at the glowing screen.

The screen displayed a YouTube video in all its shaky shot-on-a-camera-phone glory: a video of me at the Yamato, fire arcing from my hand to the Tommy Thing. As the movie screen exploded in front of me, a cheer went up from the crowd.

I watched my glamoured self as she stared at her hand, then turned and gave a tentative version of Aveda's million-watt grin. Standing tall in her ruined boots with a smoking hole that used to be a movie screen gaping behind her, she looked pretty freaking cool.

Okay, fine—*I* looked pretty freaking cool.

Yesterday I was too discombobulated to process that all those people—the stoners and the school-skippers and the girl with the messy hair—were cheering for more than the fact that they were no longer trapped in their seats watching a shitty movie. They were cheering for *me*.

The thought filled me with a surprising surge of warmth. I'd saved a crowd of people, and they'd looked at me the way I looked at Michelle Yeoh in *The Heroic Trio*. It was ridiculous. It was crazy.

It was also kind of awesome.

"That's right, Sis." Bea waved the phone again. "You are totes a viral sensation."

She tapped on the screen. "The comments are insane. Marriage proposals. Demands for new Tommy Demonbuster T-shirts. Lots of love for the whole fire power deal." She rubbed absently at her eyes, smudging blue liner onto her fingertips. "I was thinking we could run a Facebook promotion: sign up for our newsletter to see an exclusive vlog of Aveda discussing her latest takedown. First fifty sign-ups also get some kind of exclusive merch—a Tommy Demonbuster sticker, maybe. You'd have to film the vlog as Aveda, but I can set the whole thing up really easily. I mean, if you want."

I gaped at her, dumbstruck. Trying to reconcile the girl who was usually in some state of Tanaka Glare with the one who was staring back at me hopefully, her smudged eyeliner giving her the irresistible appearance of a plaintive raccoon. It was like she had found something to latch on to overnight, something to focus all her energy on. Considering that her energy was usually focused on acting out and trying to make me mad, maybe this Social Media Guru thing was doing her some good after all.

"We have a newsletter?" I finally managed, attempting to make sense of everything she'd just said.

"We do now." Her brow crinkled and she chewed on her lower lip. "I'm trying to get more sign-ups. I was thinking the vlog thing could be part of a series. Give the fans that personal connection to Aveda. Take her off the pedestal and make her one of the people."

"Wow." I smiled at her. "That's really creative. It reminds me of something Mom would think of."

She looked confused. "Mom didn't have a vlog."

"I meant the creative bit. The way you looked at something and came up with an idea just like that." I snapped my fingers. "Like when Mom found that box of buttons at the swap meet. Remember? They weren't just buttons to her. She made them into those cute figurines? Little button people? Created something strange and adorable out of something seemingly ordinary."

"Huh," Bea said. "Mom was totes Etsy before Etsy was a thing."

"Yeah. And that's you, too." I gave her an affectionate nudge.

She beamed at me. More sunshine.

"Why don't you take this idea to Aveda?" I said. "Because she'll probably want to—"

"She'll want to what?"

Bea and I sat up straighter in bed and turned to the doorway, where Aveda was shuffling in, propped up on a pair of crutches. Her ankle was now encased in an immobilizing air cast boot Nate insisted she wear.

"Because right now, she just wants to talk to you about *this*," Aveda said, brandishing her iPad as she dragged herself across the room. She heaved herself onto the bed, landing soundly on my feet. I winced. The cut on my foot from yesterday was healing pretty well, but the last thing it needed was a dramatic superheroine throwing all of her muscular body weight directly on top of it.

She waved the iPad in front of my face and I realized it was cued up to the same scene I'd just watched on Bea's phone: Me as Aveda nuking the Tommy demon.

"Pretty cool, right?" I said tentatively.

She passed me the iPad. "Read the comments." Her tone was clipped. Clearly "cool" wasn't exactly what she was thinking. I studied her for a moment. Yesterday I'd noticed that she seemed frustrated and was coping by micromanaging me . . . and maybe acting a little crazier than usual. Now that crazy flared to the surface, giving her eyes a hint of desperation.

But what could she possibly be upset about?

I scrolled past the video to the comments.

You guys?! This fire power deal is amazeballs!

I know, right? When was the last time Aveda Jupiter did something so kickass? Frankly, with the zit and everything, I was kinda worried she'd lost her mojo . . .

Facts are facts—her attacks have been looking totally same-y lately. But now . . .

Just say it: Aveda hasn't been this awesome in months! All hail the new girl on fire! It's like we've got a real, live Katniss up in here!

Motherfucking hail! Aveda Jupiter 2.0 is the new bomb diggity . . . wait, do people say "bomb diggity" anymore?

"Isn't this good?" I said, setting the iPad down on my fuzzy chenille comforter. "You said you wanted the right kind of press. And this is basically, like, Aveda Jupiter is the Most Awesome Thing Ever. Full stop."

"You were supposed to merely prep them for my impending awesomeness," she said. "Not steal the spotlight entirely."

"But everyone thinks it's you," I countered. "You and your . . . awesomeness."

She shook her head, that bit of crazy flaring in her eyes again. "You were supposed to *prep* them," she repeated, whine overtaking the steel in her voice. "And then once I got my fire power, I could take the stage and really wow everyone. But now they're talking about how I've lost my mojo."

"You will wow them," I said. "You just have to be patient."

"Too late," she said, the whine dissipating into something even more pathetic. "Aveda 2.0 is already a viral sensation." She jammed a fingernail into her mouth. "I've worked so hard," she muttered. "Given my life to keeping this city safe. And then you come in and show off that fire and within two days, all they can talk about is how much *better* you are." She glared at the iPad. "This commenter, MissionMan364—he hasn't said anything remotely complimentary about me in months."

I studied her scrunched-up face, trying to make sense of what she was rambling on about. I guess she thought that I'd make a competent stand-in, but the comments about Aveda Jupiter being super-duper incredible wouldn't *really* start up until she took over. Bitching at me for being a bad Aveda Jupiter was one thing—it gave her a sense of control over the situation and allowed her to boss me around as usual—but she hadn't anticipated what might happen if I surpassed competent stand-in mode and actually did a good job. And people started talking about it. Because even if they thought it was her . . . she knew it wasn't. She knew they were commenting positively on me-as-Aveda and dissing the *real* Aveda in the process. She knew that on top of being unable to do the one thing that gave her purpose, she had to watch someone else win praise for doing it in a way the fans deemed better. And it was clearly driving her nuts.

"It was your idea for me to do this," I reminded her.

She shrugged, pulled her finger out of her mouth, and examined her nails. They looked ragged, the ends chewed and uneven. In fact she looked different all around—like a sharp photograph gone blurry at the edges. Her hair, always so full and shiny, hung in limp hanks around her face. The zit from a few days ago had returned with a vengeance. But even more disturbing was her stooped posture, the ghost of defeat flitting through her eyes. The Aveda Jupiter bravado that usually emanated from her every pore was absent. I could only recall her looking like that in two other instances. One was after our kindergarten classmates made fun of her mom's soup dumplings. The other was whenever her parents gave her one of their dismissive "Mmms."

She looked, I realized, achingly human.

"Annie . . ." I said, without thinking.

Aveda's eyes flashed, her shields going up. "I'm fine," she spat out. "I just want to be . . . back. Back to doing what I do best. Back to being *me*."

With as much haughtiness as she could muster, she stood, grabbed her crutches, and hobbled out.

"Bea." I turned to my sister, who'd remained silent during this whole exchange, eyes wide, phone clutched to her chest. "Can you go, I don't know—"

"Make sure she's okay? Offer a little comfort? Show her some of the 'squee' comments about last month's sourdough bread factory triumph? People love the sight of her—the real her—annihilating those bunny demons."

"Yes. Great idea. Nice Social Media Guruing."

"That has nothing to do with social media, Big Sis." She rolled her eyes at me. "But thanks anyway." She gave a nod and scampered out of the room, nearly running into Lucy, who was on her way in.

Apparently my nice new room was an everyone welcome free-for-all.

"Evie? Good gravy, why aren't you up yet?" Lucy bounced onto the bed, jostling me to the side.

"Morning, Luce," I said. "Are you also here to talk about how I'm a viral sensation?"

"No. But you should probably get that looked at,

darling. It sounds dreadful." She tipped her head back against the headboard. "I wanted to inform you that I sealed the deal with Letta. She came knockin' on my door after we got home last night." One side of her mouth tilted up. "The power balladeering worked."

"Oh! That's great!" I squeezed her hand. "And a testament to the everlasting power of The Bangles. Is Letta still here? Did you leave her all alone just to share this earth-shattering news with me?"

"No." Lucy gave a dismissive wave. "Last night was fun, but her pillow talk skills are seriously lacking. Once you get past the red hair and the intriguing emo shell, she is rather dull."

I gave her an amused look. "I could've told you that."

"But!" Lucy grinned at me, eyes full of mischief. "I'm hoping my sex mojo rubs off on you so you can make proper use of my 'welcome to Jupiter HQ' present . . ."

She reached over and eased the nightstand drawer open, revealing a giant pile of condoms. There were so many of them stuffed in there, I wasn't sure how the drawer had closed in the first place.

"Lucy!" My eyes bugged out of my head. "I don't need all that!" I hissed, reaching over her and attempting to slam the drawer shut. It only closed halfway. A few of the condoms spilled onto the floor. "Or any of that."

"You do!" she protested. "I told you, this fake superhero thing is going to break your three-year dry spell. And I'm going to do everything I can to facilitate that."

I shoved at the drawer again, but that only jostled the condoms further. More of them fell to the floor, their bright wrappers sparkling luridly in the morning light.

"Lucy, I do not want—"

"Evie—oh. Hello, Lucy."

My head jerked away from the condom avalanche to see Nate lurking in the doorway, his expression turning uncertain when he spotted the two of us crammed together in bed. My heart gave an annoying little hop. And dammit, this time there was no "Eternal Flame" to blame it on.

"Did you want something?" I said, sounding more standoffish than I intended. I wondered if he noticed the half-open drawer of condoms. Or the ones on the floor.

"Yes . . . no. I mean yes." He raked a nervous hand through his hair and stepped more fully into the room. I fiddled with my comforter, running the fuzzy edge along my thumb. Lucy's eyes darted from me to Nate and back again.

"Well, I should get going," she sang out, her voice suddenly way too loud. "I have to, uh, do some things!" She winked at me and slid out of bed. I gave her an "oh, come *on*" look, but she just skipped out the door.

Leaving me alone with Nate. Which, if I'd had to pick, was at the very bottom of my List of Desirable Situations.

I wondered if Lucy suspected anything. She had taken notice of my ruined shirt the night before. I'd hastily explained it away as a fire power-related mishap, which she'd seemed to accept readily enough, what with the sprinklers going off and all.

Maybe she was just so intent on ending my dry spell that any heterosexual man who so much as entered my bedroom was a winning prospect. And Nate was even more of a prospect since she was always trying to get me to notice his hotness.

Well, I guess I'd finally noticed last night. I'd noticed *a lot*.

I blew out a long breath and pulled the comforter around me in a makeshift cocoon.

"The company doing remodeling work on Cake My Day just sent something over," Nate said. His nervousness had vanished and now I couldn't quite read his expression. I wondered if being alone with me was at the bottom of *his* List of Desirable Situations.

Dammit, Lucy.

"They found it embedded in one of the mixing bowls," Nate continued, crossing the room. He sat down next to me and deposited a smooth, round stone in the palm of my hand. I scrutinized it. It was one of his supernatural gibberish stones, but this one had two clear words etched into it:

You need

"Flip it over," Nate prompted. I did. On the back there was a single number:

3

"Wow," I said, my tone continuing on its not-entirely-intentional standoffish bent. "Real, actual words."

Nate frowned at my lack of reverence. The frown made me relax. A frown put us back in comfortable territory.

"If you ever paid attention, you'd know many of the portal stones have real, actual words on them," he grumbled. "But this is the first case where they seem to be arranged as a directive—a command. The question is: a command from whom?"

"Or for whom," I murmured, turning the stone over in my hand.

"What do you mean?" Nate said, still frowning at me. I frowned back, exasperated.

"It's just as valid a question," I said. "Correct me if I'm wrong—and I'm sure you will—but our little demon friends are usually pretty haphazard. There's no rhyme or reason to where and when they attack and they don't seem organized enough to have a leader. If a directive is being issued, that says there's now someone worth issuing directives *to*. Which could possibly be a bit of data to log for our still-amorphous 'demons changing and evolving' theory."

I gave him a challenging look, expecting him to contradict me. But his frown dissipated.

"That's true," he said. "Hmm. Interesting."

He took the stone back from me and studied it, brow

furrowed. As he stroked his thumb contemplatively over the stone's surface, I couldn't help but flash back to him stroking . . . other things the night before. A flush crept up the back of my neck.

And we were back to that damn closet tryst highlights reel.

I shifted uncomfortably and pulled my comforter-cocoon more tightly around my body, banishing any and all images from the night before from my mind.

Of course, then he had to go and ruin it.

"Evie? I wanted to talk to you . . ."

Oh, no.

He set the stone on the bed, reached over, and brushed a hand against my shoulder. The briefest of physical contact, but his touch seemed to burn its way through my comforter, leaving an indelible mark on my skin. He dropped his hand in his lap, as if he wasn't sure what to do with it.

". . . about last night."

Nooooooo.

I turned to him, silently ordering my face not to betray me. The way he was looking at me, the way his voice shaped itself around my name—rough and husky, just like the night before—made me want to come apart. But the last few days basically amounted to a series of random outbursts, impulse control problems, and emotional vomit. And now that we had possible demon evolution issues, I couldn't add this to the list. I just couldn't. I needed to have a firm handle on *something*.

"What do you want to talk about?" I said, my voice as steady as I could make it. "The fact that we were both bored and horny?"

Disbelief passed over his face. "That's your explanation? We were *horny*?"

My index finger poked out of my comforter-cocoon, jabbing into his chest. What was it about this man that constantly gave me the urge to *point*?

"Well," I said. "Weren't we?"

He glowered at me. We faced off as if frozen in place, neither of us willing to budge. After a moment of heated silence, I caught a bit of movement in his face, a faint twitch of the lips.

"Are you *laughing* at me?" I snarled, retracting my pointy finger. "This is not funny. And shouldn't we be trying to figure out this whole demon . . . thing?" I flapped my hand at the stone. "Don't you think that's more important than our debatable levels of horniness? Like, possibly panic-worthy?"

"Yes." His face sobered. "You're correct. Laughing in the midst of discussing this situation is inappropriate. But I can't really explain any of my behavior around you. You make me . . ."

"What? I make you *what*? You don't have some technobabble-y science term for it?"

"I do," he retorted. "'Completely insane.'"

His voice was resigned and puzzled with a hint of warmth, making that last bit sound more like an endearment than an insult. I squelched the heat rising in my cheeks.

"Guys?" Lucy ducked back into the room. "Um, sorry to interrupt, but we've got an emergency going on."

"A bigger emergency than a possible demon evolution?" I said.

"Yes. Well . . . sort of. It's Aveda." She hesitated, as if she couldn't quite believe what she needed to say next. "She's missing."

CHAPTER THIRTEEN

I'D NEVER RACED up a moving escalator before.

But there's a first time for everything. And boy, had these last few days brought me a lot of firsts.

We'd spent an hour trying to track Aveda down, only to receive a phone call from the security department of the San Francisco Mall. She'd been detained there, she was in some kind of trouble, and could we come by immediately?

As soon as we burst through the massive glass doors of the mall, Nate, Lucy, and I were off, clattering up the impossible-looking loop-de-loop of moving stairs that curved through all eight levels of the shopping mecca. It took the otherwise run-of-the-mill mall into sci-fi territory, a futuristic cityscape out of *Metropolis*.

"Superhero security detail coming through!" Lucy barked, leading the charge through the sea of shoppers clogging the escalator. "Move aside, please!"

"They really wouldn't tell you over the phone why Aveda's been detained by Nordstrom security?" I said, mouthing "sorry!" as I pushed past a pair of women weighed down by what appeared to be several metric tons of shopping bags. One of them gave me a dirty look.

"They wouldn't tell me anything," Lucy said. "Which is why we need to get to her as soon as possible."

Adrenaline thrummed through my system as we

shoved our way through the mass of bodies. The crowd reminded me of the Whistles crowd, thick and sweaty, but the momentum of the escalator gave me an extra lift, propelling me forward. We finally landed on the fourth floor of Nordstrom, a wonderland of heels, wedges, and boots arranged on marble platforms and spotlighted from above. A cloud of flowery perfume seemed to coat the air, and a gleaming grand piano sat near the top of the escalator, positioned on a bit of plush red carpet. Even though the lid was closed and the actual player appeared to be off duty, the mere presence of the piano gave the store that extra little bit of luxury.

"Security office is that way," Lucy said, pointing toward the back.

I decided not to ask how she knew that.

As we marched purposefully through the shoes, I spied a pair of all-too-familiar figures.

"Shit," I muttered, my adrenaline levels ratcheting upward.

Maisy Kane and Shasta were loitering outside the security office like a pair of overdressed vultures. Maisy was doing a yellow thing today: honey-colored sundress and sandals with plastic daisies on the toes. Another daisy was tucked behind her ear, as if to create the illusion that she found it growing on the street and whimsically plucked it from its urban prison. Her hair was now dyed golden blond.

Had Aveda been spotted here, doing whatever it was that had landed her in the security office?

Did Maisy have some kind of exclusive "scoop" on the incident?

Could this situation get any worse?

"Lucy," I muttered, nodding toward Maisy and Shasta. "Let me and Nate distract them. You slip into the security office and find out what's going on. And then we'll figure out how to get Aveda out of here without causing a scandal."

"Roger that," Lucy said.

I sped up, ignoring the hammering of my heart as I planted myself in front of Maisy and Shasta.

"Uh, what's up?" I said.

Terrible opener, but it got them to look at me—and away from the security office while Lucy darted through the door.

"Well, good gosh-dang! Aren't you Aveda Jupiter's escort?" Maisy's eyes immediately diverted from me to Nate, who'd positioned himself behind me, distracting them further. "Goodness, that monkey suit you were wearing at the benefit did not do justice to your physique," she purred, laying a hand on Nate's arm.

I stiffened, consumed by a stab of . . . something. The closest feeling I could liken it to was the idea that someone was trying to steal my favorite toy.

"We heard tell of an Aveda Jupiter sighting over here," Maisy continued. She linked her arm through Nate's. "I imagine you've got the inside word on that? You two seemed awfully cozy at the benefit."

"She's just doing a little shopping," I said, making my tone firm. "And she'd really like to be left alone while doing so."

"Shopping, eh?" Shasta examined her zebra-striped nails. "So she has time for that, but can't find a moment to send us that promised statement about the Yamato incident?"

Ugh. I'd completely forgotten about the statement. I tried to catch Shasta's eye, but she was really into her nails.

"I really must have a li'l ol' girl time meet-up with her," Maisy said, ignoring both me and Shasta. "I know soup dumplings are her favorite, and the most adorable place just opened up down the street from me. Probably the most authentic xiaolongbao I've had outside of Shanghai."

Oh, brother. There was something deeply ironic about

the fact that so many of the "exotic" food items that had gotten us teased and bullied by our white classmates were now fetishized by white hipsters.

I bit back a retort about 1) how terrible her exaggerated accent was and 2) how there was no way mass-produced dumplings spat out by some trendy place in Maisy's neighborhood were more "authentic" than the ones handmade by Aveda's mother.

"We could go shopping together," Maisy continued. "I have so many style ideas for her."

"Aveda doesn't need any ideas," I blurted out, unable to hold back this time. "She likes her style just the way it is." And before I could stop myself, I added, "Potential nip slips and all."

An awkward silence descended as Maisy and Shasta turned to stare at me. And for the first time since I'd known her, Maisy looked uncomfortable.

"Um, yes. Well." Maisy arranged her features back into their usual carefree expression and smoothed a nonexistent wrinkle from her bright yellow skirt. "I'm sure Aveda would love the cute vintage boutique I just found in the Mission—so much more original than the clothes you get at corporatized chains. I hate those."

"Which is why you're at the mall," I said. "And not just any mall, but the biggest, most touristy mall in the city." I didn't know where all these words were coming from, but I couldn't seem to stop them. There was that unhinging feeling again, loosening my tongue and obliterating my impulse control.

"It can be fun to mix mass fashion with your own unique POV," Maisy insisted. "I'm sure Aveda would agree with me."

"I know she wouldn't," I countered, verbal vomit going into full effect. "And do you know why?"

Maisy shrank away from me and glanced at Nate, as if to say, "Please, sir, protect me!"

"Because," I said, "if there's one thing Aveda can't

stand, it's overdressed pseudo-hipsters who pretend to be her friends and then threaten to post 'nip-slip' pictures of her on their stupid, sensationalistic, overhyped blog *things* in order to leech off her hard-earned and actually deserved fame."

Maisy's mouth formed a perfect O.

"I would never!" Her hand fluttered to her chest. "My posts about her revealing outfit were nothing but flattering. And I didn't even post the photo I had of her actual nipple, ah, revelation."

"She would never!" echoed Shasta, making an unsuccessful attempt to do her own fluttery hand thing.

"Oh. You so would." I took a step forward. Maisy dove behind Nate, her grip on his arm tightening. "Aveda has eyes everywhere. We know you were trying to stir up some kind of salacious mean girl bullshit. We *know*."

To emphasize my point, I did the I-see-you thing where I pointed at my eyes with my index and middle fingers, then pointed at Maisy, then back to me again. It was ridiculous. It was also immensely satisfying.

"Not so mousy today," Maisy murmured. "When did you decide to grow a backbone, Rude Girl?"

"It doesn't matter," I growled. It was a pretty good growl. "What matters is this: you need to leave Aveda alone and stop posting all your snarky bullshit about her appearance. Enough with the tearing down other women and encouraging everyone else to look at them through a male gaze-centric lens. Just . . . enough. And keep your grabby hands off her *escort*."

I jerked my head at Nate. Maisy retracted her claws from his arm so fast her hair daisy fell to the floor. She slunk off, Shasta trailing behind her.

"Man," I heard her mutter. "What a gosh-dang cun—"

"Was that necessary? Telling them off like that?"

I turned back around to see Nate gazing at me, his expression amused.

"What?" I said. "I got rid of them, didn't I? Plus I'm

protecting Aveda and her image. Maisy's posts totally encourage the fans to make even shittier comments than usual. I know how damaging that can be; I wrote a paper on superheroines and male gaze-centrism in grad school."

"And the bit about the 'grabby hands'?"

"I could tell Maisy was making you uncomfortable." My lips started to twitch and I tried to school them into a more stern expression. "I can't have her disrespecting you in Nordstrom, of all places."

His lips were twitching, too. "I do have a frequent shopper card."

I gaped at him. "C-card?"

He shrugged. "They have an excellent selection of black T-shirts."

"You're serious?"

He finally allowed the smile to overtake his face. "I'm *always* serious."

I lost our stand-off and laughed. He joined me with his own harsh burst of a chuckle. It was such an odd sound, but it gave me a frisson of pleasure, my heart doing that hoppy thing in my chest.

"Guys? Where'd the Evil Overlord and her minion slink off to?"

We turned to find Lucy emerging from the security office.

"We got them to leave," I said. "Is Aveda okay?"

"Yes," Lucy said. "But I need you to remember what you said earlier about getting her out of here without causing a scandal. Save the fire for later, okay?"

"What are you talking about?"

"Just . . . don't get mad at them right now."

"Wait a minute," I said. *"Them?"*

"What were you thinking?" I halted my furious pacing and glared at the two figures seated in front of me. "Scratch that—you obviously weren't."

"Any more faux-Mom clichés to bestow before we get out of here?"

"Beatrice Constance Tanaka," I spat out, well aware that this did nothing to diminish my Mom-like aura. "You do not get to talk right now."

I resumed my pacing. Pacing in the Nordstrom security office was frustrating business. There wasn't a lot of walk room in the small, gray cube. And I kept worrying about accidentally pacing into one of the giant TV screens or other pieces of complicated-looking equipment used to monitor the store. An hour ago one of these screens had captured Bea and Aveda trying to exit the mall with a pile of expensive scarves and cardigans they hadn't bothered to pay for.

"You told me to comfort her," Bea said accusingly. I could practically feel the teenage hate-rays coming off her, but I willed myself not to step back. "The bunny vids went only so far. She was sick of being cooped up, so I thought we could have some fun. Not that you'd know anything about that."

"And I assumed once the security guards learned my true identity, they'd simply let us go," Aveda interjected. "It was supposed to be a little adventure."

"An adventure in shoplifting?" I retorted.

Aveda crossed her arms over her chest. "I was tired of reading about Aveda 2.0 being so much better than the real thing," she said. "We were initially just going to go shopping, but when Beatrice suggested perhaps we should up the fun factor by doing something a bit naughty . . . well. I was just so *bored*—"

"I dared her," Bea interrupted. "I dared her to see if she could get away with it."

"And Aveda Jupiter does not back down from a dare," Aveda said.

"A *dare*?" I said, incredulous. Frustration and anger boiled inside of me, a potent stew threatening to rise up. Heat ghosted across my palm.

Not now, I thought at the fire. *This is not the time, okay?*

"I don't see what the big deal is," Bea said. "We dressed her up all incognito. So no one would recognize her."

Aveda was outfitted in a way I could only describe as bag lady meets teen runaway: crocheted hippie-dippy crop top, oversize jeans that concealed her cast, and a flashy sequined belt that had likely come directly from Bea's closet. The ensemble was topped off with a floppy-brimmed hat and a pair of sunglasses that took up a full third of her face. Her crutches were propped up against the wall next to her.

I tried another stern glare, as if the sheer power of my angry eyeballs would force them to apologize. Instead they just stared back, matching pouts in place.

My frustration flared again. My palm heated again.

Sooooo not the time, I reminded the fire.

"Fine," I said, curling and flexing my fingers. "Since nothing made it out of the store, they aren't pressing charges—as long as they can release you into the custody of a responsible adult." I pointed to myself. "Responsible adult, right here. Let's go."

I headed for exit, hoping they would follow me without protest.

As I pushed open the door, I was instantly aware of two things: Nate diving in front of me and a brilliant flash of light. I squinted, momentarily blinded. The brightly colored blurs surrounding me resolved themselves into people-like shapes. Including one particularly vibrant shape in a yellow dress.

"We spread the word about Aveda Jupiter doing a little shopping and whaddya know? The fans decided to congregate," Maisy said, shoving a mini digital video recorder in my face.

Shasta stood next to her, her red lipstick a smug slash across her face.

And around them a mob of people had closed in on

the otherwise benign Nordstrom shoe department. A buzz swept through the crowd. I tried to retreat, backing into the security office, but Bea was already pressed up behind me.

"What's going on?" she bleated.

Nate turned to Maisy. "I told you, Marley: Aveda was just leaving," he said. His hand found the small of my back.

"It's Maisy," Shasta corrected.

"No need to protect me, Nathaniel," a voice called out behind me. "I'm always happy to greet my glorious public."

And then Aveda Jupiter—the real one—was pushing her way out from behind me, half-walking, half-hobbling into the spotlight of Maisy's recorder. A delighted murmur rippled through the crowd and I was nearly blinded again by the flash of several dozen phone cameras.

"Fuck," I muttered.

I turned to Nate, hoping that some kind of resolution to this disaster in the making would be reflected in his dark eyes. But his gaze remained locked on Aveda. I scanned the crowd for Lucy and caught a glimpse of a lacy dress flitting through the far right corner of the crowd. Probably trying to find an alternate exit.

Silence had overtaken the crowd, all of whom seemed to be hypnotized by Aveda's charisma. They were waiting to see what she would do next. A sickly feeling settled in the pit of my stomach.

"Oh em gee," Bea murmured. "She is legit cray-cray."

I turned to respond and was instantly silenced by two things: the fact that Bea was now clutching Aveda's still-very-necessary crutches, and the look of flat-out admiration on her face. Apparently, "legit cray-cray" was my baby sister's ultimate role model.

"Aveda-girl!" squealed Maisy. "Give your pal Maisy a little ol' scoop! What are you doing at the Nordstrom security office? We heard you were shopping." She gave me a disdainful look. "But surely there's more to it than that."

"It's all very top secret," Aveda said. "Which is why I'm wearing this ridiculous disguise." She preened as more phone cameras went off.

"You look amazing," breathed Maisy. "But come now, give your fans a hint!"

Aveda took off her sunglasses and gave the crowd a dazzling smile.

"I'll just say one thing," she said.

The crowd seemed to lean in as one, hanging on her every word.

"Nordstrom may be home to a great many delicious clothes. But even the yummiest of sweater sets have their *demons*."

She punctuated that with a broad wink.

The crowd contemplated this for a few moments before letting loose with a titillated murmur.

"What does that even mean?" I sputtered. "I think Aveda's quip skills are out of practice."

"Forget that," hissed Nate. "We have to get her out of here. And keep her from hurting herself further in the process."

"All right, all right," I grumbled. "Let me handle this."

I took a deep breath, brushed my sickly feeling aside, and marched over to Aveda.

"This hat is remarkably useful for demon-hunting," Aveda was telling Maisy. "The wide brim forces you to focus."

I clamped a hand on Aveda's arm. She tried to jerk away, but I held on tight.

"No more questions for Miss Jupiter," I said. "She has to . . ."

BANG!

BANG BANG!

Before I could figure out what, exactly, Aveda had to do, that sound pierced the air, a harsh triple-knock that shocked everyone into silence. I whirled around, searching the crowd for the source.

BANG!

It appeared to be coming from . . . the piano? The usually benevolent Nordstrom piano perched by the escalator?

Seriously, what *now*?

The piano lid flung itself open and a blurry gray blob flew out and landed with a wet *splat* on the keyboard. It squashed against a few of the keys, producing a dissonant pseudo-chord.

"What is that?" someone shrieked. "Save us, Aveda!"

Keeping a firm grip on Aveda's arm, I moved closer to the piano, trying to get a better look, then instinctively looked up, searching for a portal. But there was nothing. Only this one gross thing, terrorizing the crowd and making a bad situation even worse.

"Demon?" Aveda murmured.

"It's . . . a hand," I said, scrutinizing the blob. "A really disgusting hand."

The thing was all pockmarked and desiccated-looking, its wrist a jagged stump ringed with dried blood. Each finger was topped by a yellowed claw.

Before anyone could congratulate me on my astounding powers of observation, the hand popped itself into the air and landed on its fingertips atop the keyboard. I noticed it had a strange mark on the index finger: a crude black line with four hash marks through it. A tattoo, maybe? Were tattoos big in the severed hand community?

A hush fell over the crowd as the hand thing stilled. Everyone was frozen in place, waiting to see what it would do next. Even Maisy was quiet.

The hand uncurled its index finger. The movement was rickety and labored, as if each joint needed a moment to adjust. As if it couldn't quite figure out what movement was.

My mouth went dry. It was that same type of movement I'd grown all too used to the past few days. Lurchy, zombie-like.

It was like the Aveda statues.

It was like Tommy.

It was . . . what was it?

The hand depressed one of the piano keys, producing a clear C note that rang out through the silence of the store. Then it started to play. Its movements were still lurchy, but it jerked itself over the full length of the keyboard, coaxing a lilting melody to life. There was something eerily familiar about the tune, but I couldn't quite place it.

It definitely wasn't "Eternal Flame."

"What the . . ." I muttered.

"Never fear, citizens! I'll take care of this!" Aveda bellowed, wrenching out of my grasp. She wobbled forward and I grabbed her arm again.

"Stop that," I hissed. "You can barely walk. Just let me—"

"Let you what?"

Before I could respond, the hand spun around and launched itself into the air, aiming directly for Aveda's neck.

I didn't think. I just leaped in front of her.

The hand landed against my neck with a *slap*, its fingers wrapping around my throat. It felt like Jell-O, cold and slick and gloppy, pressing into my windpipe with such force that white spots exploded around the edge of my vision. I was dimly aware of someone screaming, of someone yelling my name. I fell to my knees, my fingers clawing at the hand wrapped around my throat, trying to pry myself free from the Jell-O Fingers of Steel. I was dimly aware of Nate- and Lucy-shaped blobs moving toward me, but a shimmery film rose up in front of them, a thin wall of glassy material that looked like bubble solution. It wrapped itself around me, forming a dome that closed me off from everyone else. I gasped for breath, desperate for a little bit of oxygen. For air-like sustenance. For anything at all.

"Force field . . . like at the Yamato . . ."

"Can *see* this one . . . "

"No way in . . . we have to . . ."

"She's choking . . ."

I heard snippets from Nate and Lucy piercing their way through the bubble surrounding me.

"God . . . damn . . . it," I choked out, rage swelling inside of me.

Let it out, a little voice piped up in my head. *Remember how you suppressed it just now? With Bea and Aveda? Let. It. Out.*

My palm heated. I let the rage flood through me, drowning out everything else. I pressed my hand against the cold blob on my neck and felt its fingers loosen, a shocked response to that brush of warmth.

Okay, I thought at the fire, *you've got to come out slowly. So I don't incinerate my neck.*

I focused on my rage, focused on my palm, focused on channeling all my feelings in that one direction. The hand's fingers loosened further around my neck. I seized the opportunity and yanked hard, pulling it off me.

Now, I thought at the fire. *Now, now, now.*

I sent my fire blazing into the gloppy thing and flung it away from me just as it burst into flames. The bubble prison vanished.

I scrambled to my feet, gulping in mouthfuls of sweet, sweet oxygen. The hand of flames careened through the air with an ominous *whoosh*, flying dangerously close to Maisy, grabbing at her yellow skirt. She shrieked and batted at it. I made it over to her just as she managed to knock the hand to the floor. It disintegrated into a pile of smoking dust.

"Maisy!" I grabbed her hand. "Are you okay?" I gave her hand a quick once-over. There were no red marks, but a few bits of skin seemed to be flaking off, slightly discolored. Shit, had she been burned? Guilt stabbed at me. "Let me help you with—"

"I'm just fine, Rude Girl," she said, snatching her hand back. She held up her other hand. Which, of course, still contained that damn digital recorder. "Care to explain what you just did?"

"Yeah, care to explain?" echoed Shasta.

I swallowed hard. The reality I'd managed to block out the moment the hand wrapped itself around my neck came crashing back in and I realized the entire crowd was staring at me, goggle-eyed.

I'd just used "Aveda's" new power. No glamour, no disguises, no ridiculous boots. Just me. As myself. In public.

"Uh." I thought fast. "It's this . . . new facet of Aveda's power. Wherein she's able to temporarily transfer it to others. We just discovered it and I was trying it out. Temporarily."

"That's right," Aveda said, shuffling up next to me. A way-too-sweet smile was plastered across her face. "And I'd be delighted to share more about that right now—"

"Um, no," I said. Was she high? "We need to go."

"As you know, Evie, I have all the time in the world for my fans." Aveda said. She turned to Maisy. "Sorry, my assistant is so protective."

"Really, Aveda, we must leave." I placed a firm hand on her arm. "We have to get out of here, regroup, figure out what that thing was," I hissed in her ear. I cast a side-long glance at the pile of ashes on the floor. Maybe there was something in there we could dissect. "Not to mention the fact that you're putting your health—and your reputation—in danger."

"No need for histrionics," Aveda hissed back, attempting to pull out of my grasp. "I know you've gotten used to being in the spotlight, but you need to remember who the real Aveda Jupiter is."

"As if you'd ever let me forget."

"Ladies, can you speak up, please?" Maisy shoved the recorder under our noses, eager grin in place. But underneath it, I saw a flash of something else: raw hunger for a story. The sense that there was something bigger going on and she could be the one to let the world know about it. For all her faults, Maisy was really good at being nosy.

"I'm going to have to ask you to stop filming." I put a hand in front of her recorder. "Any interview time with Aveda needs to be scheduled through our press office."

"I'm okaying it," Aveda said. "It's fine."

"It is *not* fine," I insisted.

"Freedom of the blogs!" cried Shasta. "We will have our say!"

"Shush, Shast," Maisy said. "We don't need to take that tone with our good friend Aveda."

"She is not your good friend!" I said, exasperated.

"I'm everyone's friend!" protested Aveda, wrenching free from my grasp. "Friend to all fans: that's my new slogan. Make a note so we can get T-shirts made."

"You aren't even a friend to your *friends*!" I yelped, my frustration boiling over. "You blatantly ignore their advice, manipulate them into doing your bidding, then act like an idiot child when the half-baked plan you came up with actually starts to work."

Aveda's expression shifted, her eyes turning to pure ice. "You need to remember your place."

"Really?" I retorted. "Because it sure seems like I'm doing a damn good job taking yours."

"Aveda," Maisy said, her forehead crinkling, "what does that mean? And are you limping?"

"Evie." I heard Nate's warning voice behind me. But I just wanted Aveda to stop bulldozing and listen.

"You wouldn't have been able to take down that severed hand *thing*," I hissed under my breath. "Not the way I just did."

"How dare you—"

"Shut up!" I balled my fists at my sides. "Just shut up

and listen. And for once in your life, give me just a little bit of fucking credit for cleaning up your mess."

She hopped away from me and put her hands on her hips, arranging her features into their usual imperious configuration. But I noticed the spark of panic in her eyes.

"Really, Evie," she said. "I'll give you a raise if that's what you want. You don't need to throw a tantrum about it." She flashed me a big, fake smile. "You're a very competent assistant."

Molten rage coursed through me, pure and hot, and I was suddenly very aware of the fact that my palms were burning up. But I didn't care. I ceased to notice the crowd, their titillated murmuring fading to nothing more than an inconsequential burble. All I could see was Aveda in front of me. Trying to bully me into obedience. Trying to boss me around. Trying to put me in my place.

And after I'd jumped in front of her and saved her damn life.

Fuck her, I thought savagely.

"I'm more than that," I snarled.

I opened my hand and sent my fire blazing directly at Aveda's head.

I saw her eyes widen in fear, saw her stumble out of the way just in time, saw the burst of flame whiz over the crowd and incinerate a hideously expensive pair of boots.

Then I ran.

CHAPTER FOURTEEN

I FLEW OUT of Nordstrom, zipping down the escalator, darting between shoppers, pushing my way out to the bustle of the street. I didn't know where I was going. I didn't think about the fact that I usually hated exercise. All I knew was I had to keep moving.

It was the exact opposite of what had happened during that long-ago library disaster, even though my emotional response was basically the same: pure terror.

No, back then I'd been the last one standing, rooted to the spot as rubble and flame and crumbling pages swirled around me in a cruel parody of an apocalyptic blizzard. Were it not for the campus firefighter who finally hoisted my shell-shocked body over his shoulder and hauled me from the building, I might've ended up forever buried underneath the stately grounds of San Francisco College, a bitter ghost haunting thousands of undergrads.

I guess underneath the fear, I'd still prided myself on my ability to stick around during a time of crisis.

This time? There was none of that. I just ran.

When my pace finally slowed and I took in my surroundings, I realized I'd ended up back at HQ. I crawled up the stairs to my room, changed into a raggedy tank top and pajama pants, and lay down on top of the covers. I made my brain empty. Blank. I didn't want to think about what had just happened.

Ah, but that is like what happened after the library. You made yourself blank then, too. So blank you haven't really felt anything in years—

Nope. Not going to think about that, either. Not going to think about anything.

I shook my head at the bothersome little voice in the back of my mind, banished all feeling until I was completely numb.

Eventually I heard voices, rustling around, the opening and shutting of doors. I kept myself still and quiet. I didn't want to see anyone. I doubted anyone wanted to see me either. I stared out my bedroom window, studying every shade of the changing sky as San Francisco turned dusky and gray. I concentrated on counting the stars as they winked into existence, filled my mind with that task so I wouldn't have to think about anything else. I was so immersed, I barely heard the knock at my door. I held my breath, hoping whoever was on the other side would go away. Instead the door creaked open and Nate appeared.

I sat up and stared at him. Maybe if I didn't say anything, he'd leave.

"I have . . . I brought you . . ." He shook his head, as if trying to get the words straight. "Your neck."

"You brought me my neck?"

"No." He stepped into the room and held up a jar of something. "I thought you might have some bruising from that thing trying to strangle you. So I mixed up this salve."

"Oh. Okay." I couldn't think of anything better to say. Words beyond that would require me to break out of my state of numbness, and I couldn't let that happen. He crossed the room, settled in behind me, and gently moved my tangled snarl of hair to the side. Cold air hit the back of my neck and I shivered. He hesitated.

"Is it okay if I . . . I mean, you can apply this yourself, but there might be some places you can't reach—"

"You can do it." My voice was flat, monotone. Nothing to see here. Just keep numb.

Then he'll go away and you can go back to counting the stars.

His hands brushed against my neck, massaging an oily solution into my skin.

"There's a bruise right here." He touched a spot on my neck. "And this looks like a minor burn."

"That hand thing must've singed me a little before I got it off," I said.

"I thought you'd like to know that we managed to collect a sample from the dust it left behind," he said, his tone turning businesslike and clinical. "Just the tip of a thumb, but it may give us something. I've prepared it for dissection tomorrow."

His fingertips pressed against the top of my spine and I felt tension I didn't know I'd been holding evaporate. "Perhaps it can finally give us some answers about the oddities we've been seeing the past few days," he continued. "Because once again: there was no portal. And as with Tommy, no swarm of demons, just this one specimen. I suppose the hand could have imprinted on a mannequin hand or something similar, but that still doesn't answer the question of—"

"It moved like the other ones," I mumbled.

"What?" His hands brushed another bruise on my neck and I winced. Feeling, both physical and emotional, started to leak back in. My shoulders slumped.

"It moved like the other oddities—Tommy and the Aveda statues. That weird, zombie-like lurching."

"So perhaps the dissection will tell us more—"

"Nate." I couldn't bear it anymore. The gentle warmth of his hands moving against my skin made my bruises come to life, brought every single one of my repressed emotions to the surface. I couldn't shut them out, couldn't remain numb any longer. "What else happened? After I . . ."

"It was fine," he said a little too quickly. "Lucy found a fire extinguisher, Aveda made up a story about how the two of you staged the incident for the crowd as a further demonstration of her power-sharing abilities, I gathered the sample, and we managed to leave the scene without additional drama." He pressed the salve into a spot near my collarbone and I winced again. Definitely a bruise there. He massaged it a little, his hands continuing to ease my tension. "Everyone decided it would be best to retire for the night and regroup tomorrow."

His hands slid to my shoulders. Still warm, still gentle. Still there.

"Evie," he said softly. "You're shaking."

I looked down at my hands. I was.

"I used it." The words slipped out, unbidden. Like they'd been waiting until I was weak enough for them to escape my throat. "It wasn't like usual, like I was just letting it happen. And it wasn't like I was defending myself or trying to save a bunch of people from an evil demon thing. I used it on purpose. I used it *for* a terrible purpose. I didn't care that it was wrong. I didn't think about the fact that other people were there. I just knew I *could* and that was all that mattered. I was so fucking angry and I was going to show her she couldn't dismiss me, she couldn't . . ." I closed my eyes. "I used it."

"You didn't hurt anyone," he said.

"No, but . . ."

But I wanted to.

In that moment the power had coursed through my veins like wildfire, demanding to be released. Demanding that Aveda feel pain.

I'd wanted to hurt her. I'd aimed for her head.

"Bea was there," I said. Now my voice was shaking, too. "What if I get mad at her? I mean, I already do. All the time. But what if I get mad at her like I got mad at the mall? If something happened to her, I couldn't live with myself. But if something happened to her and it was my fault, I . . . I'm supposed to be taking care of her. After Mom died and Dad took off, I promised I'd be there for her. Always. I'd be there for her like our parents couldn't be. But what if me being near her is the thing that destroys her?"

I was babbling, the words pouring out of me like over-cooked hangover spew. He said nothing, just kept his hands on my shoulders.

I turned around to face him.

"This is what I've always been afraid of. That I would get angry over something petty and selfish and I would fucking use it and I would incinerate everything and people would *die*—"

That last word clogged my throat, choking me, and then I was crying, tears pouring down my face in messy, unstoppable rivulets. Goddammit.

Nate's hands—those big, gentle hands that had warmed my skin while I babbled—cupped my face, his thumbs brushing away the tears that wouldn't stop coming.

The warmth of his touch soothed me, but the tears still wouldn't stop and I cried silently, helplessly, unable to do anything else. His thumbs kept brushing the tears away: a rhythmic stroke against my flushed cheek.

"No one died," he said. "And I don't think you're petty. Or selfish."

He brushed another tear away.

"I think you're brave."

I hiccupped and the tears picked up speed, spilling and spilling and spilling.

"I think," he said, "you want to protect the people you love and you don't always know how. I think you're smart and resourceful enough to figure out how to take down a bizarre hand creature we've never seen the likes of before. I think that right before you lost your temper with Aveda, you saved people from very real danger." A ghost of a smile touched his lips. "I think you make the occasional mistake. Just like everyone."

He leaned closer, his hands still cupping my face.

"And I think," he said, his breath warm against my cheek, "that I would give anything to take away your pain right now."

I hiccupped again. "Even," I squeaked out, "your Nordstrom frequent shopper's card?"

A smile broke out over his face, slow and surprised. He touched his forehead to mine.

"Even that."

I looked up at him through wet lashes. It seemed like the most natural thing in the world for my hands to plant against his chest, to feel his heartbeat through the soft cotton of that ever-present black T-shirt. To feel it speed up at my touch.

I wasn't sure who closed the remaining sliver of space between us this time, but somehow my lips found his, somehow I was drinking him in again, the strong, clean scent of him all around me.

Our first kiss was wild, desperate: insatiable hunger expressed through lips and tongues. This one was softer, more tentative. Exploratory.

He nibbled at my upper lip, his hands sliding into my hair, pulling me closer. His mouth opened fully under mine, and I tasted the salt of my messy tears. My arms wound around his neck and my chest pressed against his, our heartbeats growing faster and more erratic in unison. Heat bloomed low in my belly and a moan escaped my throat. I repositioned myself, straddling him, wanting to feel every inch of him against me, wanting and wanting and *wanting*—

No.

I broke our kiss abruptly. "We can't," I said, my words landing in a staccato rhythm between shaky breaths.

His right hand dropped from my hair and splayed across the small of my back. I felt his fingers flex, relax, flex again. Like his hand couldn't decide what it wanted to do. He was breathing hard, his eyes dazed. There was

something irresistible about seeing him so unguarded—on the verge of losing every bit of his gruff veneer,
of going over the edge.

"It doesn't feel right?" he said. "Because you are currently experiencing a disproportionate amount of emotions and you might regret—"

"What? No!" I took a deep inhale, trying to even out
my breathing. "I don't mean, 'We can't because I'm
afraid you'll crush my delicate girl-soul—'"

"I don't think you have anything resembling a delicate—"

"I mean, we can't because I will burn you to death."

His fingers flexed against my back again and I felt another stab of *wanting,* so fierce I gasped out loud.

"Remember the closet," I managed to get out.

We just stared at each other for a moment, our breathing still jagged. Even though I knew it was a bad idea to
stay all tangled up in him, I couldn't quite bring myself
to get out of his lap.

"Evie," he finally said. "At the mall, you directed the
fire at Aveda. You controlled it."

"No need to rub it in," I muttered.

He gave me a half-smile. "On the contrary; I thought it
was impressive." He took one of my hands in his and
brushed his thumb over my palm. "Your hand isn't even
hot," he said. "Despite what just . . . happened. Between
us." Color rose in his cheeks. "Consider the changes
your power appears to have gone through the past few
days. It seems to be gaining more nuance."

I opened my mouth to protest.

But then I did consider it. Not only had I taken out
Tommy and the hand, I'd also managed to keep the fire
inside during moments of extreme stress. Like when I'd
had to deal with Maisy and Shasta outside the Nordstrom security office. Or when Nate had infuriated me
so much, I'd stalked off in a huff. Or when I'd found myself getting more and more enraged with Bea and Aveda
before the hand had attacked us . . .

Wait a minute.

In that case I'd *told* the fire to stay put.

I'd given my power an order, and it had obeyed.

And, hell, hadn't I also kind of given it an order when I'd gotten the disembodied hand off me? Telling it to come out gradually, so I wouldn't burn myself up? If anything, the moment in The Gutter closet was an anomaly.

I wiggled my fingers experimentally. My palms were still cool. Okay, so maybe my temper could use some work, but when it came to the fire power itself, was I actually gaining control?

"I'm sorry," Nate's voice broke into my thoughts. "I didn't mean to push. I'm not trying to . . . to . . ."

"To get it on with me, thereby fulfilling your weird fetish that involves burning down entire buildings and getting yourself incinerated?" I cocked an eyebrow.

"No!" He looked horrified. "I'm sorry. I'll leave. I—"

"No—don't. *I'm* sorry. I was kidding. Badly." I brought my hands to either side of his face, studying his features. Usually so harsh, they were rendered softer and less distinct by the darkness of the room. "I think you're right. My control is getting better. Much better."

His hands tightened around my hips and desire flooded my senses again, overwhelming everything.

"And I think . . . I would like to have sex right now. With you," I clarified. My breathing had gotten all shaky again.

"There's still the question of regret," he said. "You have a lot happening at the moment, a lot of conflicting emotional states, and tomorrow I don't want you to feel like—"

"Stop." I met his eyes. "I may not know much right now, but I know I want this. And I don't want to think about what it means. I want to exist in this moment and I want . . ." The full weight of everything that had happened that day washed over me. My voice broke and I swallowed. No more crying. "I want the rest of the world to disappear for a little while. Okay?"

He stared back at me and I thought he was going to move me to the side, to leave, to let my delicate girl-soul down easy. Instead, one side of his mouth tipped up and his eyes lit with tenderness, softening his face even further. He covered one of my hands with his.

"Okay."

We took a few precautions. We agreed to go slow. And at my request Nate found the fire extinguisher we kept downstairs and put it next to the bed.

And then we were back to me straddling him. We stared at each other, unsure of what to do now that we'd taken a little break from the heat of passion. I shifted uncomfortably as the silence stretched on too long.

Finally I said, "Maybe you should kiss me."

He rested his hands on my waist.

"You're the one who made the, er, final decision. That we should do this. I think *you* should kiss *me*."

"Yeah, pretty sure we're both really into my decision. I'd say there's some very convincing proof . . ." My eyes drifted downward, right below his waistband. " . . . that you're equally—"

His mouth was on mine before I could complete that thought, his hands taking charge and pulling me flush against him. The aforementioned proof pressed against the critical juncture between my legs, but before I could so much as moan, he rolled me onto my back, his hands sliding underneath my tank top, the electric brush of his fingertips raising goose bumps on the most sensitive parts of my skin.

"Are we really fighting," he said between kisses, "about *how* we're going to have sex?"

"You started it," I murmured, biting his lower lip.

"I don't think so. But I'm not going to argue with you."

He pulled back and gave me a wicked smile. "There are much better things I could be doing with my mouth right now."

Before I could fully process the fact that 1) Nate made a joke and 2) Nate made a *dirty* joke, he was making good on that promise, trailing kisses down my neck and between my breasts. Every brush of his lips was an incendiary mark, a touch that sent shockwaves coursing through me. His hands skimmed my torso, playing with the ragged hem of my old tank top, then yanking hard, instantly transforming my shirt into shreds.

"Hey." My hand jutted out, landing on his chest. "Do you really have to ruin all my shirts like that?"

He smiled at me, twisting a particularly sproingy lock of my hair around his finger and giving it a little tug. "The one I just . . . removed was almost destroyed anyway."

I bit my lip to keep my traitorous mouth from smiling back. "Take yours off, too."

His grin widened and he obliged, slipping his black cotton number over his head and revealing . . . *wow*. I knew he was fit. But even my most vivid imaginings couldn't have conjured the beautiful muscles of his chest, the way they flowed into impossibly broad shoulders. My greedy fingertips skimmed over the terrain of his bare skin. I wanted to touch it all.

We made a wordless agreement to do away with the rest of our clothes. And then he knelt between my thighs, nothing left between us but the thin cotton of his boxers and the lace of my panties. I allowed my eyes to flutter closed, wondering what was next. He was so *big*. Those broad shoulders. That gorgeous chest. I couldn't help but wonder if he was, you know . . . proportional.

I mean, he'd certainly *felt* impressive when we were pressed up against each other the night before, but I hadn't been able to really get the full picture—

"Oh." His voice broke into my porny thoughts. "Wow."

I remembered then that I was wearing neon yellow underwear. My eyes flew open.

"You trying to blind me?" His voice was laced with amusement.

I propped myself up on my elbows, getting my best glare on. "I didn't exactly expect that we would be—*oh.*"

Suddenly his tongue was stroking me through neon lace, hitting the exact right spot to send spikes of pleasure rocketing through me. I gasped hard, *want* giving way to *need.*

He lifted his head. No wicked grin this time—just pure intensity. He touched my hand. Which was still perfectly cool, no sign of fire at all.

"Are you okay?" he asked.

"Yes," I managed to squeak out.

He hooked his thumbs under the waistband of my panties and slowly dragged them off, his eyes never leaving mine.

And then I was naked in front of him.

He hesitated, his eyes roaming my body, and I felt self-conscious. I hadn't been naked in front of someone in a very long time. Not since Richard.

"Wh-what?" I stuttered. My arms crossed over my chest, trying to cover some of my bared skin. "Is something wrong?"

Maybe my breasts were lopsided. Maybe that random smattering of freckles on my left hip was off-putting. Maybe I looked weird naked.

He gently pried my crossed arms away from my body, interlacing his fingers with mine and pinning my hands on either side of my head. "No," he said softly. He leaned in, his lips brushing my ear. "I just like looking at you."

I flushed all over.

He squeezed my hands. "Still okay?" he whispered.

I took inventory. My hands remained nice and cool. The fire was staying put.

"Definitely okay," I whispered back.

He released my hands and pulled back to study me again, and now I could see the raw desire in his gaze. He slipped off his glasses and set them on the nightstand — an endearingly tidy gesture — then lowered himself along my body. He framed my hips with his hands and found me again with his tongue, marking my most intimate spot with his mouth. The pleasure had been intense even with the barrier of my panties. Now it was almost unbearable, nearly sending me over the edge. My fingernails dug into his shoulders.

I was practically panting with need as he worked his way up, planting lingering, open-mouthed kisses on my hipbone, my navel, the delicate underside of my right breast. When he finally slipped my nipple between his teeth, I almost combusted, white light exploding behind my eyes as my lashes fluttered shut, my fingers thrusting into his hair to pull him closer, my back arching so far off the bed, I felt like I might break in half.

A sharp cry of protest escaped me as he pulled away from my breast, but he stopped it with a kiss, his wall of a chest pressing against me, both of us slick with sweat, our heartbeats united again.

He pulled back and brought a hand to my face, brushing my hair out of my eyes. Gentle, even in the midst of our moment of complete inhibition-shedding.

He took my hands again, brushing his thumbs over my palms.

My palms were good to go.

All of me was good to go.

Stay put, I thought at the fire. *For the love of God: please stay fucking put.*

"Yes?" he whispered.

I wrapped my arms around his neck, bringing my lips to his ear.

"Yes."

He rolled away from me and yanked open the nightstand drawer, scrabbling around for a condom and nearly falling off the edge of the bed in the process. If I hadn't been so focused on the very serious business of having sex with him, I might have giggled.

He finally found what he was looking for and slipped off his boxers and . . .

Oh. Oh, God.

So, yes—he was *definitely* proportional.

He put the condom on and then he was back to me, his big hands lifting my hips. He slid inside of me in one long thrust and I groaned low in my throat. He felt good. So goddamn good, I could barely stand it.

He gasped my name in that hoarse, husky way that undid me completely.

And we went over the edge together.

CHAPTER FIFTEEN

THE DISEMBODIED HAND reached for my neck again.

I scuttled backward and it swiped at me, claws extended, as if it could already feel my neck in its slimy grasp. The crude tattoo on its index finger mocked me, a mysterious rune I couldn't decipher. I tried to scoot backward again, tried to get the fuck out of the way, but I couldn't gain traction. One of the claws made contact, cutting a deep groove into my wrist.

I stared at the cut. It didn't hurt. In fact, my entire arm was numb. Blood started to drip from the wound, slowly at first. Then it picked up speed: gushing, flowing. I pressed my hand over the cut, but blood poured through my fingers. And then it was everywhere, coating my entire body, a red haze obstructing my vision. I opened my mouth to scream and was choked by an onslaught of blood pouring into my mouth.

I couldn't call for help. I was drowning. I was dead. I was overtaken by the roaring in my ears, a deep growl that started low and crescendoed into a wall of sound. And then I was slipping away . . .

My eyes snapped open. I jerked my wrist up to my face. It was unblemished, unbloodied. I wasn't dead. I was in my bed, safe.

And yet the roaring in my ears was still disturbingly present. I rolled onto my side and was greeted by a wall of muscular man-flesh. A wall of muscular man-flesh emitting a snore so powerful, I could practically feel the bed frame shake.

Oh. Right.

I eased myself into a sitting position, doing my best not to wake Nate. My fuzzy comforter had twisted itself around his giant frame, a comical imitation of a too-small toga. There were things about his body I hadn't noticed in the dark of night: the muscular curve of his back, the surprising grace housed in those thick limbs, the pale latticework of scars crisscrossing over his left shoulder. I brushed a fingertip over the scars, wondering where they had come from.

He was, I thought, kind of heartbreakingly beautiful.

My fluttery thought was cut short when he let loose with another snore.

I bit my lip to keep from giggling. I was thankful to that snore for snapping me out of my nightmare. I rolled onto my back, shuddering at the memory of the hand reaching for my neck.

Three makes a trend. The phrase popped into my head out of nowhere. It had been a standby during my stint in academia, a thing professors liked to spit out to get you to better prove whatever thesis you'd been struggling to justify. And while I'd definitely struggled with it at the time, the rule was pretty sound and eventually led me to some of my best paper topics.

The Aveda statues. The Tommy demon. The hand.

All three of these things moved in similar lurching fashion. And . . . hmm. Come to think of it, the hand followed the pattern of imprinting on something very human-like. Did that mean something? What was the trend? Besides the fact that they were different from the demons we'd dealt with before?

What were they after?

Suddenly it hit me.

That's it, I thought. *Or at least . . . that's something.*

I sat up and punched Nate in the arm.

"Nate," I yelped. "Wake up." He grunted and pulled a pillow over his head.

I clambered on top of him, straddling him at the waist. "Nate."

"Mrph?"

I yanked his pillow shield away and tossed it to the side. He threw an arm over his eyes. I jounced around, batting at his chest.

"Naaaaaaate!"

He lowered his arm, eyes blinking as they adjusted to the light and took me in. I was wearing his shirt and nothing else. He'd argued that I should put it on before going to sleep so I didn't "catch cold from the freezing air seeping in through that window you insist on leaving open." I'd just wanted to pass out after the mind-blowing series of orgasms he'd given me. We'd bickered about it, but I'd ultimately given in—the shirt was soft and smelled like him.

It hit me that we were both half-naked and in the potentially awkward throes of the morning after. I decided to just motor through the theory I wanted to share without acknowledging that.

"This possible new breed of demons," I said. "I think they're stalking Aveda."

I paused to make sure he was fully awake and listening to me. He appeared to be. He was also resting his hands on my hips. Which was kind of nice. I forced myself to focus.

"In the places where we've seen these out of the ordinary demon things—Whistles, the Yamato, and the mall—Aveda was there right before the attack happened. She had to go down to Whistles the day before the party to scope out the atmosphere. She was skulking around the Nordstrom shoe department, shoplifting with Bea, right before the hand appeared."

"And what about the Yamato?" he asked. "Since when has Aveda Jupiter deigned to go to something as pedestrian as a movie?"

I poked his chest. "Every Friday, eleven a.m. matinee. She's there, usually wearing some terrible disguise. Always hoping someone will recognize her and tweet about how down-to-earth Aveda Jupiter is, going to bargain matinees and all. And how fantastic she looks in her disguise, of course." His eyes widened in surprise. "I guess that was our secret."

"What about the League benefit?" he said. He looked at me thoughtfully, his words free of their usual know-it-all air.

"What about it?"

"Didn't you see a demon on your way to the bathroom? While you were glamoured as Aveda? One of the statue demons?"

"I thought I imagined it, but . . ." I called up the image in my head and forced my brain to accept what my gut already knew was true. "It was there," I said. "I think it must've ducked out that alternate bathroom exit you and I used to leave. And . . ." A chill ran up my spine as I replayed the scene from yesterday. "And the hand at the mall: it threw itself at her. It was trying to strangle her before I stepped in the way."

He nodded slowly. "So if they are stalking Aveda . . . why? What's their goal?"

I thought about it. I'd been giddy about my possible revelation, but as I contemplated it further, dread built in my chest. "Let's think about the theory that this new evolution of demons is smarter. I mean, the hand didn't interact with us like Tommy, but it played piano, which indicates some level of intelligence beyond the usual 'I want to eat everything in sight' credo."

I looked at him to see if he was following me. He nodded.

"So if they *are* smarter, maybe they've keyed into the fact that Aveda Jupiter always takes them down," I said. "Maybe they think if they defeat her, they can take over the world. Or at least the city."

"Do you think that directive-issuing stone from Cake My Day—'You need three'—is connected?"

"Three . . ." I trailed off, a shiver running up my spine. *Three makes a trend.*

"Maybe whoever's in charge, whoever the directive was issued to, has the three they need?" I said. "The statues, the hand, and Tommy? But if so, what happens next? Does that mean they're all set to take Aveda out?"

"If that were the case, I can't help but feel they would have mounted a more ambitious initiative than sending a single demon hand to strangle her," Nate said. "And since you defeated Tommy and the hand, it's unclear what these demons actually have in their arsenal right now."

"The statue demons came back, though," I said. I gnawed my lower lip. "I swear I destroyed them all, and then one of them just showed up at the benefit. Like it resurrected itself or something. What if Tommy and the hand can do that?"

Nate nodded, thinking. "Let's see if we can make some of these connections more solid. I need to dissect the specimen from yesterday—the tip of the thumb."

"And we should bring everyone up to speed." I attempted to shove my burgeoning dread to the side. No sense in getting all freaked out until we knew more. I started to hoist myself off Nate. "Time to rally the troops. Or at least figure out if the rest of the troops are awake."

"Wait." His hands tightened around my hips. "Before you go rally, I . . ."

"What? You want your shirt back?"

"No." He gave me a slight smile, then eased himself into a sitting position. We were face to face: me still straddling him, his hands moving to my lower back. He hesitated, something unsure flitting through his eyes.

"We should have sex again," he said.

"Like . . . now?"

"No. I mean, I am not opposed to that and if you had

woken me up for sex rather than demon theory discussion, I would have been very open to it, but that's not what I . . ." He shook his head, frustrated. "I can never seem to say things right."

I thought about his gentle words to me when I couldn't stop crying the night before. His insistence that I was brave when I felt anything but. "You do okay sometimes."

He took a deep breath and let his thoughts pour out in a rush. "I think we should have sex again sometime in the near future. Possibly several times in the near future. If you want."

"Are you interested in testing my control further?" I teased. "See what does and does not provoke my flame-y reaction? Like a sexperiment?"

"No, that's not it." He didn't laugh, just regarded me steadily, his serious expression contrasting in bizarre yet appealing fashion with his sleep-tousled hair. "I am not someone who has fun very often. But I had fun last night. And I'd like to have fun with you again."

I couldn't help but smile. I hadn't had time to consider our sex status post-last night, but now that he mentioned it . . .

I'd also had fun. I totally wanted more multiple orgasms. And if our theory about this new breed of demons targeting Aveda was in any way correct, I was going to need major stress relief.

God, was I really trying to come up with a list of reasons to have *incredibly hot sex*? Which, by the way, hadn't resulted in anyone being burned to death?

"Okay," I said.

"Okay?"

"Yes. But we need a couple of ground rules."

"Such as?"

"It can't mean anything beyond the sex. I don't have the emotional bandwidth for that right now. Fun and orgasms: those are our only objectives. And no telling anyone. I'd rather not explain this, uh, arrangement to Aveda or Bea. Or even Lucy. Oh, and I still get to call it a 'sexperiment.'"

He gave me a solemn nod. "I accept your terms." He pulled me closer. "And as far as sexperimental aspects to explore . . ."

"I'm listening."

He smiled. This whole tousled, naked, "I just woke up and successfully proposed a possibly disastrous sex plan to the girl in my lap" thing he had going on was really working for me. I suppressed the big, dopey grin that was threatening to spread over my face.

"We can try different locations. Perhaps places containing elements that counteract fire, just in case."

"Like . . . what, a rainstorm?"

In one fluid motion, he slid off the bed and stood, taking me with him. "Like the shower."

This time, I didn't suppress my big, dopey grin. I didn't even try.

After my sexperimental shower, I bolted downstairs, all ready to make with the troop rallying.

Instead I stumbled into an intervention.

Lucy and Bea were clustered around the kitchen table and Scott was standing off to the side, his usual easy posture disrupted by the steady drum of his fingertips against the kitchen countertop. They were all frowning at Aveda, who was sitting in a chair across from them. Her arms were crossed over her chest and her face was screwed into an "are you kidding me?" version of her usual imperious look. There was a single empty chair positioned next to her.

I didn't have to ask who it was for.

I sat down and resisted the urge to fidget or play with my hair, which was matted against my head in an awkward half-wet, half-dry formation. Silence blanketed the air.

"Maybe you should go first, Bea," Lucy said.

"Me?" Bea frowned, swirling Froot Loops around in an overflowing bowl of milk. I was firmly anti-milk, but Bea liked to drown her cereal in the stuff. Even as a toddler, she was obstinate about this, furiously banging her spoon against her high chair to demand more. "But you're, like, the most senior person, Lucy. You should go first."

"Well, I don't know about that. Scott, you've been friends with both of them since junior high. Maybe you'd like to—"

"Technically, Bug's known them the longest, though," Scott protested, gesturing to Bea. "You know, since birth. And I heard about everything that happened yesterday secondhand—"

"Exactly," said Bea. "So you're the best person to speak to—"

"That doesn't make any sense—"

"Actually, it kind of does if you really think about it," Lucy said.

"Oh my God," I blurted out. "You guys are the absolute worst at putting on an intervention."

"Thank you," Aveda muttered under her breath. We exchanged a surprised look of solidarity.

"Okay," I said. "Let's just do this, shall we? I lost my temper yesterday, endangered people, and almost set Aveda on fire. It was a moment of extreme irrationality and it won't happen again." I turned to face Aveda. "I'm sorry. This whole being you deal is even crazier than I thought it would be. After suppressing all my emotions for so long, they're heightened, magnified, and basically all over the place. I haven't felt that much rage in forever and it just . . . came out. Right next to your head."

Surprise crossed her face, and I saw a flicker of that

piece of her that always took me back to kindergarten: that little girl barfing up thirty spam musubi while I rubbed her back. That soft underbelly that was capable of being hurt if she exposed it too much. I reached over and took her hand.

"I'm sorry," I repeated. "You know I've always been scared of hurting someone with the fire. I'm horrified that I almost did. And I'm especially horrified that it was you."

Aveda studied me for a long moment, her expression shifting between confusion and anger and vulnerability. "Thank you," she finally said. She hesitated and it seemed like she might be about to let that vulnerability take over. Instead, her shields snapped up, her eyes becoming veiled and haughty again. "I'm glad you're owning up to your mistakes, Evie," she said, dropping my hand and drawing herself up tall in her chair.

I rolled my eyes and faced Lucy, Bea, and Scott again. "I am indeed," I said. "But let's not forget who the other half of this intervention is for: you."

Aveda blinked at me. The haughtiness in her eyes was washed away by shock. Nate chose that moment to join us, his hair slick from our shower. My cheeks warmed. I'd suggested we enter the room at different times so as not to give away the fact that we'd just spent the night (and morning) together. Now it seemed like the most obvious move possible. Like I should just add "Hey, everybody, *we had sex*" to my speechifying and get it over with.

"I'm taking responsibility for losing my temper," I continued. "I am not taking responsibility for you acting like a crazy person, going on some weird shoplifting adventure . . ." I gave Bea a look. She trained her eyes on her Froot Loops. " . . . and then causing a scene and putting people in danger because you couldn't stand being out of the spotlight for even one second. I'm also not taking responsibility for you bullying me, bitching at me, and telling me to remember my *place*."

Aveda opened her mouth to protest, but I held up a silencing hand and straightened my spine, trying to project Michelle Yeoh/Invisible Girl-esque strength.

"That's shitty, Aveda," I continued. "That's a really fucking shitty thing to say to someone. And this someone . . ." I pointed to myself. " . . . is sick of you saying shitty things to her in general. This someone is supposed to be your *friend*."

Aveda's mouth opened and closed, giving her the appearance of a confused fish.

I turned to everyone.

"Did I miss anything?" I asked.

"You pretty much covered it, darling," Lucy said. "We wanted to speak to both of you about your erratic behavior yesterday and how—"

"How your personal conflicts are a hazard to the functionality of this entire operation," Bea said, as if suddenly remembering the intervention statement she'd prepared.

We all looked at her.

"What? I googled some HR worksheets," she said. "Someone has to keep things running semi-smoothly around here."

"You're right," I said, meeting Bea's gaze and mirroring her serious tone. "Our personal conflicts were a hazard. But I want to assure all of you that I've got things under control now. I'm learning how to have feelings in a far less . . . dangerous way. I regret what happened, but I'm ready to move on and I appreciate you guys supporting me in that."

"Goodness," Lucy said, grinning at me. "You really are quite talented at this intervention thing."

I couldn't help but grin back. "Thanks. It's my first."

I looked around the room, gauging everyone else's

expressions. Bea had stopped swirling her cereal around and looked like she was trying to remember more official-sounding HR speak. Scott was regarding me with respect. And Nate was unreadable.

"All right," I said briskly. "Now that we've addressed the issue of my and Aveda's mutual meltdown, there's something important I need to discuss with all of you."

I briefly explained what Nate and I had talked about: demons appearing as human-like things. Demons displaying higher than usual intelligence. Demons targeting Aveda.

"I know some of you think I've been imagining things these past few days," I said, even though "some of you" basically meant "Aveda." "Frankly, I thought I was imagining things, too. But given all that's happened, I don't think we can deny that something bizarre is going on and it's best if we figure it out and nip it in the demon-y bud. Nate's dissection of the specimen he collected yesterday will hopefully give us more information. And . . ." I took a deep breath, a vague idea of a plan taking shape in my head. "We have to draw out whatever this new force is." I turned to Bea. "What's a cool upcoming event?"

"Um, what?" Her head snapped up and she dropped her spoon in the bowl, sending milk sloshing onto the table.

"Something that everyone who's anyone in San Francisco will turn up for? Something with, like . . ." I made air quotes with my fingers, feeling supremely dorky. ". . . a 'cool factor'?"

She tapped her cereal spoon against her bowl, thinking it over. "There's that karaoke competition? The one down at The Gutter? It's gonna be *the* event of the month for the Bay Area's hippest hipsters."

"Okay." I nodded at her, remembering the Best of The Gutter flyer Lucy had pointed out a couple nights ago. "Good."

I turned to Lucy. "You're the Gutter-slash-karaoke expert around here. Can we get Aveda entered into that, do you think?"

"Kevin is a snob when it comes to karaoke," Lucy said, mulling it over. "And he's a bit thrown off because Stu didn't show up for work yesterday."

"Oh, no," I said, thinking of Stu's advanced age. "Has anyone checked on him?"

"They're trying," Lucy said. "No word yet. But in any case, as one of Kevin's best customers: yes, I think I can talk him into it. I'll be sure to note that having someone as famous as Aveda in the competition will give it even more cachet than usual."

"That's exactly what I'm hoping." I turned back to Bea. "Your prowess as Social Media Guru is going to be key over the next few days. We need to create buzz around this karaoke competition thing. Entice anyone and everyone—even the non-hipsters—to come out and cheer Aveda on. Like I said, we have to draw this new demon force out. Give it the biggest, most tempting Aveda-shaped target possible. And that target has to be me."

"What?" Aveda squawked. Still in shock from me interventioning her ass, she'd been uncharacteristically silent as we pieced together a plan. "Why?"

I met her eyes without flinching. "Because I can nuke the shit out of it."

Out of the corner of my eye, I saw Nate smile. And then there was silence. No one could disagree with that.

Well, almost no one.

"You really think you should continue posing as me after yesterday's outburst?" Aveda said. She looked around the room, challenging. "Does anyone think that?"

"It was a mutual outburst," I reminded her. "We both fucked up. And like I said: I'm sorry, I'm processing, and I'm moving on."

"We can't put you out as bait for this possible new brand of demons while you're still injured, Aveda," Lucy said.

"And it does seem like we should take care of this new breed of demons as soon as possible," Scott added, frowning at Aveda.

"Since when are you so keen to be part of the 'we' around here?" she snitted at him.

"Since I agreed to help Evie," he shot back. "But really, this seems bigger than all of us."

"It is," I said, interrupting them before they could really get into it. "And honestly, all the power usage I've been doing over the past few days feels like it's giving me control. Or at least something resembling control." I briefly recapped what Nate and I had discussed the night before, detailing the few incidents that seemed to indicate my growing control. Naturally I edited out what we'd done afterward. "In short," I concluded, "I can do this. And Scott's right: I need to do this as soon as possible. If this new force sticks around and keeps targeting you, Aveda, how long until they actually succeed in taking you out? How long until San Francisco's really and truly fucked?"

Aveda crossed her arms. I could tell she was furious, but suppressing it with all her might. "Fine," she said. "It seems I'm outvoted." She pushed herself out of her chair. "Why don't you all wake me when you actually need me again." She aimed her hand at her crutches, glaring at them, trying to use her weak telekinesis. They wouldn't budge. She let out a strangled cry of frustration, then reached over and grabbed them and clomped out of the room with as much dignity as she could muster.

Nate turned to Bea, who was playing with remnants of her cereal. "Beatrice?" he said. "Would you like to help me dissect the thumb?"

"Holy frakballs! I mean . . . yes. I am more than happy

to assist you." Bea modulated her voice to professional tones.

Nate smiled at her. "Let's go, then."

"Do I get a lab coat?" Bea asked. "And can I personalize it? I mean, nothing too flashy, but I have some sequins left over from when I bedazzled my phone. Hey, maybe I could fix up your lab coat, too? You'd be surprised how much easier it is to be productive when you look your best." She followed him out of the kitchen, chattering all the way.

I let out a long breath, crossed the room, and sat down next to Lucy. I pulled Bea's cereal bowl over and picked through the mushy milk, trying to find an intact Froot Loop. Now that I wasn't interventioning, speechifying, or otherwise putting on a tough face, I felt like a balloon with a hole poked in it, all the bravado leaking out of me like helium.

"So that's one big plan all settled," I said. "And I am starving."

Lucy chuckled. "I must say, I'm impressed."

"Agreed," said Scott, pulling a chair up to the table and plopping down in it. "The way you stood up to Aveda—finally—was . . ."

"Totally diva-ish?" I suggested.

"Smashing," Lucy corrected, beaming at me. "Seriously overdue and a really marvelous sign of personal growth. If I hadn't been so focused on our intervention, I would have applauded."

I laughed. "Thank you. I think."

Scott reached over and took my hand. "I wasn't there yesterday. Like I said, I heard the whole story secondhand," he said. "But I wanted to make sure: are you okay?"

I stared down at our intertwined fingers and was suddenly reminded of the day Jay Tran, my longstanding high school crush, had asked someone else to the prom after hinting for weeks he was going to ask me. That was way before I knew what real pain felt like, and I was convinced it was the worst thing that would ever happen to me. Aveda had stomped off to find Jay, declaring she was "going to give him a very large, very significant piece of my mind," but Scott just sat with me at our usual lunch table, holding my hand. Staying well after lunch period was over, after everyone else had gone back to class, soothing me out of my dramatic teenage emotion spiral. And then he'd asked if I wanted to go with him.

The memory gave me a surge of warmth. But it was a friendly warmth. A sibling-like warmth. A warmth that contained no trace of sexual attraction. I didn't have those kinds of feelings for him, I realized. I never would. And that was really, really okay. I squeezed his hand. "Yes," I said. "I am. Thanks for asking. And thanks for *always* asking."

He grinned at me and squeezed back. "Of course." He released my hand and stood. "So I guess if I'm officially joining the team here, I should find a room or something."

"There are a couple left upstairs," Lucy said. "Have a look." She made a shooing motion at him. He smiled, nodded at us, and exited the room.

"I thought he'd never leave," Lucy said, turning back to me. "Now we can finally talk about something more interesting."

"Like these new demons? I don't know what else we can discuss until Nate does his dissection—"

"Not that. You need to tell me in extremely filthy detail—seriously, leave nothing out—how you and Nate ended up having sex."

"*Lucy*. H-how did you . . ."

"Oh, for heaven's sake. You two are not exactly subtle. What with the blushing and the carefully timed separate entrances and the simultaneously wet hair—"

I buried my face in my hands. "Please stop talking."

"It was bound to happen sooner or later, given the

way you're always sniping at each other." She gave a delicate shudder. "Ech. Straight people."

"Then why do you want details?" I dropped my hands from my face. "What about your whole 'cocks and cauliflower' bit?"

"I'm a good friend," she said, patting my hand. Her eyes widened. "He was the one who destroyed your shirt at The Gutter, wasn't he? I knew you were doing something illicit while I was up there singing my heart out. My goodness, you're lucky I gave you all those condoms. Seems the two of you can really go at it. Like a pair of horny teenage bunny rabbits."

I slumped into a chair, wondering if there was any possibility that intense mortification would cause me to vanish, thereby truncating this conversation.

"Only you could twist the nice moment we were having into this," I said.

"That's why you love me." She beamed. "What was it like? Is he as dour and buttoned-up in the bedroom as he is everywhere else?"

"No." A smile crept over my face. "He was passionate. Enthusiastic. He made me feel like . . . like I didn't have to hold back."

I'd never felt that way before, I realized. Not in a sexual context. Richard might have been clueless about the key erogenous zones, but I'd also never been able to separate from my overactive brain and enjoy the moment with him. I'd never felt like I *could* do that. With Nate, all my inhibitions had sailed out the window.

"Luce," I said. "Aveda and Bea and Scott—do you think they know, too?"

"No. They are not attuned to matters of the heart. Not like me."

I shook my head affectionately. "There's no one like you."

"Nor you." She patted my hand again. "Now. We should draw up a detailed plan for your pre-karaoke contest workouts. I know weird is our stock in trade, but this new demon brand of weird seems . . ."

"Even weirder than usual?"

"Yes. But we can handle it, right?" She looked at me uncertainly. "*You* can handle it?"

I gave her the most confident smile I could muster. "I guess we're about to find out."

CHAPTER SIXTEEN

LUCY AND I worked out for two hours. Most of our "training" ended with me on the ground, gasping for breath. But I kept reminding myself that even if I didn't feel as brave as Michelle Yeoh/Invisible Girl, I needed to be prepared to act like her.

Afterward I darted up to my room, showered, and changed into jeans and an old T-shirt with a stretched-out neckline that drooped off my shoulders. I was just adding some fuzzy socks to my lazy ensemble when I got a text from Bea:

Dissection results in. Plz report to lab. URGENT!!!

I hustled downstairs, my mind whirling. Had they discovered something crazy or was Bea just being melodramatic?

Nate's lab really did look like a cave, its surfaces gray and gloomy and depressingly sterile. Why he enjoyed spending so much time down here was beyond me. He was leaning over a long table in the middle of the room, poking and prodding at what appeared to be pieces of the thumb specimen. Bea, meanwhile, was perched on a stool next to him, jotting down notes.

"Evie!" Bea's eyes widened. "We dissected the thumb. That thing is bananas. And the results are . . ." She looked at Nate. "Do you want to tell her?"

"You go ahead," he said.

Bea's face was so dead serious, I found myself holding my breath, my trepidation rising.

"It has human tissue," she said.

"Wh-what?" I sputtered. Holy shit. Okay, so the dramatic text had been warranted.

"But not all human. It's, like, a hybrid. Of human and something else."

"Which means . . . ?" Nate prompted.

"Which means!" Bea exclaimed, stabbing her pen at her notepad. "This wasn't an example of a demon imprinting on something human-like. This was a demon *fusing* with an actual human."

"Fusing . . ." I tried to process the information. As far as I knew, we hadn't encountered anything like that before. Then I thought about how skillfully the hand played the Nordstrom piano—and the tune it had played. A horrific realization started to take shape.

"Nate," I said, trying to keep my voice steady. "Remember how Lucy mentioned that Stu hasn't shown up for work? That they're not sure where he is? The music the hand played yesterday . . ." I swallowed hard. "It was Stu's original composition. The one he's been tinkering with for months down at The Gutter."

"Shit." Nate frowned at the thumb pieces, as if willing them to provide further answers. "All right. I'll mention that to Rose. I'm sending her our findings to see if SFPD can get us a DNA match off the thumb's human tissue. I also compared the results from the thumb with the dissection records for the humanoid demon corpses found near that first big portal. They don't match. Those corpses may have looked human, but DNA-wise, they were all demon."

I rubbed a hand over my face, my frustration rising. "So whatever this is, it's definitely new. Nothing from the past is going to give us useful clues?"

Nate nodded. "That is the logical conclusion. But I wish we had something from the other oddities we've witnessed—Aveda statue demons and the Tommy Thing—to compare these results to. Something to give us a solid connection."

Bea looked up from her pad. "As far as connecting things: Evie's observations are still solid. Like, how these guys have that weird way of moving and at least a couple of them seem all smart and stuff?"

Nate and I looked at her in surprise. She waved her pen at us. "All data is useful at some point, right? In terms of adding to the bigger picture?"

Nate hesitated, then smiled at her. "Yes," he said.

"Excuse me?" I blurted out. "Are you actually acknowledging that messy, vague, real life experience-type data is just as good as the hard facts that go in your spreadsheets?"

He cocked an eyebrow at me. "I'm coming to see that, as Beatrice says, *all* data is valuable. And methods of data collection, even if they aren't my own methods, should not be discounted. Especially if we want that bigger picture to come into focus."

I gawked at him. "Well. That's different."

"Ahem," Bea said, giving both of us a look.

I shook my head, tried to wipe the shock off my face, and refocused on what she was saying.

"So even though we don't have bits of the other oddities for dissection, we can totes speculate based on what we've seen recently," Bea continued.

I drummed my fingers on the table, trying to follow the thread. "Say we keep assuming all three things are connected," I said. "If the hand is a demon that fused with Stu, was the Tommy Thing a demon that fused with the actual Tommy? Rather than a demon merely imprinting on a cardboard Tommy standee?"

"You did mention that it acted like him. That it was upset about people not liking the movie," Nate said. "Has anyone seen the real Tommy Lemon recently?"

"He's supposedly on one of his zen retreats right now.

His social media claims he's trekking through the Andes or something," Bea said, making a face. "That's where Dad is, too, by the way. He just emailed me that he's on another vision quest with Yogini Lara." She shrugged, trying to look like she couldn't care less what Dad was up to. "Maybe he'll come back for my birthday."

"Maybe," I said. Dad had forgotten her birthday for the last four years.

"What about the statue demons?" Nate asked. "Do we think they were fused with anything?"

"They had the weird movement thing going on," I said, trying to work it out. "But they seemed to be created the same way our non-humanoid demons usually are: by coming through a portal and imprinting on the first thing they see."

"And there was a swarm of them," Bea piped up. "With the other two things, there was a single demon, and we're theorizing that it fused with a specific person: first Tommy, now Stu."

"So maybe the statues were some kind of test run or prototype—maybe they somehow had human DNA, but weren't fused with one specific human? Does that even make sense? Or are they connected to this at all?" I said. I leaned back against the long table, my frustration mounting again. We just kept coming up with more questions.

"Let's try to connect Stu and Tommy and go from there," Bea said, scribbling on her pad. "While Nate is getting the thumb tested for possible Stu DNA, I can do further research on Tommy's whereabouts—the last time he was sighted, how long this retreat thing is supposed to last."

"That sounds like a good start," I said, meaning it. I smiled at her. She gave me a tentative smile back. I felt like we were forging new territory and I had to tread carefully. "Also, Bea, can you talk to Rose, see if she and her team have observed or found anything weird the last few days? Rose Rorick? Head of the cleanup crew—"

"I know who Rose is," Bea said. "I've been taking care of the Jupiter HQ general email account while you've been busy, Evie. Rose is super smart. And she said I could come to the next portal site and she'd show me how the portal scanner thingy works." She perked up. "I've always wanted to see one of those in person. Anyway. I'll go get started on the Tommy research." She slid off her stool. "And I have to update Twitter with an ice cream coupon thingamajig. Humphry Slocombe said they'd give ten percent off to anyone who comes in and mentions Aveda's fave flavor."

"We got ice cream earlier," Nate said, filling in the blanks. "Very important for powering through research. There's some for you in the freezer."

"Thanks." I nodded at him and Bea. "That was nice of you."

Bea gave me a brisk nod in return. "I'll get on this research thing as soon as I've updated Twitter."

I watched her leave and let out the long sigh I'd been holding in. The thumb may have given us new information, but it still felt like we had a bunch of assumptions and half-theories with no real answers. And I needed more than that if I was going to take on whatever this new demon force was at the karaoke battle.

"Beatrice was very helpful," Nate said, cutting into my thoughts. He was cataloguing the pieces of dissected thumb, putting each one in a plastic baggie and labeling it with a Sharpie.

"And she hasn't yelled at me at all today," I said. "Which is a pretty novel feeling since she always seems to get madder at me than anyone. I guess it's a family thing, you know?"

"Not really," he said. "I'm not in contact with my family."

"Why not?" I said, then clapped a hand over my mouth. "Sorry. That was nosy."

"It's okay." He frowned contemplatively, then shrugged. "We don't share the same worldview."

While he worked, I wandered over to another part of the lab, trying to rearrange the information we'd gathered in my head, trying to pull a full picture into focus. I stopped at a table shoved in the corner with a pile of stones on it. Nate's Otherworld gibberish stones, I realized. They looked like they were in the process of being sorted into piles. Most of them still looked like gibberish to me, nonsensical scribbles carved into their surfaces. But some of them did indeed have real, actual words.

The You Need stone from Cake My Day was in a pile of four. I picked through the ones sitting next to it, reading their inscriptions.

Once He Sees All

The Golden Princess

Son Will Rise

Maybe the demons were secretly a bunch of wannabe haiku writers?

"Hey, Nate," I said. "What's going on over here? Did you sort these?"

I turned and gave him an inquisitive look. He had finished tagging and bagging all the thumb pieces and was standing by the lab's basin sink, washing his hands. He turned off the faucet and crossed the room to me.

"No," he said. "Beatrice did." He plucked the Golden Princess stone from the pile. "This is our most recent acquisition. Whistles management sent it over while you were training this morning. A customer found it in her mozzarella sticks."

"And these all go together?" I gestured to the pile around the You Need stone.

"That's Beatrice's theory, as all the phrases are rendered in similar letter shapes." He nodded at the neat piles. "She started cataloging them." He pointed to a piece of paper next to the stones, which had a makeshift grid rendered in Bea's loopy handwriting.

"She's making her own spreadsheet?" I arched an eyebrow. "You are a terrible influence."

He laughed. "She has an aptitude for scientific studies. She started finding patterns in the stones I'd never seen before." He pointed to one of the piles. "For instance, she thinks these are all markers of powers humans received when that first Otherworld portal opened up." He picked up one of the stones and handed it to me. "This could be Aveda."

"'Lifts Most Weakly,'" I read out loud. "Let's not show this to our fearless leader."

"Or this one," he said, pointing to another stone, "could be your Human GPS friend Mercedes."

"'Auto Track,'" I read. "Where's mine?"

"Bea thinks this one is you." He plucked a third stone from the pile. The words on it were smaller and I had to squint to make out the phrase.

"'Anger Shatters Field,'" I read.

"Because of the anger leading to a destructive action," he clarified. "It works."

"It sounds like a badly translated fortune cookie. Reminds me of a paper I wrote in grad school about the cross-cultural impact of incorrect movie subtitles."

He grinned and set the stone back in its Bea-approved pile. "If it's acceptable to you, I'd like her to continue with this. She's finally making sense of the, as you always call it, gibberish."

"Right. Gibberish." I hesitated and picked up the Anger Shatters Field stone again. I'd always been so disdainful of it all: the stones, his spreadsheets, his attempts to make sense of the Otherworld. And he'd seemed dismissive of me in turn.

But he'd just admitted that his worldview had been broadened. That he now believed all methods of gathering data were worthwhile. I'd felt a surge of triumph because he'd finally admitted my observations were valuable. And then I had promptly ignored the other side of it. Which was *my* dismissiveness.

I'd been so fixated on getting him to see that my point

of view was valid, I'd never acknowledged that his was, too.

Instead I'd spent pretty much every moment before today making flippant comments about how useless his research was.

I'd told myself it was because I was exasperated with him for refusing to go out in the field while the rest of us put ourselves on the demon-y front lines. For refusing to see anything but his black-and-white charts and grids, his numbers and data, while the rest of us dealt with the real world. But as I picked one of the stones up and felt its weight in my hand, I realized something else had been bubbling underneath the surface of my disdain the whole time. Something I'd been afraid to admit until now.

"I'm all for any Bea hobby that doesn't involve her finding new ways to be mad at me," I said slowly. I ran my thumb over the stone's smooth surface. "And about the whole gibberish thing. I've been a jerk to you. About your research. Now that we're up against some crazy demon force that seems bent on accomplishing some serious evil, well . . . I see how important it is. How everyone needs to work together on some spreadsheet action. I didn't mean to dismiss your work or you or . . ." I bit my lip, trying to put the right words together. "I was scared."

I took a deep breath and stared down at the stone in my hand. I didn't look at him; I still had more to get through.

"I didn't want to know about my power, didn't want to even think about it. I wanted to pretend it didn't exist," I said. "I think I was secretly afraid of what your research on Otherworld 'science' might reveal. What you might discover about my whole Little Miss Totally Destructive Fire Power deal. Like, if you made just one too many spreadsheets or put too many pieces together, you might find out that I'm . . . I'm . . ."

"That you're extraordinary?"

"That I'm a monster."

I'd never said those words out loud. But as they landed in the air, rushed and staccato, I knew down in my bones that they had guided me since that horrible day at the library.

What if you're a monster? What if you're a supervillain? What if you allow yourself to let go and be all unguarded and feel something for just one millisecond and everyone dies and it's all your fucking fault?

"You're not a monster." Nate reached over and took my hand. "I'm standing by extraordinary. And for the record, when I've suggested exploring your power, it's not because I think you're an experiment or a science project or whatever you want to call it. It's because I want you to see that, too. That extraordinariness."

"Thank you," I said softly. I tried to process each one of those words, to internalize them. I'd gone to the brink of monsterdom—nearly taking Aveda's head off—and come back from it. I was on the other side of almost realizing my greatest fear and I actually felt okay. I was even making plans to use the fire *more* and battle this still-nebulous demon force.

For a moment we just stood there, Nate's hand clasping mine. I reveled in the gentle warmth of that touch. In the past, any kind of heat near my palm area would've been enough to start that familiar panicky feeling spiraling through my stomach. Now it just felt . . . nice.

"You may have been, as you say, 'a jerk' to me, but I've been nothing but hostile to you throughout our acquaintanceship," Nate said, bringing me out of my thoughts. "I should apologize for that as well. And I should tell you why."

He stopped so abruptly, I wondered if there was more to that sentiment or if I'd heard wrong.

"Okay," I said, trying to be encouraging. "Why?"

He dropped my hand and rocked back on his heels, his eyes going to the ceiling. This bit of movement looked strange on him: casual and waffly and weirdly vulnerable.

"This is going to require ice cream," he finally said. He crossed over to the freezer in the corner of the lab, opened it, and pulled out a small dish with a wooden spoon stuck in it. Then he grabbed a stool and dragged it over to me.

"Sit," he ordered. "And eat this." He shoved the dish into my hands. It was the promised ice cream. "There are some things I want to tell you. But I would like to request that you not interrupt me."

I couldn't respond, because my mouth was already full of ice cream. Clever man. And it was the best flavor from Humphry Slocombe, Secret Breakfast: cornflakes and bourbon and sugar. I savored the taste and hoisted myself onto the stool and motioned for him to continue. He took a deep breath and fixed me with a piercing gaze.

"I've wanted to see you naked since the moment we met."

I nearly choked on my mouthful of ice cream.

"I'm sorry," he said. "That's one of those sentences that didn't quite come out right."

"But—" I sputtered unattractively. "How can you . . . you probably don't even remember—"

He held up a hand. "No interrupting. I do remember: You answered the door that first time I came to HQ. Your hair was coming out of its ponytail, sticking to your neck, and you were wearing a very tight T-shirt with a cartoon duck on it. And you told me, without so much as a hello—" A smile played around his lips as he went into a spot-on imitation of my put-out tone. "'The bodyguard position has been filled. We are not accepting new applications at this time.'" He ran a hand through his hair, making it stand on end in that way I used to find so odd. Now it was kind of endearing. "I have never meant to come off as disrespectful of you, the way you live your life, or the way you see the world . . . but I'm afraid that's exactly what I've done. I was trying to put as much distance between us as possible. In the past, it's been very necessary to keep my life free of distractions. And you are a very big distraction. Especially in that goddamn tight T-shirt."

He looked at the floor, stuffing his hands in his pockets. I licked my spoon and set my dish on the table next to the stones. My heart was beating very fast, and I didn't think it was from the sugar rush.

"So our sexperiment has been a long time in the making," I said. I was going for "teasing," but my tone came out more like "do me on this table right now, please."

"Indeed. But perhaps we shouldn't call it that since I just clarified that I do not think of *you* as an experiment—"

"No, no, it's a joke. A funny wordplay thing," I said quickly. "I mean, we agreed orgasms are our only purpose. We're not actually collecting hardcore data or anything."

I was babbling now. I couldn't think of what else to do.

"Hmm." He paused and placed his hands on the table on either side of me, hemming me in. I sat very still, trying not to betray how much the heat rolling off his body affected me. He cocked an eyebrow at me. "Or are we?"

Whoa. Was *he* trying to be teasing now? Because his tone was definitely matching my "do me, etc." cadence.

Should I keep going with it? Could I pull off sex kitten for more than one line? Actually, it wasn't even quite sex kitten, it was more like—

Jesus Christ.

Was I really overthinking *incredibly hot sex* again?

"I've collected an abundance of data so far," he said. He dipped a finger in the melting remnants of my ice cream. "For instance," he said, "my highly scientific analysis indicates you have a very sensitive spot right . . . here . . ." He dabbed a droplet of ice cream on the curve of my neck, right below my earlobe.

"Hey!" I protested, unprepared for that bit of cold against my skin. Before I could elaborate on that thought, he leaned in and flicked his tongue over the spot. Which was indeed quite sensitive. A giggle escaped me. "Very funny."

"It's not funny." He gave me a stern look. "It's *science*. I have also been able to discern that you turn a rather violent shade of pink right . . . here . . ." He dabbed another drop of ice cream along my collarbone. " . . . when you're aroused." He pressed his lips against my skin, gently sucking at the ice cream. The melding of the cold with the heat of his tongue created an irresistible sensation, a feeling so heady I couldn't find words superlative enough to describe it.

But I was pretty sure that bit of skin was now an exceptionally violent shade of pink.

"And here . . ." He eased the stretched-out collar of my T-shirt over my shoulder, exposing the top slope of my right breast. He dabbed the last of the ice cream just above my nipple, which remained frustratingly covered. "Here, you like teeth." He grazed the spot to demonstrate. I inhaled sharply, all of my nerve endings standing at attention.

He kept his focus on that spot, licking and sucking, even though the ice cream was long gone. Desire coursed through me so fiercely, it felt like it was jabbing at my vital organs, a repeated shock to the heart. A single thought pulsed through my brain, relentless and ridiculous.

Science is awesome!
Science! Is Awesome!
Science . . . is . . . awesome!!!

"Science . . ." I gasped out loud.

And then I felt it. That telltale warmth in my palm, that sensation that was usually accompanied by panic.

But once again I didn't feel panic.

"Nate!" I pulled back from him and held up my hand.

Right there, perched in my palm, was a perfect fireball. It was contained and still and unlike the wild bursts of flame that usually shot out of my hands. I goggled at it, unsure what to make of its seemingly docile nature.

Nate's eyes went wide.

"That," he said, "is awesome."

CHAPTER SEVENTEEN

"WOW," NATE SAID after a few moments of awed silence. Then he looked at me anxiously. "That's not . . . I wasn't trying to do that. I wasn't even thinking about your power. I meant what I said about you not being an experiment, I was going along with your 'funny word-play' idea—"

"I know. I got it." I smiled and thought back to what he'd said earlier.

I want you to see that, too. That extraordinariness.

For the first time in my life, I felt like I could see it. Or at least I wanted to. The more I figured out about my fire, the more control I gained, the more I wanted to learn about how my power worked.

I couldn't believe I actually *wanted* that.

But I did.

I fixated on the fireball, orange shot through with streaks of molten gold. It was beautiful. It was glorious. It . . . was just sitting there. Steady, steady, steady. As if awaiting its marching orders. I gently batted my hand back and forth. It remained stuck to my palm, as if affixed with glue.

"So that's different," I murmured.

"Why is it not . . ." Nate mimed the fire exploding out of my hand and flying across the room.

"I'm not sure." I closed my fingers around the fireball

and felt the heat vanish. When I opened my hand, it was gone. I flexed my fingers. Suddenly, I had an idea for an experiment of my own.

I felt emboldened by the need to see some extraordinariness.

"Let's see if I can bring it back."

"I could kiss you again."

"No. I mean . . . maybe later." I smiled at him. "Let me try something else."

I closed my eyes and summoned the feeling I'd had yesterday: the pure, unadulterated rage toward Aveda. No other thoughts, no inhibitions. I let the anger flood through me, drowning out everything else.

When I opened my hand, the fireball was there again.

"Still awesome," Nate said. "How do you think this is working?"

"You mean, what's my hypothesis?"

He smiled. "Yes."

I studied my fireball. "These past few days, I've gotten accustomed to feeling things," I said slowly. "I'm used to having a suppression reflex: kill a big emotion as soon as it starts. But ever since Tommy—ever since I let the rage out—that reflex has been breaking down." I met his eyes. "Just now, with you and, uh . . ." I gestured at the empty ice cream dish. "I was completely in touch with what I was feeling. I was *focused* on that feeling and nothing else. Does this sound insanely stupid yet?"

He held my gaze. "No."

"It's like catching the feeling. Grabbing on to it and letting it overtake me. That brings the fire." I looked at my little fireball again. "But this thing seems to be stuck to my hand. I want to try throwing it."

"Where?" Nate surveyed his precious lab, apprehensive.

"Out a window?"

"You might hit an innocent passerby."

"Into a bucket of water?"

"We own a bucket?"

"How about over there?" I nodded at the lab's basin sink. "That's like a bucket."

He considered it then nodded. "Okay."

Before I could say anything else, he scooped me up and carried me over to the sink.

"Hey!" I gave him a look. "I can manage. This fire thing doesn't impede my ability to walk."

"You should focus on keeping your hand still." He gave me a sheepish grin. "And maybe I like carrying you."

I rolled my eyes at him. We made it over to the sink and he set me down on the counter and turned on the water. I whipped my wrist back and forth, trying to separate the fireball. But it stayed stubbornly stuck to my hand.

Hmm. If pure emotion was the key to forming these fireballs, maybe pure emotion would also help move them?

I cleared my mind and tried to focus on a single feeling. I dredged up my exchange with Bea from the day before, when I'd said she reminded me of Mom: the happiness that surged through me when she smiled. Warmth, contentment. A sense of relief that maybe I hadn't fucked her up for life.

The ball floated in my palm, unmoving. I bit my lip in frustration.

Oh! That was a good one—frustration! I summoned it up: the impotence I felt over this new breed of demons. The flicker of rage that flashed through me whenever I got one of Dad's useless postcards. The burning need for Nate to rip the rest of my shirt off, exposing my attention-starved nipple . . . no! Bad example. I felt my collarbone area flush pink.

After several more seconds of deeply feeling every feeling I could think of, I shook my head.

"Shut the water off. Not happening."

I closed my hand over the fireball, extinguishing it, while Nate turned off the sink.

"Okay," I said. "So apparently I can now call my fire up on cue, which does indicate a further level of control. Which means I don't have to worry about it shooting all over the damn place. Which is pretty amazing." I paused, considering. "And just like last night, I think that level of control means I can also still . . ." I closed my eyes, channeled my frustration, and felt my palm heat.

No, I thought to myself. *Not now.*

The fire didn't appear. Triumph surged through me.

"I can keep it from coming out, too!" I crowed. "Like, regularly. Last night wasn't just a fluke." I flexed my fingers and frowned into space. "But if I can't figure out how to make my fire *move,* it takes my power from horrifically destructive to possibly useless."

"Not useless," Nate countered. "It is still fire, after all."

We shared a few moments of contemplative silence. Then he leaned in. "We don't seem to be getting much further with this hypothesis."

"Just like our new breed of demon hypothesis."

"So why don't we try that kissing thing again?"

"For science?"

"For fun."

I had no objections.

He had just managed to get my shirt almost all the way off when the lab door flew open and a very pissed-off Aveda Jupiter hobbled in on her crutches. Lucy, Bea, and Scott trailed in behind her. When they saw us, they came to a standstill.

"What?!" Aveda squawked. She gave us a once-over. "Whatever you two are doing cannot possibly be sanitary. This is supposed to be a scientific laboratory."

"We're aware," I said, rearranging my shirt so it sort of covered my torso. "Do you want to tell me why you all just barged in?"

Aveda glared at me. "Just when I think there's no

possible way you can make things worse, you go and . . . and . . ."

"And what?"

"Oh . . . em . . . gee . . ." whispered Bea, her eyes widening as she stared at me and Nate. I realized I was still tangled up in him and made a move to extricate myself, sliding down from the counter. So much for keeping our sexperiment a secret.

Weirdly I found I didn't care. Given how much I'd exposed myself the past few days—both literally and figuratively—getting caught in a hot, heavy, possibly unsanitary make-out session seemed like small potatoes. Although my baby sister probably didn't need to be seeing this. I gave Scott a meaningful look, trying to silently tell him to get Bea out of the room. But he just grinned, clearly enjoying my discomfort. Lucy snickered.

My friends were so awesome.

"Evie," Bea began, holding up her glittery phone. "You need to look at . . ."

Aveda snatched the phone from Bea and shoved it in my face. "Explain this, Evelyn."

The screen displayed Maisy's blog, her sickeningly cute logo splashed across the top. Below the logo was one of her typical headlines. Only, for once, the headline wasn't about Aveda.

It was about me.

ASSISTANTMAGEDDON!

Why Evie "Rude Girl" Tanaka Must Be Stopped!
by Maisy Kane, Bay Bridge Kiss Editrix

It's time for some real talk, 'Friscans. Now, you know your pal Maisy doesn't like to get all unfun in her reporting. But frankly? Someone's gotta address this. And I think it's best if that someone's me.

After writing yesterday's post about Aveda's mall adventure, I had a good think about what I'd observed on the scene. Sure, Aveda being able to temporarily transfer her fire power to her minions sounds cool in theory, but let's consider this—do we really want non-superheroes test driving something so gosh-dang destructive? And who is this Evie Tanaka person, anyway?

'Friscans, I think it's time I exposed some truths about Aveda's mousy little assistant, aka Rude Girl. Why, she threatened your pal Maisy right before nearly incinerating the entire Nordstrom shoe department! If I hadn't ducked just in time, I might've ended up burned to death. And crispy critters are no good at blogging!

Further reporting uncovered even more bad behavior. A reliable source at The Gutter shared a terrifying tale about a recent phone call with one of Ms. Tanaka's minions. That's right: Aveda's minions have their own minions now. Truly, the situation is out of control. Acting on Evie's orders, said minion used outright threats to nab a spot for Aveda in The Gutter's prestigious karaoke competition! Can you even wrap your brain around that one?

I've decided it's very necessary to take a stand against bullying. I've talked our source down at The Gutter into giving me the spot opposite A. Jupes in their karaoke contest. I'll be singing in symbolic protest of E's threatening ways . . . and in protest of A letting her lapdog run wild in the first place. And you can bet your buttons I'll be crowned queen of the whole shebang.

I can't help but wonder if all this is a result of that shiny new international fame going to A's head. I mean, if she's willing to let such an unhinged menace play around with her power, she's clearly not using her best judgment. Perhaps she's started to consider herself better than the rest of us.

Someone's got to show her she's not the only 'Friscan who matters. And that someone is your pal Maisy!

Shasta's Corner! Shasta (Maisy's bestie) here. I was on the scene at the mall and can confirm that Evie Tanaka is a menace to society. And a badly dressed one, at that. (Editrix's Note: Nice one, Shast! I knew you weren't a total waste of space.)

CHAPTER EIGHTEEN

"WELL?" AVEDA HISSED. "What are you going to do about this?"

"Now you want me to do something? Because yesterday you were ordering me to shut up and get back in your shadow," I retorted.

"Evie!" Bea hopped from one foot to the other. "You have to take this seriously! Aveda's already lost a couple hundred Twitter followers. And there's a whole thread on Facebook questioning her continued validity as a superhero. People trust Maisy's reporting."

"That's reporting?" Scott said. "A shitty picture and a bunch of half-assed suppositions and exaggerations?"

"Yeah, I incinerated one pair of shoes, not the whole department," I said. "And as for this karaoke thing . . ." I turned to Lucy. "Kevin's got to be Maisy's source, right? Did you threaten him when you asked for a spot in the contest?"

"Of course not," she said. "I mean, he was a bit reluctant at first. I believe his exact words were, 'Call me when Aveda can do her superhero theatrics while also singing Cher's 'Believe' over a track of AC/DC's 'You Shook Me All Night Long' and hitting every note without autotune.' But I wore him down. And possibly said I'd start a rumor about unsanitary kitchen practices if he didn't give in. I'd hardly call that a threat, though. I certainly never said I was your minion or that you told me to—"

"Right, right," I said, shaking my head. "But no one supposes and exaggerates like Maisy. Especially when she's got what she thinks is a story."

I took the phone from Aveda and studied the screen. There were two photos accompanying the post. In the first one, I was confronting Maisy in the Nordstrom shoe department: eyes wild, hair flying, pointing at her in a way that was decidedly threatening while she cowered behind Nate. This was when I'd told her to keep her "grabby hands" off Aveda's escort. Shasta must have snapped it when I wasn't looking. The second image was a lovely shot of me shooting fire at Aveda's head.

I should have been embarrassed by how unhinged I looked in these photos. But, honestly, I was kind of proud. Because I also looked . . . cool. Powerful. Like a worthy colleague for Michelle Yeoh/Invisible Girl and Co.

"What's that?" Nate asked, pointing to a spot on the first photo.

He took the phone from me and tapped the screen to zero in on Maisy's left hand, which she had brought to her chest, as if clutching invisible pearls. The back of her hand seemed to have some kind of black blotch on it.

"Is it a tattoo?" I said. "I know Maisy Kane's super alternative, but that doesn't seem like her brand of alternative."

Nate tapped the screen again, enlarging that spot of the picture. It appeared to be a tattoo of a crude symbol, a line with four hash marks through it.

Where had I seen that before?

"The hand!" I blurted out. "That same mark was on the hand that attacked at the mall." I stared at the screen, a hunch forming in my brain. I took the phone from Nate and handed it to Bea. "Do we have any photos of the Tommy Thing?" I asked her. "Or shots from the Yamato YouTube video?"

Bea's fingers flew over the screen. "Let's see . . ." She pulled up a series of freeze frames from the video.

"There." I jabbed my index finger at one of the pictures. "He has the tattoo, too. I didn't get a good look at it 'cause I was too busy running away from him."

"So there are odd things in a couple pictures, so what?" Aveda cut in. "Can we please get back to what's important?"

"Which is what, your image?" Scott said. "Unbelievable," he muttered under his breath.

Ignoring them, I turned and stared into the sink. Maybe the Aveda statues were a red herring. Or maybe they fit into the picture in some way I just couldn't see yet. But the tattoo was an actual solid connection that linked Maisy, Tommy, and Stu.

Three makes a trend.

"So these three all have this mark," I said, facing the group again. "We've hypothesized that Stu was somehow turned into a freaky demon-human hybrid and maybe Tommy was, too. Does this mean Maisy is also part of that crew?"

"You know . . ." Lucy paused thoughtfully. "She and Shasta are always there. In all of the instances connected to the new breed of demons: Whistles, the benefit, the mall. The Yamato, too: we didn't actually see them, but Shasta told us they were there. It's under the guise of reporting on Aveda, but . . . whenever these weird demons appear, they're on the scene."

Lucy met my eyes. She'd gone pale. "That night at The Gutter—remember how we had that encounter with Shasta? And then right after, she approached Stu Singh."

"Whispered in his ear and shit," I said, remembering.

Lucy nodded, going even paler. "Do you think she was recruiting him into this cult of demon-human hybrids? And is she one, too?"

"Okay, let's slow down for a minute," I said, holding up

a hand and trying to get my thoughts in order. "I don't know about Shasta. She doesn't appear to have the tattoo and it seems like she's fulfilling her usual role, supporting and enabling Maisy, so even if she's part of this—"

"She wouldn't say boo unless Maisy told her to," Bea finished.

"Right," I said. "Let's go back to the idea of Maisy, Tommy, and Stu being connected. Tommy and Stu look clearly transformed, but Maisy . . ." I frowned. "She doesn't look different. She still looks like her aggravating human self." In my head, I called up the image of Maisy waving her stupid recorder in front of my face the day before, trying to capture every moment on video. I'd missed the tattoo. Had I missed anything else? I'd been pretty close to her, had even grabbed her hand . . .

"Her *hand*," I said out loud.

Everyone looked at me quizzically.

"I thought my fire had burned it," I said, remembering how her skin had looked flaky, patchy. "But she brushed it off, acted like it didn't matter. And it didn't look *quite* burned. It just looked different. Like . . ."

"Like the skin on Tommy? On the disembodied hand?" Lucy said.

"Yes," I said. "But not that extreme. It wasn't all over her body, just in that one spot."

"As if she was controlling it, maybe?" Nate suggested. "Does that perhaps indicate that Maisy has a higher level of power than the other oddities we've observed?"

I heard Bea inhale sharply. "Evie," she said slowly, "Maisy's outfit yesterday at the mall was all yellow, right?"

"Yes. What does that have to do with this?"

"What does any of this have to do with anything?" muttered Aveda.

"Did you see that new stone from Whistles?" Bea persisted.

"Yes?"

"Yellow," Bea said, "could also be interpreted as . . . gold."

The Golden Princess.

I stopped breathing for a minute. Those three simple words acted as a trigger, forcing our scattered observations into a connected whole. I saw a picture coming together, a mishmash of images arranging itself into a possible solution.

"The yellow outfit," I muttered out loud. "The tattoo. Her patchy skin. And . . ." I paused as another memory rose up in my head. Maisy and Shasta in the bathroom at the benefit. Me in the stall, trying to hold back tears. Them cackling about my dress. Maisy saying she wanted to transcend Aveda's celebrity status. She didn't just want to be a star, she wanted to be . . .

"A princess," I said out loud.

I'd thought she was putting on airs. Now their conversation seemed to indicate something much more sinister.

"And in her blog post," Bea said, waving her phone around. "She said she was going to be 'crowned' at the karaoke contest."

"Holy shit," I said. "Maisy Kane isn't just connected to this new demon threat. I think . . . I think she's in charge."

"She's a freakin' demon princess," Bea breathed.

"A good hypothesis, considering the data," said Nate.

"I agree with you one hundred percent, darling," said Lucy.

"I guess that sort of makes sense," Aveda said reluctantly.

"How generous of you," Scott retorted.

"So obviously we're not going through with this karaoke debacle anymore," Aveda said. She tried to give her "that settles it" smile.

Only this time that did not fucking settle it.

I turned and stared at the sink again. So clean and silver and shiny. I imagined the drain was a portal to another world—not the Otherworld, but some dull dimension where everything was nice and mundane and there were no superpowers or superheroes or bloggers who were also pissed-off demon princesses. Five days ago I would've leapt through a portal to that world without a second thought.

But now? I was surprised to find I had absolutely no desire to. Zero, zilch, zip. I couldn't dredge up even the tiniest bit of longing for a mundane alternaworld. I wanted to save the crazy, colorful, occasionally fucked-up world I was already living in.

Was that personal growth or insanity?

I decided I didn't care.

"Yes, we are," I said, turning away from the sink. "Karaoke debacle is on."

Aveda glared at me. "Have you forgotten who's the actual boss, here?"

"No. But what we're facing is bigger than that. It's bigger than you, it's bigger than me. It's about saving this city from the clutches of a hipster demon princess who . . ." I hesitated. What was Maisy's endgame?

"She might be trying to take down Aveda to prime San Francisco for invasion, as you suggested earlier," Nate said, as if reading my thoughts. "Or perhaps she's set on turning the entire city into demon-human hybrids. Or maybe that 'you need three' stone was meant for her and—"

"And she already has the three she needs to take over!" yelped Bea. "Stu, Tommy, and herself!"

"But Evie took out Tommy and Stu," Lucy said. "Er, part of Stu."

"We don't know if I took them out for good," I said.

"Maybe it doesn't matter if you took them out," Bea said. "Maybe all Maisy has to do to gain ultimate power is, like, *create* these weirdo hybrid things. In which case, she can still totally count Tommy and Stu in her number."

"Okay, okay," I said. "So it's safe to say that none of

these are good options. Whatever Maisy's up to, it's not going to end well for us. Or anyone in San Francisco. We have to go through with the karaoke plan."

I looked at everyone in turn. Aveda was frowning hard, but the others looked intrigued. Hopeful. Even Bea gazed at me as if what I was saying was at least as rousing as Bill Pullman bellowing, "Today, we celebrate . . . our Independence Day!"

"Who's with me on this?" I asked.

Slowly they all raised their hands. Nate, Lucy, Scott, Bea. Everyone except Aveda. She kept glaring at me, a weighted silence settling between us.

"I see," she finally said, her voice like ice. "I guess there's a new boss in town."

She turned and stalked out of the lab as fast as her crutches would allow. I suppressed a sigh. I'd deal with her later.

I turned back to everyone else.

"I don't care if Maisy's a demon princess with a whole army of disembodied hands at her disposal. I don't care how many shitty, unflattering pictures of me she posts on her blog. And I don't care that I really can't sing."

I drew myself up tall.

"Maisy can have the internet, but she can't have the city: not while it's under the protection of Aveda Jupiter. Let's take that blowhard blogger bully *down*."

CHAPTER NINETEEN

THE NEXT WEEK whizzed by in a blur. We all went about our business and Aveda mostly avoided us, holing up in her room and mainlining way too many reruns of *Toddlers and Tiaras*. She claimed to have come around to my Big Maisy Takedown Plan, but her overall demeanor was listless and disinterested, as if the act of nodding her head in agreement was a lot of fucking work.

A couple new portals opened up around the city, but the resulting demons were of the boring, non-hybrid sort. I used them to practice my newfound ability to call up fireballs. Lucy taught me a few handy fight moves, including something called the running punch, wherein I hopped in range of my demon target, jammed my fireballed hand against it, then hopped off in the other direction. This technique nicely compensated for the fact that I still couldn't *throw* the fireballs.

On the research front, Rose told us the disembodied hand's DNA didn't have any matches in the system. But I just knew it had to be Stu. Meanwhile Bea reported that Tommy Lemon was still supposedly in the Andes and the Aveda statues were no longer being sighted around town. After menacing many a citizen—including me—the statues appeared to have vanished entirely.

Oh, and Nate and I had lots of sex. My newfound fireball control meant I was more confident about trying things out spur of the moment. There was even a day where we came very close to doing it in Lucy's car, which we'd borrowed for a routine grocery run. But the idea that we were in semi-public and semi-visible to every judgey eye in the Bay Area put a crimp in my passion. The stick, as they say, does not fall far from the mud.

Still, I was having fun. Our orgasms-only arrangement was pretty much nothing *but* fun.

We also tried to draw Maisy out in the vain hope I might be able to take down her demon ass before the karaoke contest. But she remained unmoved by Bea's tweets documenting where one might find Aveda Jupiter if one were so inclined. In fact, the usually ubiquitous Maisy Kane was barely seen in public at all. Even her blog posting was light. I started to wonder if she'd given up and returned to the Otherworld.

Until three days before the karaoke contest, when Bea received an obnoxious email with an even more obnoxious demand.

"You're sure it's from Maisy?" I asked, pacing the kitchen. "And she wants *what*?"

Bea looked up from her laptop. "As a show of good faith, she's demanding a meeting with a representative from Team Aveda to ensure the rules of the karaoke contest are understood and adhered to."

"So I'll go as me. Or Lucy can go."

"No." Bea shook her head. "She says it has to be a specific representative." Her gaze slid over to Nate, who was leaning against the counter. "It has to be him. Or she's pulling out of the contest."

"Ugh." I blew out a long, frustrated breath. "How do we know she's not bluffing?"

"Maisy Kane never bluffs," Bea said. "It's one of her Ten Commandments of Maximum Kane-osity."

"I can go," Nate said. "All I have to do is sit with her somewhere for an hour and pretend I understand karaoke, right?"

I was already shaking my head. "It could be dangerous. What if she chooses that moment to show her true demon-y colors?"

"Maisy can't risk revealing herself before the big karaoke to-do," Bea said. "That's where she wants to, as she's written on her blog, 'show San Franciscans who the real superhero is.'" She looked at me. "She's trying to rattle you before the contest. To make you give in to her demands and show you she's in charge or whatever."

Nate put a hand on my shoulder, forcing me to stop pacing. "Let's not display any weakness. I'll go."

I frowned at him. I knew Bea was probably right, but I hated the idea that Maisy was getting away with something. And if I was being honest, I really hated the idea that she was getting away with something involving the guy I was currently having amazing sex with.

But it's just sex, I reminded myself. *Orgasm purposes only, remember? No need to get all crazy-possessive.*

"Fine," I said. "But it has to be in a public place, like a restaurant. And Lucy's going with you. She'll sit a few tables away, make sure Maisy doesn't try anything sketchy. And I'll position myself somewhere nearby. Just in case."

Nate smiled. "Just in case."

For some reason, his smile irritated me even more.

"I've seen a karaoke bar before, Evie," Aveda said, casting a skeptical eye at our surroundings. The Gutter hadn't opened for the day yet and the fluorescents were turned up high. In the wake of Stu Singh's disappearance, the place was soldiering on. The piano sat on stage gathering dust between its keys, a macabre reminder of Stu's absence. Kevin had been forced to invest in an actual karaoke machine and was none too pleased about it. He also wasn't thrilled about us hanging out in the bar before business hours—Kevin believed in preserving something he called "the sanctity of the karaoke space"—and he kept sending disgruntled looks in our direction while wiping down the bartop. I'd told him Aveda needed to "properly engage with the venue for her upcoming performance." He'd grudgingly agreed, but apparently we had to put up with his snippy attitude as part of the deal.

Hopefully, it would be worth it. I figured if I showed Aveda the setup, she'd be able to visualize how heroic the Big Maisy Takedown Plan was going to make her look. Then maybe she'd stop sulking and get more enthusiastically on board with it. If I was going to pull it off, I needed everyone's support.

Of course, I hadn't thought a whole lot about *how* I was going to pull it off. You know, beyond "burn her." Or maybe "singe her enough to subdue her so she doesn't kill everyone." And we still didn't know what, exactly, being the Golden Princess meant. We didn't know if Maisy was the same as the hybrids, whether she'd ever been human, whether she was at all human now. We'd talked through the possibilities so many times, my head swirled just thinking about it. Whenever I started to consider the fact that I was about to battle a possible demon princess, that the fate of the city and possibly the entire world rested on my shoulders, my chest seized up and my brain collapsed under the weight of it all.

So I was doing my best not to think about it. After all, I'd been the one to confidently declare I was going to take Maisy down, and I needed to keep up that bold veneer for the rest of Team Aveda.

The Gutter just happened to be next door to the trendy hole-in-the-wall Maisy had chosen for her big meet-up with Nate. Which was going on right now and which I was trying not to fixate on. I glanced at my phone. Lucy was supposed to text me if Maisy pulled any demon shit. Nothing yet.

"The setting doesn't seem particularly epic," Aveda said. She frowned, peering out from under the brim of her floppy hat. She was disguised in her Bea-approved incognito getup, just in case someone happened to see us out and about. I was dressed as me: jeans, T-shirt, Chucks.

"The setting doesn't matter," I countered, sneaking another look at my phone. Still nothing. I should've been happy there were no updates. That meant all was quiet on the Maisy front. "But Aveda Jupiter busting a demon princess matters tons. In an epic sense."

"Will enough people be here to witness that?" Aveda said. She hoisted herself onto a bar stool and propped her crutches next to her. "I thought this was mostly a senior citizen haunt."

"Bea's promoted it far and wide," I assured her. "And Maisy's recent posts may be inflammatory, but they're also stirring up interest. Everyone wants to see you two face off. Hipsters, nerds, former popular kids trying to relive their glory days via a few verses of their favorite prom slow jam—they'll all be here. Ready to revel in the power of somewhat competently performed songs. And to drunkenly cheer you on."

"Hmm." Aveda cast a sidelong gaze at Kevin. "Can we drink *now*?"

"Sure, why not?" Kevin grumbled, snatching a bottle of whiskey off the shelf. "It's not like you guys are disrupting my preopening cleaning rituals or anything."

He plunked a glass in front of Aveda and poured whiskey up to the brim. Today his shirt read MIXED PLATE SPECIAL.

"Lovely." Aveda brought the glass to her lips, tossing the entire thing back in one gulp.

I glanced at my phone again. Nothing. A whole lot of nothing.

Kevin poured Aveda another drink, then pulled his phone out of his pocket and tapped on the screen, feigning boredom. "Just tell me when you want something else. I definitely don't mind putting my real work on hold to be at your beck and call."

"Pour one for Evie, too," Aveda said, waving a hand at the whiskey.

"No thanks," I said.

"Ooh, look at this!" Kevin exclaimed. He waved his phone around. "Wasn't this guy your escort to the last League benefit, Aveda? Looks like he's moving on with your karaoke rival."

"Give me that!" I said. I snatched the phone from his hand. And immediately wished I hadn't. Because right there on the screen was a Maisy Live Blog! update featuring a vibrant full-color picture of "your pal Maisy out and about with a mysterious hunk who'd prefer to keep his name from the paparazzi."

I gnawed at my lower lip. *I* knew his name.

In the picture, Nate and Maisy were seated at a cozy table at the bistro next door. Maisy was flashing her Sassy Flirt Grin, her fingertips grazing Nate's thigh. Nate, meanwhile, looked neutral. He wasn't leaning in, but he wasn't exactly recoiling, either.

"Jeez, Tanaka, what's with the major bitch-face? They make a cute couple," Kevin said, taking the phone from me. "Or is major bitch-face your default look these days, thanks to your moment in the spotlight?"

I resisted the urge to roll my eyes at him. Ever since Maisy had posted about me, I was getting mentioned a lot more on Aveda's Facebook page. Most of it was in the context of analyzing Aveda's decision-making skills: did lending me her fire represent a single bad choice or had she really lost it? Her most dedicated fans defended her fiercely, calling Maisy's reporting into question and noting that no one at the mall had actually gotten hurt. But some weren't so sure. A particularly vocal skeptic posted a rant suggesting San Francisco should "give Magnificent Mercedes another shot." Bea deleted that one before Aveda saw it.

I was reasonably certain I could win everyone back to Aveda's side with the Big Maisy Takedown Plan. If I managed to pull it off.

Aveda glanced at the picture of Nate and Maisy on the phone screen, then back at me, her eyes narrowing shrewdly. "I told you: you need a drink."

"It's two in the afternoon!" I snapped.

"Hey, this one's kind of racy," Kevin interrupted, waving his phone around again. I looked at the screen. Maisy had uploaded another Live Blog! picture. In this one she was pressing a plump strawberry to Nate's lips, her eyes widening in theatrical delight. He still looked neutral, but he was also accepting it. Taking a bite.

Well, what did I expect? For him to look disgusted, like he was about two seconds from spitting the fruit back in her face?

Yes, I thought viciously. *That's exactly how he should look.*

What the hell was wrong with me? I was thinking like an irrational, harpy-type person. Not a pseudo-superheroine with big plans for fighting a demon princess. I sternly reminded myself that Lucy would alert me if I was needed next door. For now, I would focus all my energy on snapping Aveda out of her bad attitude. Getting her on board with the Takedown would help me feel confident in my plan. I attempted to refocus. To refocus *heroically*.

"Kevin," I said, "could you leave us alone for a minute? I need to have a karaoke heart-to-heart with my boss, here."

"Sure, whatever," he said. "But you guys have to be out by seven so I can open for the night." He stuffed the phone in his pocket and stalked toward his office in the back, muttering about "entitled celebrity karaoke fakers" under his breath.

"Oh, good, now we can really drink," Aveda said, grabbing the bottle of whiskey and filling her glass.

"And how many have you had already?" I sputtered.

"Still a stick-in-the-mud," she said. "Even after everything that's happened."

"And what do you mean by that?" I planted my hands on my hips and glared at her. I had a momentary flashback to us as kids, affecting these exact same poses: her all gloaty, me righteously indignant. I didn't remember what we'd been fighting about, but I was pretty sure she'd won. As usual.

"Nothing." She turned to her drink.

"Not nothing." I set my hand in front of her glass, so she couldn't get at it. Now that I had compartmentalized my crabbiness over the Nate/Maisy situation, my crabbiness over her constant bitching slid easily into its place. "Look, I know you're going through a rough time and I think I've done a pretty okay job of trying to help. But I'm sick of your passive-aggressive sulky face. I'm trying to save the city from an evil demon princess and make you look awesome in the process. It'd be nice if you could get on board with that."

She regarded me, her expression unreadable. Then she lifted her hand and aimed it at her drink.

"That's not going to work!" I exclaimed. "Your telekinesis sucks!"

The glass wobbled, moved a fraction of an inch then went still. I heaved a sigh and removed my arm, allowing her to grab her drink.

She took a swig. "At least you've finally grown something resembling a spine. Spiney stick-in-the-mud." She choked out a bitter laugh. "Look at you. Engineering master plans. Setting things on fire—when you mean to, even. And you can finally walk in heels without falling down. You've even managed to nab yourself an extremely talented lover."

As I opened my mouth to ask how, exactly, she knew about the talented part, she said, "I have excellent hearing, Evie. You're very *vocal* when you're having a good time."

My face flushed.

"And speaking of Nate," she continued, "why don't

you check your phone for the five-trillionth time? See if there are any pretty new pictures of him and Maisy."

I flushed even harder. She still knew how to read me like no one else.

"Sounds like I'm actually doing well, then," I said, choosing to ignore that last bit. "Make up your mind: do you want me to be the best Aveda Jupiter I can be, or a really shitty Aveda Jupiter who attracts nothing but bad press? Because neither version seems to make you happy."

Aveda set her glass on the bar and frowned at it, as if she wished it would magically refill itself. "Are you going to be able to go back, Evie? Back to being your dull-ass self, with no fans and no flashy outfits and no freakishly loud sex?"

"It's not that loud," I muttered. And then, without meaning to, I glanced at my phone again. Nothing. Apparently Maisy was too busy shoving fruit in Nate's mouth to do anything evil.

"Whatever." Aveda poured herself another drink. "Now that you've had a taste, you won't be able to conceive of a world where you're not queen bee star of some dumb karaoke contest."

I felt my chest tighten, constrict. No matter what I did, she always found *something* to complain about. I was sick of it. I didn't need to deal with her bullshit on top of worrying about whatever Maisy was pulling next door. And what she might pull at the karaoke contest. As if on cue, my phone finally buzzed and a text from Lucy popped up onscreen: *Nothing evil, love. But definitely disgusting.*

Attached was a picture of Maisy scooting out of her chair just far enough to drape herself over Nate's lap. My hand tightened around the phone. She was *in his lap.*

Harsh pinpricks of anger plucked at my skin. I didn't know if they were inspired by Maisy or Aveda or both. I hopped to my feet and started pacing in a furious circle.

I felt the telltale warmth in my palm, but I kept it clenched at my side.

You don't get out unless I say so, I thought at the fireball. *Not anymore.*

"All this stuff you're describing, Aveda—I don't want it," I insisted.

She let out a horsey snort of laughter. "Of course not. Typical fucking Evie." She widened her eyes and brought a fluttery hand to her chest. "No, Annie, I don't want to be sophomore class president," she bleated in a high-pitched voice that was apparently supposed to be me. "I have no idea how I won without so much as trying, when you spent months campaigning your ass off."

I tightened my fist. "Really? You're going there? I told you, Scott stuffed the ballot box. He thought it would be funny. I didn't want that, either."

"Ah." Her eyes flashed. "Scott." She screwed her face back into the faux-innocent look. "No, Annie, I don't like Scott. I don't know why he asked me to the prom and I don't know how we ended up having sex in a car like some teen movie cliché. Too bad you had to spend the night home all by yourself, crying your eyes out."

"Oh my God." I swallowed my scream of frustration. "That's not how it . . . how can you . . ." A revelation crept around the corner of my brain. "Did *you* like Scott?"

Something soft and painful flashed through her eyes, and then her face hardened again.

"You're the one everyone loves," I said, exasperated. "You're the fabulous one. The brave one. The one who gets up and sings 'Eternal Flame' in front of the entire school just for kicks. *You're* the superhero."

"And I have to work at it every second of my life," she snapped. "Meanwhile you pretend like you don't want anything, but you still manage to get *everything.* And by just sitting there, all prim and wallflower-like. Putting in no effort whatsoever." She glared at the bartop. "Yes, people love me. They worship me. But nobody *likes* me."

She wrapped a hand around her drink, gripping it so hard her knuckles turned white. "Lucy was supposed to be my friend. Remember? I kept saying how cool I thought she was when we first hired her? You didn't even care. So naturally, she liked you better."

"You're her boss, Aveda. She's not supposed to like you."

"That's not the point!" She pushed herself off the stool, clutching the end of the bar for stability, her glare turned up to maximum. "You get everything," she repeated. "How do I know you're not going to take this from me, too?"

"I don't want it," I growled.

"Why not?" She slammed her hand against the bar.

My fists were balled so tight, they felt like they were glued shut. I wanted to scream at her until my throat was hoarse. I wanted to tell her to fuck off and then abandon her there. I wanted to go next door and physically remove Maisy from Nate's lap. I wanted to—

Bzzzzzz!

My phone buzzed so loudly, we both jumped. I snatched it off the bar and saw another text from Lucy.

Mission completed. No signs of demon. All clear, headed home.

I read the words a few times then let out a long sigh. The anger drained from my body. I slumped into the seat next to Aveda.

"Because," I said, "I'm a mess."

There was a long pause. Aveda resettled herself on her stool and cocked her head at me, confused. "What?"

I poured my own glass of whiskey.

"Look," I said, trying to make my tone as matter-of-fact as possible, "I experienced two traumatic events in a relatively compressed period of time—my mom dying and the library thing—and then I repressed all my emotions for what I thought was forever." I fiddled with my glass, swirling the whiskey around. "And now that I've let all those emotions out for fire-creating purposes . . .

I'm a mess." I waved my phone at her. "I was just freaking out over a guy—a guy who's not even mine—cozying up to a demon princess. Not because she could do something evil to him. Because she's, like, getting to touch him. Which is the most idiotic, unheroic thing ever."

I paused and took a long drink, the alcohol burning down my throat.

"I can finally control my fire, but I'll never be able to control my feelings," I continued. "Even when I was repressing them, I wasn't really controlling them. They're big and irrational and they spiral like crazy. I don't have the Oprah-esque inner strength required to rein them in." I met her eyes. "Being a superhero like Aveda Jupiter requires more than just a fire power. It requires that type of strength. It requires someone like you. You may be self-absorbed and image-obsessed and prone to tantrum-throwing in private, but when there's heroing that needs to be done, you call on that strength and step up to the plate. You put on your game face and set your feelings to the side."

She was regarding me silently, thoughtfully. She was practically docile. It was weird.

"I can make all the fire I want, but I can't actually *be* you," I said. "There's always going to be a place where my strength—what there is of it—ends. Whenever I think about this whole karaoke thing, the fact that I'm voluntarily putting myself in the path of an evil demon princess, the fact that if I don't succeed, Maisy could take over the world and kill us all or at the very least turn us into demon hybrids . . ." My voice turned shaky. "I freeze. I'm paralyzed. I don't know how you do it every damn day." I took another drink. Then I repeated: "I'm a mess."

She studied me for a long moment. As if I was changing, morphing before her eyes. Finally becoming something other than that painfully shy five-year-old she'd saved all those years ago.

"Wow, Evie," she said. "That is monumentally fucked up."

I choked on my drink, a choke that morphed into a snort, and emerged as a strangled giggle. Aveda started to giggle, too, a burbly noise that conjured memories of the two of us stuffing our faces with french fries and obsessively recounting every moment from *The Heroic Trio*.

That image—those two dorky preteen girls—just made me laugh harder. Which made her laugh harder. And then we were both doubled over, clutching the bar for support. The giggles rose in my chest like hiccups, forcing their way out, relieving the tension in my chest. Tears streamed down my cheeks.

"Oh." I scraped the back of my hand over my eyes and attempted to sit up. Aveda clutched the bar for support as her breathing evened out.

"Of course I get scared," she said. "I don't know how you could think otherwise. Our demon friends are, as you so eloquently put it, 'vicious little motherfuckers.' And these new demons seem like they could be an even bigger threat."

I nodded, a bit of tension worming its way through my chest again. They *were* a bigger threat. My whole Maisy Takedown Plan suddenly seemed incredibly inadequate.

"I get my strength from thinking about what I'm protecting," Aveda continued. "Not in big, vague terms, like 'the world.' I think about the specific things I'd miss if the world suddenly weren't there. That gives me a goal. It makes me forget about my fear long enough to kick some ass."

"Specific things like the adoration of your fans? The perks of being the beloved daughter of San Francisco?"

"No. Though I have perhaps gotten caught up in that these past few years." She gave me a wry smile. "I'm thinking of things like french fries. *The Heroic Trio*." She touched my hand. "And for the record, I think you're wrong about your own strength. There are different kinds of strength and there are different ways to be a hero. What about the way you've taken care of Bea all this time? That's incredibly strong."

"Eh." I waved a hand. "Not exactly world-saving strong."

"I disagree." She gave me her patented imperious look. "You're incredibly compassionate, annoyingly persistent, and you've got the fucking fire all up in you, Evelyn. A demon princess is no match for that."

A surge of warmth ran through me and I couldn't help but laugh. "Thank you. But for the record: I'm giving that fire to you as soon as Scott can perfect the transfer. Even with all this inspirational talk, and even though I've learned a lot more about how the power works, I still don't want your job." I smiled at her and firmly brushed my tension to the side. If I fixated on the world-saving ramifications of the karaoke contest, I was going to explode. So I changed the subject.

"Hey, Annie," I said hesitantly. "What's this Scott thing? Did you like him? 'Cause I can tell you there's nothing between him and me. Nothing like that, anyway."

She chewed on her fingernails, staring off into space. "It was more than that. More than like." She looked into her drink, refusing to meet my eyes. "There was a time right after I became Aveda Jupiter. You were still at grad school and I didn't have HQ yet. I was trying to maximize my living space for my new superhero duties, so Scott came over one night to help me move some furniture around in my apartment—remember that disgusting little place on Church?" She smiled at the memory. "We'd had a lot of beer and he was trying to move an end table into the corner and I was like, 'Why would you do that? It's an *end* table, it goes on the *end* of something.' I tried to jostle it away from him and suddenly we were standing very close together. And he kissed me."

My jaw was nearly on the floor. I hastily shut my mouth.

"It was such a kiss." She smiled again. "Well. You must know what a good kisser he is, Evie. From prom night."

I bit my tongue.

"I had always wanted him so badly," she continued. "All through high school. Even before he got those muscles. And when he kissed me, it was like the culmination of every teenage fantasy I'd ever had. Like . . ."

"Like the scene in *The Heroic Trio* where the cute scientist and Invisible Girl talk about lilies? But it's really about their feelings for each other?"

"Yes!" She finally met my eyes. "Exactly like that."

I toyed with my empty glass. "I don't understand. Why aren't you guys together, then? What happened to your dreamy teen movie ending?"

She turned back to her drink. "When we finally broke apart, the way he looked at me . . . he was so earnest. So adoring. I was deliriously happy for one full minute. And then all I could think was, 'He looked at Evie that way, too. He looked at her that way *first*. And he only kissed me because she's not here.'"

She gnawed on her nails again. "I pushed him away and asked him what the hell he was thinking. I told him that I was Aveda Jupiter now, for God's sake. And Aveda Jupiter can't be seen with some low-rent surfer mage. Aveda Jupiter has an image to consider."

"Was that the first time you used the, ah, third person sentence construction?"

She gave me a tight smile. "I think it was. We got in a huge screaming match. I said some things, he said some things. The end result is we'd barely spoken until you forced us back together."

"Annie." I covered my hand with hers. "First of all, he never looked at me that way. The prom sex was bad. Really, really bad." I remembered then that I'd tried to tell her just how bad the sex had been the day after prom, but she'd been dismissive, saying things like "well, the first time is supposed to be less than perfect" and "I do hope you and Scott won't let this distraction interfere with our plans for my junior class president campaign" and that had been that. At the time I'd thought she was just being her usual competitive self. After all, I'd managed to lose my virginity before she had and she prided herself on doing everything first. Now I realized she'd been covering. She'd been *hurt*.

I thought back to Scott's reactions to Aveda, the way she seemed to get under his skin like no one else. The way he'd teased her mercilessly in junior high, always trying to get her attention. If I had learned anything these past two weeks, it was that sometimes the person who drove you the most crazy was also the person you secretly, desperately wanted to bone. "I think he still has feelings for you," I said. "Maybe if you guys talked—"

"It's too late. We missed our moment. Or rather, I fucked that moment up."

I squeezed her hand, not sure what to say.

"Well, then," I said. "Let's see if we can get some french fries up in this joint. And spam musubi. And definitely more drinks." I hopped down from my stool and set off to find Kevin.

"Lots more," she agreed. "That will also help distract you from your freaked-out feelings about the karaoke battle." She hesitated. "So the prom sex was really that bad, then? You're not just saying that to make me feel better?"

"Oh my God," I said. "The badness was epic."

CHAPTER TWENTY

AVEDA AND I stumbled home when the marine layer moved in, casting a sheen of gray sludge over everything. It looked like it was going to rain. The chill didn't invade our bones as it usually would, however, thanks to the warming glow of the alcohol we'd both consumed. Aveda was wobbly on her crutches, but I managed to sling her arm around my shoulder and drag her back to her room.

"That was fun," she murmured, as I flopped her into bed and tucked her under the covers. I smiled and made sure to prop her crutches where she could reach them.

I stumbled upstairs and teetered down the hall, swaying back and forth, my hand jutting out to steady myself against the wall. I stared at my hand, watching it blur in and out of focus.

Okay. So maybe I was a *leetle* bit drunk.

Go back to your room, I told myself sternly, using my best inner schoolmarm voice. I sounded like I was scolding Bea. *Go back to your room and pass out and . . . and . . .*

No. I shook my head, as if the stern, schoolmarmish Evie was standing in front of me, glaring through fussy librarian glasses. *No. Nonono.* I shook a defiant finger at Invisible Schoolmarm Evie. I had much betterer . . . *better* ideas. Better, funner, *sex* ideas that involved showing

Nate he didn't need to be going after any demon princess tail. No matter how cute and blond that tail might be. I pushed off from the wall and staggered down the hall to rap on his bedroom door.

Was this, like, a booty call? I hadn't made an actual call or anything. My call was right down the hall.

Ha! I thought. *Rhyming!*

I giggled out loud and clapped a hand over my mouth. Didn't want to be getting in trouble with Schoolmarm Evie.

Nate answered the door, confusion passing over his face as he scanned my swaying form. He was adorably disheveled: hair all messed up, glasses sliding down his nose. And wearing nothing but pristine black pajama pants.

I hazily realized I'd never encountered his pajamas. Our recreational time together was usually unencumbered by clothing. But *of course* his pajamas were black. I giggled again. Then clapped a hand over my mouth. Again.

"Oh!" I said, way too loudly. "Were you sleeping?"

"No." He opened the door wider so I could come in. "Are you drunk?"

Instead of stepping inside, I pitched forward, landing with both hands on his chest. Which was totally beautiful and totally naked. Totally ready for my better, funner SEX PLANS.

"I'm just a little tipsy." I held my thumb and forefinger a centimeter apart, indicating my level of tipsiness. "How was your meeting?"

"Awful." His mouth tipped up into an amused grin. He took me by the shoulders and guided me over to the bed. "Sit. I'll be right back."

What? Where was he going?! We hadn't done my SEX PLANS yet.

I sat on his bed. I'd never been in here. His room was spartan, bare. Not much in the way of decoration, unless you counted the clothes-drying rack in the corner, which contained a few carefully hung black T-shirts.

Ha! I thought. *Of course he line dries.*

I glanced down at the bed I was sitting on. Well, sort of . . . swaying on. It was a narrow twin with a plain gray cover and it was perfectly made. I poked a wobbly finger at one of the hospital corners.

The creak of the door announced Nate's return and I jumped, as if I'd been caught doing something illicit. He padded over to the bed and handed me a bowl of something. I squinted at it.

Oh! Lucky Charms. My favorite. And good, fortifying pre-SEX food.

"Eat this." He indicated the bowl. "Drink this." He set a glass of water on a rickety chair sitting next to his bed, which seemed to be serving as a makeshift nightstand. "And take this." He put a couple of Advils next to the glass.

I picked through the bowl, ferreting out the purple horseshoes and tossing them to the side. "Did you know these are called 'marbits'? Like, marshmallow bits. Lucky Charms has a patent on that."

Nate's eyes followed my horseshoe excavation. "Let me guess: you wrote a paper in grad school about it."

"Did not!" I jabbed him in the arm with my marbit-sticky finger. "Some things, I just know." I giggled at my obvious mental superiority and dug into the bowl.

Nate swept the purple bits into a wastebasket next to the bed and sat down beside me.

"And are the purple marbits dangerous in some fashion?" he asked.

"What? No. I just don't like them."

He grinned at me, now fully amused, and a tiny flutter bloomed in my chest. Maybe I could make him laugh. I *loooooved* making him laugh. It wasn't a gimme like it was with, say, Lucy. You had to work for that shit.

All lingering thoughts of the pictures of him and Maisy and my nerves about the Big Maisy Takedown Plan dropped out of my head. She didn't matter. All that mattered was this neat-as-a-pin room containing me and him and my attempts to make him laugh.

"They're all the same, though." He nodded at the marbits. "All equally terrible for you. Just with different food coloring."

I made the "wrong" buzzer sound through my mouthful of magical deliciousness and then he did laugh and it was the best thing ever. I drank in that deep, rumbly sound, giddy pride washing over me.

Then suddenly my head was too heavy and my eyes seemed like they were being dragged closed by invisible weights.

"Guuuuhhh." I set my empty bowl on the chair-nightstand and popped the Advil in my mouth. I listed to the side and managed to flop onto my back in the middle of the bed. My limbs felt like they were filled with warm sand.

"Mmm," I sighed, my eyes fluttering closed. *"Sex."*

He laughed again, and I felt the bedspread being maneuvered from its tucked-in position so he could pull it over me.

"Go to sleep," he said, brushing his lips against my cheek.

"Wait." I grabbed his arm. "Stay with me."

"You're right in the middle of the mattress. And taking up every available inch of space." I could hear the smile in his voice.

I scooted over, tugging at his arm. He allowed himself to be pulled into bed. I ran my fingertips over his gorgeous shoulders, tracing those mysterious threads of scar tissue. "When are you going to tell me about this?" I slurred. "Like, were you an international superspy with a penchant for bar brawls or did you just fall off your bike or something? 'Cause if someone hurt you, I will totally kick . . . their . . . ass . . ."

"Go to sleep," he repeated, mock sternly. He pulled me close, fitting my body against his. My head drooped onto his shoulder. As my breathing started to deepen, his clean, soapy scent settled around me like a blanket.

I drifted off, cradled in the warmth of him, my sugary breakfast treat soaking up the alcohol in my stomach.

And I thought, *Right now is perfect.*

I woke up with a headache. But thanks to Nate's Advil and cereal cocktail, it was a mild one.

"How do you feel?" Nate murmured. We were entwined on his narrow bed, both of us still half-asleep. The room was very warm and I could hear the pitter-pat of rain against the window. I sat up slowly, my sluggish brain kicking into gear.

"Not bad," I said. I suddenly felt self-conscious. "Um. Sorry for barging in on you last night."

"I don't mind." He gave me a half-smile. "Barge in any time." He surveyed our cramped formation. "I should probably get a bigger bed."

I smiled back, but my self-consciousness flared. I was still clad in yesterday's rumpled drinking ensemble. My skin felt sticky and I instinctively knew my hair was a mess.

I shifted and allowed my gaze to drift over to his chair-nightstand. My empty cereal bowl was still there, but now I noticed something sitting next to it. Something small and gray and familiar. "Is that one of the stones?" I asked.

"Yes." He plucked it from its spot and handed it to me. It was the You Need stone. Those two words stared back at me ominously. I wondered if Maisy had ever received this mysterious directive. "I wanted to show you this yesterday when Lucy and I returned to HQ, but you were otherwise occupied with Aveda. And then last night you were . . ." He smiled. " . . . not exactly coherent." He nodded at the stone. "Turn it over."

I did. And despite the uncomfortable warmth of the

room, my blood ran cold. The number, that creepy 3, was no longer there. It had been replaced by a 1. Somehow, this tiny shard from the Otherworld had changed. Possibly overnight.

"When did this happen?" I asked.

"I'm not sure. I only noticed it yesterday."

I ran my thumb over the stone's smooth surface. "You should show Scott. He can figure out if there's a magical explanation. Like if it's enchanted or something. And Lucy—she might be able to connect it to something we've seen in the field. And obviously Bea since she's been cataloging the stones."

"I plan to," he said. "But I wanted to see if you had any theories first. You always see things differently than I do; it makes for a balanced perspective."

"It does?" My voice somehow sounded both squeaky and raspy and my throat was dry. I needed water.

"Yes. I tend to see hard facts with no shading. You see nuance, how those facts might be affected by real life experiences, by people's impressions—in other words, a more human side. These two elements work very well together. *We* work well together." He smiled and I felt self-conscious again. What was wrong with me? I'd been gleefully naked with him countless times at this point. Yet now, fully clothed and discussing actual meaningful topics, I couldn't seem to get even a little bit comfortable. Maybe I was more hungover than I'd initially thought.

I forced myself to concentrate on the stone.

"One from three," I said. "We've speculated that this is a directive. And Bea theorized that Maisy had already created the three she needed to take over: herself, Stu, and Tommy. But say Maisy doesn't count herself in that number. She's the princess, the leader. And we still don't know her exact origin: maybe she's always been a demon. So maybe she's only created two hybrids. Which means . . ."

"She still needs one more," Nate said.

"And if the stone is counting down like this, which we've never seen a stone do before?" I looked at him for confirmation. He nodded. "Then that last one is probably important. When she gets that last one . . . that's when something really horrible happens." My headache pounded against my temples, no longer mild. "Maybe she's planning on getting this final person at the karaoke thing, turning them into a hybrid on the spot. That seems like a place where she could do it in as show-offy a manner as possible."

I curled my fingers around the stone. The tension I'd managed to brush to the side the day before returned with a vengeance, causing my chest to seize. I forced a breath out. Maisy was, in theory, more dangerous than anything I'd taken on yet. Whatever powers she possessed were likely to be way more impressive than the grabby claws of the Tommy demon or the cold fingers of Stu's disembodied hand. I could get seriously hurt. I could die, probably. Or if I fucked up, other people could die. I—

No. Stop. I bit my lip hard enough to draw blood and thought back to Aveda's words at the bar. *I get my strength from thinking about what I'm protecting. All the things I'd miss if the world suddenly weren't there.*

"Hey." Nate took the stone from me and set it back on the chair-nightstand. "What's wrong?"

"Nothing." I smiled weakly, but nausea spiraled through my stomach. "Wow, look at the time." I wasn't wearing a watch. "I should go. Bea wants to discuss the song list for my big karaoke debut. And you probably want to talk to everyone else about that, huh?" I gestured to the stone.

His hand slid under the covers to take mine. The room seemed to be growing warmer, and not in a sexy "it's gettin' hot in here" kind of way. More like an oppressive, walls closing in kind of way. And his bed was so narrow,

so small. It was impossible to get comfortable. The nausea settled in, taking up permanent residence in the pit
of my gut. I tried to follow Aveda's advice, to build
strength by thinking of things I'd miss.

Lucky Charms. Spam musubi. Lucy's high-pitched
giggle. Orgasms. Neon underwear. Bea's purple boots.
Nate . . . Nate's . . .

"It's six in the morning. No one else is awake yet,"
Nate said. He released my hand and wrapped an arm
around my waist. "And you look like you could use some
distraction." He leaned in and brushed his lips against
my collarbone. "Stay here. We'll have . . ." He lifted a
suggestive eyebrow. " . . . breakfast. And you can help
me shop for a new bed online."

I laughed, but it sounded false. "Not right now. Bea's
an early riser and I need to talk to her. And anyway, I
look disgusting." I gestured to my unkempt appearance.
My voice, like my laugh, sounded weird. Like it was
coming from someone else's body.

"I think you look perfect." He brushed a curl off my
face.

"Well, I feel disgusting," I countered, pulling away. I
awkwardly maneuvered myself out of bed by scooting
down to the foot of the mattress and hopping to the
floor.

"Wait." He stood and faced me. "Seriously. What's
wrong?"

"I told you: nothing." My voice was harsher than I intended. The nausea-anxiety mix was swirling around
like crazy.

"Are you acting strangely because you're worried
about the karaoke contest?" he asked. "Because you
don't have to go through with this Maisy thing. We can
come up with another plan."

I stiffened. Why was he bringing up Maisy? I mean, of
course I was thinking about her. I was getting ready to
battle her and the fate of the entire city hung in the bal-

ance and it was freaking me the fuck out. I idly wondered if she'd been trying to freak me out further by draping herself all over him yesterday. She knew he was Aveda Jupiter's "escort," that Aveda might have special mushy feelings for him . . .

Fuck it. I didn't want to think about any of this. I just wanted to go back to my own room.

"I'm not worried," I said, trying to project confidence. "I want to take her down."

He hesitated. "I've been thinking about it. And I'm not sure *I* want you to."

"Why not? Because you have such a deep, personal connection to Maisy Kane after your big meeting?"

"What?" He looked confused.

"Because it was so fun to sensuously eat strawberries off the perfectly manicured fingertips of a demon princess? Who, in case you've forgotten, is totally evil and totally our enemy?" I knew I sounded ridiculous, but I couldn't seem to stop the words from spilling out of my mouth. Why wouldn't he just let me leave?

"No, of course not. The whole experience could best be described as pure torture."

"Then how come you looked like you were having fun?"

"I was merely trying not to antagonize her. Why are you acting this way?"

"I'm not acting any way. I—"

"Are you jealous?"

"*Yes.*" The word shot out of my mouth before I could stop it. I forced myself to relax my shoulders. "Which is stupid since we have much bigger concerns right now. And anyway, we're not even together. Not like that."

He looked confused again. "Yes, we are."

"No. We're just using each other for orgasms. We agreed on that."

His face darkened. "And clearly things have changed."

"No, they haven't!"

"Evie—"

"We agreed! And we've never discussed changing that agreement."

"We spend every night together." His voice was low and controlled, but I could hear the anger percolating there. "We have intellectually stimulating conversations. I have observed details about you that are intimate but not sexual: the fact that you eat cereal at all hours of the day, for example. The evidence suggests that we—"

"Evidence?!" I gaped at him. "You can't use 'evidence' to determine dating status! That may work for tracking demons and tracking fire powers, but it doesn't work for this!"

"You're jealous because I was seen in close contact with another woman," he pressed. His eyes were locked on me with such intensity, I had to take a step back. "And I'm jealous of your longstanding friendship with Scott because he is another heterosexual male who—"

"Scott? How can you be jealous of Scott? We only slept together that one time—"

"You slept together?" His face darkened further. "Recently?"

"No, at prom, and . . . you know what, it doesn't matter!" I snapped. "None of this matters. This is just sex and you can't use some scientific algorithm to make it into something else!"

"It's already something else!" He grabbed my hand and pulled it to his chest. His heartbeat slammed against my palm. "And I don't understand why you're so deadset on insisting it's not. You are the most stubborn, pigheaded, infuriating—" He stopped, trying to get ahold of himself. He squeezed my hand and I felt his heartbeat speed up. "I don't want you to participate in the karaoke contest because I'm worried Maisy has something big planned for that night. That something terrible is going to happen to you." He squeezed my hand again and there were so many emotions swirling in the dark depths of his eyes, his gaze pierced me like a physical shock. "And I can't bear that thought, Evie. I *can't*."

His voice cracked on that last word. My heart smacked against my breastbone over and over and over again. I was still anxious and nauseous and I felt like I was going to throw up all over him and my brain was screaming at me to run, run, run.

"It doesn't matter what you can or can't bear," I said, trying to hold myself together. "You don't get to make this decision for me."

"I know that—"

"And anyway, I can't be distracted by all this . . . stuff right now." I wrenched my hand away. "I have to focus. If Maisy does have something planned for that night, I need to be ready. This stupid fucking karaoke battle is important."

"It *is* important. That's why we should talk about—"

"No, we shouldn't!" I stomped toward the door. "There's no 'we'!"

"Yes, there is!" he bellowed.

I stomped back to my bedroom and pushed open the door to find Bea arranging a series of large spreadsheets on an easel, all of them displaying rubrics of data on which karaoke songs should and should not find a place in my performance.

"There you are," she said, clapping her hands together. "So first we have to talk about how Maisy owns the boy band repertoire. Don't attempt anything in that wheel-house."

Anger was still churning through me. "Not even One Direction?" I said.

Her eyes nearly bugged out of her head. "Especially not One Direction. She'll annihilate you. The songs you choose matter. This isn't just about you taking down Maisy the Demon Princess. It's about *how* you take her down. That's the story that will spread far and wide and be documented on every form of social media. Aveda

Jupiter has been gaining an international audience ever since 'she' got a fire power. That means you're essentially performing on an international stage. You've got to have a sense of showmanship. And that means . . ." She trailed off, frowning. "Evie. Are you crying?"

"No," I said automatically. I lifted a hand to my face. It was wet. "Oh, shit."

I crossed the room and slumped onto my bed. "Keep talking. I seem to be having some kind of allergic reaction. Maybe it's the rain."

She left her spreadsheets behind and sat down next to me, then laid a tentative hand on my arm. "What's wrong?"

"Nothing," I said, my voice robotic. "Let's just keep going with this karaoke discussion."

"No."

"No?"

"You're my sister," she said. "We're supposed to talk about stuff, even when it's stuff you don't think is appropriate for my supposedly innocent ears."

I couldn't seem to process anything she was saying. My anger was dissipating, but I still felt sick. She jabbed me in the arm.

"Talk to meeeeeeeeee."

Any confessional resistance I might've once possessed had been thoroughly destroyed in the last two weeks. So that was all it took to get me to start yammering.

"I had a fight with Nate. But I was feeling weird before that. Kind of sick. Anxious. Possibly hungover." I scrubbed a hand across my face. "Maybe I need to throw up."

Bea chewed her lower lip. "What was the fight with Nate about?"

"Nothing. Everything. You're too young for me to talk about this."

She gave me her best Tanaka Glare. "I'll be seventeen in a few days. And don't forget about my birthday breakfast. I still haven't heard back from Dad, but you have no excuse for not being there. Now. Answer the question."

I bit my nail off. "It was about whether we're dating or just, um . . ."

"Having sex?"

I nodded. It sounded pretty dumb when you said it out loud like that.

"But you said you started feeling gross before that?" Her expression was so deadly serious, I had the deranged urge to laugh. Beatrice Tanaka, Feelings Detective. "What were you talking about when the weird feelings started?"

I thought about it. I'd woken up feeling a little gross. And despite my best efforts, I'd managed to totally freak out about the Big Maisy Takedown Plan. But my cocktail of bizarre emotions had taken off sometime between those two things. Right before he'd shown me the stone.

What on Earth had we been talking about?

"His bed," I said, replaying our inane conversation. "He wants to get a new bed. I have no idea why that would make me anxious."

Bea smiled smugly. "Sounds intimate."

"Talking about furniture while fully clothed? Doesn't seem as intimate as some of the other things we've done."

"Oh em gee, that is way more intimate!" She gave me a look. "Nate is a creature of extreme routine, Evie. Just look at his wardrobe. And he's talking about buying a whole new piece of furniture?"

"His bed is really small . . ."

"And he wants a bigger one so you can fit in it!" she crowed. "Like, fit in it all the time. That's what freaked you out. And that stoked the fires of your whole dating-slash-not dating fight." She clapped her hands on my shoulders and gave me an intense look. "I knew this would happen. He looks exactly like the guy in that movie you and Aveda used to watch."

"The scientist? In *The Heroic Trio*?"

"Yes."

He did. How had I never noticed it before?

Oh, God.

Bea's grip on my shoulders tightened. "So first, once you let your emotions come out after shoving them down for so long, your body figured out it was attracted to him. And now your body's taken the next step and figured out you *really* like him. For more than, like, sexual purposes. So your brain's trying to catch up. That disconnect probably made you react to him in a super irrational way."

I opened my mouth to respond, but she kept barreling on.

"And your anxiety over the Maisy battle is just adding to your stress on top of everything right now, all your emotional stuff. Which probably made your reaction even worse."

"How do you know I have anxiety about—"

"Well, of course you do. The whole demon princess situation is super scary and you're trying to deny it's scary rather than just accepting that it's okay to be freaked. That you *should* be freaked."

I slumped over, resting my forehead on my knees. I couldn't even begin to process the thought of Nate and I existing beyond our just orgasms arrangement.

Why couldn't I do that?

"Evie." I felt her hand on my back. A rush of warmth washed over me, making me feel momentarily soothed.

Unfortunately, then she started talking again.

"I know sometimes you think you can get rid of feelings you don't think you should be having," she said. "I know because I do it, too. Like with Mom. I still feel sad sometimes and it's like, why? I shouldn't still feel this sad. It's been almost five years. I should be moving on. But just because I think that in the most logical part of my brain space, it doesn't make me less sad."

My heart clenched. "Bea . . ."

"You're scared. If you let yourself care about someone too hard, they might go away. They might die or leave, like Mom and Dad." She rubbed my back and I felt that rush of warmth again. "That's not gonna stop you from caring, though. So you might as well give in."

I lifted my head and looked at her. She was still ultra-serious, trying to gauge my reaction. "You sound so smart," I blurted out.

She gave a long-suffering sigh. "I've always been brilliant. I got all As this semester without going to class once."

I should have scolded her, but curiosity got the better of me. "How?"

"I homeschooled myself." She grinned. "I called the school and pretended I was you and I informed them I have a very rare and contagious disorder and I needed to be quarantined all semester. They sent me my work, I sent it back. I aced all the tests and did extra credit in math. The end."

"A generic and extremely sudden 'disorder'? They bought that?"

She shrugged. "Schools have to be super-sensitive nowadays. Otherwise I could totes sue them for discrimination. Against my disorder."

"But . . . but . . ." I spluttered, not sure what to address first. "Don't you miss your friends?"

"I don't have any friends. Well, not at school. Not anymore." She looked down at the bedspread. "Aveda's my friend. And Lucy. Scott and Nate."

I scrutinized her. Even after everything that'd happened with Mom and Dad, I'd always assumed she'd stayed the same: popular and selfish, the tempestuous life of the party. But now I saw that she was nearly as lost as I was.

She was kind of a mess, too.

"Mom would be proud of you," I said. "Balancing

school with a real job and managing to kick ass at both? Pretty awesome."

A small smile crept over her face. "Does that mean I can still have my disorder next semester?"

"We'll see." I squeezed her hand and left the rest of my thought unspoken.

If there is another semester. If I manage to keep Maisy from totally destroying the city and all.

"For now, why don't we talk about that song list?" I said. "And my showmanship."

She hopped up and trotted over to her spreadsheets. "So are you gonna go for it with Nate? 'Cause you should. Let him buy the bigger bed."

That heady stew of feelings was still swirling around in my stomach. I wasn't sure of anything and I especially wasn't sure of that.

"I can't believe I just talked to you about all that." It was an artful dodge of her question, but it was also the truth: for the first time, we'd spoken as something other than enforcer and inmate. I'd acknowledged that she was growing up. And much as I hated to admit it, I was probably going to have to keep doing that.

"I can believe it," she said. "So. Ready to get started?" She gestured to her spreadsheets and looked at me hopefully, purple-streaked cap of hair listing to the side.

This, I realized, was what I'd miss if the world suddenly weren't there. Her looking at me like that, as if I was actually capable of fighting a demon princess and saving us all.

Maybe I was. In any case, I had to try.

I took a deep breath and felt something resembling strength take root in my veins.

"Okay," I said, "tell me more about the boy bands."

CHAPTER TWENTY-ONE

I'D LIKE TO be able to say I took the mature route. That I took Bea's words to heart and untangled my feelings and conveyed them to Nate in a calm, precise, thoroughly grown-up manner.

Instead, I avoided him for two whole days.

I claimed I was busy, I was stressed, I had to spend all my time on the seventy-three "essential vocal warmups" Bea had assigned. And when he looked back at me with a flicker of hurt in those dark eyes, I pretended I didn't notice and walked away.

Yeah, I took pretty much the most immature route available to me.

I didn't avoid all my actual feelings on the matter, though. I allowed my anxiety and uncertainty and fear to flourish, to build and swirl and roil, and then I channeled all of it into practice fireballs. So there was that.

Anyway, my future relationship status seemed like kind of a silly thing to be consumed by when I had more pressing concerns. City-saving, demon princess-busting concerns. We hadn't uncovered any new information about the stone with the mysterious changing number. It had stayed at 1, though, so at least Maisy hadn't gotten her claws into any new humans. Presumably. There was nothing left to do but kick her ass at karaoke.

"Remember: showmanship." Bea rubbed my shoul-

ders as she murmured last-minute words of encourage-
ment in my ear, as if I was a championship boxer and she
was my cigar-chomping coach. "Maisy has her fanbase,
but you're the city's hero, its beloved daughter. San
Franciscans feel like you belong to them."

"Don't I know it," I muttered, scanning The Gutter.

The place was packed. Bea's social media blasts appeared to have worked their magic, as had Maisy's increasingly contentious blog posts. "Aveda Jupiter clearly
needs to be taught a lesson in humility," she'd noted in
one of them. "Rest assured, I have been practicing my
karaoke shiznitz like a mofo."

The usual seniors were in attendance tonight, but Maisy's hipster crowd was also well represented, a tight cluster
of girls in cat-eye glasses and dudes wearing little straw
hats, all of them ironically drinking Pabst Blue Ribbon. I
caught a glimpse of Shasta's bangs in the mix. We still didn't
know how—or if—she was involved, but Lucy had vowed
to keep an eye on her during the proceedings. The hardcore Aveda junkies were crammed into another corner,
many of them wearing gigantic T-shirts emblazoned with
comic book logos. Giant Dude from the Whistles incident
was there, his braying laugh cutting through the crowd
noise. The usual tables and chairs had been cleared to the
side to create space for a makeshift dance floor.

My plan still had a key flaw I couldn't quite wrap my
brain around: Maisy was going to have to fully show her
demon side before I could retaliate in any way. Otherwise it'd just look like I was attacking a poor, helpless
human. I was going to have to goad her into showing all
her supernaturally evil colors. And I didn't know how,
exactly, to do that.

To counter Maisy's boy band extravaganza, Bea had
put together a slate of sassy lady empowerment themes.
The grand finale was an extended version of TLC's "No
Scrubs," a dizzying showstopper that required me to sing
all three parts, harmonize with myself, and sort of rap.

My crew was stationed all over the room, being various degrees of helpful. Lucy darted through the bar, checking for signs of demon activity. Nate and Scott stood a few feet away from me: heads bent, locked in conversation. Nate was gesticulating emphatically about something. I wondered if he was talking about me. The ache I didn't want to acknowledge swelled around my heart. I shoved it down hard.

Best to save all my emotions for the show.

"Hey." Aveda hobbled up next to me on her crutches. Because she had to be glamoured as something, she was glamoured as me. No one cared if Aveda's trouble-making assistant was injured, though I noticed a few of Maisy's fans giving her the stink-eye. The effect was disconcerting as she smiled my smile, then took my hand and gave it a squeeze. "You're gonna do great, okay?"

"Thank you." I'd ducked into her room more than a few times the past couple days when I'd been avoiding Nate. We'd talked about all manner of inconsequential things and pulled out our old yearbooks and taken a trip down Bad Hair Memory Lane. We'd even watched *The Heroic Trio* a couple times on her iPad. It had been nice.

As Aveda hobbled back to the bar area, another familiar figure approached.

"Hey, Rose!" Bea exclaimed. "We've got a Patsy Cline number queued up just for you."

"I can't wait," Rose said, giving her a slight smile. She nodded at me. "Aveda." Rose was dressed casually tonight. I'd never seen her in jeans before. But they were, of course, perfectly pressed, with a sharp crease running down the center.

"Bea tells me you might need backup tonight?" Rose said.

I frowned. No one outside of Team Aveda knew about our Maisy suspicions. "Backup?"

"In one of our email exchanges, Bea indicated—"

"Um, that we really should have some extra form of

security on-site since this is such a big deal event and all," Bea said. "Lucy's only one woman."

"Right." I nodded at Rose. "Thank you."

She nodded back then took note of the dimming lights. "Looks like we're about to start," she said.

The crowd noise faded to a burble as Kevin bounded onstage clutching a gold-sequined mic. "Welcome, welcome, welcome!" he crowed. "And can I just say it is fantastic to see so many karaoke enthusiasts in one place?"

He grinned as the crowd cheered. Tonight, his T-shirt proclaimed HAPANESE, BITCHES.

"We've got quite the battle for you tonight!" he continued, swaggering across the stage. "The city's preeminent lifestyle blogger . . ." He gestured to Maisy, who preened for her following. " . . . versus our favorite superhero!" He pointed at me and I popped a theatrical "ta-da!" pose. The crowd screamed its approval. (For me? For her? Maybe just for the idea that they were about to witness a nasty catfight as rendered through song.)

I had selected my own superhero getup: a short, sparkly dress, a matching sparkly hair clip, and a pair of strappy heels that laced up my legs. And I'd practiced walking in them, so I was prepared. Maisy, meanwhile, had gone for some kind of ironic eighties athlete statement, and was outfitted in running shorts, a tank top, and thick white knee socks with jaunty red stripes banding their way around her calves. I felt like those stripes were mocking me.

Kevin stopped in the middle of the stage and motioned for the crowd to hush.

"Before we get started," he said, "I've got a little surprise for these lovely ladies."

Um, surprise? Oh, no. Nonono. The surprise was supposed to be, when, exactly, Maisy was going to go full demon. I didn't think I could handle any surprises beyond that.

Kevin paused and planted a hand on his hip.

"As Karaoke Master," Kevin continued, "I decided to spice things up. Who wants to see a battle where the contestants merely alternate full songs, am I right? Boooooooring."

Oh, no, I thought. *Not boring at all, Kevin. In fact, that's exactly what I prepared for and I really wish you would do me a fucking solid and abide by the original rules of this contest. You know, so I can focus on the evil-fighting bit.*

"Instead, we're gonna do the songs random roulette style," he said. "Song stealing is allowed. Whoever owns the entire sequence and makes it her bitch wins."

Um, what?

I frantically scanned my brain, trying to remember if Lucy had said anything about song roulette. I looked at Bea, hoping she'd have answers. But her eyes were glued to the stage, wide and panicky. Even she didn't know what to make of this.

"A serious wrench in the master plan," Lucy said, sidling up next to me. "But never fear, darling: I sneaked a peek at the karaoke machine and all the songs are the ones you prepared for. They'll just be smashed into each other in random order. Listen for yours and you should be fine. And don't forget the running punch move I taught you!"

With that, she shoved me toward the stage. I stumbled and felt my wobbly legs carry me forward. Kevin placed a microphone in my sweaty hand.

And then it was just me and Maisy underneath the hot lights, staring out into the sea of faces before us. I could practically feel the malevolence—the sheer satisfaction of her impending victory—rolling off her. I clutched my microphone harder, willing its slippery plastic surface to stay glued to my hand.

What if my fire won't work?

What if I die?

What if everyone else dies?

I was jolted out of my thoughts when the first song blared out of the speakers. It was so loud, it sounded like a random collection of yelps and drumbeats and I was keenly aware of Maisy throwing me a challenging look, as if to say, "Better jump on this shit before I do." I realized the song was one of mine: "Single Ladies" by Beyoncé. Bea claimed the "oh-oh-ohs" punctuating the chorus made it an easy ham-it-up song, so I rallied, shoving the microphone into my face and singing as loudly as possible.

I vamped my way through the first verse, thrusting my hips all over the place while trying to keep an eye on Maisy for demon signs. She remained surprisingly docile: mic dangling carelessly from her hand, her expression unreadable. Maybe she was waiting for *her* song to throw out all the stops.

As I sang, a gaggle of girls pushed their way to the front, doing a drunk, enthusiastic version of Beyoncé's hand-flippy dance. Hey, crowd participation! Unexpected. And kind of cool. Maybe Bea's tutorial on showmanship was paying off.

"We are over the moon for Jupiter!" one of the girls screamed.

I flipped my hand back at her and kept singing, my gaze roaming the rest of the crowd. I zeroed in on Nate leaning against the bar, trying to suppress a highly amused grin. Emboldened by my dance circle of fangirls, I gave a particularly emphatic hip thrust. Unable to hold back any longer, he laughed. The dance circle let loose with a "WHOOOOOO" and a wave of triumph surged through me.

Then I was unceremoniously shoved to the side.

My knees buckled. I stumbled and nearly wiped out on the floor.

And there was Maisy, stomping a sneakered foot in front of me and bringing her microphone to her lips and giving me the smuggest look of all time ever. Her voice captured my last series of "oh-oh-ohs" as I focused on staying upright. The crowd went crazy. She'd stolen the song.

Shit. I'd made a crucial mistake. I'd gotten wrapped up in my showmanship and taken my eyes off her.

The Beyoncé song cut out mid-"oh," only to be replaced by the dulcet opening bars of the classic Backstreet Boys power ballad "I Want It That Way." Maisy's eyes narrowed in sultry fashion as she switched gears. The crowd went quiet, transfixed by her. She looked around the room, connecting with each of them in turn.

Wow, I thought. *Maisy is a total master of the starefuck. Better than Lucy, even.*

I tried to think of how I could provoke her, how I could rattle her and get her to show her true self. But I was distracted.

Because goddammit, her voice was stunning.

It soared over the audience, grabbing hold of notes and spinning them into new shapes, turning the song into a master class of vocal ornamentation.

She bent down on one knee and extended a hand to a cute guy at the edge of the stage sporting a raggedy Green Lantern T-shirt. She was charming *my* demographic. The cute guy ate it up, his eyes going all big as Maisy belted out the chorus, pulling him closer.

So karaoke was the one thing she didn't do ironically.

Meanwhile I was just standing there with my mouth hanging open, hoping her demon side would come out. Which it was showing absolutely no signs of doing.

Maybe we had been wrong. Maybe it wasn't her. Maybe I was about to lose this thing in every sense of the word.

I was so screwed.

I mean, even I was into Maisy's masterful rendition of the song. In fact, I was so mesmerized I didn't notice when the "oh-ohs" of my "Single Ladies" chorus blared back into being.

I needed to take the song back. Even if Maisy wasn't the demon we were looking for, I had to keep myself in the game for the sake of Aveda's fanbase. I stepped forward and raised the microphone and spat out the last few words of the chorus. A little off-key, but still loud enough to have an impact. I forced my voice to right itself, to be less shaky. My dance circle of fangirls cheered.

And suddenly Maisy was in front of me again, flinging a hand out. Her hand connected with my microphone. And my microphone smashed into my face. Bright lights exploded behind my eyeballs and pain stabbed through me.

"Oops!" she trilled. "Sorry. I was just so into my expressive hand gestures."

I instinctively clapped a hand over my face and spun around so my back was to the audience. Hot blood dribbled through my fingertips. *Fuck*.

I stumbled forward. Not sure where I was going, not sure of anything, really, except that blood was pouring through my fingers and splattering down the front of my sparkly dress and the audience sure as hell didn't want to see *that*.

The "oh-oh-ohs" soldiered on, pounding into my head with merciless force. They were loud, proud, and all I could hear. I tripped over something and fell to my knees, the skin of my bare legs scraping against the stage.

Pain. Blood. I felt like I was falling and falling and falling, a dizzying concerto of "oh-oh-oh" wrapping itself around me like a vice. My breathing was too harsh, too fast, too everything. My face wouldn't stop hurting. And the blood pouring out of my nose was thick and vicious and unstoppable.

Shit, shit, shit.

I was dimly aware of a pair of knee socks sidling up to me, their jaunty red stripes like two streaks of blood.

"Pro tip," the socks whispered. "Never turn your back to the audience. I'm giving you that bit of gosh-dang advice because we're friends and all." I turned more fully toward the socks, trying to see Maisy. But everything I could see seemed to be coated in blood.

Then something swooped down at me, something gray and pockmarked with giant claws and . . . and . . . fuck. Holy fuck. It was just like the hand that had leaped out of the piano at Nordstrom. And it was *Maisy's* hand.

She was the fucking demon princess.

The claw snatched the sparkly clip out of my hair.

And with that, the "oh-oh-ohs" cut out and the Backstreet Boys cut in and now all I could hear was Maisy's incredible voice seducing the crowd, their cheers nearly drowning out her amazing performance.

I fisted my hand at my side, trying desperately to call up my fireball. But my emotions were everywhere, scattered bits of feeling littering my psyche. Panic thrummed through me and I tried to grab on to that, tried to use it. But I couldn't. I couldn't focus.

I was losing. I'd already lost. I'd finally managed to completely and thoroughly tank Aveda Jupiter, superhero. She was gonna kill me. And then Maisy was gonna kill me. And then we were all gonna die.

I was visualizing a scenario wherein San Francisco was now ruled by Maisy Kane, Perky Demon Princess Overlord, and we were all forced to wear ironic knee socks, when all of a sudden, the Backstreet Boys cut out and a familiar strain of plinky piano notes cut in.

"Eternal Flame."

An avalanche of images smashed into my brain.

Aveda snatching the mic at that freshman year dance, singing with all her heart.

Lucy belting out the song while I stuffed my face with nachos.

Nate lifting me off the ground and carrying me into The Gutter closet and kissing me and kissing me and kissing me.

My breathing slowed, my mind focusing on each of

these memories in turn, a spark of something small and sure worming its way through the despair swirling through me.

Think of all the things you'd miss if the world suddenly weren't there.

That spark pushed me to my feet, forced me to turn and face the crowd. And finally I felt heat start to pool in my hand.

Maisy was standing near the front of the stage, looking most put out at having been cut off from her boy band serenade.

Why wasn't she singing? How the fuck did she not know The Bangles?

I noticed she was also holding her arm behind her back.

I was not fully conscious of everything my body was doing, but I felt myself rip a piece of fabric from my sparkly hem and bring it to my nose, sopping up the blood. The front of the dress was soaked with the stuff, as if I'd just suffered an explosive chest wound. The crowd regarded me with some strange brew of awe and horror. I must have looked like a monster movie victim.

No, I thought, my brain finally catching up to my body. *I'm the fucking monster. And you know what? That's awesome.*

I strode to the front of the stage, planting myself in the center, wiping the remaining blood from my nose. The heat in my hand was ratcheting upward. Any minute now. *Any minute.*

I turned to Maisy, hissing through gritted teeth so only she would hear me.

"You don't have to do . . . whatever you're going to do. If any part of you was ever human . . . I mean, look at all these people. They're innocent. Just come with me and—"

"*No,*" she growled.

She backed away from me. I sang directly to her. My voice was not stunning. But it was strong and sure and bolstered by the fact that I was standing there covered in blood. Out of the corner of my eye, I spotted my friends in the crowd, trying to shove their way to the front.

I put my entire soul into the song. The crowd gave over to awe and cheered.

I felt raw power coursing through me. My hand was getting hotter. It was almost time. If I could just get Maisy to reveal that damn arm.

My little dance circle resurrected itself on the side of the stage, going so far as to make punk-rock devil horns in my direction. During a power ballad.

Fine. If Maisy wasn't going to reveal the arm on her own, I was going to *make* her do it. I'd grab it with my fireballed hand and show the world. Then I'd try the singe-and-subdue-her thing. I focused on the adrenaline flowing through me. Then I dramatically extended my right hand and opened it, revealing my perfect fireball.

The crowd cheered. It sounded like one unified voice.

I thrust my hand at Maisy. She darted out of the way and glared at me.

"All right, Super-Bitch," she snarled. "Let's play."

She swung her arm in front of her and slashed at me, her claws ripping through my sparkly skirt.

The crowd screamed. I stepped toward her, my hand outstretched, trying to grab her. But she darted out of my way again, her giant claw waving menacingly in front of her.

"You think that piddly little flame thing is any match for me?" she screamed. "I'm a freakin' demon princess! My power will destroy you and everyone in this bar! Everyone in this gosh-dang *city*!"

She turned to the crowd and snarled, then extended her claw outward, slashing at the people next to the stage. Her claw expanded, growing on the spot and ballooning out from her body, giant-size talons threatening to take out an entire section of the crowd. The terrified screams of the crowd got louder and louder, so loud they nearly drowned out the music, so loud the floor seemed to shake, as if the entire bar was about to be upended, as if . . .

Wait a second.

The bar *was* shaking. The ground *was* shaking. *We were shaking.*

"Earthquake!" someone screamed.

The unified voice turned into a panicked mob, pushing and shoving at each other, not sure where to go. I threw myself in front of Maisy and thrust my hand at her again, determined to make contact, determined to get her to *stop*.

And then my fireball was arcing away from me, shooting up at the ceiling, a bright, beautiful phoenix of color and heat.

It *moved*.

The fireball smashed into the ceiling, sparks flying, and then careened downward. It landed directly on Maisy Kane. And just like the Tommy Demon, she combusted on the spot.

I looked out at the crowd, but they were still only paying attention to shoving their way toward the exit. The sprinklers chose that moment to activate. Water soaked the mob and they pushed each other harder.

I was rooted to the ground, eyes fixed on the spot where my fireball had just exploded.

How had it moved? How . . .

A raw rush of energy coursed through my veins. I was soaked to the bone and covered in blood and possibly about to be swallowed whole by the shaking earth.

I had just incinerated a demon princess.

And I felt fucking fantastic.

So I started singing again.

I sang louder and louder, and the crowd quieted, transfixed by my literally earth-shaking performance. They stopped shoving each other.

And just like that, the ground stilled. The sprinklers shut off just in time for my last verse. A confused, relieved murmur rippled through the crowd and the cheers started up again as I sang my way to the big finish, high note strong and clear and perfectly executed. As the crowd roared, my gaze swept the stage. There was nothing but one solitary knee sock and my sparkly hair clip.

I scooped up my clip and defiantly refastened it in my hair, then planted a hand on my blood-caked hip.

"Hey, everybody," I said. "Did you see the part where I . . ."

"Took out an evil demon masquerading as a gossip blogger who just tried to kill us all?!" bellowed Giant Dude. He held up his phone. "I recorded that shit."

The crowd unleashed a deafening cheer, hipsters and geeks and oldsters united at last. These were *my* people. This was *my* city. And I'd just taken it back.

I laughed, that sense of giddy power humming through me. I found Bea and Aveda and Scott in the crowd, arms thrown around each other, jumping up and down in exultation. I saw Lucy clap Rose on the back and flash me a thumbs-up. And then I saw Nate pushing his way to the front, trying to get to the stage. To me. His usual stoicism was replaced by a look of complete panic and his soaked T-shirt clung to his body, his muscular chest fully outlined in a way that bordered on indecent.

A fierce bolt of lust stoked my power rush even more.

I tossed the mic to the side and took a flying leap, launching myself at him. I smacked into him and his arms went around me, hoisting me off the ground. I could feel his heartbeat against my fingertips, pulsing faster as I locked my legs around his waist.

"You're okay," he gasped, as if reassuring himself. "You're okay."

I kissed him hard. My mouth was open and wet and wanting—no warm-up, no breathless anticipation. Just pure need, heightened by the blaze of adrenaline singing through my veins. He stiffened in surprise. But then his mouth opened to mine, his need matching my own.

The crowd screamed around us, a drunken mob fueled by a wild night that was being capped off by the beloved daughter of San Francisco dry-humping some dude on the dance floor.

How's that for showmanship?

CHAPTER TWENTY-TWO

"OW." I WINCED as Nate's fingertips brushed my swollen nose.

Me, Nate, Aveda, Bea, Lucy, and Scott were crammed into The Gutter's minuscule kitchen, breaking down the events of the last hour and doing our best to dry off using Kevin's supply of Gutter swag hoodies ("You will, of course, have to pay for those," he'd sniffed). The thin material of my dress had mostly aired out, but I could feel my damp hair starting to curl around my ears as my glamour faded. Snippets of sound wafted in from the party in the bar, drunken celebratory screams mixed in with the off-key stylings of patrons trying karaoke mash-ups.

I stole a glance at Nate. We'd reset to our awkward state as soon as the dance floor make-out moment passed. He was touching me very carefully as he examined my face for injuries. Very professional, very doctorly, his eyes keeping me at a distance.

"So how do we know Maisy's gone for good?" I said.

"She did go up in flames, love," Lucy pointed out. "That's not a bad sign. Particularly since Tommy and Stu don't seem to have returned after meeting a similar fate."

I shook my head. "I wish I could have convinced her to . . ."

"Talk it out?" Lucy said.

"Not try to kill everyone?" Scott said.

"Well, yeah," I said. "I figured that's what I'd do after the whole singe-and-subdue-her thing."

"Yeah, it really didn't seem like she was up for anything like that," Bea chimed in.

"She was about to do some serious damage to everyone here," said Aveda. "And she would have if you hadn't stopped her."

I nodded. The image of someone I thought I'd known for so long going up in flames was disconcerting, to say the least. But I guess I hadn't really *known* her. I'd thought she was a very grating, very human gossip blogger. Instead, she was apparently a demon princess bent on mass murder.

"Nothing broken," Nate said tersely. He stood, striding with purpose to the back of the kitchen.

"Can we talk about the part where you apparently figured out how to move that fire?" Scott said. "What happened?"

"I don't know." I flexed my fingers, examining my palm. "After so much trying, it happened when I wasn't trying at all. Something clicked."

"Whatever happened, it was an impressive display of badassery," said Aveda. "You should be out there enjoying the moment, Evie."

I noticed Scott giving her a look of surprise.

"Or *you* could enjoy it," I said. "Deglamour yourself and we'll switch outfits and you can go greet your adoring public."

"Oh em gee!" Bea shrieked, waving her phone around. "That public has increased, like, a thousandfold. That video of you incinerating Maisy has gone even more viral than the Yamato one. I can't keep track of all the new Facebook fans."

Nate strode back to us and handed me an ice pack and a bowl of something. I was suddenly starving. I set the pack to the side, focusing on the bowl. Lucky Charms.

"And Aveda's just been invited to be the official ribbon-cutter for San Francisco's Small Business Crawl," Bea continued, typing on her phone. "Total prestige position. I'd say tonight's a win."

I couldn't think of how to respond. Right after my karaoke triumph, I'd felt electrified. As if my fire and the sheer awesomeness of The Bangles had come together to totally defeat evil.

But what if Maisy came back? What if this wasn't the end? The thought cut through my sense of victory, making me jittery.

I stared into my bowl and absently swirled my index finger through the mix of processed sugars, searching for the purple bits. I saw pink, yellow, green. No purple.

No purple.

My head snapped up, my eyes going to Nate. He was leaning against the counter, avoiding my gaze.

"We can count tonight as a win for now," I said, setting the bowl to the side. "But we still don't know how Maisy—or this new breed of demon-human hybrid things she created—works. We can't let our guard down and we have to keep trying to learn more about them."

"Oh, speaking of!" Bea put the phone down and rummaged around in her pocket. "I brought the You Need stone with me to monitor that number. You know, see if it ticked down further." She frowned, reaching deeper into her pocket. "Except . . ." The color drained from her face. "It's not here. It must've fallen out of my pocket." She gave me a stricken look. "Evie, I'm so sorry. I—"

"It's okay," I said gently. I was bone-tired and in the grand scheme of things, losing a stone seemed fairly minor. "I'm not sure what more it would be able to tell us at this point. We can ask Kevin to keep an eye out for it." I turned to Aveda. "I'm going home. Do you want my dress?" I gestured to my blood-crusted finery. "You could be, you know . . . you. Just make sure you're sitting down so they don't notice your limp. And you'll need to hide your cast. Maybe you can sit behind the bar or something."

Her eyes drifted to the doorway, lingering on the snippets of party.

"No," she said. "I think I just want to hang out. Have a few drinks. With people. If, um, people want to stay." She threw Lucy and Bea and Scott a hopeful look. "I think Rose is still out there, too. You sure you don't want to stay, Evie? We could make you look like someone else if you don't want to be Aveda, either."

"Nah." I stretched. "You guys go on." I turned to Bea. "Soda. Nothing else."

Lucy tossed her keys to Nate. "Take my car. We'll cab it later."

"Oh. That's okay." A huge yawn escaped me. "I'll make it back myself. Nate can stay."

Nate met my eyes, no longer keeping me at a distance. The cramped space of the kitchen suddenly felt too warm.

"Does this look like something I'd enjoy?" he said, inclining his head toward the party. The sound of someone screeching "FREEBIRD!" rocketed its way through the kitchen door.

Point taken. Instead we'd have to settle for the most awkward car ride home ever.

The silence in the car was worse than I'd expected. It wasn't even a pure silence, since Lucy's rattletrap of a vehicle emitted a yowling hum as it carried us home. And it was raining again. Mist dotted the car windows, distorting the deserted late-night streets with a mosaic-like overlay.

"I can't believe I just won a karaoke contest," I blurted out. It was a dumb thing to say, but I wanted some other sound in the air, something to break the bubble of awkwardness. My fingers wrapped tightly around the cereal bowl in my lap. I'd decided to bring my Lucky Charms with me. I was still starving. Yet I couldn't bring myself to eat a single bite.

"I believe the word Bea used was 'shredded,'" Nate said. My head jerked up. I wasn't expecting him to respond. "I'm not sure what that means," he added.

"I don't understand, like, eighty percent of what she says," I said. "It's all about the context clues."

"So when she said she was 'scouting The Gutter for some major boy band bootie,' what does that mean?"

A helpless laugh burbled out of me. "I think it means I'm glad she's with responsible adults, at least one of whom is armed."

"You're not worried?"

"No." I answered without even thinking about it.

I searched myself, deep down. I wasn't worried. Two weeks ago the suggestion of Bea so much as glancing at a boy would've sent me into a panic spiral, would've sparked the need for me to lock her in her room or send her to a convent. Then again I couldn't imagine the me of two weeks ago winning a karaoke contest. Or entering a karaoke contest. Or tossing around fireballs and incinerating a demon princess. Exhilaration surged up inside me—that same unhinged feeling I'd had just hours earlier, when my fire took flight and Maisy exploded and the ground shook beneath my feet. I stared down into my bowl of cereal. *No purple.*

My gaze drifted over to Nate. His hands were precisely positioned at two and ten o'clock on the steering wheel, eyes focused on the rainy street.

"Stop the car." The words spilled out of my mouth like a string of fireworks, cutting through the car's persistent hum.

"What? Why?" His eyes didn't leave the road. "We're almost—"

"*Stop the car.*"

He looked around, trying to find a safe place amongst

the unwieldy sea of parked cars, then deftly moved us into a loading zone.

"What is it? Are you worried about Bea? I didn't mean to scare you, I was just—"

"Not Bea." I shook my head vehemently and stared out the front window. I gripped my cereal bowl, watching as the rain morphed from mist to storm, water smacking against the car, droplets expanding to splashes. Exhilaration was still whooshing through me, but it was pierced by fear. I had a sudden, vivid image of water bursting through the windshield, flooding the car and taking me under.

I squeezed my eyes shut, as if this would make me invisible.

"Nate, I . . . I want to try."

I let my little sentence sit there in the open air. Set free, his for the taking.

Instead, there was more silence.

"I'm going to need you to elaborate," he finally said, his tone gentle but confused.

"I want to try . . . us." I closed my eyes even tighter, until fireworks bloomed in front of my pupils. "You and me. Together. Actually together, not just for orgasm purposes. Like, maybe we would go on an actual date or something. Or maybe we'd never make it out the door, because . . . sex. Not that I only like you for sex. I like that you're good and decent and kind. That you always look surprised when you laugh, like you genuinely weren't expecting to laugh, ever. That you don't think I'm weird because I pick things out of my cereal. That you pick things out of my cereal for me. And *God*, I love your mouth. Okay, so that part is about sex, technically, but . . ." I took a mighty inhale, trying to motor through. "Aveda said the other day that I always pretend I don't want things. I know it's because I'm scared. And I know I've been saying that a lot lately, but that's what these last two weeks have taught me, bit by bit: that everything comes back to me being scared of actually living my life in any kind of full, meaningful way. Every time I've experienced a fully living life-type emotion in the past, it's led to something bad, whether that's torching the library or being consumed with grief because my parents are gone or loving Bea so much that it takes over my entire being and she resents me at every turn. But now I'm realizing that awesome stuff can come from big emotions, too, and shutting myself off from feelings altogether—shutting *down* like I did with you—is keeping me from the awesome stuff." I swallowed hard. "I'm tired of being scared and I'm tired of pretending I don't want things. There are things I want *so badly*. I want to not be scared of my fire-freak status. I want Bea to be okay. I want the world to be safe from vengeful demon princesses like Maisy. And I want you. I want *all* of you. I will totally help you shop for a new bed."

Tears gathered behind my squeezed-shut eyelids. I forced myself to open my eyes, to blink the tears back. To breathe deeply. I didn't know how to end this latest bout of emotional vomit, so I just said, "What do you think?"

Silence descended on us again, punctuated by the smack of rain against the windows. This silence seemed to stretch on forever, rebuilding our bubble of awkwardness. My tears loomed, ready to make a break for it.

When he finally spoke, his tone was not gentle or accepting or placating. It was completely exasperated.

"Evie . . ."

"No, it's okay," I interrupted, my eyes still trained forward. "I get it. I freaked out and pushed you away and then I'm, like, throwing myself on top of you on the dance floor and then I yelled at you to pull the car over for no good reason and . . . and . . . I know I drive you crazy. Like, all the time. I can hear it in your voice right now. I wouldn't want to date me either. I absolutely respect your decision. I—"

"Evie." His voice was even more exasperated now. I felt his hand curling around mine. "Will you look at me, please?"

I turned in my seat, reluctantly meeting his eyes. His gaze was sweet and earnest and so tender I thought my heart might split in two.

"It's not like you're the only one who's been acting irrationally," he said. "I'm sorry I was so strange and insistent about our dating status. I was out of my mind with worry about what might happen to you tonight and I don't have a lot of experience with these sorts of situations and as we've established, I'm not very good at putting words together. Using evidence to determine what was going on with us . . . it's the only way I know how to do things. I realize now I should have told you what I wanted and asked you how you felt. I was trying to make you hear me by not hearing *you*." He brushed my damp hair off my face. "But please hear this: I'm on board. I'm on board for everything. I don't know how you've managed to miss this, but I *like* you driving me crazy. You don't have to talk me into it. You don't have to dramatically chase me through the rain. I'm *here*. Now if you're done trying to convince me of something I'm already convinced of, I'm going to kiss you. Okay?"

"Okay," I said, my voice faint. "But I was definitely going to chase you through the—*mrph*."

His hands tangled in my hair as his mouth claimed mine. It was a continuation of our kiss on the dance floor. All fierce need with no warm-up.

I stretched over the space between our seats, trying to bring us just one iota closer. A craving sparked low in my belly, a craving for his hands all over me, shaping and stroking the spots he'd gotten to know so well.

No matter how much I contorted myself, I was still not

close enough, so I tossed my bowl of cereal into the backseat and clambered over the gap between us, hefting myself into his lap. My foot jutted out, smacking against the parking brake, and the car moved, rolling backward down the steep hill.

Nate's hand snaked around me, closing over the brake and yanking it upward just as we were about to smack into a parked car.

"Always an adventure with you," he murmured, his lips finding mine again.

I responded by pressing myself more firmly into him, sucking at his lower lip. I slid my hand down the front of his jeans and stroked, my fingers closing around the long, hard length of him. He shuddered against me.

"Evie," he gasped against my mouth. I felt a thrill at how out-of-control he already sounded. "Glove compartment," he choked out.

Um, what? "Glove compartment"? As dirty talk went, that wasn't particularly hot.

"Open the glove compartment," he managed.

I reached over and did as I was told and was rewarded with an avalanche of condoms. They slid onto the floor in one slithery, multicolored mass.

"What?" I squeaked. "Does Lucy just have piles of these things waiting for me everywhere?"

"I put those there." He was still breathing hard, but managed a smile. "After the day we almost . . . in the car . . ."

I looked at the mass of condoms still spilling onto the floor. "You were certainly ambitious."

His smile widened. "I was hopeful."

I couldn't help but smile back. I reached behind me and yanked down the zipper of my dress. It had a built-in bra, so I wasn't wearing anything underneath.

Nate's eyes went wide as the dress fell to my waist. He was giving me that look that made me melt, that look that had my heart rising in my throat and all available oxygen fleeing my lungs.

"Wow," I said teasingly, trying not to show him how much that look got to me. "We've been apart for all of two days and you're looking at me like you've never seen breasts before."

His eyes locked with mine. "You take my breath away. Every time."

He pulled me close and kissed me. Exhilaration sang through me again, but this time there was no fear.

I wasn't afraid of anything anymore.

CHAPTER TWENTY-THREE

I'M GOING TO *have nightmares.*

The thought swam through my brain before I passed out in bed with Nate wrapped around me.

Because even though I'd managed to incinerate a demon threat and fulfill the dubious bucket list item of having sex in a haphazardly parked car, I had been so overloaded with thoughts and feelings and terrifying images throughout the night, I figured it was inevitable that some of them would re-form in my subconscious as a fucked-up Voltron of a dream tableau.

But I'm ready for it, I thought as I drifted off. *I've conquered my fears and I can do anything. Bring it on, brain!*

I even made a rallying fist-pump in my sleep.

But there were no nightmares. My sleep was dreamless. When I woke up, I felt rested and happy and ready to have regular ol' bed sex with my newly minted boyfriend.

I rolled over to press myself against him in a suggestive manner. And then I noticed he was shaking.

I sat up. He was curled into a fetal position, facing away from me, and every part of him seemed to be thrashing. His limbs jerked and his fists clutched the sheets so hard, his knuckles turned white. He was completely silent, which made the whole thing more disconcerting. He looked like he was caught in a seizure.

I touched his shoulder.

No response. Only shaking.

Panic shot through me. Had Maisy come back? Was she doing this?

Was she going to take him away from me?

No, you idiot, I thought, forcing myself to think rationally. *He's having a nightmare. He saw a lot of fucked up shit last night, too.*

I gripped his shoulder more firmly. "Nate. Wake up."

More silence. More shaking.

I grasped both of his shoulders and leaned close to his ear. "Wake up *now*. Please."

Still nothing. My panic threatened to flare. I shoved it back and shook him as hard as I could.

"Wake up, dammit! Or I'll . . . I'll *burn your Nordstrom frequent shopper card*!"

His eyes flew open and his breath whooshed out in one violent gasp. His hands wrapped around my arms and he met my eyes with a stare so blank, I wondered if he recognized me.

I gently disentangled myself from his grasp and brought my hands to his face. His skin felt clammy. But at least he wasn't shaking anymore.

"You were having a nightmare," I said. I stroked my thumbs over his cheekbones. "At least I think that's what it was."

He wouldn't stop looking at me with that freaky expressionless gaze. Worry rose like bile in my throat.

"Nate?" I tried to make my voice soft, soothing. I didn't want him to hear any of that worry.

His eyes finally seemed to focus. "Yes," he said, his voice hoarse. "It was a nightmare." His arms went around me and he pulled me against his chest. His heartbeat thudded in my ear, amplified and way too fast.

"About last night?" I pressed.

"No." He sounded surprised. "I . . ."

He trailed off and paused for what seemed like an

eternity. Which made my panic rise again. I pulled out of his embrace and faced him.

"Because maybe Maisy did something to you that . . . that . . ." I couldn't bring myself to complete that thought.

"What? Oh, Evie—no. It's nothing like that." He tried to give me a half-smile, but his eyes looked haunted. "There's a specific kind of nightmare I have sometimes."

I nodded, but I was still studying him carefully, trying to discern what was wrong. He looked disoriented, like he wasn't fully inhabiting his body.

"The other night, you asked about my scars," he continued. He met my gaze. "And one of your theories was correct."

"The superspy thing?" I said, even though I knew that wasn't right.

"Someone hurt me." His tone was measured and steady. "A long time ago. And once in a while I have a dream where I remember."

He looked like he wanted to say more, but didn't know how.

"I want to tell you . . ." he began, but his voice cracked. His breathing sped up, becoming distorted and uneven. His eyes were full of old pain he didn't want to pass on to me.

I didn't say anything. I slid my arms around his neck and held him. Then I leaned back against the headboard and pulled him with me, positioning us so his head rested on my shoulder. I ran my fingers through his hair, feeling his staccato breath against my neck. Eventually, it started to even out and I felt like I could speak.

"You don't have to tell me everything right now," I said. "But it's like you said last night. About how you're here. I'm here, too. I know it took me a little longer to figure things out, but I'm not going anywhere."

His arm tightened around my waist and I felt his big body relax against me. And I realized I wasn't the only one scared of this "not just orgasms" thing between us.

"I'm not going anywhere," I repeated softly.

I kept stroking his hair, willing his breathing to even out further. Within this moment of quiet contemplation, I was surprised to feel a hot surge of anger—a sharp, bitter thing out of place in the current calm of the room.

How could anyone hurt this man, so sweet and gentle beneath his gruff exterior? If I ever found the person responsible for his pain, they'd better be prepared to either run really fast or suddenly develop magical abilities that rendered them fireproof.

My palm heated at the thought, anger pooling in my chest.

Calm down, I told the fire. *This isn't the time.*

I focused on holding him. Our breathing eventually matched up, and we had both started to drift back to sleep when the bedroom door flew open and Lucy barged in.

"Morning," she said, breezing over to the bed and plopping herself down next to me. "I was going to ask why the backseat of my car is covered in Lucky Charms and panties, but . . ." She gave us a pointed look. "I guess I have my answer."

"We can clean that up later," Nate muttered, rubbing sleep from his eyes.

"This came for you, Evie." Lucy tossed a padded manila envelope in my lap. "Fan mail, perhaps? From someone who enjoyed your ragey pictures on Maisy's blog?"

I rolled my eyes at her and glanced at the postmark. Peru.

"Now, about my backseat," Lucy said.

I tuned out while she and Nate discussed the most effective car upholstery cleaning methods and slit the envelope open. It contained two plane tickets and a folded letter. And as I read the letter, the anger I'd banished moments earlier rose up again.

Evelyn and Beatrice: I received Beatrice's email regarding her birthday celebration and must send my regrets as

*I am about to embark on Chakra Balance Step #5 in my
training at Yogini Lara's Mind-Body-Spirit Wellness Retreat. I do, however, wish to reconnect with both of you on
a higher plane of spiritual awareness. Yogini Lara says
this is crucial to my inner foundation becoming whole
again. Enclosed, please find two plane tickets to Peru (the
current locale of our retreat space) as well as a birthday
present for Beatrice. Downward Dog be with you,*

Dad

I stared at the plane tickets, then back at the letter. It
was the most words we'd gotten from him since he left.

"Birthday present?" I muttered. I tipped the envelope
upside down and a flimsy bracelet made of pink plastic
hearts tumbled out. The rage that had been percolating
in my chest blossomed. "Christ, Dad," I murmured.
"Bea's not a little kid. And she hates pink."

I clenched my hands, soothing the fire, telling it to stay
put. It was just so *him*. Thinking he could fix something
with a plane ticket and a shitty birthday present. And
thinking about it in terms of how it helped his "spiritual
awareness" rather than how it might heal us.

What would happen if we actually went to him? Bea
would love the fact that he'd sent her a birthday present
at all, that he'd remembered the tiniest detail about her
life. But I could see, all too clearly, what would happen
next. Once we joined him, Dad would proceed to get
wrapped up in the Yogini Lara-ness of it all and Bea
would be neglected, ignored. And eventually, crushed.

I couldn't let that happen. She had come so far, she
was doing so well . . .

And honestly, so was I.

I swept the envelope and its contents into the wastebasket next to my bed.

"Nothing important?" Nate asked. His hand slid under the covers to take mine.

"No," I said, managing a quick smile. "Why don't we
get dressed and clean up Lucy's car?"

"Evie!" Now Aveda was barging in with Scott trailing behind her. "I have something very important to show you!" she crowed.

Really, I was going to have to think about installing some kind of industrial-strength lock on my bedroom door. At least Nate and I were both sort of clothed—him in boxers, me in his shirt again.

Aveda's hair was frizzy and tangled, her eyes bright with glee. And she was standing upright with no assistance.

"Where are your crutches?" I asked. "And your cast?"

"Never mind that. I want you to watch the hell out of this."

She raised her hand and aimed it at the empty water glass on my nightstand. I instinctively reached over to get it for her. But there was no need.

The glass flew across the room and smashed into the wall.

"What . . ." I sat up straight, my eyes blinking rapidly. "Have you been practicing or something?" I exchanged a bewildered look with Nate and Lucy.

"No." She beamed, flexing her fingers. "It just kind of happened. Reached for my toothbrush this morning and it sailed across the sink and snapped into my hand. And I can do multiple objects, too!" She lifted her hand again and the mess of glass came to life, rising from the ground in a sparkling field of jagged edges and light.

"Wow." I flinched. "Can you put that down, please?"

"Spoilsport." She dropped her hand, allowing the glass to cascade back to the floor.

"Did Scott figure out some kind of power-enhancing spell?" I said, grasping for an explanation.

"No." Aveda stamped her foot. "Come on, people. Use your borderline-competent powers of deduction."

"We just woke up," Nate said. "Please enlighten us."

"Last night's earthquake," Aveda said. "Remember how Evie was suddenly able to throw her fireballs? How she'd been trying for days and they'd stayed all stuck to her hand and then right in time for the big karaoke finale, right when the earthquake happened . . . *bam*." Aveda mimed throwing a fireball at the ceiling. "She did it. That's a whole new dimension of control for her. And my telekinesis is way stronger. We've both leveled up."

I opened my mouth to protest then realized that wasn't a bad explanation.

"Your powers aren't connected to natural phenomena," Nate said.

"But they are connected to unnatural phenomena," I said, working it out. "That first demon portal opening up all those years ago caused an earthquake. Maybe something like that happened again. Maybe defeating Maisy triggered it."

"Another portal?" Lucy said. "Does that mean we have more humanoid demon corpses to contend with? Or worse, humanoid demons?"

"I checked in with Bea. She said Rose's team is scoping out the area where the earthquake was centered," Aveda said. "They haven't found anything. No corpses, no portals. No reports of demon activity since Evie busted Maisy's ass. But they're keeping an eye on things and will be in touch with us."

"Rose is up and about after staying out so late with us at The Gutter last night?" Lucy mused. "Impressive."

"I wouldn't have pegged her for it, but that girl has quite the arsenal of dirty jokes," Aveda said. "Especially after you get some bourbon in her."

"Okay," I said. "So this level up business may be due to another portal, but we're not sure why. And there's no physical evidence of said portal. Sounds like this requires . . ."

"Further scientific research?" Nate asked.

"Yes." I smiled at him.

"Gross." Aveda made an exaggerated retching sound.

"You two need to cut it out with that cutesy stuff before you thoroughly ensicken the entire team."

I rolled my eyes. "You're the one who barged into my bedroom. Plus, 'ensicken'? That's not even a word."

"Look it up." She stuck her tongue out at me. "Your picture is next to the Wikipedia entry."

I grinned at her. It was nice having some of our junior high-era banter back. With the added twist that I was now unwilling to let her walk all over me.

"What about Scott?" Lucy piped up. "Did he get a level up too?"

"Yup." Scott leaned against the doorframe. "As soon as Annie discovered this new wrinkle in her power, I decided to test mine. Notice anything different about her ankle?" Aveda twisted her foot around to demonstrate.

"You're healed," I realized. "That's why you don't have your crutches."

"It seems I can now do higher-level spells," Scott said. "I'm still working out what all I can do, but the first thing I tried was a healing spell. All I had to do was touch her ankle and—"

"And it's fixed!" Aveda exclaimed, rocking back on her heels. "So obviously I can return now. No more hobbling around on the sidelines."

She looked at me hopefully, as if seeking permission. Or at the very least, advice. It threw me, because it was so unlike something the uninjured version of Aveda Jupiter would do. Maybe the past weeks had changed her as much as they'd changed me.

"I mean, your ass looks good in leather pants, Evie. But not as good as mine."

Okay, so maybe she hadn't changed *too* much. But she gave me a small, teasing smile to soften her words.

"Nate will need to do a full medical exam to make sure you're fully recovered," I said. "And Lucy will have to put you through some basic training. Why don't you take over at that Small Business Crawl thing Bea mentioned last night? That'll give you a week to prep."

"Okay." Her head bobbed eagerly.

Scott stepped forward. "There's also the question of . . ." He hesitated.

"Of what?" Lucy asked.

"The power transfer spell." He looked from me to Aveda then back again. "With this power level up, I should be able to do it now, no problem."

No. The response popped into my head, unbidden.

Before I could say anything, Aveda spoke up.

"Now that my power's awesome, I don't need the fire," she said. "We can spin the telekinesis as an improvement. Fire can be kind of, I don't know, destructive? Makes people uncomfortable."

I resisted the urge to disagree with her. The enthusiastic response from the karaoke crowd last night seemed to indicate otherwise.

Then again, why should I disagree with her? Thanks to this new development, I was getting everything I wanted. My days of fake superheroing were about to come to a close, I could finally control my fire, and I had a really hot boyfriend whose fingertips were now trailing suggestively down my back.

And yet, there was no sweet relief flooding through me. No sensation of a weight being lifted from my soul. I felt tense and twitchy and like I had something else to say, but couldn't quite say it.

Maybe I was just reeling from the slew of new developments in the last twenty-four hours. Or hell, from the last two weeks. I'd been through so much: emotionally, physically, supernaturally. I'd fought hard, I'd pushed through my fear. And now I'd finally arrived at my goal. It'd been such a hurricane of events and I was still processing and said goal didn't feel real yet. It'd probably be weird if I *wasn't* experiencing a little twitchiness.

"Sounds like a plan," I said. "Now why don't we take

this party out of my room and downstairs to Bea's birth-day breakfast?"

I smiled at everyone.

But that twitchy feeling stayed with me for the rest of the day.

From the official website of Demon City Tours:

To the Potential Guests of Demon City Tours

We are doing our best to accommodate all requests, but please note that our tours are booked until further notice. To get on the waiting list, fill out the contact form below with your name, email, and the number of guests in your party and someone will get back to you. Thank you for your patience and understanding!

To respond to our newest frequently asked questions:

1. Yes, we have added the Yamato Theater and The Gutter to our list of stops.

2. No, we cannot guarantee a viewing and/or demonstration of Aveda Jupiter's fire power. We also can still not guarantee an appearance by Ms. Jupiter herself.

Most Recent Reviews of Demon City Tours

"This isn't really a review since I couldn't even get a spot on the tour for my upcoming San Francisco vacation. If you ask me, Demon City Tours needs to add more staff and vehicles. Clearly, everyone wants to see the new, improved, and super-fiery Aveda Jupiter in action! Aveda, if you're reading this: I love you! I may be #263 on the waiting list, but I'm definitely your #1 fan!"

—Jenn F., Timberlake, Ohio

CHAPTER TWENTY-FOUR

"YOU'RE SURE IT'S not too much?" Aveda twirled in front of me, the sequins accentuating her body sparkling in the morning light. She was debuting a new outfit, a glittery bodysuit thing that made her look like a mermaid going to a rave. Her hair was twisted into an elaborate nest of braids on top of her head and a trail of stars painted on her left cheekbone completed the ensemble. Bea had put together the entire look based on her own algorithm combining social media stats with the latest fashion trends.

"It's not too much." I squeezed her hand. "You look fantastic."

And she did. Glowing and gorgeous. San Francisco's perfect daughter.

It had been a week since we'd gotten our power level up, and the real Aveda Jupiter was about to return. Nate and I were with her at the starting point of the Small Business Crawl, which just happened to be Pussy Queen, Shasta's snooty underwear store. I noticed Shasta had invested in a garish new Pussy Queen sign featuring the slogan "a fine lingerie shoppe." If I were about to go on as Aveda Jupiter, I'd probably accidentally blurt out that adding extra letters to words in order to make them appear classy was really fucking stupid.

But I wasn't about to go on. Aveda was.

The past week had been quiet. No new portals had opened up. I wondered if this was a new status quo; if, in light of the destruction of their princess, the demons of the Otherworld would withdraw from San Francisco altogether. My pessimistic side told me that was way too easy.

Still, I'd allowed myself to relax a little. As my fabulous Aveda Jupiter lifestyle got farther and farther away from me, I wondered what it would be like to settle into a normal routine. Especially now that I didn't have to worry about burning down any more buildings.

I had to admit: when I thought about fully embracing normalcy, I felt a little twinge of discontent. It was that same twinge I'd experienced when Aveda had declared her return to superherodom, and I couldn't quite figure out what it meant. I knew I didn't actually want to *be* her. The sheer pageantry of her existence was definitely not my speed. And I'd always wanted to be normal. So what was wrong with me?

Aveda squeezed my hand a little too hard, snapping me out of my thoughts. She hopped from foot to foot, her face apprehensive. We were positioned off to the side of the store, Nate standing in front of Aveda to shield her from view while Lucy threaded her way through the crowd, checking for security risks. Shasta stood under her hideous new sign, her red-lipsticked mouth stretched into a grin. She was clad in a blue polka-dot fifties-style dress, the skirt swishing back and forth as she moved. I wondered how she was coping without Maisy. After the Big Maisy Takedown, Rose brought Shasta in for questioning. She'd claimed not to know anything about Maisy's powers, that she'd thought Maisy was only trying to rule the city in a figurative sense. She'd even offered up her DNA, which had tested all human.

Still, she'd lost a best friend who'd given her a sort of coolness by association thing. That had to hurt.

"Welcome, everyone!" she screamed, her smile widening even further.

"Remember," I said to Aveda, "you don't have to put on any power displays today. Just be yourself."

We'd decided to hold off on telling the public about the change in Aveda's power until there was an organic opportunity for her to use telekinesis. Then Bea would send out a press release about how the fire had been replaced with something even better.

Well. Something different. Not necessarily *better*.

Aveda lifted a hand to her mouth then quickly lowered it before she could bite her nails. "What if I've forgotten how to talk in front of people?"

"Never. And if you freeze up, just steal a trick from that horrible kiddie beauty pageant show you can't stop watching. It's not too late for you to get a spray tan."

"Glitz pageants are serious business, Evie," she sniffed, her voice finally taking on its usual imperious cast. "I will have you know . . . oh. You're making fun of me, aren't you?"

"A little bit." I gave her a push. "Now get up there. I think this is your cue . . ."

"And here she is!" bellowed Shasta. "Our honored guest and ribbon cutter for the Small Business Crawl: Aveda Jupiter!"

Aveda glided up to the store entrance, waving to the crowd with both hands. They ate it up, camera-phones flashing as they took in the glitter of her costume, the brightness of her smile, the sheer scope of the hair sculpture sitting on top of her head.

Then she tripped over an uneven bit of pavement.

"Oh, shit!" I leapt forward as she stumbled, her palms nearly planting on the ground before she clumsily righted herself.

"She's okay," Nate murmured.

"Aveda!" Shasta exclaimed, her mouth shaping itself

into a look of worry. She wasn't as good at the whole fake concern thing as Maisy was. "Are you all right?"

"I'm perfect!" Aveda flashed her dazzling smile and brushed aside a strand of hair that had escaped from her nest of braids.

"Jeez," I said to Nate. "Now that I've actually walked in those shoes, watching her do it is way more stressful."

"I don't know if you noticed, but I got a new sign for my shop," Shasta said as Aveda joined her next to the store entrance.

"Lovely!" Aveda said.

"I wanted to have something extra-special for your appearance," Shasta continued. "And we all know how much you adore borderline tacky displays of glitz." She gave Aveda's outfit a once-over. "Well. Maybe not so borderline."

"That I do," Aveda said without missing a beat. "Though for the record, I would like to note that Aveda Jupiter is not keen on adding extra letters to words just for the heck of it." She gestured to Shasta's sign. "Proper spelling is very important."

That got a big laugh and a few "hell, yeahs" from the crowd.

"Wow," Nate said. "That was actually kind of honest? Unrehearsed? Like something she just blurted out. She may be taking a page from your book."

"I doubt that," I said. "Unless she's also planning on doing something horrifically embarrassing."

"I am fairly certain only you can pull off 'horrifically embarrassing.'"

"From now on, I'm only going to embarrass myself in private."

He slipped his arms around my waist from behind, pulling me against him. "I like the sound of that."

I rolled my eyes. But I was smiling.

"Now," said Aveda, "where is this ribbon I'm supposed to be cutting?"

"Oh, uh . . ." Shasta's eyes darted back and forth. "There's no physical ribbon."

Aveda cocked an eyebrow. "What does that mean?"

"We're trying to reduce waste," Shasta said. "So the ribbon is a metaphorical one. But before we begin, would you like to say a few words? You've been through so much lately! How are you holding up?" She gave Aveda and the crowd a big grin. I noticed there was lipstick on her teeth.

"Time for Aveda to slip in the 'protecting San Francisco is my duty, my love, and my life' bit," I murmured to Nate. "Remind everyone that Aveda Jupiter always holds up just fine."

Aveda opened her mouth, then hesitated. "You know, Shasta," she said slowly. "You're right. It has been a rather challenging couple of weeks."

I blinked in disbelief. Was she actually admitting to something resembling weakness? In public?

Aveda looked out into the crowd, her gaze finally resting on me. "I can honestly say I couldn't have gotten through it without my incredibly patient team. Particularly my best friend, Evie Tanaka. Not to mention Rose Rorick and her hardworking demon cleanup crew. I'm lucky to have such dedicated compatriots in the ongoing fight to keep San Francisco safe."

I couldn't help but grin back at Aveda, warmth surging through me.

"Well. That's different," I said.

I leaned back against Nate, studying Aveda. There was definitely a surreal quality to watching her in public after embodying her. Like I was watching the sparkly glitz pageant version of myself.

But the real me was in the crowd, drinking in the warmth of the sun and Nate's arms around me.

I thought again about the whole being normal thing.

Here I was, spending a nice day with my boyfriend. I'd just given my friend a decent pep talk. And my little sister was at home making nerdy spreadsheets instead of trying to drunkenly take over a karaoke bar.

These were all normal things. Nice, normal things.

And, you know, I could be normal without being mundane. I'd finally accepted my own supernaturalness; had embraced it, even. I could still use my fire, but for everyday-type stuff. Like lighting candles. Going camping. Heating up Hot Pockets when the microwave was broken. The possibilities were endless! The *normal* possibilities! The—

My giddy train of thought was interrupted when I caught a flash of something familiar out of the corner of my eye. I craned my neck, scanning the crowd. It was probably nothing.

But just for a moment, I was sure I'd seen Stu Singh's signature fedora.

Eh. Well. Lots of people wore fedoras. Especially in San Francisco.

"Everything okay?" Nate asked.

"Yup." I allowed my head to drop back against his chest. "I think I'm just tired—whoa."

My head swiveled to the other side and I broke away from him, standing on my toes, trying to see through the crowd.

This time I'd seen a flash of gold. A daisy. Just like the one Maisy had worn during our mall confrontation.

Nate frowned. "Are you sure you're okay?"

"Yes. Sorry. I'm going to get some water."

I darted off before he could protest, pushing my way through the crowd, trying to spot the elusive bit of gold. That Maisy gold.

I was so intent on zoning in on any flash of yellow I could find, I nearly ran into Lucy.

"Hey!" She grabbed my shoulders, steadying me. "What's wrong?"

"I thought I saw Maisy. I know that sounds nuts," I continued, as her eyes widened.

"Let's not discount that theory," Lucy said. "Who knows what evil demon princesses are capable of?"

We started elbowing our way through the swarm of people. I kept almost pouncing on people with random hair adornments, some of which were not even in the flower family. After I nearly tackled a woman wearing a very un-daisy-like beret, I stopped moving and turned to Lucy.

"I think I imagined—"

"You're looking for me."

A watery voice echoed in my ear.

I turned and my heart leapt into my throat.

It was Maisy. Cowering at the edge of the crowd, her back turned to all the Small Business Crawl attendees, so they couldn't see how . . . different she looked. Her skin was gray and flaky and her eyes were sunken and underlined with bruise-like smudges. Her mouth sat at a crooked angle, as if it had been pasted onto her face. And her arms were rotting and desiccated and topped off with evil-looking claws. A wilted daisy drooped over her ear.

"Maisy," I whispered. I reached toward her and she winced.

"Don't do that," she said in her awful, inhuman voice. *"Don't say my name—"*

BOOM!

Suddenly the world went black and I was falling into an endless pit of nothingness and I couldn't see anything, I couldn't see, I—

SMACK.

The world came back into focus as I landed on concrete, jarring my entire bone structure. I blinked once, twice.

I was still in front of Pussy Queen. But now I was surrounded by a bubble-like dome similar to the one that had blocked me off while the disembodied hand tried to strangle me at the mall.

A force field, I realized. *It's another fucking force field.*

Outside the bubble dome, people were milling about as if nothing had changed, as if they couldn't see us.

I looked around frantically. Nate was lying a few feet away from me, shocked but conscious. Aveda was sprawled next to him, her eyes blinking. Lucy was passed out behind me, but still breathing. Maisy—or whatever thing Maisy was now—stood in front of us, wringing her dead-looking hands.

"You shouldn't have . . ." she started.

But then there was a blinding burst of light.

And there was Shasta. She appeared next to Maisy and loomed over us. Her eyes sparked with a malevolence so pure, it knocked the wind out of me. Maisy moved to stand just behind her.

"Maisy?" I choked out, as if maybe she could explain.

"Dammit," Shasta growled. "It's always about Maisy, isn't it? Even when it's my event. Even when I did all the work. Even when that bitch is *fucking dead.*" She shook her head in frustration and started pacing back and forth, her high heels clicking against the ground. Maisy, still silent, watched her nervously.

"God, you people are idiots," Shasta snarled. "Especially you."

I thought she was talking to me, but then I realized her eyes were focused on a spot to my left.

"You don't recognize me, do you?" she said, her mouth twisting into a cruel mockery of a smile. "I looked so different all those years ago. But I always knew it was you, Nathaniel."

My stomach turned.

Nate's harsh features tensed up in shock and then slackened into a dull sort of realization.

And then he said, "Hello, Mother."

CHAPTER TWENTY-FIVE

WHAT THE FUCK.

That was the only thought my brain was capable of. But you know what? It seemed warranted.

What. The. Fuck.

My adorable, dorky, bespectacled boyfriend was related to Shasta? Who was apparently evil and way older than she looked and somehow in charge of this whole demon-human hybrid operation?

Was she a hybrid, too? Or something even worse?

"Leave them alone," Nate growled. "I'll go with you, but they don't need to be part of this."

Shasta threw her head back and cackled, a sound like a glass bottle being shattered over a rock. Maisy, who was still standing behind her, winced.

"Oh, Nathaniel," Shasta said. "'Nathaniel' . . . what an adorably mundane human name you gave yourself, by the way. Nothing like the one *I* gave you. Don't worry, I'll come for you later. Ever since I saw you at the League benefit—and really, it was so nice to reconnect—I've planned on bringing us back together. But for now I've got other things to worry about."

I tried to look at him, to gauge his expression. Shasta snapped her fingers, and as I turned my head, I was hit by a searing pain. It was like being stabbed all over by a million knives.

"Ah, do you like that?" Shasta said. "It's taken me years, but I've finally perfected how my force fields function in your world. If you move, it will hurt like a bitch and probably damage all your internal organs. And if you keep trying to move through the pain, you'll eventually die." She flipped her hair, obviously pleased with herself. "My latest field is so brilliant, it doesn't take up physical space—it exists on a whole other plane of the Earthly dimension. So they can't see us. Or accidentally walk into us." She gestured to the crowd in front of Pussy Queen. "They think I escorted Aveda inside after the sun got to be too much for the poor dear. Superheroes are quite delicate, aren't they?"

She grinned. There was still lipstick on her teeth.

"What do you want?" Aveda asked. I was heartened to hear her usual imperious tone.

"Isn't it obvious?" Shasta strode toward Aveda, her heels clicking ominously. I willed myself not to shrink away from her as she came to a stop and planted her hands on her hips, looming over us. "As you may have realized—or maybe not, since you're all so stupid—I've been slowly infiltrating San Francisco society, one local celeb at a time." Shasta snapped her fingers, and gray, rotting versions of Stu Singh and Tommy Lemon appeared behind her. "I know you thought you took out my demon-human hybrids, Aveda," Shasta said smugly. "But these guys can easily reconstitute themselves after being burned to bits. And their limbs can be detached—" She nodded at Stu, who gamely demonstrated by breaking his arm off and waving it around. "Or expanded." She grinned at Maisy, who held out her taloned hand. It inflated before our eyes, just as it had during our karaoke battle, morphing into a gigantic, menacing claw. I shuddered. Apparently Shasta's minions could move through the force field, no problem.

"Why, Tommy managed to inflate his entire being during your Yamato face-off so he was nearly as big as the movie screen—pretty cool, eh?" Shasta said, grinning as Maisy deflated her hand back to normal size.

Do something, I thought frantically. *You have to do something. You have to—*

What? What could I do? Set Shasta on fire? I'd landed with both arms twisted awkwardly underneath me and the force field was making it impossible to move. If I tried to conjure up a fireball from my current position, I'd incinerate myself.

"But back to what I want," Shasta purred. "I need one final minion. And it's you, Aveda. It *has* to be you."

She reached down, grabbed Aveda's arm, and dragged her away from us. Aveda cried out as the force field stabbed into her.

"No!" I screamed. I attempted to sit up and nearly passed out from the pain. My stupid arms were still pinned beneath me.

"Mother," Nate said. "Please."

"Oh, hush up, all of you," Shasta said irritably. She dumped Aveda in front of her minions. "I need peace and quiet for my hybridization ritual."

Shasta grabbed Aveda's arm again and started to yank her into a standing position. Aveda screamed.

Do something. Do something. You have to—

"Your plan sucks," I blurted out. I had no idea why I'd said that. I didn't even know what her plan was, exactly. But my haphazard insult had the desired effect. Shasta dropped Aveda's arm, whipped around, and glared at me.

"Excuse me?" she hissed. "My plan is amazing: fabulous demon princess reinvents herself as a successful businesswoman, cozies up to the Bay Area's most notable figures and converts them into demon-human hybrids, thereby creating her own cabal to run the city. What sucks about that?"

"Just the city?" I countered. "Not, like, the world?" All I could think was this was like the dopey *Heroic Trio* villain who only wanted to take over China.

"We'll start with San Francisco," Shasta said. "And move on to the world from there. Now if you will kindly stop interrupting me . . ."

This time, she didn't bother with Aveda's arm. She just grabbed Aveda by the hair and wrenched, attempting to pull her to her feet. Aveda's face twisted in pain and she screamed again, but she resisted with all her might, planting her hands on the ground and dragging her weight forward, pulling Shasta toward her. Shasta blew out a frustrated breath and let go.

I couldn't help but wonder why none of Shasta's minions were helping her. They were all just sort of frowning in her direction, looking put out.

Okay, I thought, trying to get my scattered thoughts in order. *Maybe I can use that.*

I desperately wanted to look at Nate, but I knew the force field would retaliate. I had no idea what he knew about all this, what he even was, what . . .

No. Don't think about that. The priority right now is getting us out of this. The priority is making sure we don't die or get turned into freaky hybrids.

I refocused on Shasta.

"You're not even going to get San Francisco," I said, making my voice as clear and confident as possible. Shasta seemed unable to resist responding to bitchy taunts. Maybe I could stall her with a whole mess of bitchy taunts, inch one of my arms out from under me, and then nuke her ass. I didn't know if she, like her hybrids, had the ability to reconstitute herself, but I was guessing that going up in flames would at least distract her for a moment. And if I moved slowly, maybe it wouldn't be as painful. I dragged my arm a tiny bit to the side.

Fucking ow.

So moving was going to be a one millimeter at a time kind of thing.

"That's right," Aveda said. "You're *not* going to be

able to get San Francisco. I don't think you realize just how particular San Franciscans are." I looked at her in surprise. Her voice was shaky, but she met my eyes and gave me a little nod, then winced. She knew what I was trying to do. "Look at the figures you targeted," she continued. "You've got a third-rate actor, a super-annoying blogger, and a dude who plays piano at an establishment that would charitably be referred to as a 'hole.'"

"No offense," I said to Stu Singh.

Stu held up a desiccated hand, indicating we were cool.

"Whatever." Shasta flapped a hand at her minions. "They think my plan is brilliant."

"Wee-eeelllll . . ." Tommy Lemon shifted uncomfortably, his glassy eyes going to the ground. His voice had the same watery, inhuman quality as Maisy's.

"That doesn't sound like a vote of confidence to me," I said, trying to egg Tommy on.

"Your plan sounded brilliant initially," Tommy said to Shasta. "But we didn't realize it had strings."

"You get to be fucking immortal," she snarled. "What are the strings?"

"I'm guessing the bit where you had to disappear from the public eye and pretend to be in the Andes maybe wasn't the greatest thing for a big movie star?" I coaxed.

"That's right," Tommy said, nodding eagerly. "This mysterious retreat hasn't been sitting well with my fans. They just want more movies, ya know?"

"We also didn't realize we'd have to look like this all the time," Maisy said. She frowned at her flaky gray hands. "Honestly, Shast, I don't know how you expect us to be this gosh-dang powerful cabal when we can't even go out in public."

"People will adapt," growled Shasta. "Once they realize we're in charge—"

"Once nothing," Aveda said. "I know it's a little racist, but the public tends to prefer it when your skin stays on your body."

Shasta glowered at her. "I think you'll feel differently once you've been hybridized. Now. We should really get started." Apparently resigned to the fact that she wasn't going to be able to get Aveda to stand, Shasta knelt down next to her.

I attempted to move my arm again. The force field stabbed me so hard, I gasped out loud.

"Evie," murmured Nate.

I ignored him. I couldn't think about him right now. If I thought about him even a little bit, I would come apart.

"Why do you want a minion who clearly wants nothing to do with you?" I said, trying to divert Shasta's attention back to me. "It sounds like these other guys went willingly, but Aveda is about as un-minion-like as you can get. For a demon princess, you lack foresight."

Shasta sprang to her feet, rage sparking in her eyes. "I have plenty of foresight," she growled. "I've been working on this plan for years!"

Years? My thought process came to a screeching halt. *What did she mean by . . . Was she . . .*

Shit. Of course.

"As in eight years?" I guessed. "You're one of the original humanoid demons? The ones who came through the first big portal?"

"I *opened* that portal." She threw me a scathing look. "And I actually came here way before that, for research purposes. The demon elders were looking to expand their empire, and I knew if I could find the perfect realm to invade and annex, they'd finally give me the respect I deserve. You know, promote me from demon princess to queen. And your realm was just so . . . shiny. So full of beautiful things and beautiful dresses and beautiful people." For a moment, her rage dissipated, and she gave a blissful sigh. "I knew if I could become one of those beautiful people, I'd be able to enslave humanity and the elders would allow me to rule your realm forever."

"You thought you could enslave humanity by being

beautiful?" Aveda said, her voice heavy with skepticism. She met my eyes. When Aveda and I were kids, our co-dependent connection meant we could communicate entire paragraphs of thought in a single look. I tried to do that now: *Just keep Shasta evil monologuing. She seems to be really into bragging about this damn plan of hers and if she keeps doing that, I know I can drag my arm out from under me and set her on fire and save us all.*

I tried shifting the weight of my torso, freeing my arm a bit.

That's it. That's it . . . I moved my arm a fraction of an inch then stopped when the force field pain hit me. It felt like it was seeping through my skin, wrapping itself around my lungs and squeezing.

"Ugh, Shast." Maisy rolled her sunken eyes. "You're explaining things all wrong, as usual." She turned to us. "She thought she could just magically become one of our human-type celebrities. Entrance all of us that way. She didn't understand that becoming a celebrity requires panache."

"And some kind of talent," Tommy chimed in. "That's what I've been trying to advise her on—the actorly side of things."

"So you came here from the Otherworld through your own portal for, uh, research," I said, trying to keep Shasta talking.

"Correct," Shasta said. She examined her nails, now in full evil monologue mode. I resisted the urge to roll my eyes. I mean, yes, I *wanted* her to be in full evil monologue mode, but I was starting to see why her minions looked so fed up. I noted that Maisy looked especially fed up. Something else I could use.

"It was a very experimental one-person portal," Shasta continued. "But I knew if I worked hard, I'd eventually be capable of bigger, better things."

"So then, eight years ago, once you'd deemed us suitable for invading, you opened a way larger, scarier portal from the Earth side. And brought a whole posse of humanoid demons through." I had another sudden, desperate urge to look at Nate, to see if he knew any of this already. But I couldn't risk the force field pain. I needed to conserve any pain-tolerating abilities I might have for getting my stubborn arm out from underneath me.

Shasta beamed. "Every celebrity needs an entourage."

"But obviously something went wrong," Aveda snarked. "Because your entourage ended up dead."

I noticed she was attempting to drag herself away from Shasta and the minions, but she was making about as much progress as I was in trying to move my arm. I met her eyes again. *It's okay*, I tried to tell her. *Stop moving. Save your strength. I got this.*

Shasta's face darkened. "I may not have had my bigger portal-opening spell entirely worked out, particularly from the human world side . . ."

"Yeah, to say the least," Maisy snorted. "Your stupid portal snapped shut immediately and killed your entire invasion team and trapped you here with no meaningful way of communicating with the Otherworld."

"And I didn't let that stop me!" Shasta exclaimed, throwing her arms out dramatically. "If anything, I was even more determined to rule you humans."

"Whoa," Tommy said. "You're hitting that line a little hard. Remember what we talked about with dramatic monologues? You gotta loosen up, connect with people, be more real—"

"Shut up," Shasta snapped. She turned back to me. "Anyway. In order to properly annex your realm, I needed to regain access to the Otherworld and open a permanent portal between here and there. I figured out how to open portals all over the city—"

"Which were smaller and weaker?" I said, catching Maisy's eye and giving her a skeptical look.

Maisy snorted in agreement. "And so unstable that only your mindless little puppy-demons could get through," she said. "Not exactly as threatening as the big, bad humanoid demons, eh?"

"But threatening in their own way," Shasta said peevishly. "I mean, yes, we keep them as pets in the Otherworld, but they do adore the taste of human flesh."

"If you're such an important demon princess and you were trapped here, why didn't these so-called elders try to rescue you?" Aveda said.

She had stopped moving, at least for the moment. I dragged my arm a bit more to the side. Now it was trapped right under my tailbone. The force field pain was starting to make me lightheaded. Tiny white dots danced in front of my eyes and I tried to blink them away.

Shasta's eyes shifted from side to side. "Well," she said slowly, "they did attempt to open more portals from the Otherworld, but they kind of couldn't because . . . um . . ."

"Because that portal attempt from eight years ago was just that botched?" I guessed, lifting a knowing eyebrow at Maisy.

"So botched!" Maisy crowed in agreement. "It totally shut down their ability to open *anything* from the Otherworld side."

Shasta glared at her. "You need to remember who's in charge, here."

Maisy gave her an injured look. "I'm a princess, too. A demon-human hybrid princess."

"Only because I decreed it," Shasta said. She gave us a smug smile. "You'll notice I even allowed her to keep her human appearance until the karaoke contest. Well, mostly. I gave her a bit of flaky skin so she could start to feel the glory of being demonified."

"Allowed me to?" Maisy snorted. "Shast, you know there's a certain amount of time between when you decide to hybridize someone and when the turn fully takes place. And that we scheduled it so *my* turn would happen during that climactic karaoke moment."

"Wait." I looked at them in disbelief, momentarily distracted from my excruciating arm-moving project. "Aveda had already used her fire power to defeat Tommy and Stu's hand at that point. What made you think things would be different with Maisy?"

Shasta gave me a "duh" look. "You sure are inquisitive today, Rude Girl. Maisy was my third hybrid. I figured I'd perfected the hybridization process, so she'd be strong enough to take Aveda out." She frowned at Maisy. "Who knew my chosen princess would be such a disappointment? After her defeat, I had to figure out how to mask my DNA, just so I wouldn't be found out by your stupid human police."

"The Otherworld higher-ups are the ones who decreed I become a princess," Maisy shot back. "They recognized my charisma and sent you that Golden Princess stone to make it happen."

"So that stone was a directive, too," I murmured. The puzzle was coming together in a totally unsettling way. But I couldn't get caught up in that. I had to focus on sending my fire blazing in Shasta's direction. I shifted my arm again and braced myself for the inevitable pain. My elbow was jutting out from under my torso now.

"Yes, yes," Shasta said. "Those stones are the only things the elders have been able to send through my, as Maisy refers to them, 'puppy-demon' portals. The stones used to be merely informational, but recently, they've started sending me little bits of advice for taking over your world."

"Or they were trying to give you proper instruction since you keep fucking up," Maisy muttered. "Exact instructions, in fact: 'Make the human-demon hybrids, already. No, you can't use an Aveda statue, you have to make them out of actual humans. Hey, here are step-by-step instructions on *how* to make them.' Oh, yeah," she said, noting my look of surprise, "there were tons of stones you guys didn't find."

"So the statues were a sort of prototype that didn't work out?" Aveda said. Our eyes locked again. *We're nearly there,* I thought. *Blabby Demon Almost Queen just needs to talk for a few seconds more. And then my arm will be free . . .*

Shasta shrugged. "Well, they did nothing to increase my power, but they succeeded in scaring you, didn't they? I had to round them up and destroy them once I realized they weren't working out, but that wasn't nearly as big a crimp in my plan as Team Aveda getting to some of the stones before I did. Luckily we managed to recover this particular stone when it fell out of that purple-haired brat's pocket at The Gutter." She brandished the You Need stone at us, then flipped it over so we could see the number.

1

My stomach clenched and my brain started working overtime. The stone must've started at 4—but by the time it came our way, Tommy had already been converted. Stu and Maisy had ticked the number down to 1. Nate and I had assumed that whoever was in charge planned on creating the last hybrid at the karaoke contest. But actually, she planned on doing it now.

We had been wrong about so many things.

"Enough chatter!" Shasta snapped, even though she was the one who had been doing most of the chattering. She tucked the stone into her pocket. "Let's get this final hybrid thing going." She knelt next to Aveda again and grabbed her arm.

"Wait!" I cried.

Shasta gave me an exasperated look. "What *now*?"

"Um." I scoured my brain, frantically searching for what else I could possibly use to stall her. My arm was almost free, dammit. If I could just move it a little bit more . . . "If you were trying to take Aveda down before, then why do you want her as your minion now? That seems like . . . not the best life choice you could make?"

"Not the best life choices are kind of her specialty," Maisy muttered.

Shasta gave a long-suffering sigh. "Originally, I was trying to knock her out so I wouldn't have any competition for my obvious future role as ultimate San Francisco celeb. I got my hybrids to stalk and attack her, and after a bit, they were even able to follow her patterns, predict where she'd be." She smiled down at Aveda, her face lighting with exaggerated benevolence. "But now I see that she's the one who can make our cabal complete. And even if she's a little reluctant now, I know I can convince her once hybridization takes hold. She's better than human. She deserves to be part of this. Part of us."

Aveda tried to pull away from Shasta. "But none of these people want to be part of *you*," she spat out, gesturing to Maisy and Co. "Not anymore. So why would I?"

"It might be more fun if you were with us, Aveda," Maisy piped up, picking at her falling-off skin. "We could finally be true best friends."

"She is not your best friend, Maisy!" shrieked Shasta. She dropped Aveda's arm, scrambled to her feet, and stamped on the ground so hard, one of her heels snapped off. "I am! That was the whole point. We were supposed to be awesome besties taking on San Francisco together. Instead you hogged all the attention for yourself and treated me like a second-rate sidekick!"

Maisy cast a meaningful look at Shasta's broken shoe. "If the cheap knock-off stiletto fits . . ."

I dragged my arm a bit further, managing to free it completely from the weight of my torso. The pain of the force field was burning through my entire body now, a near constant presence. But I had to keep going.

Almost there, almost there . . .

"I think I've had just about enough of your sass-mouth," Shasta said, taking a threatening step toward Maisy. Her features turned malevolent.

My palm was facing the ground. I just had to turn it over.

"Let's get back to Aveda!" Maisy said brightly. "That's why we're here, right?"

"Right." Shasta turned back to Aveda. "I can make you immortal. If I'm interpreting the message on this stone correctly, once I have my four hybrids, I'll be strong enough to open that permanent portal to the Otherworld, the whole demon population will invade, and we'll rule San Francisco together!"

There was a moment of resounding silence.

Shasta stomped the foot wearing the broken shoe, nearly toppling over in the process. "Together," she growled out of the side of her mouth, prompting Maisy and Co. to half-heartedly echo, "Yes, yes . . . together . . . right . . ."

"No." Aveda's voice was hoarse with pain, but she still managed to sound like she was dealing with an overzealous—but ultimately harmless—fan. Shasta's gaze darkened.

I managed to flip my hand partway over. *Goddammit. Ow.* Okay. Just one more bit of movement . . .

"So tiresome," Shasta said. Her eyes shifted to me. I stilled my hand. "What about you? You're no Aveda, but you showed promise during that little incident at the mall. Are you still test-driving the fire power?"

"No," Nate growled, finally speaking up. He'd gone so quiet, I'd nearly forgotten he was there. With great effort, he hauled himself in front of me. "Mother. I told you: you can take me. I'll be your final minion . . ."

"We're not minions; we're partners!" chirped Maisy.

". . . if you let them go."

Shasta looked thoughtful. "I was thinking more along the lines of you joining me as minion *support*, Nathaniel. You know, help them adjust to their new lifestyle. But there would be a certain poetic justice to you being one of my actual minions. I still need someone like Aveda, though. She brings me prestige."

I started to ease my hand all the way over, channeling all the fear and confusion I was feeling toward my palm.

I can do this, I can do this . . .

"You know what?" Shasta said, her tone light with a false whimsy. "I don't see why I can't have both. I just need to make some room." And with that, she snapped her fingers and Tommy Lemon disintegrated before our eyes.

It should've been a quick thing, disintegration. The turning of someone into dust in the blink of an eye. But this moment seemed to last forever as Tommy screamed and shriveled, his flaky skin crumbling, his eyes caving in on themselves.

"Stop it!" I screamed.

I harnessed the stew of emotions bubbling inside of me and flipped my palm all the way over. My fireball ignited, brilliant and bright. I gritted my teeth through the force-field pain and flicked my wrist, sending the fire flying in Shasta's direction.

I expected to see fear register on her face, but she just smiled. And then she snapped her fingers again.

It all happened in an instant. The bubble-like prison of the force field melted away and suddenly we were back among the crowd, the noise of the busy street crashing into me.

Shasta darted out of the way and my fire flew past her, smashing into Pussy Queen's new sign.

I heard screams, saw people flailing away from the flames. I felt terror rise up inside me, that same all-consuming terror I'd felt at the library so long ago. Back then, I'd been rooted to the spot, unable to do anything but stare as the fear overtook me.

This time I channeled the fear, used it to push myself to my feet. I looked around frantically for Nate or Aveda or Lucy. My gaze finally landed on a fire hydrant. I dove through the crowd and smashed my still-hot hand against it. The valve melted and the water sluiced out, sending a powerful spray at the flames.

The fire died, but the crowd was still frantic, pushing and shoving as smoke and ash drifted through the air. Smoke clouded my lungs, making me dizzy. As my vision swam and I felt myself listing to the side, I spotted Shasta hauling an unconscious Aveda into her shop.

"Not to worry, everyone!" she called out. "Aveda was just experimenting with her fire power. And now she needs a nap."

With that, she slammed the door behind them.

And I passed out.

CHAPTER TWENTY-SIX

I WOKE UP in my bed, pillows surrounding me like a fort. For one elated moment, I deluded myself into thinking it was all a dream and the entire household was about to barge in and bury me in their various problems and neuroses and demands. And everything was going to be fine.

And then a barrage of images from the last few hours crashed into me and I knew nothing would be fine ever again.

Shasta kidnapping Aveda.

Tommy Lemon disintegrating on the spot.

And Nate . . .

What was he?

I shook off my grogginess. I needed answers.

I pushed myself out of bed and marched down the hall to Nate's room. I flung open the door without knocking. He was standing next to his bed, his back to me.

"Go downstairs," he said, without turning around. His voice was low and steady, devoid of inflection. "You and Lucy lost consciousness at different points during the confrontation. I called Scott and we got you back here and you both appear to be fine. Everyone else is down in the kitchen, trying to come up with a game plan to recover Aveda."

"And you're . . . what? Brooding?" I put my hand on

his shoulder, forcing him to turn. His eyes were cold and expressionless, and he looked at me like I was a specimen he was studying from afar. I noticed a satchel on the bed. It appeared to be stuffed full of black clothes.

"No," he said. "I'm leaving."

My grip on his shoulder tightened. "You're leaving now? When Aveda's missing and we're right in the middle of a city-shattering crisis and you owe me about fourteen kazillion explanations? I don't think so."

He frowned. "You should want me to go. My presence here puts you in danger." His tone was so flat and clinical and *reasonable*, it made me want to scream. Where was the man who had surprised me with his passion, his depth of feeling?

Or was he a man at all?

I released him and crossed my arms over my chest. "Tell me," I said. "I will surround you with a fucking wall of fire before I let you leave here without at least telling me what you are and why you lied about it. On a scale of wannabe demon queen to minion, where do you fall? Make me a spreadsheet so I really get the picture."

His gaze remained steady. "I'm mostly human."

I glared at him. "Keep going."

He hesitated and seemed to be on the verge of pushing past me and walking out. Instead he let out a long breath and started talking.

"Like Mother said, she came here years ago." His voice was still flat. "Her portal-opening spells were experimental and unorthodox, but the demon elders approved of her ambition, and were hopeful she'd be successful in expanding their empire."

His words were so precise, so carefully chosen. As if he'd memorized a passage from a particularly dull history book and was spitting it back out with no real connection to what he was saying. I resisted the urge to grab him by the shoulders again and shake him. He had to be feeling *something* underneath that stoic façade.

"Before she opened the big portal—the one from eight years ago—she was able to maintain sporadic contact with the Otherworld from Earth," he continued. "Once she'd determined your realm was suitable for invasion, she began devising a plan to open a permanent conduit between the two worlds. And one of her first experiments . . ." He paused and his eyes drifted to the floor. " . . . was me."

"Like she . . . bred?" I couldn't help but shudder. The idea of Shasta breeding with anyone, human or not, wasn't something I wanted to think about.

"Yes. She enspelled a human man, then sent him away once she got pregnant," Nate continued. He met my eyes and I saw a flash of uncertainty. It disappeared quickly as he resorted back to that infuriatingly calm tone. "The elders told her that if she had a child with one foot in the human world, she'd be able to add its demon powers to hers, thereby strengthening her enough to successfully open that permanent portal."

"Seriously, 'thereby'?" I spat out, my anger bubbling over. "Can you cut it with the lecture speak and talk to me like a normal . . ."

"Human?" he retorted. That hint of uncertainty flashed through his eyes again. "I believe we've established that is *not* what I am. But my demon side didn't assert itself like Mother expected it to. I was born—"

"Mostly human," I finished. I swallowed hard, trying to tamp down on my rage. "So what does that mean?"

"It means I have a small amount of demon DNA. I've done tests on myself. Strangely it was my human side that asserted itself."

"And do you have a special demon superpower?" Now my voice was starting to take on the same calm, clinical cadence as his. I didn't know what else to do, how else to keep from lashing out at him completely. Maybe if I had all the puzzle pieces, I could put them together in a way that would show me how to kick Shasta's ass. And maybe then I'd be able to figure out how to shock Nate out of Cold Scientist Robot mode and make him help me with that. I tried to latch onto that sense of purpose.

Just get the facts. Then remind him that this isn't who he is. You know *this isn't who he is.*

"A very minor one," he said. "It's an enhanced observational ability: I see things in more detail than the average person. It helps with my work, but nothing beyond that. It's nothing like Mother's."

"Back up." I held up a hand. "What is Shasta's power, exactly?"

"She can access certain types of Otherworld magic, like Scott. This actually gives her a number of different abilities, among them the power to perform the portal-opening spells in the first place and the power to change her appearance at will. That's why I didn't recognize her—the last time I saw her, she was a wrinkled crone."

"And do all humanoid demons have a bunch of powers or is Shasta just really freakin' special?"

"From what I know, yes, they all have multiple powers," he said. "Though magic-based powers are especially prized. That's what makes her royalty."

I worked that bit of information out in my head. I was amassing Fun Demon Factoids like Pokemon. The key to saving Aveda—and the whole damn city—had to be in there somewhere. "So when the powers were distributed to humans from the demons who came through the first portal—"

"The multiple powers from each demon were split up among humans," he confirmed.

"Only one per customer," I murmured.

"And when split up, not terribly impressive. Except for yours."

I shook my head. Out of all the powers, *I* got the good one? That seemed wrong on so many levels. "Lucky me. So did she still try to add your power to hers? How does that work?"

"She has to make physical contact with me and form a magical bond between us. In theory my power then gives hers a boost. Like I'm . . ."

"A battery?" I filled in. I felt ridiculous, like we were calmly completing some kind of Demon Mad Libs form. I balled my fists at my sides and once again, shoved down the urge to scream at him.

"Sort of. And yes, she did try. When I was a child, she tried to use magic to alter me, to enhance my demon side. She used . . . a particularly painful spell. She tried it over and over and over again and each time it was worse. She tried it for ten years." As his story got more horrific, his voice got more dispassionate. "That's what gave me the scars on my shoulder."

My throat tightened. I was still angry and I was holding onto my fact-gathering sense of purpose with all my might, but the image of him as a helpless child forced to endure unspeakable pain brought tears to my eyes.

"How did you escape?"

"She'd mostly given up on me by the time I was eleven. She kept ranting at me about how humans were so weak, so useless. But she turned her invasion plans elsewhere," he said. "When I was eighteen, she thought she'd figured out how to open the big portal without adding to her strength. Which, as we now know, was incorrect since that portal was unsuccessful. When it snapped closed, it took so much out of her that she passed out for three whole days. I walked out the door and never went back. I gave myself a generic name, made a human life, and went to medical school."

"You turned to science," I murmured. "Trying to make meaning out of all this demon crazy."

"Something like that."

I shifted from foot to foot. My brain was like a Kitchen-Aid mixer that had been packed with a mishmash of incomprehensible info and turned on high. How could I even begin to make sense of it all?

"So from what Shasta said today, this new demon-human hybrid thing is going to strengthen her enough to finally open that permanent portal."

"Yes." He shook his head. "Imagine, if my demon side had asserted itself more fully and her spell had worked on me all those years ago, she might've been able to accomplish her goals much sooner."

"You wanted to work for Aveda because it would help you track all the supernatural goings-on in the city, maybe let you know what Shasta was up to," I guessed. "But you never went out in the field, never appeared in public, never even allowed yourself to be photographed, because you were worried she'd find you."

He gave me a curt nod. "And over the years, I allowed myself to be lulled into a false sense of security. Because the demon threat had become so benign and Aveda always took care of it. And frankly, I'd always harbored the hope that Mother hadn't been merely unconscious when I walked away; that maybe she'd died. That those smaller portals were the work of someone else. Like you, I tricked myself into thinking I could be a normal human. And then I actually went out on a mission and that's where she saw me."

"The benefit," I said, remembering how Shasta mentioned reconnecting with him. "The one you escorted me to."

"Yes. I agreed to go to that damn benefit because . . ." He trailed off, trying to maintain control. But I saw emotion flaring in his eyes.

Now was my chance. I had to make him fight with me, yell at me. I had to make him show me he was still the person I thought I'd gotten to know so intimately.

"Because of what?" I challenged.

"Because of you," he spat out. "Because I couldn't stand the thought of you in danger. Because growing up the way I did, I never knew what it meant to feel alive. I always assumed I'd spend my entire life not knowing. And then I met *you . . .*"

I grabbed his hand. "So don't go."

He was already shaking his head. "I have to." He schooled his features back into a look of detachment. "And you're wasting precious time arguing with me." He freed his hand from mine and turned back to his satchel. "When we started to piece together this new demon threat, I didn't think it was her. After failing so thoroughly to make me into the son she wanted, she swore she'd never again attempt a plan involving 'weakling humans.' I embraced the theory that she'd died, that this was something else. When Maisy showed so much . . . interest in me, that seemed to settle it. Not even Mother is that twisted."

He zipped up his satchel and turned to me. "You heard her, Evie: she wants me for her one of her minions. She may have a new and improved version of demon-human 'children,' but she won't be able to resist the idea of making her first failed project into a success. If I leave now and get far away from here, she won't be able to complete her plan and maybe you'll be safe. All of you. Think of Bea." His tone wasn't pleading or anxious. It was, once again, cold and logical. It enraged me. And I couldn't hold back any longer.

"Don't you dare use her against me," I hissed. Heat was zinging into my palm like an overactive Fourth of July sparkler.

Not now, I snarled at the fire.

I put a hand on his chest and locked my eyes with his, determined to reach him. "You believed in me when no one else did. You always thought I could be a real hero. And now I believe in you. I know you're braver than this. I know you don't want to run away. I know you're suppressing every single emotion you have because you think it somehow makes you stronger. And I also know

that is the biggest crock of tortured hero bullshit ever
invented. I know because *I* fucking invented that." My
fist closed around the fabric of his shirt, pulling him
closer. His eyes were still devoid of emotion. "Stay. Fight
with us. Fight with *me*."

He paused for a very long moment. Then he shook me
off.

"Good-bye," he said softly. And he slung the satchel
over his shoulder and left.

I stood there for a moment, wondering if there was
any way I could set something very small on fire in order
to release the anger churning through me.

I settled for letting out a strangled scream of frustration.

Then I squared my shoulders and marched downstairs.
Moping, crying, sulking: none of these things even entered my brain space.

Because even though my heart was breaking, I still
had a city to save.

As I got closer to the kitchen, I heard yelling.

"Just concentrate on this right now, love. I'm sure she
didn't mean to—"

"Oh, I'm sure she *did*."

I walked into the kitchen to find Lucy and Bea in the
midst of what appeared to be an ill-timed stand-off. Scott
was sitting at the kitchen table with his head in his hands.

"Guys—" I started.

"How could you?" hissed Bea, zeroing in on me. Her
face was white with rage and her fury hung in the air like
a physical thing, forcing me to take a step back.

I held up my hands, attempting to placate her. "Whatever you're upset about, it's not a good time."

"You threw away my plane ticket. My plane ticket to
Dad."

Dammit. How had she found out about that? I'd taken the stupid trash out myself.

"Let's talk about this later," I said, keeping my tone as firm as possible. "It's not as important as—"

"You didn't even *mention* it to me."

"Because I knew it would end badly," I said, my frustration boiling over. "You know how he is, Bea."

"He sent me an email asking if I was coming," she said, pointing an accusatory finger at her laptop, which was sitting on the kitchen table. "And he said—"

"Why would you trust anything he says? The man abandoned us."

"Why should I trust anything *you* say?" she countered. "Since you covered up the fact that he asked us to come to him."

"Beatrice. Seriously. Can you please just—"

"No. I won't 'just' anything." She advanced on me again, hands balled at her sides, eyes flashing with rage. I recoiled. I felt like that rage was piercing me in the heart. "I've listened and I've worked hard and I've followed you around like a stupid little puppy dog and you lied to me about the most important thing."

She pushed past me. "I'm done!" she screamed over her shoulder, her stompy feet echoing through the hall.

"Lucy," I murmured. "Scott. She's not going to talk to me. Can one of you . . . ?"

"I'll go," Scott said, rising to his feet. He looked like he hadn't slept in a month. "Evie. You have to get her back."

I knew he didn't mean Bea. I squeezed his arm. "I will."

As he left, I sat down at the kitchen table, studying Bea's computer. I took a deep breath and tried to channel all my feelings about Bea and Nate and everything else toward my ultimate goal: Beat Shasta. Save the city.

I saw that Bea had started a document that was helpfully labeled "SHASTA = BAD GUY :(FACTS AND TRIVIA!"

"She hadn't gotten very far when that email from your dad arrived," Lucy said, sitting down next to me. "Where did Nate go? He told us he was going to his lab to do some research, and then he just disappeared." I didn't respond. I realized she'd been passed out when the revelation of Nate's heritage had come up. And Scott and Bea hadn't even been there. Aveda and I were the only ones who knew.

I zeroed in on the single note in Bea's document: the URL for Maisy's blog. I clicked on it.

As far as I knew, Maisy's blog had been dormant since the karaoke contest. But as it loaded, I noted it had gone through a significant change. Now it was called . . .

"The Pussy Blog?" I choked out.

Lucy peered over my shoulder. "Looks like Shasta's trying to take over *everything*."

I looked at the screen in disbelief. Maisy may have been annoying, but at least she had a sense of style. This new version of her blog was boring and basic; an endless stream of photos of Shasta posing in her shop, topped off by headlines rendered in truly unfortunate fonts. The top photo caught my eye. It displayed Shasta hugging a half-conscious Aveda to her side. The timestamp showed it was from earlier today.

"So she's holing up at her shop," I said. "But we need a way to get through her force fields. If she incapacitates us, it's going to be a repeat of today. I can't incinerate her if I can't control where I'm aiming."

Lucy frowned. "Maybe Scott has a spell?"

"Maybe." Even with his enhanced power, I was worried about Scott effectively performing a new spell when he was so torn up over Aveda.

I clicked around on Bea's computer, allowing my mind to wander. How did you break a force field? I clicked on one of Bea's minimized documents and it brought up a spreadsheet. I squinted at it. It was a formalized version of her handwritten document categorizing the Otherworld stones. I smiled ruefully, remembering the day I'd found the scribbled version in Nate's lab.

Then I remembered something else.

I stood up so suddenly, I knocked my chair over.

"Evie?" Lucy said, but I was already bolting down to the lab. I dashed over to the table with Bea's piles of stones and pawed through them. I located the one I was looking for and scooped it up, reading the words etched on its surface.

Anger Shatters Field.

I ran back to the kitchen.

"This is it," I said, waving the stone at Lucy. "It's me. Bea and Nate thought this was a vague explanation of my power. But now I think it means I can shatter force fields if my fireballs come specifically from anger. Today it didn't work because I was utilizing fear."

I was practically giddy that I'd found the solution. All I had to do was get mad. And I could totally do that.

Lucy insisted on gathering an arsenal of weapons before we left. While she was working on that, I attempted to draw up some sort of game plan and picked through the rest of the stones to see if I'd missed anything else important. But I kept coming back to the same thing: just get mad. Get *mad*.

Right before we headed out the door, I refreshed Maisy's blog to see if Shasta had left us more clues. A new picture popped up. This one had a timestamp of just a few seconds earlier.

The background and setup were the same. It was still Shasta's lingerie shop, and Shasta herself was still at the forefront of the photo. But this time she had her arm locked around someone else. Someone tall and sulky-looking.

Lucy gave a little yelp. "She's got Bea?! How did that happen? Where'd Scott go?"

The feelings I'd been so focused on channeling exploded to the surface. Anger bubbled through me, thick and toxic.

"Yeah," I said. "I don't think getting mad's going to be a problem."

CHAPTER TWENTY-SEVEN

I LET MY anger power me all the way to Pussy Queen, stomping through the ten-block walk with Lucy hot on my heels.

The lingerie shop's entrance was charred thanks to its earlier encounter with my fireball. I stared at it, gearing myself up.

I could take Shasta down. I could save my friends. I could save the whole freakin' city. I *could*, dammit.

I was suddenly aware that I looked extremely un-superhero-like. I was wearing jeans and the cartoon duck T-shirt and my hair had been stuffed into a half-assed ponytail.

I was still a mess, inside and out.

But it didn't matter. *No one* could match my rage right now. And I wasn't trying to shove it down or repress or ignore it. I was going to *use* it.

"Just so you know: I'm not entirely sure incinerating Shasta will destroy her," I said to Lucy. "Her hybrids have the ability to reconstitute themselves. She might, too."

Lucy planted her hands on her hips. She had strapped swords and knives and nunchucks all over her body. She looked like an adorable pixie Rambo. "Then some other solution will present itself, love," she said. "Half a plan is better than no plan. And we've got at least sixty percent of a plan."

I took her hand and squeezed it. "You don't have to go in there with me, you know."

"Yes, I do." She smiled. "Save your martyr-esque declarations for some weaker soul."

I gave her a grateful nod. And with that, we burst through the door.

I'd barely gotten a look at the now infamous Pussy Queen—which was an unremarkable series of racks of boring pastel underwear, no neon in sight—when Shasta threw a force field around us. She snapped her fingers and once again, my limbs froze up. She had changed into a fresh vintage dress, I noted, a figure-hugging black sheath from the forties. She gave us a sly smile, her bright red mouth a slash against her pale skin.

"At least she fixed her lipstick," muttered Lucy.

I took stock of everyone else in the room, even though the mere act of turning my head was agony. Maisy and Stu were positioned behind Shasta, their aggravated expressions indicating they'd had enough of this whole minion business. Aveda was sitting on the floor, looking dazed, like she wasn't quite aware of what was going on. Scott was sprawled next to her, unconscious. I didn't see Bea, but I was surprised to discover one more person in the room: a black-clad figure whose eyes widened the moment he saw me.

"Nate," I gasped.

"What are you doing here?" he snarled, his face darkening. "You're supposed to be—"

"What? Sitting on my ass at HQ agonizing over the specifics of my plan to take out your mom?"

"Yes," he spat out. "That's exactly what you're supposed to be doing. Giving me enough time to—"

"To offer yourself up as the sole sacrifice, thereby distracting me from the fact that I need four whole minions, not just one?" Shasta droned. "Blah, blah, blah. Nathaniel, really. Your plea to join me is so touching, but how stupid do you think I am?"

"Can anyone take a crack at that question?" muttered Maisy.

Nate turned to Shasta. "As I was trying to explain, Mother, you can now successfully accomplish what you tried all those years ago: my power is finally strong enough to add to yours and guarantee your success in opening the portal."

Shasta rolled her eyes. "And you know that because . . . ?"

He opened his hand to reveal two of the portal stones. I craned my neck, trying to see them.

" 'Son Will Rise,' " Shasta read. " 'Once He Sees All.' "

I remembered those stones from the same pile as "You Need" and "The Golden Princess." Nate was obviously the "son." But what did the rest of it mean?

"Duh," said Maisy, as if reading my thoughts. "Those two stones go together, Shast. His observation power must've gotten the same level up as all the other human abilities when you tried opening the earthquake portal on the night of the karaoke contest." She waved a desiccated hand at Shasta. "The portal might've closed right away, but that blast of super-special Otherworld energy that came through enhanced everyone's powers. Including his. He's your 'son' and now he can 'rise.' Because the level up means he 'sees all.' "

Nate nodded. "You don't need anyone else," he said to Shasta.

He'd never intended to flee the city, I realized. He was trying to sacrifice himself. And I knew him well enough to tell that he had something up his sleeve that ensured Shasta would not, in fact, be successful in opening her damn portal. That he was trying to trick her in order to save us all.

If we got out of this, I was going to yell at him so hard for trying to play angsty, overdramatic hero. Didn't he know that was *my* job?

Shasta examined her lacquered nails. "A tempting offer. But I like to have insurance. I will take you, Nathaniel, but I see no point in giving up my other two minions."

She jerked her head at Maisy and Stu. "And since I have a willing party to complete my little foursome . . ."

She nodded toward the dressing room. I turned my head, the force field pressing painfully against me.

Bea stepped out from behind the curtains, adjusting a dress that was a carbon copy of Shasta's black forties number. "Thanks for the dress, Shast!" she sang out. "It's so me."

I felt a whoosh of relief that she was okay. It was instantly replaced by rage.

"Beatrice Constance Tanaka!" I snapped. "What the hell do you think you're doing?"

Bea met my gaze, her eyes narrowing into that perfect Tanaka Glare.

"Shasta's going to make me immortal," she said. "A big, important immortal type person! It's gonna be frakballs awesome!"

"That is not awesome," I said. I attempted to lunge for her and the force field retaliated, stabbing me everywhere. "That is frakballs *stupid*! Do the minions look like they're having a good time?"

Maisy mouthed "nope." Stu frowned miserably.

"They will be," Shasta said. "Once we rule the city. And eventually the world."

"Yeah," said Bea. "And anyway, Aveda doesn't want it."

She gestured to Aveda, who raised her head and blinked a few times, as if trying to come out of a trance.

"Ah, yes," said Shasta. "A wrinkle in my plan." She smiled at me. "As it turns out, there was something to what you were saying earlier. My other minions accepted willingly. I didn't realize that was a requirement until I tried to turn Aveda and it didn't take."

"You didn't realize a lot of things," muttered Maisy.

"Unfortunately Aveda still seems to be in a daze from my efforts," Shasta continued. "And then this one showed up trying to find Beatrice, even though she didn't want to be found." She nodded toward Scott's limp body. "He resisted my force field so much, it knocked him unconscious. Or maybe he's dead by now. I'm not sure."

I gritted my teeth, tamping down on my urge to lunge at her.

"Luckily Beatrice is more adventurous than Aveda," Shasta said. "She approached me about minion-dom after seeing my delightful blog pictures . . ."

"'Delightful' isn't the word I'd use," muttered Maisy.

". . . and realizing that being your little toady for the rest of her life would simply not do," Shasta continued.

"Bea." Nate stepped forward. "Trust me, you don't want this."

She glared at him. "You're just as bad a liar as Evie, Mr. Demon Spawn."

"I'm trying to help you," he said.

Bea shrugged. "I don't need anyone's help. I want to be different. Special."

"Well, you'll be a demonified version of yourself with dead skin, no free will, and a lifelong debt to a pissed-off demon princess who also happens to be a psycho hosebeast," I spat out. "That's definitely *special*."

"Shut up," Bea growled. "Why are you always trying to mess stuff up for me?"

"And what about your friends over there, don't you care about them?" I said. "Your new mentor just said she might have killed Scott."

A ghost of uncertainty passed over Bea's features. Then she hardened again. "I'll fix him when I'm immortal," she said. "No big whoop."

I was pretty sure that wasn't within the realm of minion powers, but I bit back a retort and focused on my rage, that pure feeling bubbling up inside me. I harnessed it, concentrated on the heat flaring in my palm.

Anger shatters field, I chanted inside my head. *Anger shatters field.*

My hands were balled into tight fists. Somehow, Shasta's dumb force fields kept catching me in positions that were not optimal for fireball-throwing. I had to open my hand gradually. Otherwise the pain would knock me out. I eased my fingers back, wincing as the stabbing sensation overtook me again.

"You can do it, love," murmured Lucy.

Shasta extended a hand to Bea. "Let's get started, shall we?"

"No." Nate planted himself between Shasta and Bea. "Take me first."

Shasta shrugged. "Very well. I mean, you're already your own sort of hybrid, so I technically don't need to perform this part of the ritual on you, but I suppose I can make you look like the others. It would be nice to have a matched set." She nodded at Stu and Maisy's gray, flaky appearance. "You can be next, Beatrice."

"Aw, man," Bea pouted.

I eased my fingers open just a little more. The pain nearly blinded me.

Shasta grasped Nate's hand in hers and looked deeply into his eyes. She started to chant a string of complicated-sounding words I didn't understand.

"Evie," Lucy said. "Look down and to the left if you can manage it. What is that?"

I moved my head and winced at the inevitable pain. A stark black slash had appeared on the floor. And it was growing, oozing outward like a blob of tar.

Shasta glanced at the slash, her eyes glowing with pleasure. "That's my portal: the one that will finally connect San Francisco to the Otherworld forever."

I swallowed. As portals went, it was far less aesthetically pleasing than the sparkly gold things we usually saw. Bea stared at it. Her expression of defiance wavered, and I felt uncertainty roll off her. Shasta refocused on Nate, the gibberish words flowing from her lips. I turned my concentration back to my hand, back to the rage I was trying to harness.

Anger shatters field.

I opened my hand, screamed in pain, and let the fireball loose. It zipped toward Shasta's head, ready to fuck her up and take her out forever . . . and then bounced against the edge of the force field and disappeared.

My jaw dropped.

"Ah, yes," Shasta said merrily. "I'm afraid your fire doesn't work inside the force field anymore." She gave me a malicious grin. "And it is *your* fire, isn't it? Maisy and I have suspected as much since the mall incident."

"I suspected," Maisy said. "You jumped on the bandwagon. Like you always do."

"So unfortunate that you of all people got that power," Shasta said to me. "It belonged to the one real bruiser in my invasion party. All his powers were centered around pure force. It was such a shame to see those powers split up among you weakling humans. Though his other abilities are not nearly as forceful on their own." She shook her head regretfully. "Fire is so wasted on a little nothing like you. But in any case, if you keep trying to use it, you'll have to move. And as I've already noted, if you move too much, you'll die." She grinned. "Of course, if you don't die that way, I have plenty of other ideas."

"What?" squeaked Bea. "Shast, you never said anything about . . . about . . ."

"About what? Killing your loser sister who's done nothing but lie to you?" Shasta said. "You should be thanking me."

Bea shook her head. "I really don't think —"

"Oh, hush up, you'll get used to the idea," Shasta said. "Now let me complete my ritual so we can get this city-ruling thing up and running." She grasped Nate's arm tighter. He started to shake.

Bea took an involuntary step back, fear pulsing through her. It radiated from her and hung in the air, a near tangible thing that I could feel . . .

That I could feel.

A series of images piled into my brain, a mixed-up puzzle arranging itself into a cohesive whole.

Bea beaming at me when I told her she was like Mom, her warmth instantly brightening the room.

Bea telling me to go for it with Nate and gently rubbing my back, her calm settling my soul.

Bea screaming at me for lying to her about Dad, her anger hanging in the air like a living thing, forcing me to recoil.

She was like a reverse empath. Her emotions could change the feel of a space, could alter things in ways I was only starting to understand. Could they also alter something as seemingly immovable as a force field? Was that what the level up portal had given her?

Anger shatters field.

It wasn't me. It was her.

But she was still frightened, nowhere close to angry. She took another step back from Shasta and Nate, her body hunching over in terror.

I could change that. If there was one thing I was really good at, it was pissing her off.

I glanced at the black slash of the portal. It was getting wider.

"Lucy," I whispered. "When the force field shatters, get Bea out of the way."

"On it," she whispered back. "But how are you going to—"

"Trust me." I raised my voice again. "Bea. Remember how I lied to you?"

"What?" Her eyes went to me, saucer-like and scared.

"I lied. I fucked you over."

Her eyes darted back and forth. "Oh. Well, I don't know about that."

"I kept you from Dad. Remember? You should hate me. If it wasn't for me, maybe you'd be with him right now. Maybe you wouldn't feel so alone."

She looked confused. "Maybe."

"You would be having tons of father-daughter bonding time."

She frowned. "That would be nice."

"If only I hadn't been so selfish."

Her eyes got a little mad. "You're always selfish."

"You could have told him how much you like the present he sent you and—"

"Present?" Her face morphed into the full-on Tanaka Glare and there was that anger, rolling off her in great, toxic waves. Waves I could definitely feel. "HE HAD A PRESENT FOR ME?!?"

Her scream rang out through the store and I saw the force field shatter in front of me, its bubble-like gloss melting away.

I charged forward, free of the pain at last, and slammed myself against Nate.

His eyes went wide with shock as my shoulder connected with his ribs. He was so much bigger than me, but I had the element of surprise—and the fact that my shoulder was really pointy—on my side.

He stumbled away from Shasta. I locked my hands around her arms.

"What . . . ?" She tried to wriggle out of my gasp, but I held on tight.

"You can't have any of them!" I roared.

She bared her teeth at me. "Wanna bet?"

She snapped her fingers and another force field rose around Bea and Lucy. Lucy stopped moving immediately, but Bea fought, arms and legs thrashing, her face a mask of fury. I saw pain register in her eyes. And then she went limp.

"No!" I screamed.

"I can do that to all of them," Shasta hissed. "To everyone you love. To every single person in this stupid city. I *will* rule."

"When there's no one left to rule over?" I growled,

tightening my grip on her arms. "Seriously: you come up with the worst fucking plans ever."

And then I sent my fire blazing directly into her.

Unlike her hybrids, she didn't disintegrate. Her hair was a flare of orange, her dress a field of red. She threw her head back and screamed: a horrible, inhuman sound. I tried to push her away from me, but she held on tight, determined to take me with her.

"The portal!" Maisy screamed. "Push her into the gosh-dang portal, Rude Girl!"

I moved myself forward, propelling Shasta toward the portal. She was still clinging to me like a leech, so I held on equally hard, hoping I could gain leverage. We hovered near that slash of black. I closed my eyes and summoned every scrap of strength I had left, every memory of the people I loved, every bit of determination to keep my city safe.

And I shoved. I shoved *hard*.

Shasta's fingertips scrabbled against my arm, trying to find purchase. And then she tripped over her too-high heel and fell backward into the black hole, screaming and horrible and on fire.

I tried to jump back. But as Shasta fell, a bolt of light shot out of the portal and hit me in the chest.

I screamed as fire licked at my skin, but I couldn't tell if it was my fire or demon fire. I felt myself being swept to the side by a powerful force and my feet slipped from under me and I knew I was going to hit the ground hard and I was pretty sure I was about to be dead.

When I finally smacked into something, it wasn't ground. It was human muscle and black cotton and a clean, comforting scent I inhaled greedily, wondering if these were my final breaths.

It was Nate, cradling me in his arms.

I tried to sit up, but it felt like there was a weight pressing down on my chest. Had Shasta conjured up one final force field? My vision blurred in and out. I felt searing pain and a strange, wet warmth. I coughed and tasted blood.

"Bea . . . ?" I gasped. "Aveda? Lucy and Scott?"

"They're okay," Nate said. His voice was choked with panic. "Everyone's okay. Evie—"

"Do not get emotional, doctor," I heard Aveda say, her voice shaky. "Just fix her."

"She's losing blood," he said. "Evie, don't try to move, okay? We're going to get you back to the house and we're going to . . . to . . ."

I blinked, trying with all my might to get my surroundings to come into focus. I saw a blurry Aveda shaking Scott awake. He looked freaked out, but alive. I saw a blurry Lucy dragging a near-unconscious Bea toward me. Bea's head lolled onto Lucy's shoulder, her eyes fluttering open and closed.

I was overtaken by a bone-deep sense of warmth.

My family, I thought. *This is my family.*

And suddenly I knew they were going to be okay. I knew Bea, especially, was going to be okay. She was surrounded by this weird little unit of people who loved her, who would take care of her forever, who would band together to defeat any evil. I knew that in my heart and soul. And as I glowed with that knowledge, I felt strong—strong in that Oprah-level, superhero-worthy way—for the first time in my life.

Too bad I was having this stunning revelation just as I was about to die.

I turned back to Nate and reached a shaky hand up to touch his face.

He'd never left me. He'd fought for me. He'd fought *with* me.

"Hey," I croaked. "I love you."

"Gross," I heard half-conscious Bea murmur.

When darkness finally washed over me, I was smiling.

CHAPTER TWENTY-EIGHT

MY EYES SNAPPED OPEN and I was instantly aware of three things: 1) I wasn't dead. 2) There were mysterious weights pressing down on my limbs. 3) I had to pee like a motherfucker.

I lifted my head and looked around blearily, trying to get a grip on my surroundings. I was in my bed, wearing what appeared to be one of Nate's T-shirts. My right arm was pinned to the mattress by Nate, his arms locked around my waist, soft snores escaping his lips. Lucy was on top of my left shoulder, her lashes fluttering against her cheeks as she breathed in and out. And Bea was sleeping curled around my feet, as if protecting them from nefarious toe fetish demons.

"They wouldn't leave you."

I turned and found Aveda sitting in a rocking chair next to the bed. She gave me a gentle half-smile. With her face scrubbed of makeup, she looked heartbreakingly young. I was hit by a wave of nostalgia, an image of two preteen girls giggling over french fries and wondering what life might have in store for them. I opened my mouth to say something about that. Instead I said, "I have to pee like a motherfucker."

Without waiting for her response, I wriggled free from my sleeping captors, bolted to the bathroom, and experienced sweet relief.

When I returned to the bedroom, Aveda pulled another chair next to hers and gestured for me to sit. The Great Snoring Trio continued to snore.

"How long was I out for?" I said. "A few days? A week?"

Aveda gave me an amused look. "Just overnight. You were about two seconds from death, but we got you back here in time and your injury ended up being fixable. The energy bolt that smacked you in the chest was some kind of supernatural feedback from shoving all that fire into the portal. It gave you a sizable gash, but Nate was able to stop the bleeding and Scott used a healing spell. They worked very well together, actually. Look down your shirt."

I pulled the cotton away from my body and glanced downward. A long scar extended from the center of my chest to the area just above my left breast. It appeared to be fading already. Now that I knew it was there, it seemed to pulse with dull, muted pain.

"Speaking of Nate: interesting backstory he's got there," Aveda said. "But given that he's obviously on the side of good, none of us really care."

I smiled and let the shirt fall back against my skin. "What happened to Maisy and Stu?"

"They're alive," she said. "They still appear to be hybridized, but they're alive. And Maisy . . . well, see for yourself."

She pulled out her phone, tapped something on the screen, and passed it to me. The screen displayed Maisy's blog, now fully restored to its former glory, but with a new title.

"Diary of a Reformed Half-Demon Princess?" I said. Maisy's disintegrating gray face grinned at me from the top of the screen.

"She's making it her mission to show the world that not all demons are evil. And to show the demons themselves that they don't *have* to be evil."

"And conveniently this will get her way more attention than her gossip-mongering ever could?"

"Naturally," Aveda said. "It's blown up overnight and already has three times the traffic of her old blog."

I laughed. "You've gotta admire her ingenuity. And I owe her one for telling me to shove Shasta into the portal."

"Indeed," said Aveda. "Look at the first post."

I turned back to the screen and skimmed through. The post was a breathless account of how Maisy had flirted with evil, but eventually saw the error of her ways and "assisted the city's two most glamorous superheroines in taking down a wannabe demon queen."

"Now that I've experienced firsthand what it's like to be a superheroine, I fully understand the multitude of challenges involved!" the post concluded. "In retrospect, all the snarky digs I've made in the past about my best friend Aveda's appearance seem small, irrelevant, and horribly sexist. My second best friend Evie Tanaka— San Francisco's thrilling new heroine!—helped me see the narrow focus of my male gaze-centric lens. Rest assured, you won't find any more of those types of posts on this blog. And any comments in that vein will be summarily deleted."

"Using her power for good, sort of," I murmured.

Aveda grinned. "Sort of. I think it's more like 'using her power for whatever will make her the most popular gosh-dang celeb she can be.' Not that I can really throw stones on that front."

At the bottom of the post, there was a photo. This one depicted me shoving Shasta into the portal. Fire was everywhere: shooting out of my hands, engulfing Shasta in a mighty blaze. I looked determined, powerful. And really, really angry.

Aveda was sitting on the floor in the background of the photo, her face dazed. I noticed her hand was raised. And I remembered that just as the energy bolt hit me in the chest, I'd felt as if I was being swept to the side.

"You telekinesised me! You . . ." I looked up from the phone screen, goggling at her. "The bolt could've hit me a lot harder, but it didn't. Because you moved me. You saved my life."

"I did," she said. "And Maisy somehow got a picture of it. But I want you to look at a different aspect of this shot." She tapped the phone screen. "Look how *cool* we look together, Evie."

I turned back to the screen. We did look incredibly cool. And as I studied the picture, I realized something else: I had totally mastered The Tanaka Glare.

"I want you to do this with me," Aveda said.

My head jerked up. Her face was earnest. No trace of snark or manipulation or deception.

"We don't know what the consequences of Shasta's actions will be," she continued. "That portal in the lingerie shop hasn't closed yet. Nothing's come through and it appears to be essentially dead as far as supernatural goings-on, so we don't think it's an active conduit to the Otherworld. That said, it's completely different from any other portal we've seen. Its appearance, its placement on the ground instead of the ceiling, the way it smacked you in the chest. Nate and Bea have taken some debris to analyze, and Rose's team is monitoring it around the clock. But it seems more than likely that this city will still need superheroes. I think we would make an excellent team. We have awesome powers and a long, storied past and a bond like no other. You and I could be like . . ."

"Like *The Heroic Trio*?"

She grinned and finished the thought: "Except there's only two of us."

I cocked an eyebrow at her. "I'm surprised you'd want there to be *two* of us."

"Point taken." She paused for a long moment, conflicting emotions playing over her face. "Look. I know I got so caught up in the fan worship and the whole 'being the most perfect Aveda Jupiter ever' thing that I forgot why I wanted to do this in the first place. I forgot that being heroic isn't about obsessing over your adoring public and what they're saying about you and what you think they want you to be. I forgot that sometimes it's just about—"

"Being crazy and unguarded and brave enough to stuff your face with spam musubi?" I said, teasing.

"Yes." She gave me a small smile. "I forgot about that moment when we first saw *The Heroic Trio*. And when everybody started paying attention to you-as-me, well . . ." She looked down and toyed with the frizzy ends of her hair. "I felt irrelevant. Like I'd been stripped of any power I'd ever had, any sense of identity I'd ever worked for. Because if I'm not Aveda Jupiter, who am I? No one. Not really."

"You've always been someone to me," I said softly.

Her smile turned wry. "You know how I say I've always been there for you? How I repeat that like some kind of deranged parrot?" She sounded out each word carefully, as if she couldn't quite believe they were coming out of her mouth. "You've always been there for me, too. You rubbed my back when I puked up all that freaking spam musubi. You went along with my ridiculous 'pose as me' plan, even though the very idea of using your fire terrified you. And now you're still here. Despite everything I've done to push you away." She reached over, took my hand, and squeezed it. "You were right. At the intervention. I've been a terrible friend. Not just recently, but for a good, long while now. I'm sorry."

I looked down at our clasped hands. I squeezed back. Then I took a deep breath and said a single word: "Okay."

She looked confused. "Okay?"

"Okay, I'll do this with you," I said. I smiled at her and we exchanged one of those looks from long ago. A look that somehow conveyed our entire existence together, stretching back to the spam musubi and rocketing forward to our helpless giggle fit that day we'd finally had it out at the bar. We'd come apart and come back to each other. We could finally use our shared history to grow stronger together instead of allowing it to keep us frozen in the past.

Aveda's grin overtook her entire face. "And by the way, Maisy already gave you your own superhero moniker." She tapped the phone screen.

"'Rude Fire Girl'?" I yelped. "Am I stuck with that?"

"Afraid so. So you're sure about this? I don't have to talk you into it, coax you out of your natural state of wallflowerism?"

I scrolled back to the picture of us on the phone screen. "That moment when I thought I was dying, I should've felt awful," I said. "I mean, with the dying and all. But I didn't. I felt peaceful. Free. Like I was dying doing exactly what I'm supposed to be doing, being exactly who I'm supposed to be." I met her eyes. "I've never felt like I had a real purpose. I mean, for years, I've definitely tried to give myself one. But it was always something small and containable and easy to fixate on. Like, 'don't cry' and 'get Bea fed' and 'don't get mad and destroy any more buildings' and 'fulfill all of Aveda's needs so she doesn't throw a temper tantrum and destroy several thousand dollars' worth of designer clothes and boxing bags.'"

I ignored the look she gave me.

"But this . . ." I harnessed my peaceful feelings and channeled them into my palm, then opened my hand to reveal a perfect fireball. "This is a purpose—*my* purpose. Using this powerful thing that's inside of me to protect our city. To make things as right as I can make them. And to save the people I love." I snapped my hand closed, extinguishing the fire.

"Show off," Aveda said.

I smiled at her. "I'm finally accepting that I'm not normal—and I don't want to be." I paused, studying the picture. "But I'm doing this my way. No spandex. No pageantry. No dumb catchphrases. And I'm wearing this." I pointed to my T-shirt-jeans-Chucks combo in the picture.

"So boring," Aveda said. "At least let me do something with your hair."

"Nope." I pulled at a particularly unruly curl and watched her grimace. "You said it yourself: there's more than one way to be a hero. And no fighting over who's the Michelle Yeoh in our little duo. 'Cause it's definitely me."

Aveda studied me, her gaze turning serious. "You're more than that," she said. "You're *you*."

Something welled up in my chest, a messy knot of emotions that felt as if it had been lodged there for years. I swallowed hard. Aveda squeezed my hand again, then made her tone light: "Michelle better recognize."

I couldn't help but laugh, the knot of emotions dissipating. Then she laughed. And then we were on our way back to giggle fit territory.

We were still giggling when Scott walked in toting a pair of coffees. "Ladies," he said, giving us his easy grin. He handed one of the coffees to Aveda then gently squeezed my shoulder. "Please don't ever scare me like that again."

I put my hand on top of his and squeezed back.

"I'm sorry I was passed out for what sounds like a truly incredible battle," he continued. "Though Annie's been reenacting the best parts for me while the rest of you were sleeping." He grinned at Aveda. I expected her to roll her eyes at him, but she smiled back.

Well. That was interesting.

"By 'reenacting,' he means I've mostly been reading Maisy's blog post out loud," Aveda said.

"What about Maisy?" Bea sat up in bed, rubbing the

sleep from her eyes. "Do I need to update Twitter?" She blinked a few times, her eyes finally landing on me.

"Evie!" she shrieked, cannonballing herself over Nate and Lucy and landing in front of me. She wrapped her arms around my legs, holding on tight. "I'm sorry," she said, her voice muffled against my knees. "I'm so, so sorry." She lifted her head to look at me. "You made me really mad and I acted like an idiot. But you have to know . . ." Her eyes filled with tears. "I love you the most," she said, hugging my legs tighter. "The very, very most."

"I know." I stroked her hair off her face, marveling once again at how much she looked like Mom. "I love you the most, too. That's probably why we make each other the most mad."

"Yeah." She smiled ruefully. "Oh, and I emailed Dad to tell him you were hurt and he was just, like, 'Namaste.' What does that even mean?" Her eyes went dark and I felt a little wave of anger roll off her.

I remembered the reverse empath power I'd realized she possessed. I was apparently the only one who knew how key she'd been in yesterday's battle. I replayed the scene in my head. The force field had shattered when she screamed. Maybe that's how her post-earthquake level up worked: once she vocalized her feelings, she could break supernaturally-based stuff.

I wondered what else her power could do. I wondered if she'd see it as a burden or a gift. And in that moment, I decided I didn't want her to have to decide just yet. I knew I had to talk to her about it at some point. I couldn't make the same mistake I had by keeping Dad's letter from her. I needed to let her grow up, even though every fiber of my being screamed to protect her at every turn.

I *would* tell her about it. But not today.

"Who needs Dad?" I said. "Not when we've got all these dorks to take care of." I gestured around the room.

Aveda. Scott. Nate and Lucy, who were finally waking up. Bea beamed at me, her mood jerking back to happy. She bounced over to the bed, giving Lucy a shake. "Get up! Let Evie have the bed!"

"Come on, people," Aveda said, getting to her feet. "Let's leave Nate and Evie alone. I'm sure they want to have some kind of disgusting moment together."

Lucy shook off Bea's "helpful" hands, crossed the room, and engulfed me in a fierce hug. "No more of this almost dying business, darling," she said sternly. "I really must insist." She released me and headed for the door, beckoning for Aveda and Bea and Scott to follow. "Let's get breakfast. I'm famished."

"I texted Rose," Aveda said. "She's going to meet us."

"To discuss this new portal business?" Lucy asked.

"Sure, that," Aveda said. "Plus I think she likes you, Lucy."

"Oh, she totally does!" Bea crowed. "She couldn't stop talking to you that night we all hung out after the karaoke battle. And Rose doesn't talk much in the first place."

"Well. I'm not sure what I think about that," Lucy said. But she sounded intrigued.

Just as the door was about to close behind them, I noticed Scott's hand drifting up to the small of Aveda's back. She gave him a surprised look, but she didn't protest.

I wondered what they'd talked about while I was asleep.

I turned back to Nate. He was sitting on the edge of the bed now, staring at me intently.

"Thanks for working with Scott to patch me up," I said. The space between us felt awkward and loaded and I wasn't sure where else to start.

He nodded, his expression unreadable. "You shouldn't sustain any permanent damage other than a scar. But a healing spell this major apparently takes a lot out of the person being healed, so you'll need to rest up for a bit. About—"

"Four to six weeks?"

"More like a few days." He matched my tentative smile.

"Still. Maybe Aveda should pretend to be *me*."

"Maybe." His smile disappeared and he scrubbed a weary hand over his face.

"So did you actually get a power level up like the rest of us?" I said, still grasping for words to fill the air with. "Or was that just part of your ruse?"

"I did," he said. "My power used to be quite mild. For instance, I'd be able to tell you the exact measurements of the shirt you're wearing and that it's made out of a cotton-poly blend rather than pure cotton. That's how it was with the stones, too. I could tell what they were made of, how big they were. But those observations consumed me and kept me from noticing other things. Like the connections Beatrice discovered."

"And now . . . ?"

He studied me. "Now I can tell you exactly how many threads make up the shirt, every single spot that's so much as slightly faded, the date it was crafted. It's like I'm seeing things with an added dimension."

"Like 4D?" I said, trying for teasing. "Can you also see *through* the shirt? Because I don't think anyone other than me will appreciate that."

I expected him to laugh, but his expression turned grim. "No," he said. He hesitated then took a deep breath. "Evie, I need to talk to you about . . . I want to stay here. In my capacity as physician. Everyone seems fine with that, despite the fact that I hid my unusual heritage. And I did have a plan for ensuring Shasta wouldn't succeed."

"I know," I said. "I never thought—"

"Once I realized what those stones meant, I thought I could get her attention with my offer, then push her into the portal while she was turning me," he barreled on. "Let the portal take us both. Anyway, like I said: I want to stay here. But I also want you to know you don't have to . . ." He trailed off and raked a nervous hand through his hair, making it stand on end. "I realize you're probably angry at me for a lot of things. And I'm not going to . . . to fixate on anything you said when you thought you were dying. Those are extreme circumstances."

I frowned. What was he saying? He was flustered and unscientific and stuttery and it was weirding me out. He looked away.

And then I got it.

This big, beautiful man—*my* big, beautiful man—was scared to believe my (almost) dying words were some of the truest I'd ever spoken. I stood and put my hands on my hips. My heart felt like it was crumpling and expanding all at once.

"You think I don't love you?" I stalked across the room and planted myself in front of him. "You think I was in some kind of over-emotional, melodramatic headspace and coughed up whatever random sentiment happened to pop into my head? Just for kicks?"

I took his face in my hands, stroking my thumbs over his harsh features. His eyes were so unsure.

"I lied to you," he said. "I didn't tell you who I really am."

"I know who you are. I also know I gave you my whole heart that first night we made love. And if you try to give it back to me, I will kick . . . your . . . *ass*."

I kissed him. I put every bit of emotion I had into it, trying to show him exactly how I felt. "Come on," I murmured against his lips. "This is my 'back from the almost dead' kiss. Make it good."

He gave a surprised laugh. That deep, unexpected sound rumbled through my body, making me feel warm all over. And then, finally, his arms went around my waist and he pulled me into his lap and kissed me back. Fully, thoroughly, passionately.

When we broke apart, he smiled at me and there wasn't a bit of uncertainty left. He looked sure.

"I love you, too," he said.

Tears filled my eyes, but for once, I didn't try to blink them away. I let them stream down my face as we sat there, him holding me like he never wanted to let go. He pressed his lips against my neck, finding that sensitive spot. My nerve endings perked up and I let out a happy sigh.

Then I took his hand and slipped it under my shirt.

"Evie!" He laughed and gave me an admonishing look. "You're injured."

"Not that injured," I said. "Can't I get a note from my doctor?"

"Hmm." His fingertips skimmed over my skin and he ran them across the scar that had formed right above my heart.

When he spoke again, his voice was husky. "Your doctor isn't sure you're up to such . . . potentially strenuous activity."

"Of course I am." I grinned and leaned in to kiss him again. "I'm a superhero."

ACKNOWLEDGMENTS

I am lucky to be part of many formidable superhero teams. Thank you to the Shamers, the Girl Gang, the Heroine Club, the 9 Pinesers, the Cluster, and the Badass Asian Lady Mafia of Los Angeles. You are my own personal X-Men, Justice League, and Sailor Senshi all rolled into one, and this book would not exist without you.

Thank you to my agent, Diana Fox, and my editor, Betsy Wollheim, for believing in this book, helping me make it the best it could be, and loving Evie and Co. as much as I do. And thank you to Brynn Arenz, Isabel Kaufman, Katie Hoffman, Sarah Guan, Josh Starr, Alexis Nixon, Nita Basu, and everyone at DAW and Fox Literary for everything you've done along the way.

Thank you to Seanan McGuire and Amber Benson for being the best fairy godsisters a girl could ask for.

Thank you to Jenn Fujikawa for inspiring demonic cupcakes and being my not-so-secret twin, to Jenny Yang for soothing my rep sweats with apple soda and tater tot waffles, and to Dr. Andrea Letamendi for providing crucial insight into the psychology of superheroes—and the psychology of angsty writers.

Thank you to Tom Wong for showing me that our superpowers work better when we're together, to Erik Patterson for detailed reads of sex scenes, and to Javier Grillo-Marxuach for assisting in crucial nacho research.

Thank you to Amy Ratcliffe for offering running commentary and wanting to hug Evie, to Liza Palmer for Shaming through the holidays and doing fight choreography at Fuddruckers, and to Autumn Massey for being the Fastest Beta Reader in the West.

Thank you to Keiko Agena and Julia Cho for making Evie's voice sing (and swear and do a lot of other things) early on.

Thank you to Kate Rorick for saying, "Yes, you can" and to Sarah Watson for saying, "No, really: I *know* you can."

Thank you to everyone who fed this book with thoughtful critique, cartoon pastries, and/or katsu drenched in curry: Jeff Lester, Christine Dinh, Christy Black, Mel Caylo, Margaret Dunlap, Cecil Castellucci, Nick Brandt, Caroline Pruett, Elizabeth Diane Benson, and Sina Grace.

Thank you to Jason Chan for taking care of my girls and bringing them to such beautiful life on the cover—they look exactly how I imagined them.

Thank you to the wonderful readers of *One Con Glory* for getting me here.

Thank you to my family for being my family: Dad, Steve, Marjorie, Alice, Philip, and all the other Kuhns, Yoneyamas, Chens, and Coffeys.

Thank you to Jeff Chen for things beyond what words can express. I love you.